Praise for *New York Times* and *USA TODAY* bestselling author Vicki Lewis Thompson

"Vicki Lewis Thompson is one of those rare, gifted writers with the ability to touch her readers' hearts and their funny bones."
—#1 *New York Times* and *USA TODAY* bestselling author Debbie Macomber

"Once again master storyteller Vicki Lewis Thompson dishes up a sizzling romantic romp guaranteed to spice up our reading pleasure."
—*RT Book Reviews*

"Ms. Thompson does a wonderful job of blending the erotic with romance that is sometimes tender, sometimes funny and always exciting."
—Diana Risso, *Romance Reviews Today*

"When you pick up a book that bears the name of Vicki Lewis Thompson on the cover, you can expect a great read. She...will make you laugh, cry, need a cold shower and most important fall in love."
—*Fallen Angel Reviews*

New York Times and USA TODAY Bestselling Author

Vicki Lewis Thompson

Two in the Saddle

Boone's Bounty

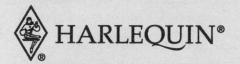

HARLEQUIN®

TORONTO • NEW YORK • LONDON
AMSTERDAM • PARIS • SYDNEY • HAMBURG
STOCKHOLM • ATHENS • TOKYO • MILAN • MADRID
PRAGUE • WARSAW • BUDAPEST • AUCKLAND

Recycling programs
for this product may
not exist in your area.

ISBN-13: 978-0-373-68801-2

TWO IN THE SADDLE & BOONE'S BOUNTY

Copyright © 2010 by Harlequin Books S.A.

The publisher acknowledges the copyright holder of the individual works
as follows:

TWO IN THE SADDLE
Copyright © 2000 by Vicki Lewis Thompson

BOONE'S BOUNTY
Copyright © 2000 by Vicki Lewis Thompson

This edition published by arrangement with Harlequin Books S.A.

For questions and comments about the quality of this book
please contact us at Customer_eCare@Harlequin.ca.

www.eHarlequin.com

Printed in U.S.A.

CONTENTS

TWO IN THE SADDLE

CHAPTER ONE

WEDDINGS MADE Travis Evans nervous.

Standing at the altar of the Huerfano Community Church with his good buddy Sebastian Daniels was like hanging out with a guy who had chicken pox. One wrong move on Travis's part and bam! He'd catch the marriage bug. And that would mean the end of life as he knew it.

But somebody had to be there for Sebastian. By rights Sebastian should have had four guys lined up to give him moral support, but he and Matty hadn't been willing to wait for folks to rearrange their schedules.

Sebastian's brother Ed was stuck in Alaska, and as for the three cowboys who made up Sebastian's inner circle, only Travis was available. Nat Grady was overseas working in a small, war-torn country with a name Travis had trouble pronouncing. Boone Conner was on the road in New Mexico with his mobile horse-shoeing business and tracking him down had been impossible.

So Travis was Sebastian's best man, which was just as well, Travis thought, because that balanced out the wedding party. Matty's family hadn't been able to make it on such short notice, either, so her only attendant was Gwen Hawthorne, maid of honor. Or matron. Travis wasn't sure which it was when a woman was divorced. Divorced and marriage-shy. It was a hell of a promising combination, in Travis's opinion. Too bad Gwen hated his guts.

Even though Sebastian and Matty were light in the wedding-party department, they weren't short of wedding guests. The tiny clapboard church was packed. The men had dusted off their best Western-cut suits, and the women…. Travis sighed with longing. The women looked like a bouquet of Colorado wildflowers in their pastel-colored outfits. The air was still cool on this May afternoon, but the women of Huerfano had dressed for spring.

Travis loved how warmer weather invited the ladies to bare a little more of their delectable skin, and ordinarily he would have taken delight in the number of eligible females within range of his smile. But weddings were a dangerous time to flirt. Weddings gave single women *ideas.*

The minister, Pete McDowell, had been a hell-raiser in his youth according to what Travis had heard, but he'd entered the ministry and reformed. With his neatly trimmed gray beard and long robe, he looked like the sort of person who could tie the knot good and tight.

Besides, everybody agreed Pete had been born with a voice that belonged either in the pulpit or on the radio. He turned now and nodded toward the church organist, Sarah Jane Ashfelder, who began to play.

Out of habit, Travis glanced over and winked at her. She blushed and bobbled a chord. Immediately he regretted the wink, partly because he'd flustered her and partly because everybody in the valley knew Sarah Jane was desperately seeking a husband. A wink from him while Sarah Jane was playing the organ at a wedding gave the wrong impression all the way around.

"Got the ring?" Sebastian whispered out of the corner of his mouth.

It was about the hundredth time Sebastian had asked since this morning, but Travis cut him some slack. A guy had a right to be wrecked on his wedding day. "Yeah, I've got it," he murmured. "How're you holding up?"

"Shaking like a newborn calf."

"This is a good move, Sebastian." Travis thoroughly believed that. Even though he wasn't interested in matrimony himself, it fit some guys like a glove. Sebastian was one of those guys. And Matty Lang was perfect for him.

"I know it's a good move," Sebastian said softly. "But I'm no good at public displays like this. This collar itches, and my coat's too tight across the shoulders. I—"

A baby's loud wail rose above the deep tones of the organ. The congregation turned toward the back of the church, their murmurs of curiosity getting louder as they strained to see where the noise was coming from.

"That would be Lizzie, kicking up a fuss in the vestibule," Travis said. "I knew it was a mistake, making her part of this shindig."

"It is *not* a mistake," Sebastian said in a low voice, although he could have spoken normally and not been heard above the bellowing organ, the screaming baby and the excited chatter of the guests. This baby had been the subject of much speculation, and folks were obviously dying to see her.

"She's not even four months old," Travis pointed out. "That's too little to be in a wedding."

"No, it's not. She's advanced for her age. Besides, Elizabeth brought Matty and me together. She belongs here. We forgot the pacifier, is all. I want my daughter to be part of this."

Travis felt like strangling Sebastian with his string tie. The guy wouldn't give up his wrongheaded insistence that he was Lizzie's father. "She's not your daughter. She's mine, as you damned well know." Travis was dead sure about it. The evidence was in the note he'd received three weeks ago in Utah, a note he'd now memorized.

Dear Travis,
I'm counting on you to be a godfather to my daughter Elizabeth until I can return for her. Your playful approach to life is just what she needs right now. I've left her with Sebastian at the Rocking D. Believe me, I wouldn't do this if I weren't in desperate circumstances.

In deepest gratitude,
Jessica

Lizzie was his, all right. Maybe he couldn't remember the specifics of that night when he, Sebastian, Boone and Jessica had celebrated the anniversary of their escape from an avalanche, but he was the likely candidate for fatherhood.

He recalled that all the guys had been drunk, drunk enough to make passes at Jessica, even though she was only a friend. And like a good friend, she'd driven them back to their cabin and tucked each of them in bed. He remembered her leaning over him, a smile on her face. He must have coaxed her in there with him, and that was when Lizzie had been conceived.

And yes, Sebastian had received a similar note asking him to be a godfather when Jessica left the baby on his doorstep. But Sebastian wasn't the type to get wasted and make love without protection. Travis hadn't ever done that before, either, but it wasn't out of the realm of possibility for him the way it was for Sebastian.

Nevertheless, Sebastian had taken credit for that baby and wouldn't give up. He was presently glaring at Travis, his jaw clenched. "She's my baby. She's got the Daniels nose."

"In your dreams. She looks exactly like a picture of my mother at that age."

Sarah Jane launched into the wedding march, pulling out all the stops to drown out the baby's cries.

"Oh, yeah?" Sebastian said. "Then I guess I never showed you a picture of *my* mother at that age. She—"

"Gentlemen." Pete McDowell lifted his eyebrows in censure. "I don't think this is the time or the place to argue your paternity issues. The processional has begun."

Sebastian gulped and faced the back of the church.

Travis turned in that direction, too. Sure enough, here came Gwen pushing the antique baby buggy she'd unearthed from the attic of her Victorian house. People on both sides of the aisle craned their necks hoping for a glimpse of the mystery baby that two men claimed to have fathered.

Gwen had pushed Lizzie down the aisle in the buggy during the rehearsal, and the little girl had seemed to love it. But today was a different story, apparently. Today Lizzie was having nothing to do with that buggy.

Gwen had decorated it with flowers and ribbons so

it looked real pretty, and she'd found a way to hook her bridal bouquet onto the buggy handle. Lizzie didn't seem to appreciate any of Gwen's efforts. But it wasn't the buggy decorations that held Travis's gaze. One glimpse of Gwen and his hormones snapped to attention.

She wore a dress the same color as new aspen leaves, and the pale green looked amazing against her golden skin. He vaguely remembered hearing that she had Cheyenne ancestors somewhere in her family tree. That also explained her jet-black hair, worn up today in some elaborate arrangement that mystified and tantalized him. She'd woven green ribbons and flowers through her shiny curls, making her look like a Native American princess—a modern princess who knew her way around a curling iron.

Travis licked his lips. He was of the firm belief that women spent all that time putting their hair up hoping that some man would itch to take it down. And he did.

The sleeves of her dress were long, with little conservative buttons at the wrists, but the neckline wasn't even remotely conservative. Travis stared at the most spectacular cleavage he'd seen in a coon's age. He sighed as he calculated the odds of ever enjoying that bounty. She was the only single woman in the valley he hadn't been able to charm.

And that frustrated him, especially at this moment when Gwen was walking toward him displaying her wares so effectively. Travis was relatively unacquainted with frustration, considering that women seemed to enjoy giving him what he wanted when he wanted it.

Because he was used to having his needs satisfied in short order, he'd never realized that rejection could be a more powerful aphrodisiac than acceptance. Good thing these fancy pants Sebastian had rented for him had pleats.

Gwen held her head high and smiled as she pushed the buggy containing the screaming baby, but Travis noticed the tension around her eyes. And then, for one electric moment, her dark gaze met his. Her silent plea for help might have been unconscious, but it was unmistakable.

Without thinking, Travis reacted. He crossed in front of Sebastian and the minister and met Gwen as she reached the altar.

She paused, and her eyes widened as he lifted a squalling Lizzie out of the buggy and cradled her against the shoulder of his tux.

They'd decked the baby out in a white eyelet dress and white booties, which was reasonable, but some idiot had decided to torment her by putting a bow on an elastic band around her head. No wonder she was upset. Travis took the bow off and kissed the little girl's damp cheek.

Gwen cleared her throat. "Travis—"

"Go on over to your spot," Travis murmured, tucking the bow gizmo in his pocket. "I'll handle her."

"But—"

"Go on. I'll get her to stop." And in fact he already had. Lizzie snuffled against his shoulder and grabbed on to his lapel as if she didn't plan to let go. He smiled at Gwen. "See?"

Gwen shook her head. "Unreal," she muttered.

He shrugged. "Most girls like me." With a wink at Gwen he returned to his place holding Lizzie.

Gwen didn't want to be touched by the picture of Travis standing at the altar letting a baby slobber on his tux. On her way to the front of the church, in addition to worrying about Elizabeth's crying, she'd noticed that Travis looked like a god up there. She'd known he was mouth-watering in jeans, but she hadn't been prepared for the sight of him in a tux.

Because she loved everything Victorian, she had a weakness for a man in a tuxedo, a man who looked as if he'd stepped out of another era. Dressing Travis in a tie and tails and setting him smack-dab in front of her should be against the law.

She'd nearly forgotten Elizabeth's wailing as she took in the allure of the high, white collar emphasizing his strong neck, the black coat stretched tight across his broad shoulders, and the snug fit of his dove-gray vest. Vests were made for men built like Travis. The delicate pink rosebud in his lapel only emphasized his virility.

In order to get her hormones under control, she'd convinced herself that Travis was vain as a peacock. She visualized him preening in front of the mirror, combing his rich brown hair, gazing into the tawny depths of those bedroom eyes of his and winking at his reflection before he walked out to face his admirers. But a peacock wouldn't let a baby suck on the shoulder of his coat. A peacock wouldn't let that same baby pull on his string tie until it came undone. A peacock wouldn't have come to Gwen and Elizabeth's rescue in the first place.

The organ music swelled, and with some effort Gwen turned her gaze away from Travis and Elizabeth in order to give Matty the respect and attention she deserved.

Matty came down the aisle, regal in the simple white gown Gwen had insisted she wear, despite this being a second marriage. Gwen had advised her on the flowers, too, and the old-fashioned bouquet of rosebuds, lavender and ivy was exactly right for Matty. Watching her, Gwen felt her throat tighten with happiness, pride, and a trace of longing.

Her friend had never looked more radiant. The expression of pure love on Matty's face made Gwen yearn for something she hadn't wished for in a very long time—a love of her own. Both she and Matty had hooked up with scoundrels the first time around, but Matty hadn't let that stop her from dreaming. Now she had a man who would lay down his life for her.

Gwen swallowed the lump in her throat. Men like Sebastian Daniels were rare, and she knew it. The rancher's good looks could have served him well as a lady-killer, but instead he was humble, sweet, and adorably dense about the effect he had on women. He was the exact opposite of Travis, who was all too aware that women swooned when he walked by.

But Gwen would not swoon. By God, she would not swoon.

As Matty joined Sebastian at the altar, Gwen sneaked a peek at Travis to see how he was getting along with Elizabeth. He was rumpled and damned sexy-looking from dealing with the baby. He'd removed his boutonniere, probably so Elizabeth wouldn't stick herself on the pin or try to eat the rosebud. Gwen was impressed with his caution.

Continuing to keep the baby entertained, he played nosey-nosey with her, and she chuckled, a low sound of feminine delight. No doubt about it, Travis had a way with the fairer sex, regardless of age.

On a hunch, Gwen glanced around the small church. The men were watching the ceremony. But as she'd expected, the women, ranging from eight to eighty, were watching Travis. From their expressions of open adoration, Gwen figured Travis would be booked up for the rest of the summer on the basis of this one little scene.

Well, good. The busier he was, the less chance she'd have of running into him. And she wanted to steer clear of Travis Evans. She certainly did. Definitely. The sexual tingle she felt every time she looked at him would go away eventually, especially if she didn't have to look at him very often. This wedding would be the worst of it. After today, she'd have clear sailing.

But today was a challenge, because she caught herself constantly glancing over at Travis, right along with every other woman in the church. He was strong medicine, especially with that baby.

Maybe he realized the baby was a terrific prop. That thought gave her some comfort. If he was using the baby to get women's attention, then that made him...calculating. She had no use for a calculating man. Yes, he probably had ulterior motives for holding Elizabeth. What a grandstander, playing with that baby and making every woman in the place drool.

"Gwen," Matty whispered.

Gwen blinked.

"The ring," Matty said, her tone amused.

Hot embarrassment flooded through Gwen. She'd lost her place in the proceedings. "Coming right up," she murmured as she reached in the buggy, found the small box she'd put there and took out the ring. She'd planned to have it ready and waiting when the time came, but she'd become so absorbed with Travis, she'd blown her assignment. Damn that tuxedo-wearing, baby-holding cowboy, anyway.

With new determination she focused on Sebastian and Matty. From her position she could only see the back of Matty's head, golden curls covered in white tulle. But with her height advantage she could peer right over Matty and watch Sebastian's face.

And sure enough, he was giving his new bride *The Look*. Gwen couldn't define it exactly, but it was a potent combination of love, respect, devotion, lust, appreciation, and a few more emotions she hadn't identified yet. Sebastian's expression left no doubt in anyone's mind that Matty was his one and only.

The lump returned to Gwen's throat. If she were completely honest with herself, she'd have to say that no one, not even her ex, had ever given her *The Look*. She wondered if she'd go through life without ever experiencing such a moment.

Pull yourself together she lectured herself. *Count your blessings*. She lived in a gem of a Victorian house and had been lucky enough to keep it after the divorce by opening a bed and breakfast. It turned out she loved the business, although at times she wondered if caring for her guests only took the place of caring for the family she'd always wanted.

But the house gave her roots. The itinerant life of her archeologist parents wasn't for her, and she'd hated the constant moving as a child. She tallied each year spent in Huerfano with pride, and she was now up to seven, more years than she'd ever stayed in one place in her life.

Maybe running a B&B didn't stack up well against her parents' international reputation, or her brother's prestigious job running a museum in Boston. Maybe they sometimes reminded her that she was twenty-nine and hadn't done anything with her life. But she wasn't giving up her house, no matter what anybody said.

"You may kiss the bride," Pete McDowell said.

A collective sigh went up from the congregation as Sebastian lifted Matty's veil and cupped her face in his big rancher's hands.

The tender moment lasted long enough to bring a mist of tears to Gwen's eyes. Then Elizabeth began chortling and wiggling in Travis's arms.

Scene-stealer, Gwen thought, and she wasn't sure whether she meant Elizabeth or Travis. She wondered what would happen with that little baby. Her mother, Jessica Franklin, seemed to be on the run from something or someone and wanted her daughter out of danger. Jessica had been gone for six weeks, long enough for Matty and Sebastian to bond with Elizabeth.

Personally, Gwen figured Travis was the baby's father, not Sebastian. But in the event Jessica never returned, Sebastian and Matty would provide a better home for the little girl than a playboy like Travis. Even Travis agreed on that point. Still, he seemed quite possessive of the baby and argued every time Sebastian tried to claim paternity.

But neither of them would find out who was Elizabeth's father until Jessica chose to tell them. She'd called a few times to check on Elizabeth, but she'd never stayed on the line long enough to answer any questions.

Gwen had never encountered something this strange, but maybe Jessica knew what she was doing. Elizabeth was safe and surrounded by people who loved her, including Gwen, although she was trying not to get too attached.

She'd learned detachment during a childhood of constant moving, losing both friends and familiar surroundings. So she'd kept in mind that Jessica could appear at any time and take the baby away, although she might have a fight on her hands at this point. Even from Travis. And he was good with the baby, Gwen admitted grudgingly. Still, he couldn't be counted on. Not in the long run.

"I give you Mr. and Mrs. Sebastian Daniels," Pete McDowell said in his deep, booming voice.

The congregation broke into applause and Sarah Jane launched into the recessional.

Gwen blinked back tears as Matty and Sebastian walked back down the aisle, arm in arm. She was so happy for her friend. And maybe a little sorry for herself, but she'd get over it.

Then she looked across at Travis. With sentiment running high at this moment, she was in no shape to deal with him, but deal with him she must.

It wouldn't be for long. A walk down the aisle, a dance at the reception, and she'd be free of her obligation to fraternize with him. And it would be good riddance.

She pushed the buggy toward the center aisle. As Travis met her there with Elizabeth, Gwen inclined her head toward the buggy, indicating Travis could put Elizabeth back inside.

"I don't want to risk it," he murmured.

"Suit yourself." Pushing the buggy required two hands. During rehearsal they'd linked arms and each put a hand on the wooden handle to push the buggy back down the aisle.

But that wouldn't work now. Travis couldn't hold the

baby, link arms with Gwen, and lend a hand pushing the buggy, so Gwen decided they could forego linking arms. Just as well.

She used both hands to push the buggy, expecting Travis to simply fall in step beside her. Instead he shifted Elizabeth to his outside arm and slipped his free arm around Gwen's waist. Instantly her heart started chugging like a freight train.

"That's not necessary," she said, a smile pasted on her face for the benefit of the congregation. Looks of envy came shooting at her from all sides.

"Yes, it is."

"No, it's not." She tried to ease away. She was entirely too close to him and his spicy aftershave, especially after she'd just witnessed the emotional joining of her two best friends.

"Yes, it is." His grip tightened at her waist, sending shock waves all through her body. "We're supposed to look as if we're together."

"Casually together, not plastered together." Oh, but his hand felt good right there. She registered the imprint of each of his fingers through the soft material of her dress.

"Take it easy, sweetheart."

"I am most definitely *not* your sweetheart." And if her nerves jumped at his words, that was only because nobody had spoken an endearment to her in a while.

"Too bad for both of us. Listen, I know you hate me and this is torture for you, but we're almost done."

Oh, it was torture, all right. Torture of the highest order. And how she wished that hate was the emotion she was feeling for this man.

CHAPTER TWO

TRAVIS HAD ACTED on impulse, tucking Gwen against him as they proceeded up the aisle. Pure devilment had made him do it, probably, knowing how much she loathed him. Funny, though, once they were hip to hip, he felt her tremble.

He recognized that tremble. Women tended to do that when he touched them, but he wouldn't have expected that reaction from Gwen, who'd let him know she wasn't even slightly interested.

So when she started squawking about his behavior he held her tighter, to test her reaction to increased contact. Sure enough, that quiver got worse, and her skin flushed pink.

He noticed the color in her cheeks, and because he was a healthy male animal, he also noticed the color spread to the swell of her breasts above the green material of her dress. The way he figured it, if a woman chose to wear a neckline like that, she could expect a man to look his fill. He indulged for as long as he dared, which was only a few seconds, considering he and Gwen were in a very public place.

When he forced himself to look away, he was trembling a bit himself. Fantasies of unzipping her dress and sampling those generous breasts swirled through his mind, affecting his breathing.

She wasn't breathing so easy herself, and her agitation stirred up the erotic, cinnamon-flavored perfume she wore, which excited him even more. By the time they reached the back of the church and moved through the doors into the vestibule where Matty and Sebastian stood waiting, Travis had decided it might be worth his time to cut through the barbed wire Gwen had strung around herself to keep him out.

So what if he wasn't husband material? He'd taught several women that good sex didn't have to lead to everlasting love. Mutual enjoyment was justification enough for climbing between the sheets, in his opinion. Gwen needed to expand her options, and he was the guy to help her. If Lizzie hadn't been twisting his ear during the entire walk down the aisle, it would have been an outstanding interlude.

If he'd had any doubt about Gwen's reaction to him, she erased it once they passed through the main chapel doors. She wrenched away from him as if she'd been cuddled up to a hot stove. An indifferent woman wouldn't have made such a big production out of escaping.

Avoiding his gaze, she abandoned the buggy and rushed over to hug Matty. "I'm so happy for you!" she said.

Travis knew Gwen's sentiments were sincere, but there was a quivery edge to her voice, as if she might not be in complete control of herself. That pleased him. After their walk down the aisle, he'd had to take a few deep breaths, himself. He caught Matty looking at him over Gwen's shoulder, and he shrugged.

Then he pried Lizzie's fingers from his ear before walking over and holding out his hand to Sebastian. "Well, it's too late to turn back now, buddy."

Sebastian was grinning all over as he clasped Travis's hand. "We really did it, didn't we?"

"I do believe you did. Congratulations. You roped yourself a keeper." He turned to Matty, who looked happier than he'd ever seen her. He'd been her head wrangler at the Leaning L through the bad years with Butch, and the lonely years after Butch crashed his plane into a mountain. Technically she was his boss, but he loved her like a sister, and he was pleased as punch that she and Sebastian had finally figured out they were meant to be more than good neighbors.

Continuing to balance Lizzie in one arm, he leaned down and gave Matty a kiss on the cheek. "I hope you know you've hitched up with the stubbornest cowpoke in the valley," he murmured. "If he gives you any problems, let me know and I'll kick his butt for you."

"I'll keep that in mind," Matty said, her blue eyes twinkling.

"Nice going, Travis." Sebastian clapped him on the back. "I had Matty convinced I was perfect, but you had to open your yap and ruin my image."

"My pleasure." Travis smiled, then winced as Lizzie crowed happily, grabbed his nose and pinched hard. "The kid's got the instincts of a steer wrestler," he said as he peeled her fingers away.

Matty laughed. "I've taught her all she knows. I'm hoping she'll have that nose thing perfected by the time she's eighteen."

Travis figured now wasn't the time to mention there was a chance Lizzie wouldn't grow up on the Rocking D. Matty was more attached to this baby than she knew. "She's got the nose thing perfected now," he said, grabbing Lizzie's hand before she could latch on again.

Matty held out her arms. "Let me hold her while we take care of this reception line business. You've been tortured enough."

"That's a matter of opinion," Gwen said.

Travis shot her a look. The old defiance was back in her dark eyes, but he wasn't intimidated by it any-more. Underneath all her bluster was a woman aching to be kissed, and kissed well. He wondered if he might find the opportunity to take care of that before the night was out.

"Lizzie's okay with me," Travis said. "She'll be fine, now that we got rid of that bow apparatus."

"I knew that bow was a bad idea," Matty said, glancing at her new husband, "but Sebastian insisted on making her look like a girl."

"I *liked* the bow," Sebastian said, a stubborn gleam in his eye.

"Well, she didn't," Matty said. "And I'm proud of her for sticking to her guns." She turned back to Travis. "Hand over that little dickens. I miss her already."

Travis eyed Matty's white dress. He had a rough idea what the dress cost, and he'd heard some talk about keeping it for the next generation of brides in the Daniels family. He didn't think Lizzie's baby drool would improve the dress any. "I'll hang on to her. That outfit of yours is a keepsake, and this tux is only rented. Might as well keep the mess concentrated in one spot."

Matty looked down at her dress. "You have a point. I'm not used to being dolled up like this, and I keep for-getting I have to be careful." She smiled at Travis. "Thank you for your sacrifice. You saved the day."

"Sacrifice?" Gwen said. "Ha. He eats this stuff with a spoon. He—"

"Maybe we'd better set up our reception line," Matty said quickly. "People are heading this way. Gwen, you'll be first, then Travis, then Sebastian, then—"

"*There's* that adorable baby!" shrieked Donna Rathbone, kindergarten teacher and one of Travis's former girlfriends.

Donna had called him her teacher's pet, he remembered. He had fond memories of hot summer nights about two years ago. Donna hurried through the double doors of the main chapel and headed straight for him, followed by half the congregation, all female, and all jabbering about the baby.

"Then again, maybe we should put Travis first in line," Matty said as the women enveloped him in a sea of pastels and perfume.

MATTY AND Sebastian had decided to hold the reception inside a large tent on the Rocking D, and from Gwen's vantage point at the head table, the whole town seemed to be packed inside the tent's white canvas walls. Tiny clear lights strung from the tent poles sparkled in celebration and centerpieces of spring flowers bloomed on each linen-covered table. The bar was open and the buffet table was crowded with food.

Sensual pleasures teased Gwen from all sides—succulent barbecued beef and rich red wine, the seductive beat of a country tune, the scent of juniper every time the breeze lifted a tent flap a few inches. And then there was Travis in his rumpled tux, an attraction more compelling than the bride and groom, apparently.

Women surrounded him constantly, whether he happened to be holding Elizabeth or not. He was a very busy man as he tended to his many admirers, and yet every few minutes he'd pause, find Gwen in the throng, and send her a smile or a wink.

She tried to be unaffected…and failed. It was heady stuff to be singled out by the man who was clearly adored by every woman in the room. But the dinner part of the reception had nearly ended, and soon the dancing would begin, which meant she'd be expected to dance with Travis. And no matter how seductive the atmosphere, no matter how appealing the man, she must not give in to his considerable charms.

She'd known Travis would be trouble the first day she'd laid eyes on him while paying a visit to Matty's ranch. About four years earlier, she and Matty had met over the yarn counter at Coogan's Department Store and discovered they both had a passion for weaving. Their friendship had blossomed.

Gwen had taken up the craft as a way to heal after her divorce from Derek. Eventually she discovered that Matty used her floor loom as therapy while she dealt with an unhappy marriage, which gave the two women even more in common.

They enjoyed each other's company tremendously, and the only fly in the ointment had been Gwen's occasional forced interaction with Matty's head wrangler. Travis reminded her way too much of Derek. He pushed all the same buttons Derek had, making her pulse race with a look, her breath catch with a devilish grin. But Gwen had no intention of losing her heart to another rascal too handsome for his own good.

Fortunately Travis spent winters at his place in Utah, which meant Gwen only had to deal with him during the summer. Because summer was high season at Hawthorne House, she was usually too busy to socialize much. She'd been so subtle about avoiding Travis that even Matty hadn't known of her vulnerability until recently…until Elizabeth had turned all their lives topsy-turvy.

The baby was presently sitting on Sebastian's lap while Matty played patty-cake with her. Gwen smiled at the picture they made. No doubt about it, Elizabeth had totally changed Matty and Sebastian's life, fortunately for the better. But Matty and Sebastian belonged together. Gwen and Travis did not, and she'd be wise to keep that firmly in mind.

Travis returned to his place at the head table just as the band finished a tune. He signaled to the band, picked up his wineglass and raised it. "Ladies and gentlemen, may I have your attention?"

That would be no problem for the ladies, Gwen thought. At the sound of Travis's rich baritone, they'd all turned toward him like daisies to sunlight.

"I'd like to propose a toast to the bride and groom." He grinned. "You know, this is gonna be like shooting fish in a barrel, Sebastian."

"Roast him, Travis!" called one of the ranchers from a table in the back of the room.

Gwen rolled her eyes. Travis would make a joke of this, the way he made a joke of everything.

"Well, you folks ain't heard nothin' until you've heard Sebastian Daniels croon *Ghost Riders in the Sky*," Travis said. "If I'd been writing your vows, buddy, I would've made Matty promise to love, cherish, and put up with a round of *Ghost Riders* every blessed morning in the shower. Oh, and I don't want to forget the yodeling. Did you tell her about that, yet?"

Gwen laughed along with everyone else, including Matty and Sebastian.

Travis cleared his throat and Gwen prepared herself for more jokes.

But Travis was no longer smiling, and his tone had changed. "Yodeling aside, I've known Sebastian Daniels for a lot of years, and he's one hell of a friend. If you're in trouble, this is the man to call. His heart's bigger than the whole Sangre de Cristo range."

Gwen stared at Travis. Just when she thought she knew what to expect from him, he did the exact opposite.

"Sebastian loves this land," Travis said. "Until recently, I didn't think he could love anything, or anyone, more than this paradise he calls the Rocking D. But I was wrong. His fondness for this ranch is a drop in the bucket compared to the way he feels about the woman sitting next to him."

Emotion clogged Gwen's throat. She could take anything from Travis except heartfelt sincerity.

"And he's found his soul mate in Matty," Travis continued. "Matty is true-blue, the straightest shooter I've ever known. If there is such a thing as a match made in heaven, you're looking at it. God bless, Matty and Sebastian. I'm proud to be here."

Gwen was destroyed. She clapped furiously and blinked back tears. Then she took a quick sip of wine to toast the newlyweds and grabbed a napkin to dab at her eyes.

The band started playing a waltz, and Sebastian handed Elizabeth to Travis. "Thanks," he said, his voice suspiciously hoarse. "That was…damned nice."

"Outstanding," Matty said, sniffing.

"I meant every word," Travis said. "Now go have that first dance, Mr. and Mrs. Daniels. You deserve it." He sat down next to Gwen and propped Elizabeth on his lap. "What'd you think?" He sounded as if he actually cared.

"Great." Gwen took another gulp of her wine and choked on it. She snatched up her napkin again and held it over her mouth while she coughed.

"Easy, now." With one arm wrapped around Elizabeth, he leaned over and patted Gwen on the back. "Didn't mean to make you nervous."

She glanced at him. The hell he didn't. At least she had an excuse for the tears in her eyes as she continued to cough and gasp for breath.

"And now let's have the best man and the maid of honor on the floor," announced the band leader.

Travis leaned closer. "Are you up to it?"

She coughed once more. "Sure," she said hoarsely. "But what about Elizabeth?"

"We'll take her along." He stood and pulled back Gwen's chair.

Stupid her, she was disappointed that they were taking Elizabeth. What a dope she was, feeling sorry because she wouldn't have Travis all to herself. She was twenty times safer if they danced with Elizabeth cradled between them, and safety was important. Self-preservation was imperative.

Unfortunately Travis's speech had derailed her protective instincts and stirred up needs she would do well to bury, especially when she was around this man.

Travis guided her with a hand at her elbow as they wound through the tables to the dance floor. Once again Gwen became aware of the envy coming at her in waves.

She and Travis would dance this one, obligatory number. After that, he'd be mobbed and she wouldn't have to worry about protecting herself from his advances. She should be happy about that, not depressed.

"How about if you hold Lizzie?" Travis asked as they stepped onto the temporary dance floor that had been erected in one corner of the tent. "Then I can hold both of you." Without waiting for an answer, he transferred the baby neatly into Gwen's arms.

Elizabeth was growing limp and her eyes drooped with fatigue.

Gwen cradled the little girl in her arms, and with a yawn Elizabeth laid her head trustingly on Gwen's shoulder and closed her eyes. Gwen's heart swelled with pleasure as she turned her head and brushed a kiss against the baby's velvet cheek.

In the past few weeks, Gwen had tried to keep some distance from this cherub, but she was afraid that distance had just disappeared. She'd fallen in love with the baby like everyone else who came within Elizabeth's charmed circle. If Elizabeth ever left Huerfano, the town would be wall-to-wall with broken hearts.

"Perfect," Travis murmured, as he wrapped his arms around Gwen and Elizabeth and gently led them into a slow, swaying dance.

The baby sighed and gave in to sleep, relaxing completely against Gwen.

The dance should have been harmless, even platonic, Gwen thought. But she hadn't counted on having to look directly into Travis's eyes while they moved to the music. Cheek-to-cheek would have been one kind of sensual temptation, but gazing into those golden eyes seemed even more intimate.

He held her gaze, and even though his arms cradled her loosely, she felt cinched in tight by the warmth in his eyes. She couldn't glance away without seeming cowardly, or nervous, or lacking in confidence.

"You don't have to be afraid of me, Gwen," he said.

She lifted her chin. "I'm not."

In sleep, Elizabeth's hand slipped down and rested on the swell of Gwen's breast. The innocent touch ignited Gwen's already heated nerve endings.

Travis glanced down with a hint of a smile. Then his gaze moved back up and lingered on Gwen's mouth before returning to her eyes. There was a flicker of heat in the tawny depths that hadn't been there before. "Yeah, you're afraid," he said. "The pulse in your throat is going like sixties. But I won't hurt you."

She swallowed and tried to calm her breathing. Her senses filled with the scent of baby powder mingled with the spicy aroma of Travis's aftershave. A baby and a man to love—she hadn't realized how much she wanted that. Longing washed over her. "That's right, you won't hurt me, because I won't give you the chance."

"You know, there's a big difference between me and your ex."

"I don't want to talk about Derek."

"We won't. I have something to tell you about me."

She tried not to respond to the caressing tone in his voice. "I know all I need to know about you."

"I don't think so. Otherwise you wouldn't be afraid. Gwen, the only way people get hurt is when promises are broken. I won't do that."

She shivered at the way he spoke her name. "Because you don't make promises?"

"Not the forever kind." His fingers traced lazy patterns over her back. "But I can promise to make love to you honestly, thoroughly, and tenderly for whatever time we decide to spend together."

She didn't want him to know he was arousing her, but those eyes probably saw everything—her rapid breathing, her beating pulse, her flushed skin.

"If we both know what to expect going in, then nobody gets hurt," he murmured.

Oh, he was good. She wanted him to kiss her so much she could taste it. "I'll bet there are several women with broken hearts who wouldn't agree with your reasoning."

"Then they lied to themselves. I never lied to them."

His mouth was beautiful, she thought. Every woman should have a chance to kiss a mouth like that once in her life. And if the rest of him lived up to the sensuous promise of his mouth....

"You're thinking about it," he said. "That's a start."

"I'm thinking about what an arrogant man you are." Excitingly arrogant. She wondered if she was capable of lovemaking with no strings. Pleasure without promises. For the long run, it didn't fit into her dreams. But a forever man seemed like a distant and unreachable goal, and in the meantime she could allow herself to enjoy...no, it was too risky. But the fact that she was even wondering what it would be like to have an affair with Travis meant that he'd breached her defenses.

"I'm far from arrogant," he said, subtly caressing her back. "I can't afford to be when you have all the power."

"Ha. You're a world-class flirt, Travis. I can't even play in your league."

"You're selling yourself short. When I saw you come down the aisle of the church in that dynamite dress, my knees almost gave out. I'm a desperate man, Gwen, begging you to soften your heart."

She was getting soft, all right. Soft in the head, heart, everywhere. Outrageous though his compliments were, they were having an effect. Soon she'd be putty in his hands. "I don't want to be another notch on your belt," she said.

He smiled, slow and sexy, his eyes alight with banked passion. "Then let me be a notch in yours."

CHAPTER THREE

TRAVIS PRIDED HIMSELF on his ability to handle a room full of women and make each one of them feel special, but this reception was taxing his powers. And to be truthful, his heart wasn't in the effort. Flattering as it was to have all these ladies asking him to dance, he would have preferred a quiet little bar, a jukebox and Gwen in his arms.

He wasn't happy about the fact that she was out on the floor nearly as often as he was, and that she seemed to be having such a good time. Damn it, she wanted *him*. He'd seen it in her eyes when they'd shared that one frustrating dance, and he'd hoped for another dance with her once Elizabeth was tucked into the little bassinet Sebastian had set up in a corner. No telling where another dance might lead, considering the look in her eyes following the first one. He was eager to stoke the fire he'd started.

Instead he'd been besieged by the female population of Huerfano. He'd danced with nearly every woman in the room, and he'd been offered enough pieces of wedding cake to open his own bakery. Apparently his stint with Lizzie at the altar combined with his wedding toast had made him a very popular guy. Ordinarily he would have loved it, but tonight he was in a strange, one-woman kind of mood.

He was so busy that he barely had time to get himself a fresh beer. Finally he excused himself from Donna, the kindergarten teacher, and headed for the bar.

"Hey, Romeo." Sebastian caught his arm as he was heading back into the fray, a cold long-neck in one hand. "Got a minute?" He glanced at Travis's beer. "I'll buy you a drink."

Travis grinned, turned back to the bartender and lifted his bottle. "Get another one of these for the bridegroom, would you? The poor guy needs to live it up while he still has the chance."

"Yeah, I've got it tough," Sebastian said as he took the offered beer. "Not every guy could handle being married to a goddess, but fortunately I'm up to the job. Come on, let's get some air."

"I can see right off that my speech gave you a swelled head." Travis followed Sebastian outside. The air was cold, but it felt good after all the exercise he'd been getting on the dance floor. "Keep it up and I'll be obliged to round up a few guys to toss you in the horse trough."

"You think *I've* got a swelled head?" Sebastian leaned against the fender of the caterer's truck and unfastened the top button of his tux shirt. The string tie had been abandoned long ago. "After all the attention you've been getting tonight, it'll take three men and a boy to cram your hat on in the morning." He lifted his beer toward Travis and smiled. "Here's to one hell of a wedding."

Travis clinked his bottle to Sebastian's. "A great party for a great reason." He took a long swallow.

Sebastian sipped his beer and looked up at the night sky. "Full moon."

"I ordered it special."

Sebastian laughed. "Funny thing is, I believe you."

"Hey, I can do anything I set my mind to."

"Uh, huh. Evans, you really should work on that lack of confidence problem."

"I know what I know."

"Okay, you're amazing. But listen, I've been going over this honeymoon trip again, and I really think I ought to hire somebody to help you with Elizabeth while Matty and I are in Denver. We don't leave until noon, so I'm sure I could find somebody if I started calling around in the morning."

Travis stiffened. "You don't trust me with her."

"Sure I do. Well, maybe I didn't at first, but you've got the basics down. I'm worried about what you'll do if something goes wrong, though. We'd be at least three hours getting home, assuming we even got the message right away, and—"

"You are such an old granny, Daniels. I swear. I can handle it. If it's major I'll go to Doc Harrison. If it's minor, I'll go to Gwen." He'd just now thought of that, but the idea appealed to him. Not that he wanted any emergency to crop up concerning Lizzie. But the combination of him and the baby seemed to melt women's hearts. It might have a thawing effect on Gwen, too. Yeah, he just might have to consult Gwen on some baby-care question.

"What's up with you and Gwen, anyway?"

"What do you mean?" Travis took another swig of his beer, so he'd look cool and casual as he answered the question.

"I thought you two were like oil and water, but you were blending together pretty good during that dance earlier tonight."

"I think she's figured out I don't have horns and a forked tail, after all."

Sebastian gazed at him. "You do anything to hurt that woman, and Matty'll be the one with the pitchfork, aiming it straight at your sorry ass."

Travis blew out a breath. "Why does everybody think I'm out to break women's hearts?"

"It couldn't be on account of all the women you've left in tears, now could it?"

"Look, I've told each and every one of them I'm not in for the long haul. Is it my fault they won't listen?"

Sebastian took a drink of his beer and glanced up at the moon. "I told Matty I couldn't get serious, either, because of the baby and thinking I'd have to ask Jessica to marry me. That didn't stop Matty from getting hurt." He glanced back at Travis. "You can't order a woman not to fall in love with you."

Travis shifted uncomfortably under Sebastian's scrutiny. "I don't want Gwen to fall in love with me. I just—"

"Yeah, I know what you just. That dress she's wearing would make a monk leave his order."

Travis grinned. "Or revive a corpse at a wake."

Sebastian chuckled. "Or replace Viagra."

"I'm only human."

"I know all about your humanity," Sebastian said. "You're a legend in your own time. But go easy on this, okay? Gwen's a sweet lady and she had a rough few years with that husband of hers."

"I promise to be careful. We won't do anything that's not in our mutual best interests."

Sebastian nodded. "Good. And one other thing. If Jessica comes back while Matty and I are in Denver, you make her stay at the ranch until we can get home, okay?"

"Damn right I will. Jessica has some explaining to do, to all of us." And telling them who was Lizzie's father was the first thing, Travis thought. But he knew in his heart the little girl was his. Looks aside, Lizzie had his temperament. She was smart, easygoing and loved everybody.

"If I'm not convinced Jessica's in a position to take care of Elizabeth," Sebastian said, "I'm going to see what I can do about keeping the baby with us. I've checked into it, and abandoning your kid puts you on shaky legal ground."

Travis rubbed the back of his neck. "I still can't figure why she'd do that. It doesn't seem like the kind of thing the Jessica we know would even think of. Hell, it was her grit that saved Nat's life after the avalanche. Something pretty nasty must have scared the daylights out of her, to make her leave her kid like this."

"Yeah, and I want to find out what." Sebastian took another swig of his beer. "I've decided to hire a private investigator while we're in Denver."

"Good. I'll go halves with you on the fee. This is dragging out way too long."

"And it damned near made me lose Matty." Sebastian cocked an ear toward the tent. "And speaking of Matty, we'd better get back in. I think the bouquet and garter-throwing is about to start."

"Hey, you go ahead. I'd sooner catch a rattlesnake with my bare hands than that garter."

Sebastian laughed and shook his head. "I don't know what your problem is, Evans. You're twenty-eight, for crying out loud. The carefree single life must be getting old by now."

"Nah. It's terrific."

"So's marriage. Or at least I plan on it being terrific, this time around."

"For you, maybe. Not for this cowboy." Travis tipped the bottle back for a deep swallow of beer.

"Well, you gotta come back in and pretend to try for the garter. You're the best man, which means you should act like you're part of the proceedings. It'll look bad if you're not there."

"I'll be in shortly." Travis lifted his bottle. "And thanks for the beer."

"It'll come out of your paycheck. Don't forget— now that Matty and I are combining our spreads, you'll be working for me."

Travis clutched his chest and staggered backward in mock horror. "Don't tell me I have to start calling you *boss?*"

"Or Your Royal Highness. Whichever comes easier."

"How about Your Royal Pain in the Ass?" Travis grinned. "That comes real easy."

Sebastian rolled his eyes. "When I throw the garter, I'm aiming for you, hotshot. You need a woman to trim your wick. Now get your butt in there."

"Shortly."

"Insubordination already." Sebastian sighed and went back inside the tent.

Travis figured he'd stall around outside and appear at the tail end of the garter-throwing. He wasn't overly superstitious, but a guy couldn't be too careful.

He'd thought about marriage, more than he'd ever admit to Sebastian, and he'd reasoned out that it was too complicated given his present circumstances. A promise was a promise, and he'd made a huge one to his dad before the old man died six years ago. Travis intended to honor that promise and take care of his mother, who depended on him something fierce.

She managed okay during the summer months, when she could walk to the little country store down the road from their place. In the winter, though, when the snow was up to her armpits, she needed Travis there to shovel the walkways and drive her where she had to go.

No one in this valley knew anything about his life in Utah, and that's the way he liked it. If folks around here thought he was a devil-may-care playboy, that was fine with him. But the truth was that keeping his mother healthy and happy took all of his resources. He couldn't imagine having enough energy left for a wife.

GWEN HADN'T PLANNED to take part in the bouquet tossing, but Matty had informed her it was obligatory. So she moved to the back of the crowd of women, figuring Matty wouldn't heave the thing that far.

As the women stood there laughing and joking, Matty turned her back and sent the flowers sailing... right over everybody's head. Gwen was forced to leap up and snag it or the beautiful bouquet would have landed on the floor. For a split second she considered letting that happen, but that would have created an awkward moment. With skills learned on the volleyball court as a kid, she pulled down the prize.

Everybody in the room cheered, and Gwen stood there holding the bouquet and feeling like a doofus. She was immensely grateful when the attention returned to Matty for the garter removal ceremony.

Amid a chorus of wolf whistles, Matty propped one foot on a chair and pulled back her skirt.

Sebastian quickly and efficiently divested her of the garter. Twirling it neatly around one finger, he turned toward the circle of men. "Show's over, gents. And let that be the last whistle I hear any of you aim in my wife's direction. *Comprende?*"

"Killjoy!" called out one of the cowboys.

"No, *husband,*" Sebastian replied with a dangerous-looking smile. "Now, where the hell's Evans?"

Gwen glanced around and realized that Travis hadn't come back in with Sebastian. She'd seen the two men head outside. Embarrassingly enough, she'd been aware of every move Travis had made that night. None of them had been in her direction.

"Evans?" one of the men said with a laugh. "You'll never get that ol' boy within twenty feet of a wedding garter. Toss that thing my way, Daniels. I could use another dance with the Maid of Honor."

"Not if I get to that lace thingamajig first," said the cowboy next to him.

"You'll have to get past me," said a third man.

Gratifying as it was to have men squabbling over the right to dance with her, Gwen couldn't work up a smidgen of enthusiasm for any of them. And damn, but she wished she could. They were nice guys, steady guys.

Apparently she hadn't meditated enough on the dangers of being attracted to a rogue. The only man in the vicinity who held her interest was the last man she should spend time with. Fortunately he was still outside and wasn't in the running for the garter.

"I guess we'll have to do this without Evans," Sebastian said. "And watch those elbows. I'd like to think we're all gentlemen here," he added with a grin.

"I'd like to think so, too, but I don't," said the first cowboy. "And that garter's mine."

"May the best man win." Sebastian aimed the garter into the air like a slingshot.

"Somebody called?" Travis stepped into the tent.

"Now that's cutting it close," Sebastian muttered as he let the garter fly.

Gwen knew Travis had amazing reflexes. He could rope and tie a calf faster than anybody in the valley, and he wasn't shy about saying so. But the lightning moves he demonstrated as he snatched the garter out of the air left the women gasping and the men swearing.

"What'd you do that for?" complained Jason Litchfield, a lanky cowhand who'd been hitting on Gwen all night. "Everybody knows you're not lookin' to get tied down, and catching that thing means you'll be the next one hitched."

Travis shrugged and tucked the garter in his pocket as he started toward Gwen. "Maybe, maybe not. But I've been wanting to dance with the maid of honor all night, and you boys have been keeping her so busy, I haven't been able to get close."

Gwen stood frozen in place, her heart beating like a rabbit's. There would be no baby between them this time.

Just before Travis reached her, Sebastian came over and clapped him on the back. "Congratulations on catching that garter. It would do my heart good to see you finally settle down with the right woman."

Travis glanced at him. "It'll take more than a garter to get me to the altar, buddy."

"Oh, I'm sure it will." Sebastian winked at Gwen. "But it's a start. Now if you'll excuse me, I'm going to find the previous owner of that garter and take her for a turn around the floor."

Travis gazed at Gwen. Then he swept out an arm and bowed. "May I have this dance?"

"I guess so." She put her hand in his and allowed him to lead her to the dance floor. Just the casual interlacing of their fingers quickened her breath. "You worked hard enough for it."

"Piece of cake. Hand-eye coordination has always been easy for me."

"And you're so modest about it, too."

He chuckled and swung her into his arms.

She rested the hand holding the bridal bouquet on his shoulder, and with every swirl of the waltz step, the fragrance of roses and lavender drifted around them, toying with her senses. She'd expected an aggressively sexual man like Travis to pull her in close and get all the body contact he could manage. Instead he kept several inches between them, guiding her with a firm hand at her waist while cupping her right hand gently, yet expertly, in his.

But once again, he held her captive with his gaze. And Travis could do more with his eyes than any man she'd ever met. She'd danced with many partners tonight, and all of them had pulled her in tight, blatantly announcing their sexual interest with their bodies. Not one of them had made her sizzle.

She was sizzling now. The spot where Travis pressed the small of her back became an erogenous zone, sending arousing signals to every part of her body. His eyes seduced her, inviting her to imagine making love with him. His rhythmic skill on the dance floor hinted at his legendary skill in the bedroom.

She'd heard the whispered rumors about Travis, and

her imagination filled in the rest. She guessed that he was the kind of lover women dreamed of in their deepest, most erotic moments. The kind even *she* had dreamed of, but never planned to have.

Because he was dangerous. He could break her heart so that it would never heal. And yet…he could make her secret fantasies come true, teach her things about her own sensuality that no other man could. But he would not stay. He would never stay.

The silence between them became heavy with unspoken desire. She struggled to break the spell. "I'm amazed you went for the garter," she said. "I guess you're not superstitious."

"I am sort of superstitious." His grip at her waist tightened a fraction. "But this looked like the only way I was going to get another dance with you. I decided it might be worth tempting fate."

She swallowed. "And is it?"

"Oh, I think it will be." His glance swept her face, slid down her throat, settled for a second longer than was polite on her breasts. Then he returned his gaze to her eyes. Hunger flickered there as he drew her a bare inch closer, so that the bodice of her dress brushed the front of his tux shirt, catching lightly on the pearl studs with each movement.

The contact was faint, subtle. Yet her nipples tightened and her breathing grew labored.

"Is that bed and breakfast of yours full?" he murmured.

"Why?" She had to keep her head. "Are you angling for personal service?"

"Nope." He drew her in a little bit more, causing her sensitive breasts to be crushed gently against the hard wall of his chest. "Just wondered how business was."

She could feel his heartbeat, rapid like hers. She should push away from him, but couldn't make herself do it. For the first time in months, maybe years, she felt alive again. "Business is a little slow right now." She cleared the hoarseness from her throat. "The skiers are gone, and the summer season doesn't usually get going until after Memorial Day."

"Hmm." Neatly, without fanfare, he broke eye contact, snugged her up close and laid his cheek against hers. "So what do you do with yourself all day?"

She closed her eyes against the wash of passion that left her shaking. "I weave," she whispered. With each movement they made, she felt the nudge of his erection. Her body moistened, pulsed, yearned.

His lips touched her ear. "I like the blanket you made Lizzie. It's so soft."

"Mmm." Oh, she ached as she'd never ached in her life.

His voice was like velvet. "Say yes, Gwen. Say yes and let me love you."

Her heart thundered in her chest. She didn't hear the music stop.

But Travis obviously had, because he slowly released her and drew back to look deeply into her eyes. Heat burned in his gaze, and his hands at her waist quivered with urgency. "Please say yes," he whispered. "I need you."

She couldn't speak. His obvious desire called out to her, teasing her with the promise of fantasies fulfilled, begging her to forget everything else and be swept away by shared passion. Calling upon the last scrap of sanity left in her fevered brain, she shook her head.

CHAPTER FOUR

TRAVIS DIDN'T TAKE Gwen's rejection personally. And because he was an expert at reading women, he didn't even believe it. Other guys might get themselves into trouble with no-means-yes situations and either miss an opportunity or, worse yet, force the issue and get slapped.

Travis had never missed an opportunity, and he'd never been slapped. He'd been told by some of his drinking buddies that he should give a clinic on how to understand a lady, no matter what words came out of her pretty mouth.

The secret could be summed up in two words—body language. When he'd propositioned Gwen, and he'd done a damn fine job of it, too, she'd shaken her head no. But he'd be a fool to accept that.

At the same time she was shaking her head, her skin was flushed and hot, her pupils were dilated, her mouth was parted and her breathing was uneven. She was leaning so far toward him that she was in danger of toppling over. Or into his arms. Gwen might think she was saying no with that shake of her head, but the rest of her was screaming yes.

But now was not the time to touch her. Now was not the time to challenge her decision, either.

"Okay," he murmured. "I'll respect that."

Her eyes widened. "You will?" Disappointment was written all over her face.

He bit his tongue to keep from laughing. "Of course. What sort of a jerk do you think I am? I gave it my best shot and you're still not interested. I'm not about to make a fool out of myself."

She straightened and moved back a pace. "Uh, that's good. Because you would have if you'd kept insisting." She rubbed a hand over the soft green material stretched across her rib cage, as if calming butterflies in her stomach. "It's good we got that settled."

He nodded, taking note of the pulse beating rapidly at the base of her throat. "Right. I like to know where I stand."

Longing shone in her eyes, but she glanced away. "Well, now you do." She gave him one more quick look. "I'd better check with Matty and see if she needs anything."

"You do that."

"Travis!" a woman called from across the room. "The next dance is mine!"

Travis turned, recognizing Donna's voice. "Absolutely!" he called out in reply. When he turned back, Gwen was gone.

ABOUT AN HOUR later Gwen lined up with the rest of the guests to pelt Matty and Sebastian with birdseed while the newlyweds made their way over to the ranch house. She headed up a line on one side of the tent entrance and Travis stood across from her in the other line.

Resisting Travis had been for the best, Gwen told herself. She just wished he hadn't given up so quickly.

And he definitely seemed to have given up. He'd spent the past hour dancing and flirting with his many admirers, not that she'd noticed, or anything. Ha. Her jaw ached from gritting her teeth.

She watched him joking with Donna, who seemed to have the inside track at the moment. Gwen had to admit that Travis's pursuit this evening had been one of the more exciting episodes in her life.

Maybe *the* most exciting episode, now that she thought about it. She didn't exactly lead a thrill-packed life. The word *dull* came to mind. But she hadn't been able to figure out how to have both stability and excitement, so she'd chosen stability.

Travis had offered her a chance for a little excitement, and chicken that she was, she'd refused him. Deep down, she was afraid she wasn't wild enough for Travis. He'd probably tire of her quickly, and then he'd be the one to call it quits. Like Derek. How embarrassing.

If she could simply enjoy his attentions and then cut off the relationship before he did, she might have considered his offer. But she'd hung on to Derek way too long, and she could easily make the same mistake with Travis. Besides, Travis was no longer extending his offer, so debating the issue in her head was stupid and unproductive.

"Here they come!" yelled Travis. "Man your birdseed!"

Gwen poured the contents of her little packet into her hand. Matty and Sebastian, carrying a blanket-covered Elizabeth, emerged from the tent into the light of the full moon. As they hurried through the gauntlet amid cheers and shouts, Gwen tossed the birdseed into the air and silently wished them all the babies they wanted.

And she would play the role of Auntie Gwen. She would weave blankets for each one, she thought, and offer to baby-sit, and bake them cinnamon rolls. Maybe it was better to spoil someone else's children instead of having the constant hassle of having your own. Maybe. But she didn't really think so.

Once Matty, Sebastian and the baby were inside the ranch house, the guests began their round of goodbyes. Following Matty's instructions, Gwen gave away the centerpieces and any extra favors. As she moved through the departing crowd, she noticed that several women besides Donna hung around Travis, as if hoping he might pick one to take home with him. Not wanting to know whether he did or not, she went back into the tent to help the caterers pack up and make sure nobody had left any belongings behind.

Finally the caterers removed all the coffee urns and bagged up all the table linens. At the last moment Gwen snatched up Matty's bridal bouquet so it wouldn't accidentally be tossed in one of the large plastic garbage bags by mistake.

As she listened to the catering truck pull away, she gazed around the silent, empty tent and sighed. Nothing more to do except throw the switch on the small white lights and go home. The party, as they said, was over.

"You look tired."

Gwen whirled to find Travis walking toward her. A night of partying had left him looking appealingly disheveled, and the glow from the tiny white lights overhead added a roguish sparkle to his gaze. But he'd said he'd respect her wishes, so he wasn't here to try and seduce her.

Her heart began to pound anyway. "I thought everyone had left by now."

"Everyone but me. I thought I'd better stay and find out if there's anything more to do."

"That's nice of you, but I think we're fine." She should get the hell out of here while the getting was good. "All that's left is turning out the lights." She stroked the rose petals of the bouquet, needing something to do with her hands. "The rental company will come out tomorrow to pick up the tables and chairs and the tent."

He nodded and glanced around at the bare tables. "It looked pretty."

"It really did." Being alone with him was starting to have an effect, making her tremble. She clutched the bouquet more tightly. "Listen, I probably should go—"

"Yeah, me, too. So that's it? You're sure there's nothing else?"

She didn't know how he'd managed to get so close to her, but before she realized it, he was near enough that she could see the gold flecks in his warm brown eyes. And if that wasn't a seductive look he was giving her, she'd never seen one before.

Her pulse raced. "Nothing else. It went like clock-work."

"Yeah, it did. But I have a nagging feeling we forgot something." His beautiful mouth curved in a soft smile.

That mouth. That talented mouth. She wanted to know what his kiss would be like. And he saw through her. She was sure of it. He knew that right this minute, she was imagining the way his lips would taste.

"You know that feeling?" he said. "That you've missed some detail?"

She struggled to take a breath. "I don't have that feeling."

"I do," he murmured. His gaze drifted to the bouquet she held like a shield between them. He stroked a rosebud, loosening the pink petals with deft fingers. Then he plucked one free and lifted it to her mouth, slowly brushing it over her bottom lip.

She grew dizzy. "Go away, Travis," she whispered.

"Can't, Gwen." The rose petal fluttered to the ground as he cupped her jaw, holding her steady as he lowered his head. "I just remembered what I forgot."

She could still escape, she thought wildly as his breath drifted warm and sweet across her mouth. She could still pull back and run away, still save herself if she just....

Too late. Ahhh…way too late. Way too good. The mouth of an angel…the tongue of a devil. Oh, *yes*.

Later she might regret this moment, but no woman could think of regret when a man was kissing her like this. He was delicious, tasting of wine and wedding cake and the wild, heady flavor of desire. And he knew what he was doing. Oh boy, did he know. Everyone had a special talent, and it seemed she'd just discovered his. She wrapped greedy arms around him and pulled him close, body to heated body, while his mouth worked magic on hers.

His kiss became a messenger, sending urgent signals to her breasts, her inner thighs, her throbbing womb. She grew taut, moist, ready. Resistance was a dim memory eclipsed by the glowing prospect of surrender.

He lifted his lips a fraction from hers. "Come home with me."

Yes. She gasped for air so that she could give him an answer, the only possible answer now that he'd kissed her so thoroughly and left her body thrumming with need.

"Hey, is anybody still here?"

Travis released her immediately and they both turned as Sebastian walked into the tent.

Gwen's cheeks warmed. She put more distance between her and Travis and clutched the bouquet in both hands to disguise how she was shaking.

Sebastian took one look at them and backed up a couple of steps. "Whoops. Sorry. We saw the lights were still on and Matty asked me to come out and check on the situation. Sorry."

Travis cleared his throat. "We'll, uh, make sure the lights are out when we leave."

"I knew that," Sebastian said, backing up into the shadows outside the tent.

"Didn't suppose you'd be taking time to glance out the window on your wedding night," Travis said.

His comment blew like a cool breeze through Gwen's fevered brain. Matty and Sebastian were enjoying a wedding night, but all Travis had offered was an affair. That just wasn't good enough.

"Elizabeth woke up and started fussing," Sebastian said. "Listen, I'll just go on back, okay? Travis, I'll see you up at the house about eleven in the morning."

"I'll be there."

"See you then. Sorry for the interruption."

Gwen took a deep breath. "I'll be going now, too, Sebastian. Maybe you'd be willing to walk me to my truck." She headed for the entrance with a determined step.

"Sure," Sebastian said. "But—"

"I'm sure Travis knows how to shut off the lights."

"I do," Travis said, "but I was hoping—"

"It's been a long evening." She glanced over her shoulder at him and forced herself to ignore the hard tug of sexual desire. "Good night, Travis."

His gaze was hot enough to melt steel. "Good night, Gwen."

He was darned potent. If Sebastian hadn't been there, she might have forgotten her principles and run back into his arms. But Sebastian's presence reminded her of what she really wanted from a man—forever. Tempting as he was, Travis didn't fill the bill.

THE FOLLOWING NIGHT Travis sank into Sebastian's old pine rocker and leaned his head back in complete exhaustion. Fleafarm, Sebastian's mixed breed, and Sadie, Matty's Great Dane, plopped at his feet.

Travis didn't remember being this tired even after a day of branding. Babies were a hell of a lot of work, but there were compensations. Lizzie was a smart little dickens. In no time at all, he'd taught her to blow an outstanding raspberry.

Her new trick had been kind of a liability when he'd tried to feed her cereal tonight, but they'd had fun playing with the stuff. He'd let her paint his face with it until he looked like some undead character from a horror flick.

Then she'd needed a bath, and some time to play on the baby gym he'd bought her last week. And finally he'd given her a bottle, changed her diaper again, and tucked her into bed. She was asleep at last, and Travis wondered if he had enough energy left to fix himself a sandwich.

As he contemplated whether he'd take the time to eat or give up and crawl into bed, he thought about Gwen. He'd fully intended to do a quick follow-up with her this afternoon after he was settled into his baby-sitting routine. He'd figured he and Lizzie would pay a little afternoon social call to Hawthorne House and see if they could get invited for dinner.

His plan had fizzled. He'd spent the time Lizzie was sleeping running a load of baby clothes through the washer and dryer, and by the time she woke up from her nap it was time to check on the horses, feed the dogs, and feed Lizzie. Thank God Matty had moved her saddle horses up to the Rocking D, or he'd have run himself ragged going back and forth between her barn and Sebastian's.

But it would be a busier week than he'd thought, that was for sure. Unfortunately, the longer he went without seeing Gwen, the more likely she'd go cold on him again. He'd had her warmed up pretty good last night, and he'd been in a state of semi-arousal ever since. He'd welcome some relief for that condition, but he wouldn't be getting it tonight.

Doggone Sebastian's hide, anyway. But you couldn't land into a guy right before his honeymoon, so Travis hadn't even had the satisfaction of yelling at Sebastian for ruining the moment. Besides, Travis wasn't convinced it had been an accident. Matty didn't want him getting involved with Gwen. If she'd noticed his truck and Gwen's still parked by the tent, she might have sent Sebastian out on purpose.

Travis sighed. Kissing Gwen had turned out to be better than he'd expected. She'd reminded him of what kissing had been like when he'd first discovered it and had been totally fascinated with the pleasure of exploring a girl's mouth. Later on in his education, he'd progressed to other areas of a woman's anatomy, and he'd been guilty of downgrading kissing to a preliminary step leading to more interesting activities.

With Gwen he could imagine kissing as an end in itself. Or at least something to pass the time for a good long while. Her mouth was soft and supple, full in a way that made him want to nibble, welcoming in a way that made him want to thrust deep with his tongue. She tasted sweet and spicy, which was the way he'd imagine she'd be in bed.

The crotch of his jeans grew tight. Apparently he wasn't as exhausted as he'd thought. He'd better think of something else besides taking Gwen to bed if he wanted to sleep tonight. He wondered if she was frustrated too. She might be, but he doubted she'd show her hand enough to drive over here tonight, even if he called and asked her to.

Still, it was a thought. He could say he wanted her to check out something to do with Lizzie. No, that would be too underhanded. He was doing fine with Lizzie.

He could be bold and say he couldn't stop thinking about her, which was true. Maybe, if he explained that he was stuck here, she'd take pity on him and consider—

The ringing phone sent adrenaline pumping through him. The dogs leaped up, too, and the three of them hurried to the kitchen. Travis grabbed the cordless receiver from its cradle, hoping that his prayers were about to be answered. "Hello?" He sounded too eager, but he couldn't help that. He was eager.

"Who is this?"

He paused. The caller was a woman, but it definitely wasn't Gwen. He went on alert. "That depends on who you are."

"Jessica."

He should have known. Sebastian had warned him she often called late at night.

"It's Travis, Jessica." He headed for Sebastian's office, where the tracing equipment was set up. "Listen, you need to get back here. Whatever you're afraid of—"

"I can't be near Elizabeth. It's not safe for her. Is she okay?"

"She's fine. But I deserve to know if I'm her—"

Click.

Travis clenched the receiver and swore softly. So much for tracing the call. Even if he'd been prepared to do it, she hadn't stayed on the line long enough. And even if she had, he wasn't in a position to go tearing off in search of her. She could be hundreds of miles away. And once she'd made the call, she'd probably leave the area, anyway. That's what he'd do if he didn't want to be found.

He returned to the kitchen and hung up the phone. In the process he glanced at the list of numbers tacked to the small bulletin board Matty had hung on the wall. She'd made several small changes like that in the past couple of weeks, putting her stamp on Sebastian's house. Her floor loom now occupied a corner of the living room, and one of her favorite paintings of a mare and foal hung over the fireplace.

She'd directed Travis's attention to the list of phone numbers at least four times before she and Sebastian had left for Denver that morning. Doc Harrison had top billing and was in red, no less. Next came the vet. Then relatives. Then Gwen.

Travis stared at Gwen's number for several long seconds. After all, he did have news. Jessica had called again.

He picked up the receiver and punched in Gwen's number. It rang twice before he thought to glance at the clock, and by then it was too late. He'd already disturbed her at an ungodly hour.

"Hawthorne House." She didn't sound the least bit sleepy.

"It's Travis." He wondered if she was still awake because she was frustrated and edgy, too. He hoped so.

"Is the baby okay?" she asked quickly.

"She's perfect. I just got a call from Jessica."

"You did?" Excitement laced her response. "Did she say anything new?"

"Only that it wasn't safe for her to be around Lizzie. But we'd kind of figured that."

"So she didn't say..."

"Who fathered Lizzie? Nope. But I guess it doesn't matter. I know she's mine."

"You sound proud of the fact."

He thought about that. "I guess I am," he said with some surprise. "I know it shouldn't have happened in the first place, but now that Lizzie's here, I'm not sorry. I'm gonna spend as much time as possible with her while she's growing up."

"Imagine that. Travis Evans making a commitment to a female."

She was getting snippy, he thought. His idea of inviting her over might be a pipe dream. "I make commitments to women all the time."

"Sure you do."

"If I'm involved with a woman, she's the only one in my life during that time. That's a commitment."

"Pardon me if I'm underwhelmed by such virtue."

He wished he had her right in front of him instead of on the telephone. Talking wasn't getting them anywhere. Action was what they both needed. "Not everybody is cut out for marriage. At least I'm honest about that."

"Okay, then let me be equally honest with you. Get lost."

He'd decided that her sass was a defense against her strong feelings for him. "Then I guess you aren't planning to drop by tonight to keep me company."

"In your dreams."

"Oh, you'll be in my dreams, all right. Last night you were the main feature."

"Funny, but I didn't dream at all last night." She sounded like the damned Queen of England.

He was beginning to like that snooty attitude of hers. It would make her surrender that much sweeter. "Of course you didn't dream. You were wide awake and frustrated, wishing I was there."

"Travis, your ego is huge!"

He grinned. "True, but women tell me it matches my...personality."

"I'm hanging up this phone."

"Good. Hang up and drive over. You sound tense. Let me give you a massage. I use the heel of my hand on the big muscles, and my fingers for some of the smaller ones. And there's a spot on your inner thigh that—"

A gentle click on the other end of the line told him she'd hung up. He wished he could believe she was on her way to the Rocking D, but he doubted it. He'd have to go to her, and with the way Lizzie kept him hopping, that would be more difficult than he'd thought.

CHAPTER FIVE

GWEN TOOK OFF the tea towel she'd draped over the mixing bowl sitting on her kitchen counter. Then she punched her fist into the swollen mound of dough inside. It was the most satisfaction she'd had all day.

Dressed in her favorite at-home outfit of soft, faded sweats, her hair caught in a casual topknot, she was consoling herself by making comfort food—her famous cinnamon rolls.

And she definitely needed comfort this afternoon. After Travis's provocative phone call two nights ago, he'd dropped out of sight. She wished he'd dropped out of mind, too, but no such luck. In addition to battling frustration over Travis, she'd had to deal with the latest e-mail from her mother, who was currently on a dig near Cairo.

Her mother had wanted to know when Gwen was planning to stop "playing house" and continue her academic career. Gwen was the only member of the family without a college degree and an intellectual job, and that had bothered her mother for years.

After sprinkling flour on the butcher-block surface, Gwen scooped the dough out and began kneading it with firm, vigorous strokes. She was good at this, damn it. It might not be rocket science, but she took satisfaction in turning out a cinnamon roll that made her guests groan with delight.

Her mother might be able to identify a pre-Columbian artifact at a thousand paces, but when she'd tackled baking from scratch, her yeast had died and her cinnamon rolls had been hard as hockey pucks. She'd pronounced the whole exercise not worth her time in the first place, claiming that people ate too much of that stuff anyway.

Intellectually, Gwen had known that her mother dissed baking because she couldn't do it. Her mother had laughingly called Gwen a throwback who for some strange reason excelled at anything domestic. The subtle put-down might have salvaged her mother's ego, but it hadn't done much for Gwen's.

This morning's e-mail probably bothered her more because she wasn't sleeping well. She tried to blame her insomnia on not having enough to do now that Matty and Sebastian's wedding was over. No guests were due until the following weekend, and she didn't dare plant her seedlings in the garden until the frost warnings were over for the season. Her weaving, which had never failed to calm her, was failing her now. She needed the big muscle movement of cleaning up after guests, planting veggies or…or having sex.

Well, *that* wouldn't be happening, so she might as well get her sensory kicks out of kneading dough. And it was sensual, she admitted as she pushed the heel of her hand into the soft, yielding surface. On the phone the other night Travis had said he used the heel of his hand on the big muscles, and his fingers on the smaller ones….

And just like that, her mind leaped back inside the squirrel cage. It spun around chasing the subject of Travis while her hands followed the familiar steps of making cinnamon rolls. The action of the marble rolling pin flattening the dough reminded her of the way Travis had stroked her back while they danced. She remembered the silkiness of his kiss when she slid a knife into a stick of softened butter and spread the butter over the dough.

Butter was a more erotic substance than she'd realized, and she grew fascinated with the creamy slide of it as she moved the knife blade over the pliable surface of the dough. She wondered how butter would feel on her skin, how it would feel to have someone lick it off.

A certain someone.

The scent of sugar and cinnamon reminded her of Travis's aftershave. She sprinkled raisins over the surface of the buttered dough and rolled it into a cylinder—a cylinder that fit her hand with the same thickness and heft as…oh, dear. She was hopeless.

She blew out an impatient breath and sliced the cylinder deliberately into sections. Fate had played a cruel trick on her, giving her a talent for creating a hearth and home, then making her susceptible to rogues who never intended to settle down.

She'd thought Derek had cured her of her weakness for a knowing wink and a sexy smile. After suffering through the insensitive behavior of her husband, she should run in the opposite direction when a man tried his devilish ways on her. Yet here she was, longing for another bad boy as if she hadn't learned a single thing during her marriage.

Travis would never know how close she'd come to driving out to the Rocking D the night he'd called. Good thing she hadn't, because his silence for the past two days indicated that he'd lost interest already. Maybe he didn't have time to fool with someone who didn't fall immediately into his clutches. Maybe he'd moved on to Donna, who would have driven out to the ranch before Travis had time to hang up the phone.

The doorbell rang as she put the rolls in the oven. Telling herself to expect the mailman or a solicitor, she deliberately took her time rinsing the flour off her hands and wiping them dry before walking down the hall toward the front door. The door's oval stained-glass insert gave her an indistinct picture of the person on the other side, but her heart recognized Travis and the baby immediately. Her pulse kicked into high gear.

She paused to take a deep breath and tamp down her eagerness. Travis was difficult enough to manage when he wasn't quite sure of himself. If he suspected she'd been thinking of him for two solid days, the situation would be out of control in no time. No doubt he'd brought the baby over as a ploy to soften her resistance. Little did he know he didn't need the baby to make Gwen as pliable as the dough she'd just been shaping.

But she straightened her spine and reminded herself he hadn't contacted her for two days. And for the time being, she still had her pride.

Turning the polished brass knob, she opened the door and promptly forgot all her resolutions as compassion swept over her. A cool spring breeze blew across the porch, and Travis had wrapped Elizabeth in a light blanket as he cradled her against his chest. She was fussing, and he looked completely done in.

"Lizzie has caught a cold," he said. "If you don't want to expose yourself to her germs, that's okay, but—"

"Come in." Gwen stepped back from the door and held out her arms. "And let me have that poor baby."

Travis looked as if she'd offered him a million dollars. "Thanks, Gwen. You don't know how much this means to me." He settled the squirming baby in her arms. "I've just been to Doc Harrison's for a diagnosis and Coogan's Department Store for supplies. The doc says it's nothing to worry about, but I'm fit to be tied."

"Poor Elizabeth," Gwen crooned as she unwrapped the baby and noticed that her button nose was red and her usually bright eyes dull. "I'll bet she picked up something at the wedding."

Travis closed the door. "That's what the doc says. He told me not to worry, that babies catch colds all the time, but I purely hate this."

"Of course you do." Gwen noticed Elizabeth's nose was running. "Come on back to the kitchen. I'll get a tissue." She hurried down the hall and ducked into the downstairs bathroom to grab a tissue from the wicker dispenser on the vanity. "Poor sweetie," she murmured, wiping the tiny nose gently as she continued on into the kitchen.

Travis stood in the middle of the room looking endearingly unsure of himself. And damned sexy. He wore old jeans with the same flair as he wore a tuxedo.

But he was nervous. She could tell by the way he took off his Stetson and ran his fingers through his hair before clamping his hat on his head again. Travis wasn't the sort to fool with his clothes. He was usually too busy being swashbuckling.

Today he didn't seem the least interested in charming her. All his attention was focused on the baby. "Do you think we should call Matty and Sebastian?" he asked. "Doc said it's not necessary, but I think maybe—"

"Let's not," Gwen said. "We'd probably scare them to death, and she'll no doubt be all better by the time they get home, anyway."

Elizabeth began to fret.

Gwen jiggled her and wiped her nose again. "Poor darling. It's not fun having a stuffy nose, is it?" She glanced up at Travis. "Did you bring her bottle with you?"

"Yeah. Her diaper bag's out in the truck, but it's hard to get her to drink when her nose is clogged up. I bought apple juice because the doc thought I should give her some, and Nellie Coogan sold me this thingamajig that looks like a tiny turkey baster. Nellie said you use it to suck the stuff out of her nose, but I'd be scared spitless to use it on her. I bought a small jar of Vaseline for her sore nose, and a humidifier. And one of those Barney guys."

Gwen blinked. "I was with you all the way until you got to Barney."

"He's that dinosaur on TV. Kids go wild for him."

"I know that much." Gwen rocked Elizabeth, trying to distract the baby from her discomfort. "I have kids staying here at Hawthorne House sometimes. But what does Barney have to do with getting over a cold?"

"When you're sick, you need a poor-me present," he said with the first show of confidence he'd displayed since he'd appeared on her doorstep. "Everybody knows that."

"Oh." Gwen held back a smile. "Of course."

Travis glanced at Elizabeth, who was making pitiful little noises of unhappiness. "So you really don't think we should call Matty and Sebastian? They called last night and I told them everything was fine. Then this morning Lizzie was all stuffed up. Maybe they'd want to know."

Gwen thought of how excited Matty had been while she planned for her week in the big city. She and Gwen had shopped for days buying slinky dresses for nights out on the town, and revealing negligees for private moments in the honeymoon suite of one of Denver's finest hotels. Matty had never been treated to such luxury.

"I hate to tell them," Gwen said. "This is a special time for both of them, and if Doc Harrison said Elizabeth's not in any danger, it seems a shame to get them upset. They might even think they should come home. And I honestly don't think having them home would make a bit of difference. This will just have to run its course."

"But what if she gets worse? The doc didn't rule that out."

"Well, then you can call them, I guess. But I think calling them now is premature."

Travis stuck his hands in his hip pockets and blew out a breath. Then he glanced at her. "Okay, I'll accept that. But I'm scared to take her back out to the ranch and be there alone with her. It's a good twenty-minute drive to town, and if she suddenly got bad, I'd—"

"You want to leave her here with me, don't you?" Gwen discovered she wouldn't mind in the least. In fact, she'd welcome the chance to have Elizabeth, even if she did have a cold. In the years of running the bed and breakfast, Gwen had encountered her share of sick babies, and the prospect of taking care of Elizabeth while she was under the weather didn't worry her nearly as much as it obviously did Travis.

"Not exactly." Travis looked her straight in the eye. "This is going to sound suspicious to you, all things considered. But I swear I don't mean anything under-handed by it. I'm caught in the middle here. I'm afraid to be out on the Rocking D alone with Lizzie, so far from town and Doc Harrison, but I don't think I could stand leaving her with you overnight, either. I want to be with her, in case she gets worse."

Reaction shivered up Gwen's spine. He'd never looked at her like that, with no twinkle in his golden eyes, no hidden agenda lurking behind his steady gaze. She couldn't doubt his sincerity or his deep concern for the baby, and yet…how could she possibly invite him to stay here? And how could she not?

"I wouldn't blame you for turning me down," Travis said. "But I don't know what else to do."

"You could have taken her to Donna's," Gwen said quietly. "After all, she's a kindergarten teacher."

He shook his head. "Donna doesn't know Lizzie like you do. She only saw her for the first time at the wedding. And Matty's not all that fond of Donna, to be honest. Thinks she's overbearing and pushy. Matty would expect me to ask for your help, not Donna's. As far as Matty's concerned, you're practically family."

Gwen wiped Elizabeth's nose again and kissed the top of her head. She did feel connected to this little girl, which probably wasn't wise, considering the baby wouldn't ever be Gwen's, in any sense of the word. "That's nice to hear."

"I don't know if you'll believe me, but I promise to behave myself. All I care about is getting Lizzie well and staying close to the doctor in case she needs something."

Gwen looked into his eyes. In times past, he'd made her heart flutter with his rakish glances, but he'd never stirred her so deeply as now, when the only emotion she saw was loving concern for the baby he believed to be his. Perhaps she'd been hasty in judging him as superficial. In his worry over Elizabeth, he seemed to have completely forgotten his sexual needs.

"You can both stay." She mentally crossed her fingers and hoped she'd be strong enough to weather this. "It does seem like the best way to make sure Elizabeth will be safe and well."

His shoulders sagged in relief. "I don't know what I would have done if you'd said no."

"I'm doing this for Lizzie, and for Matty and Sebastian."

A ghost of a grin crossed his handsome face. "Oh, I don't doubt that. Without Lizzie, I probably wouldn't have made it past your front door today."

"True enough." And she wanted him to keep right on believing that. "Maybe you'd better bring in her diaper bag and all the things you bought."

"Yeah." He started out of the kitchen and paused. "You said you sometimes have kids here. Do you have a crib around?"

"I do. But what about your chores at the ranch? Is everything all right out there for the next twenty-four hours?"

He looked stricken. "My God, you're right. I forgot about the dogs and the horses. I can't believe I did that. I'd...I'd appreciate it if you wouldn't let Matty and Sebastian know that I forgot about the animals."

"You've been worried, and I'm sure they'd want your top priority to be Elizabeth." She was touched that he'd been so preoccupied with the baby. And there was no doubt in her mind that he hadn't planned this overnight stay. He'd panicked and brought Elizabeth straight in to see Doc Harrison, not thinking beyond the baby's immediate needs.

"If it's okay with you," he said, "after I bring in Lizzie's stuff, I'll take a quick run out there and put the dogs in the barn. I can pick up a toothbrush and a razor while I'm at it, and call Len down the road. He could run over and feed all the animals in the morning."

"That's fine." *A toothbrush and a razor.* The announced items made his impending presence in her house more real, and she shivered again.

"Thank you, Gwen. This means more than I can say." He looked around at the house as if seeing it for the first time. "It's real nice here."

"I like it."

"And something smells great."

"Oh! The cinnamon rolls!" She'd totally forgotten them. Talk about being preoccupied. She *never* forgot what was in the oven, which was why she never bothered to set a timer. She hurried forward and put Elizabeth into his arms. "Hold her for a minute."

"Sure."

She got the rolls out in the nick of time. They were plump and golden-brown, oozing with warm raisins and caramelized sugar. She set them on the counter to cool and went to retrieve Elizabeth.

"Are those for something in particular?" Travis asked as he handed over the baby.

"No. I just felt like making them." She cradled Elizabeth against her shoulder and patted her back.

"Gonna put frosting on them?"

"I always do." She couldn't help smiling at the longing in his eyes when he glanced over at the rolls. "I'd be willing to share them, if you like."

He grinned. "I'd like. If a guy's gonna be noble, he oughta at least get a consolation prize."

Before she could think of an answer, he was out the door headed for his truck. And it appeared he hadn't completely forgotten about his sexual needs, after all.

WHEN TRAVIS drove up to Gwen's house a second time, he'd calmed down considerably, enough to notice things. Although he'd driven past this two-story Victorian lots of times, he'd never paid much attention to it because Gwen had seemed like a stuck-up woman with a stuck-up house. Funny how things worked out. As of now, they were both the answer to his prayers.

The house he'd always considered too fussy had become the prettiest place on the block because it was only a short drive from Doc Harrison's office, and because Gwen was allowing him to stay here with Lizzie. Two weeks ago he would have said the exterior paint job made the house look like a goddamned Christmas tree, but this afternoon, he thought the grayish-green siding and the red-orange gingerbread trim were just about perfect.

He even liked the canary-yellow she'd used here and there as an accent color. In a week or two the daffodils would be blooming in the flower garden, which would go real good with the yellow on the posts and along the eaves. A couple of blue spruces that looked as old as the house stood on either side of her walkway, and he took a deep, appreciative breath as he went up to the porch.

The wicker porch furniture might be a little too girlie for him, but it looked comfortable, and when he rang the doorbell, it had a nice, deep chime to it. Best of all, he could still smell those cinnamon rolls.

Gwen answered the door by herself, without Lizzie.

The old panic came back and he moved quickly into the house. "Where is she?"

"I finally got her to sleep. I don't know how long it'll last, but for now—"

"Let me see. I want to make sure she's breathing."

"If you wake her up, so help me, I'll throttle you. It took me forever to get her to drift off."

"I won't wake her up! Where is she?"

"Upstairs."

Still carrying his duffel bag with his overnight stuff in it, he started toward the staircase just beyond the entry hall.

"Wait a minute!" She grabbed his arm. "You sound like a herd of buffalo. Take off your boots."

"Oh, for crying out loud." He set down his duffel, grabbed the newel post and quickly tugged off his boots. Then he took the stairs two at a time. When he got to the top, he realized he had no idea which bedroom she was in. He spun around and nearly knocked Gwen back down the stairs. "Sorry." He steadied her before she could take a header. "Which room?"

"The first one on the left," she murmured. "And keep your voice down."

He glanced at the closed bedroom door and saw little puffs of smoke coming underneath it. "It's on fire!"

"No!" Gwen clutched his arm. "Damn it, you're going to wake her up. That's not smoke, it's steam from the humidifier. I set it up in there so she could breathe easier."

"Oh." He glanced down at her. "Sorry. But you should have warned me."

"You bought the thing. I figured you'd know what it did."

"How would I know? If I get sick, I just drink some Jack Daniel's and I'm right as rain."

She gazed at him. "Then I'm very glad I'm helping

you take care of Elizabeth. We're not dosing her with alcohol."

"Of course we're not. I'm not stupid." Without waiting to see if she'd agree or disagree, he headed for the closed door and eased it open. Steam billowed out, and he could hear the hiss of the machine. He wished it didn't remind him of going through a haunted house back when he was a kid. He hadn't been very manly going through that foggy place, and he didn't feel particularly manly now, facing this illness of Lizzie's.

If she really was asleep in this clouded-up room, that was a good thing. But she was a greenhorn when it came to this head cold business, and he kept wondering if she knew how to breathe out of her mouth or if she could somehow get mucus stuck in her throat and choke. He wasn't sure if you were born knowing how to deal with mucus.

Once inside the room, he knew for a fact she was breathing. He could hear her rasping away, poor little baby. He crept over to the fancy white crib in the corner of the bedroom and stopped just short of it to study her.

Sure enough, she was asleep on her tummy, her little bottom pushed up in the air the way she'd taken to doing. She was breathing through her mouth, so at least he could relax on that score. She was drooling onto the sheet and her cheeks looked flushed.

Damn, but he wanted her to be better. He'd give anything if he could be sick instead of her. A cold was no problem for him. He'd like to get his hands on the idiot who had come to the wedding spreading germs to this little, innocent baby. That person should be strung up.

"Satisfied?" Gwen whispered.

He turned and realized Gwen was standing beside

him. He also realized something he'd been too worried to notice when he came through the door. She wasn't dressed in the old sweats she'd had on when he'd arrived the first time. Instead she wore a white silky blouse buttoned just to the swell of her cleavage, and green slacks that fit her behind in an outstanding way. And her long, glossy hair was down around her shoulders. And there was red lipstick on those soft, kissable lips.

His body stirred and tightened. Vaguely he remembered promising something in order to get Gwen to let him stay here. As he stared at her, he finally remembered what it was. He'd promised to behave himself.

CHAPTER SIX

VANITY HAD GOTTEN the better of her, Gwen had to admit. Even in the misty twilight created by the late afternoon and fog from the humidifier, she could see the change in Travis's expression as he looked at her, really looked at her, for the first time.

She should have stayed in her old sweats, which sent the message that she wasn't interested. She would have stayed in her grubbies, too, if Elizabeth hadn't gone to sleep. But once the baby had drifted off, Gwen had glanced in the beveled mirror that hung above the bedroom's antique dresser and winced at her ragtag appearance.

She'd tried to talk herself out of changing clothes the entire time she spent frosting the cinnamon rolls. She'd continued the internal discussion while she washed up the dishes she'd used and took a container of her homemade lasagna out of the freezer for dinner. But when she'd done every imaginable chore in the kitchen and Travis still hadn't arrived, she gave up the fight and went into her private suite off the kitchen to put on a different outfit.

Once she'd started the transformation, she hadn't been able to stop primping. She'd brushed and curled her hair and put on makeup. She'd even taken an emery board to her fingernails. Any bystander would assume she had a hot date coming up.

As the mist swirled around them, Travis shoved back his hat and looked his fill. Under his scrutiny, she was embarrassed to be caught going to so much trouble to look good. "I could use a cup of coffee," she murmured, and started out of the room.

"Yeah, me, too." His voice sounded husky.

As she went down the stairs, she heard the click of the bedroom door as he closed it behind him.

"Which room is mine?" he called softly. "I'll put my duffel in there." Intimate whispers. A shared roof. A common concern. An explosive combination.

"The one next to Elizabeth's," she said over her shoulder.

"Where's yours?"

She paused, her hand on the banister, her heart hammering. She didn't turn around, but she could feel his gaze on her. "Why?"

"Idle curiosity."

She didn't think there was anything idle about it, but his question was her own stupid fault. She hadn't been able to stand the thought of appearing dowdy in his presence, but she'd changed the rules when she'd changed clothes. Now she'd have to deal with his renewed sex drive. She turned to glance up at him and hoped her expression gave nothing away. She needed to regain a measure of control over the situation, and she wouldn't do it by acknowledging that his question meant anything at all. "I have a suite downstairs," she said in a matter-of-fact tone, "so that I have some privacy when I have guests."

He nodded, his expression bland. "Good idea."

"I'll go make that coffee." Quickening her pace, she descended the stairs and headed for the kitchen. Not that she was escaping anything by doing so. She'd barely started the coffee brewing when he appeared, minus his duffel and his hat.

And with a gleam in his eye. "Sure smells great in here, between the cinnamon rolls and the coffee," he said.

"Thanks." As she busied herself getting cups and saucers from the cupboard, she adopted her best hostess manner—friendly but reserved. "I could serve you in the library, if you'd like."

"You don't have to *serve* me at all." He walked over to the counter where the cinnamon rolls were still in their pans. "I can have some of these, right?"

"As many as you want."

"Good." He picked up one of the pans, reached inside and tore a roll free with his fingers, stirring up the sweet yeasty aroma. Then he lifted it in her direction. "Here's to you." Then he took a big bite, closed his eyes and moaned in satisfaction.

Desire slammed into her, and the cups and saucers she held rattled in her grip.

He opened his eyes and gazed at her as he chewed slowly and swallowed. "This is so good, it's probably illegal," he said before taking another bite.

"P-people usually like them." Terrific. She was stuttering. And blushing, if the heat in her cheeks was any clue. She was also in danger of dropping the delicate cups and saucers in her hand. To prevent that, she set them down on the sturdy work table in the middle of the kitchen.

Crossing to the coffeepot, she picked up the carafe. The next logical step would be to actually pour coffee into the cups, but she was quivering too much to do that yet, so she stalled. "How do you like your coffee?"

"With cream, if you have some. Damn, these rolls are good." He finished off his first one and licked the stickiness from his fingers.

The action of his tongue gave her another jolt that settled with swift determination between her thighs. "I have cream." She turned in relief to the refrigerator and opened the door. The cool air felt wonderful against her heated skin. If she stood there a moment, maybe she'd regain her composure.

She was probably acting like an idiot, but surely any red-blooded woman would be in turmoil after watching his reaction after taking a bite of a cinnamon roll. And the sensuous way he'd licked his fingers belonged in an X-rated movie. Travis eating a cinnamon roll was the most erotic thing she'd ever seen.

"If you're out, that's okay."

"Out?" She realized that she'd totally forgotten why she'd opened the refrigerator in the first place.

"Of cream."

Cream. She'd been staring at the container for at least thirty seconds without seeing it. "It's right here. I was taking a little inventory of my supplies while I was at it." She pulled the cream carton from the shelf and closed the refrigerator door with careful efficiency.

"Gwen, are you okay?"

She turned to him with what she hoped was a pleasant smile, an easygoing smile, perhaps even a jaunty smile. "I'm fine."

He gestured behind her. "The reason I ask is that you just put the coffee in the refrigerator."

Hot embarrassment flooded through her. "Oh, dear."

She plopped the cream on the counter and jerked open the refrigerator door. Sure enough, the coffee carafe sat on the top shelf where the cream had been.

"Iced coffee is good, too." He was right behind her, and his voice was dangerously close to her ear.

"I want it hot." She grabbed the carafe and realized what she'd said. "My coffee," she amended quickly. "I like hot coffee."

"I like it any way I can get it." His body brushed hers and his spicy scent teased her senses as he reached around her and nudged the refrigerator door closed.

Her pulse raced and the carafe trembled in her grip. "Be careful," she said, her voice quivering. "I have hot coffee here."

"Are you about to throw it on me?" He drew her hair aside and nibbled at her earlobe.

She gulped for air as the gentle rake of his teeth drove her insane. "Travis, this isn't what I—"

"You fixed yourself up for me," he murmured as he caressed the nape of her neck. "Don't tell me this isn't what you want. We both know better."

"I don't know what I was thinking!" she wailed. Her knees threatened to give way as he kissed the tender spot behind her ear.

"Then let me tell you what you were thinking." His warm breath tickled her skin as he slid his arm around her waist and drew her back until she made easy but definite contact with his erection. "You were thinking that we wouldn't be taking care of Lizzie every minute." He cupped her breast softly, teasingly. "You were thinking that we might need a way to pass the time." Only a slight tremble in his voice betrayed his excitement. Otherwise he seemed in perfect control.

She groaned and closed her eyes. The quiver in his voice told her he was going wild inside, as she was. Yet he touched her with such finesse, such exquisite restraint. He must know that when a woman was completely aroused, a light caress had more power than a heavy hand. Oh, yes. He knew that a slow approach would hypnotize, robbing her of the will to resist. Of course he knew. He was an expert at this sort of thing.

Her mind emptied of everything except his hand at her breast, his lips brushing the outer rim of her ear. Her body grew as limp and cooperative as a rag doll's. "I'm…going to drop this…coffeepot," she whispered.

"No, you're not." His voice was tight with strain as he took the carafe from her nerveless fingers. It clicked down on the kitchen table behind him.

"Travis—"

His breathing harshened. "You're going to let me love you." He slipped a silk-covered button of her blouse from its loop.

"No," she said softly, knowing it was a token protest that meant nothing. He was in command.

"Yes," he murmured.

Her heart raced with anticipation. The house was completely, utterly still, except for the fevered rasp of their breathing. Travis took his time, dropping butterfly kisses along her shoulder as her blouse gradually fell away. Another button gave way, and another. Her breasts ached with the need to be touched.

And then a baby's cough broke the silence.

Travis's hand stilled.

Elizabeth coughed again and started to cry.

Travis kissed Gwen's neck firmly and quickly, then

released her. Without a word he left the kitchen and started up the stairs.

Fumbling to refasten her blouse, Gwen followed him on wobbly legs as the baby's coughs became louder and her wails higher pitched. She met Travis coming down the stairs with a flushed and unhappy Elizabeth in his arms.

"What can we do?" he asked.

"Try cleaning out her nose and giving her some juice, I guess."

"She feels hot."

"We'll take her temperature, then. I have a thermometer in my bathroom. Bring her in there." She retraced her steps back through the kitchen and opened the door into her suite.

When the house was built at the turn of the century, the rooms had been used as maid's quarters. Gwen had a small sitting room, a bedroom and a bathroom that were off-limits to guests. She'd meant to keep them off-limits to Travis, too, yet the scene in the kitchen had demonstrated how easily she could give up her promises to herself.

"Try rocking her in the rocker while I get the thermometer." She hurried into her bathroom and took the thermometer out of an oak cabinet. A couple of years ago she'd replaced her old one with a digital model that registered by placing it the patient's ear. She'd justified it as a service for guests with children, but lately she'd begun to realize her "guest" purchases were really for the family she longed for.

The wooden rocking horse in a bedroom upstairs, the toy train on the library mantel and the children's books scattered on shelves throughout the house had all been collected in hopes she'd someday become a mother. If she allowed herself to get sidetracked with a confirmed bachelor like Travis, she was in danger of being involved with him when Mr. Right came along. She really needed to stay away from Travis Evans.

Yet when she walked into the sitting room and found him rocking Elizabeth in the delicate antique chair padded with ruffled chintz cushions, her heart squeezed in a way that didn't bode well for staying away. He cuddled the fussy baby against his broad chest and dabbed at her nose with a tissue he'd taken from a box on the table beside him.

And he was singing to her. Off-key.

He glanced up and grinned sheepishly. "I'm a lousy singer, but Lizzie never seems to care. It usually helps her quiet down."

Gwen swallowed the lump in her throat. It wasn't fair that a man who was so good with women and children should refuse to become a husband. "I'm sure it does." She walked over to the rocker and crouched beside it. "Let's see what her temperature is." Murmuring to the baby, she eased the thermometer cautiously into her outer ear.

"Doc Harrison has one like that, too."

His voice rippled over her nerve endings. He could probably recite names from the phone book and get a response from her. Or from any woman. Perhaps that bothered her the most—knowing he'd used his seductive techniques on so many other lovers. She longed to believe that the chemistry between her and Travis was unique, but that would be fooling herself, which was a dangerous thing to do.

She glanced at the numbers on the thermometer. "A hundred degrees. That's not too bad."

"You're sure that thing's working?"

"Pretty sure."

"Test it on me to make sure. It could be broken." He cupped his hand around Elizabeth's soft cheek. "She feels hot to me."

"Okay. Let me sterilize it first." She returned to the bathroom and tried not to think of the tender way his fingers had curved around Elizabeth's cheek. Gwen ached with longing. Travis's touch against her bare skin would be heaven…and hell, because he would be a temporary lover.

After she'd sterilized the tip of the thermometer, she returned to the sitting room and crouched beside the rocker again. "Hold still. This might tickle."

He angled his head. "I'm not ticklish. Do it." He continued to stroke the baby's cheek, and it seemed to have a calming effect on her. She still coughed every so often, but she stopped crying.

It wasn't surprising, Gwen thought as she prepared to insert the thermometer in his ear. Travis had an amazing ability to get females to do what he wanted them to do. He was one of the most appealing male specimens she'd ever known.

Even his ears were attractive. She liked the way his thick brown hair fell into a soft wave right there. As she slid the thermometer carefully into the outer channel, she imagined finger-combing his hair back and outlining the curve of his ear with her tongue. It wasn't an appropriate thought considering he was holding a sick baby, but Travis inspired inappropriate thoughts.

And he definitely had nicely formed ears. She suspected that everything about Travis was nicely formed. Her womb tightened at the thought.

"Mmm." He closed his eyes. "Feels sort of sexy."

"That's because you think everything feels sexy."

"Just about everything does, if you do it right."

Zing. A painfully sweet sensation settled between her thighs. "Ninety-eight-point-six," she said as calmly as she could manage. She lifted the thermometer from his ear. "It's working." She stood and moved away from his commanding force field.

He gazed down at Elizabeth and sighed. "I wish I could do some hocus-pocus and get her well."

"It's a cliché, but love is sometimes the best medicine."

Travis looked up at her. "Then she'll be better real quick. I'm crazy about this little kid."

Gwen experienced a sudden and unworthy stab of jealousy. She was ashamed of herself, resenting his feelings for Elizabeth. Gwen loved the baby, too, and was thrilled that Travis was so devoted to her. After all, Elizabeth had a tough situation—a mother on the run and an uncertain family future, depending on who her father was. The baby needed all the luck and love she could get.

Gwen laid down the thermometer. "Why don't I go upstairs and get the suction bulb so we can take care of her nose? Then we'll give her some juice."

"Is it okay if I stay here? She's used to the rocker at the ranch, and I think this makes her feel more at home."

"Sure. I'll be right back." As Gwen left the room, she wondered if she'd ever find a man with Travis's obvious capacity to love…and a desire to stay.

LIZZIE WASN'T the only one who felt at home in this cozy suite of rooms, Travis thought. Gwen had a real gift for putting things together so a person felt welcome.

He pictured sharing a meal at the drop-leaf table, or enjoying some serious cuddling on the love seat in front of the small fireplace.

Sure, the decoration scheme was a little flowery, but even though he was a guy, flowers appealed to him. Actually they had the potential to get him hot. Flowers had always seemed like sex symbols to him.

Besides, he liked the idea of making love to a woman in her surroundings. It felt as if he'd penetrated her inner sanctum, breached the last of her defenses, touched the core of who she was. That turned him on.

He'd always been careful, though, not to let a woman touch the core of who *he* was. Maybe that wasn't fair, but it was the way things had to be. He could afford to fall in lust, but not in love.

From that standpoint, Gwen made him nervous. His need for her felt different, more urgent, less manageable than his other affairs. At the beginning of a relationship, he usually pictured the end of it and started preparing for that inevitable day. But the end of this relationship wouldn't come into focus for him.

In his lap, Lizzie coughed. He lifted her to his shoulder and patted her back as she coughed again. Poor little tyke. He didn't approve of a system that let babies catch colds. If he was in charge of the world, nobody would get sick until they were at least twenty-one and could treat it with booze.

Maybe Lizzie was throwing off his normal sense of timing with Gwen, he thought. It sure was possible, especially considering how Lizzie's illness made him feel raw inside. Maybe he only thought he needed Gwen more because she represented help with the baby.

Then again, maybe it was those damned cinnamon

rolls. He'd never tasted anything so fantastic in his life. They were almost as good as sex. Almost.

Gwen came back into the room holding a small towel and a basin with the suction doohickey inside it. There was nothing deliberately sexy about the way she moved, and there was definitely nothing sexy about the job she proposed to do. He winced thinking about it, in fact. And yet he couldn't stop looking at the swell of her breasts or the curve of her hips. She was so womanly he could barely stand it.

She picked up one of the two ladder-backed chairs flanking the drop-leaf table and carried it over next to the rocker. "She probably isn't going to like this."

Travis eyed the rubber bulb with suspicion. "Then let's skip it. What if you suck out something important?"

She smiled. "I don't think that's possible. I read the directions, and we're not applying much pressure. And if we don't do this, she'll have trouble drinking from a bottle."

"I know. This morning I tried to teach her to blow out of her nose, but she didn't get the picture. She can sneeze, but she can't blow yet. I showed her about twenty times, but she just stared at me."

"She's just too little for some of these tricks. Come on, let's try this thing. Prop her up in your lap."

"Okay." Travis surrendered to the inevitable. The doc had said they needed to get some fluids in the baby, and she couldn't drink as long as her nose was plugged. "Here we go, Lizzie." He propped her so she was facing Gwen. "Remember, this isn't me doing this. It's your mean Auntie Gwen."

"Thank you, Benedict Arnold." Gwen picked up the bulb.

Travis cringed. "This is a gross concept, you know that?"

"Then don't watch."

"I don't believe I will." By turning his head to the right, he could look at Gwen's cleavage, instead. That was an excellent distraction until Lizzie started to yell. He glanced back at the sputtering, red-faced baby as Gwen pulled away from her. "Hey! You hurt her."

"She probably didn't like the sensation, but one nostril is free. Hold her so I can do the other one."

"But listen to her! She hates this."

"She'll be happier when she can breathe again." Gwen looked him in the eye. "She won't go through her life pain and hassle-free, Travis. Sometimes she'll have to suffer a little in order to make progress."

"Says who?"

Gwen smiled and shook her head. "It's a fact of life."

"Not when I'm around."

"Then it's a good thing you won't ever see a woman give birth. You'd probably outlaw the process forever."

Travis had thought about what women had to go through to bring kids into the world, about what Jessica had gone through, alone, to produce Lizzie. The concept did make him flinch and feel slightly sick to his stomach.

"You might be right," he said. Then he gazed at Lizzie. "But I would have given anything to see her born," he added quietly.

CHAPTER SEVEN

ONE BY ONE, Travis was knocking down Gwen's preconceived ideas about him. The man she'd thought she knew would never have admitted regret at not being there when his baby was born. She'd been attracted to him when she thought he was sexy but not very sensitive. Sexy and sensitive might be more than she could handle.

She finished cleaning out Elizabeth's nose. "There. Now let's try a bottle of juice."

"Would you be able to take her for a little while?" Travis asked. "My arm is cramping up. Old steer wrestling injury."

"Sure thing." She set down the basin and lifted Elizabeth into her arms. The baby's breathing was still wheezy, but sounded a little clearer than it had before.

"That's better." Travis stood, rolled his shoulder and flexed his fingers. "It stiffens up on me if I stay in one position too long." He held out his arms. "I can take her back now, if you want."

"That's okay. I'll feed her." Once again, Gwen had been caught staring, fascinated by the ripple of muscles when he rolled his shoulder and the grace in those long, talented fingers. And if she wasn't mistaken, he'd just admitted a physical weakness, a very unmacho thing to do. "Have you ever tried massage?" she asked.

He glanced at her, that gleam back in his eyes. "Are you offering?"

She swallowed. "Uh, no." She sat down in the rocker, positioned the towel over her shoulder and propped Elizabeth there, so the baby could breathe easier. The seat cushion still held Travis's warmth, and Gwen began to tingle in a very specific spot. "I don't really know anything about massage."

"I do. I could teach you what to do."

She just bet he could. She wished she'd waited to sit down until the rocker cushion had cooled off. The heat he'd left there was doing things to her that made her blush. "We'll see. Better go get her bottle of juice ready before she plugs up again. I put all that stuff in the kitchen."

"I saw it. Be right back."

Once he was out the door she sighed and relaxed back against the rocker. She would get through this episode one moment at a time and hope, for her own sake, that she didn't end up in bed with this man.

She adjusted Elizabeth's position against her shoulder to give the little girl maximum chance to breathe without so much effort. Elizabeth coughed and laid her head on Gwen's shoulder.

"You're exhausted, aren't you, sweetheart?" Gwen murmured. "Can't sleep, can't eat. It's almost like being in love." She had the unwelcome thought that she hadn't been sleeping or eating well recently, either.

"Who's in love?" Travis asked as he came back with the bottle of apple juice in his hand.

"Matty and Sebastian," Gwen answered quickly. She settled Elizabeth in the crook of her arm and took the bottle Travis handed her. "I've never seen two people so much in love." She offered the bottle to Elizabeth, and the baby took the nipple, which was a good sign.

Travis snorted. "They're not only in love, they're in la-la land. It got so I had to keep a close eye on ol' Sebastian, because his mind wasn't on his work. Twice he dumped oats in the watering trough, which made a hellacious mess."

"I know what you mean." Gwen kept her attention on Elizabeth, and although the baby snuffled a little while she drank, she was drinking, which was the main thing. "When Matty and I went to Canon City to look for clothes, she was driving down the street raving about how wonderful Sebastian is and nearly stripped the gears on her truck."

Travis blew out a breath. "I was wondering why her truck wasn't shifting so smooth. I ran it yesterday so it wouldn't sit idle all week. I'll bet she's got some teeth missing in those gears."

"It's possible." Gwen smiled, remembering how excited and totally brainless Matty had been in those last few days before the wedding.

"I have to say this love business is scary," Travis said.

Gwen glanced up. "I take it you've never…"

"Not to the point where I'd start rubbing Bag Balm on the hood of my truck, thinking it was car wax. Sebastian did that, too." He paused. "I guess you've been in love, seeing as how you got married."

Gwen thought about Derek. She'd been crazy about him once. Love had made her blind, deaf and dumb. "I have been in love." She gazed down at Elizabeth. "If you're lucky, you fall for someone who feels the same about you."

"Hey, he must have if he asked you to marry him."

"Maybe he did, in his own way, but he wasn't the faithful type." Gwen tilted the bottle a fraction to keep the apple juice flowing. "Unfortunately he didn't realize that until after he put a ring on my finger."

"Do you still love him?"

The roughened timbre of his voice made her look up. If she didn't know better, she'd swear he was worried about her answer. Yet he shouldn't care if she still loved Derek or not. Sex and love were two different things to Travis, and he only wanted one of them from her.

Before she could answer, Elizabeth began to cough and gag.

Gwen immediately handed the bottle to Travis and hoisted the baby to her shoulder again. She patted her firmly as the baby continued to cough and wheeze.

"Is she okay?" Travis hovered near. "Want me to call the doc?"

"I think she got some down the wrong drain." She stood and walked back and forth with Elizabeth, jiggling and patting.

Eventually the baby's coughing became a burp. Then she began taking shallow, raspy breaths.

"Do you think her fever's worse?" Travis came close and laid his hand over Elizabeth's forehead. "Maybe we should take her temperature again."

"Let's wait a bit on that," Gwen said. Having Travis so close made her tremble, even when he was only there to check on the baby. She put some distance between them. "I really think she just needs time to fight this. Maybe we should try changing her and putting her down again."

"I'll do that. Let me take her." He scooped her out of Gwen's arms.

In the process he brushed a hand across her breast. Gwen was sure it was an accident. The touch was too casual to be intentional. When Travis wanted to caress a woman, he wouldn't be sly about it. Still, the contact made her nipple pucker in reaction.

"I'll come upstairs with you," she said, following him through the kitchen and into the hallway. As long as she concentrated on the sick child, she could resist him, she told herself. "I want to try putting a rolled blanket under the crib mattress, to elevate the bed so she won't be so horizontal. I think she might be able to breathe easier that way."

"Good idea." His sock feet whispered over the carpet runner on the stairs and a loose board squeaked under his weight. "You should fix that."

"Actually I sort of like it. A squeaky step lets me know when my guests are coming downstairs. That way they don't catch me by surprise." And that would go for Travis, too, she thought. A squeak from the stairs tonight and she'd know she was in trouble.

"Have you ever had anybody stay here that worried you?"

"No." *Not until now.* "I check on the people who make reservations. If I find anything suspicious, I call them back and tell them I've made a mistake and I'm full at that time."

"That's good, but it might not be enough. If word gets out that you're running the place alone...."

"I know some basic self-defense techniques." Gwen didn't know how to take his obvious concern for her safety. On a surface level, she wanted to brush it off as being condescending and typically male. But on a deeper level she liked it. Derek had always assumed she could take care of herself, and she could, but there was something gratifying about a man who took a protective stance.

"I think a dog would be a great idea." He turned left into Elizabeth's bedroom. "A big dog."

"I don't have much of a yard." Gwen followed him and went over to retrieve the blanket that lay folded across the foot of the room's queen-size bed.

"No problem. Take Fido for runs in the park. Or bring him out when you come to see Matty and Sebastian." Travis put Elizabeth on her back in the crib and she began to complain. "Hey, Lizzie, what's up, kid?" He levered the side down and started unsnapping the baby's sleeper. "Easy does it, darlin'. Got to change your britches."

Travis was so casual about the future, Gwen thought. When she came out to visit Matty and Sebastian, Travis would be there every summer, because in addition to being one of Sebastian's best friends, he now worked for the combined spreads. Travis would be in her future as long as she remained friends with Matty and Sebastian. If Travis became her lover, no matter how long it lasted, he would be a very complicated part of that future.

She held the blanket to her chest as she watched him change Elizabeth's diaper with efficient movements. He'd obviously taken the time to learn how so he'd be as proficient at this as he was at everything else he chose to do.

With no difficulty he found what he needed in the diaper bag, and he kept the baby so constantly entertained she had little time to fuss. When her sleeper was off, he leaned down and vibrated his lips against her tummy. Sick as she was, she began to chuckle and make little crowing noises.

Travis always seemed to know the right sensual move to make, Gwen thought. A touch, a kiss, or a teasing caress always came at the right moment. His timing was impeccable.

He fished a bedraggled sock monkey out of the diaper bag and gave it to Elizabeth to hold. "Look who I found! Bruce!"

The baby squealed in delight and waved the monkey around, whapping it against Travis's cheek.

"You missed your Bruce, didn't you?" Travis said. "No wonder you couldn't sleep."

"Shoot, I didn't even think about looking in the bag for that monkey," Gwen said. "He's bound to help the situation."

"Gotta have Bruce," Travis said as he took off the wet diaper.

"I found out Sebastian used to have a sock monkey named Bruce," Gwen said. "Now that he's named this one Bruce, I suppose when Elizabeth has kids, she'll give them a sock monkey named Bruce. A hundred years from now, her descendants will still be getting sock monkeys named Bruce."

Travis's movements stilled and he glanced over his shoulder at Gwen. "Good Lord. If Lizzie is really my kid, then someday I could be a granddaddy."

Gwen couldn't help chuckling at the astonishment in his expression. "Does that prospect horrify you?"

"No," he said thoughtfully. He turned back to his work. "No, it doesn't horrify me. It probably should, but it doesn't."

Gwen longed to have him explain exactly why he'd decided not to get married. From her viewpoint, he was ripe for such a commitment. But he'd be suspicious of a question like that coming from her, so she didn't ask it.

"Here's a blanket to tuck under the head of the crib mattress," she said, laying it on the top of the dresser next to the crib. "I'm going to get more water for the humidifier and then I'll see about some dinner for us."

"That would be great." He glanced over at her. "I'm feeling a lot calmer about Lizzie than I was a few hours ago. Thanks for all you've done."

"I haven't done much."

"You were here when I needed you."

The words were more potent than he probably meant them to be, she thought. "Glad I could be of help." Then she left the room before she said or did something really dumb.

AN HOUR LATER Travis had polished off a second helping of lasagna and wondered if he had room for a cinnamon roll or two for dessert. Gwen could cook like nobody's business, and he'd gotten a kick out of eating off of antique china in her small formal dining room.

He'd checked on Lizzie in between courses of lasagna, and she was sleeping pretty soundly. Gwen had put on a new pot of coffee and the atmosphere in the house was downright cozy.

He glanced across the table at Gwen. During the meal he'd managed to find out a little about her folks and gathered that they'd pressured her to do something more high-toned than run a bed and breakfast in a small town like Huerfano. He thought Gwen and this place were a perfect fit, and she seemed to love the role of hostess. He hoped she wouldn't let her folks talk her into selling the house and becoming scholarly like them, or a big-city hotshot like her brother. She seemed cut out for this life.

Besides, Huerfano would be a sadder place if Gwen ever left it, he thought. He didn't like the idea at all.

He laid his cloth napkin beside his plate. "You're something, you know that?"

"I'm really not going to bed with you," she said quietly. "So you can just stop giving me that look."

He laughed in surprise. "What look?"

"Don't you suppose I can see what's going on in that fertile mind of yours? You were smiling that smile. Tell me you weren't sitting over there thinking of how to maneuver us into bed, now that Elizabeth's asleep and dinner's over."

Never mind that for most of the meal he'd been contemplating exactly what she'd just accused him of. At this very minute he'd been thinking very pure thoughts, and he reacted with the outrage of the innocent. "I was thinking how well you run this bed and breakfast!"

"Oh, right. I believe the word *bed* figured into your scheme, but the rest of it is horse manure."

He'd never been a fan of defensive tactics. In any tussle, he preferred going on the offense as quickly as possible. He leaned forward. "Since you've brought up the subject, let's talk about your outfit."

Wariness lit her dark eyes. "It's nothing special."

"Oh, really? When I first arrived this afternoon you were in a baggy old sweat suit."

"You caught me by surprise."

"I realize that." And her clothes wouldn't have made any difference to him. He would have been turned on by seeing her in sweats, once the immediate danger had passed with Lizzie, but he decided not to say that and prejudice his case. "Anyway, I come back later to find you in a silky blouse and snug-fitting pants. Your hair is down and you have on lipstick. What's that supposed to mean?"

Her cheeks grew very pink. "Probably a knee-jerk reaction to having guests. I'm in the habit of getting fixed up when someone's going to be here overnight."

"I'm not a guest," he said softly. "Or would you like me to pay for tonight? If so, name your price. I'd be happy to empty my bank account for what you've done for Lizzie."

"Of course I don't want you to pay! Don't be ridiculous. I'm doing this to help out with Elizabeth while Matty and Sebastian are gone. You know that."

"I thought I did. You've turned me down flat twice now, so I figured in return for your cooperation with Lizzie, you'd expect me to keep my hands off you. And that's what I promised. Then I saw how you were dressed when I came back from the ranch, and I took another look at the whole program."

She was blushing furiously by this point. "All right! So I didn't want to spend the evening with you looking like a scrub woman. Is that such a crime? I have some pride in my personal appearance, and I—"

"Stop playing games. It doesn't suit you. You want me to want you, Gwen."

She stared at him and her throat moved in a nervous swallow.

That nervous movement caused a wave of tenderness to sweep over him. "It's okay," he murmured. "I'm flattered that you do. And no question about it, I want you. But fair is fair. You can't wave a red cape in front of a bull and not expect him to charge."

She threw down her napkin and pushed back her chair. "And you love to get women to wave that red cape, don't you? You present a challenge they can't resist, and it's not fair to do that, either, considering your agenda!"

"I don't know what you mean. I'm always up-front about—"

"Oh, yes, you certainly are!" She stood, and her voice quivered. "And you think that makes it all right, don't you? You issue your famous disclaimer. You make sure that a woman knows she might satisfy you for a while, but eventually you'll leave her, because *nobody* is woman enough for you."

"That's not true. I—"

"It's absolutely true." Her dark eyes flashed. "To even be considered for the short-term with you is supposed to be an honor, isn't it? And I fell for that kind of thinking, which is why I changed clothes! God help me, I wanted to join the Travis Evans fan club!"

He couldn't believe she so completely misunderstood him. "You've got it backward. The women in my life have been too good for *me*."

She rolled her eyes. "Oh, I'm sure."

"I swear, I leave for their benefit, not mine! Some guys are thoroughbreds, good for the long race, a lifetime together. When it comes to relationships, I'm a quarterhorse!"

"Try telling that to Donna. Do you think she's convinced that she's too good for you, and that's why you dropped her?"

He stood and braced both hands on the table. "I did *not drop her.* I never drop a lady. Never. When I think she's getting too serious, I ease back a little. If she still comes on strong and starts dragging me past the jewelry store window, I have a talk with her."

"How considerate."

"I think it is!" His blood was pumping now. Too bad he was also getting aroused. That was inconvenient. "I try to keep things like they were. If she can't do that, I send her a dozen roses and let her know that we can't go on like we have been, but she'll always be in my heart."

"Your heart must look like a Denver freeway at rush hour!"

He shoved away from the table, more wounded than he wanted her to know. She made him out to be some arrogant bastard, when all he'd ever wanted was to bring women pleasure. "I cherish every woman I've ever made love to."

"A friend of mine cherishes her Beanie Babies, too." Gwen crossed her arms. "At last count, she had two hundred and sixteen of those suckers."

"I have not made love to two hundred and sixteen women, damn it!"

"Yet! Give you time. You're a collector, as much as my friend is, and I'll be damned if I'm going to be part of that collection."

"Fine with me." But it wasn't. The fire in her made him want to grab her and kiss her senseless. Normally, when a woman got this uppity, especially before they'd even made love, he gave it up as not worth the hassle. He couldn't seem to walk away from Gwen, though. He wanted to convince her that he was a good guy. And that was a bad sign.

She tossed her head, and her glossy dark hair shone in the light from the crystal chandelier. "I'll admit that you tempt me, both because you're sexy as hell and because you present a challenge."

Maybe that's all she was to him, too, he thought. A challenge. Until now he'd batted a thousand. Whenever he'd put as much effort into a woman as he had with Gwen, he'd ended up in bed with her. There had been no exceptions. But he'd been good to those ladies, damn it. He'd treated them right, and he'd let them down easy. Lots of guys, including her ex, hadn't been so careful.

She wasn't finished ripping him a new one, though. "Around these parts," she said, "if you're an eligible female it's bad enough to be loved and left by the great Travis Evans, but at least you know you made the grade. It's a real blow to be passed over completely. So, at least I have it on record that you want me."

And he did. Still. Even after she'd drawn and quartered him.

She fixed him with a bold stare. "I think I'll just quit while I'm ahead."

Rejected. Again. Hell. He worked hard to look nonchalant about it. "Does that mean you do or do not want help with the dishes?"

CHAPTER EIGHT

IF THE DOORBELL hadn't chimed at that moment, Gwen was afraid she would have started throwing dishes at Travis instead of asking him to help wash them. And her dishes were carefully gathered antiques, mismatched on purpose and irreplaceable. Her urge to throw them showed just how out of control she'd become when it came to this man.

"Excuse me." As she left the dining room and walked down the hallway to the front door she took a deep breath. Too bad she hadn't been able to just say *no* instead of delivering a dissertation on the subject of Travis's life-style. A simple rejection would have left her with more dignity.

She reached for the doorknob.

"Wait!" Travis called from the dining room door. "Don't open it."

She turned. "Why not?"

He strode down the hall toward her. "Sebastian and I figure whoever's after Jessica might somehow find out about Lizzie and come after her, too."

"Oh." What a ghastly thought. No wonder his mind had been on security measures for her bed and break-fast. "I didn't realize."

"We haven't made a point of saying so, but we're

careful. Security is second nature to me at the ranch, but the change of scene made me forget for a minute. Don't you have one of those peephole things so you can check who's outside?"

"No. It would ruin the look of the door. Besides, in the daytime I can pretty well guess who's out there by looking through the glass. It's only at night that I can't see as well."

Travis blew out a breath. "Then wait a sec." He walked into the parlor on the left, where he moved the curtain aside to check the porch. "It's Donna. Go ahead and let her in."

Donna. Donna sure as hell wasn't paying her a visit, Gwen thought. They were only passing acquaintances. No doubt Travis's truck parked outside had caught the woman's attention. Gwen wondered if the kindergarten teacher had received a dozen kiss-off roses, and if Donna was still in Travis's heart. Chances were good that Donna had once been in Travis's bed, and the thought made Gwen clench her teeth.

She opened the door. "Donna! What a surprise." She stepped back from the doorway. "Come in."

"Excuse me for bothering you, Gwen."

As Donna stepped into the entry, Gwen thought how petite and doll-like she looked. But she also had generous breasts, so the doll she most resembled was Barbie. Maybe gym-teacher Barbie, considering Donna's short, practical haircut.

"No bother." Gwen closed the door.

"I noticed Travis's truck out front and wondered if he happened to be here. I need to talk with him about something and this would save me a trip out to the ranch."

And the woman had apparently forgotten how to dial a phone, Gwen thought.

Travis walked out of the parlor. "What can I do for you, Donna?"

Gwen glanced at him. *Bad choice of words, cowboy.*

"Oh, well, hello, Travis." Donna's cheeks turned pink. Then her gaze dropped to his sock-covered feet and her cheeks were even pinker when she looked up. She shot a furtive glance at Gwen. "I, uh, hope I wasn't interrupting anything."

"Not a thing," Travis said. "I took off my boots so I wouldn't clomp around and wake up Lizzie. She's asleep upstairs."

"Let me take your coat, Donna," Gwen said. When Donna handed it to her, she hooked it on the brass coat tree in the entry. "I have some fresh-baked cinnamon rolls, if you'd like one. And I think there's some coffee left from dinner."

Donna glanced from Gwen to Travis. "You and the baby are staying here?"

"At least for tonight. Lizzie's sick."

"Oh, *no*."

"'Fraid so. I wanted to be close to Doc Harrison in case we needed him. Gwen was nice enough to let us use a couple of her guest rooms and feed me some dinner."

He seemed awfully eager to clarify that he wasn't sharing a bedroom with his hostess, Gwen thought with some irritation. And he had said he had a rule about being faithful to someone until he moved on. Maybe now that she'd made her position clear, he'd decided to reconnect with Donna.

Well, that was fine with her. Donna could make a

fool of herself if she wanted to, but Gwen wasn't
planning on it. "Why don't you two go on in the parlor
and I'll bring in coffee and cinnamon rolls?" she said.

"That would be very nice." Donna smiled and
walked into the parlor. No offer of help, no suggestion
that they could all gather in the kitchen. Donna seemed
happy to put Gwen in the role of obliging servant and
get her out of the way.

"I'll help you," Travis said.

"I wouldn't dream of it." Gwen gave him a scorch-
ing look. "Go entertain your guest, Travis."

He lifted his eyebrows, then shrugged and turned to
follow Donna into the parlor.

Normally Gwen loved serving people. She drew great
satisfaction from arranging a tray with her silver coffeepot, her china sugar and creamer and her antique cups
and saucers. Ordinarily serving in the parlor called for
lace-trimmed napkins and dainty silver napkin rings.
This time she came close to slapping some discount
paper napkins on the tray along with the carton of
creamer and some old sugar packets from the last time
she'd bought take-out coffee at the Huerfano Shop 'n Go.

But she had her pride.

She arranged the tray with more care than usual, in
fact. She took time to warm the cinnamon rolls and
place them in a linen-draped basket that had an oven-
hot stone at the bottom to keep the rolls warm. Fresh
coffee, not the leftovers from dinner, went into the silver
pot, and she rubbed a spot of tarnish from the handle
before she picked up the loaded tray and walked down
the hall to the parlor.

She suspected Donna had relished every minute
alone with Travis, but if the two of them had had the

bad manners to make out on Gwen's fainting couch, she'd order them both out of the house. A person could only be expected to put up with so much.

Bracing herself for a cozy scene, she walked into the parlor and found Travis sitting on the Victorian velvet sofa alone. "Is Donna in the bathroom?" Gwen asked as she set the tray on the table in front of the sofa.

"No, she went home."

Gwen's head came up. "Home? Already?"

"She didn't get the answer she wanted, so she left." He leaned forward. "That smells great. You must have warmed up the rolls."

"Yeah, I did," Gwen said, still perplexed as she glanced at the front door, half-expecting Donna to reappear. "She really went home?"

"She really did. Can I pour this coffee?"

"Sure." Gwen looked at him. "I thought I'd come in here and find the two of you acting very friendly."

He poured the coffee without spilling a drop. "Goes to show what you know. Should I pour you some?"

"Okay." She was dying to know what he'd said that had caused Donna to leave.

He glanced at her. "Are you going to come and sit down or drink it standing up?"

"I'll sit down." She walked around the low table and sat next to him on the crushed velvet as she tried to solve the mystery of Donna's quick exit without having to ask. She had a suspicion the answer had to do with her, which made her heart beat a little faster. It was almost as if Travis wanted to continue to be alone with her.

He poured a dollop of cream into her coffee, gave it a quick stir and put the spoon into his own cup before handing over hers.

"How did you know how I like it?" Her hands weren't entirely steady as she took the coffee.

"I've watched you." He added cream to his cup.

"When?"

"Lots of times." He stirred his coffee with deliberation. "At the wedding reception. Tonight at dinner. You always take it like that." He tapped his spoon on the rim of the cup and laid it in the saucer before smiling at her. "Right?"

"Right." She shouldn't be impressed with the fact that he'd taken the time to notice a small detail like how she liked her coffee. But she was. "It isn't fair that you're so darned charming."

He lifted the linen covering on the basket of rolls. "Donna didn't think I was so darned charming when I told her I couldn't spend next weekend with her at her parents' cabin. Oh, God, these smell incredible."

Gwen's insides wouldn't settle down. So Donna had been here to stake a claim. "I'm sure you could get away. Matty and Sebastian will be back, and—"

"Oh, I can get away." He paused in the act of taking a cinnamon roll from the basket and looked up at her. "But I'm not going to. In spite of all the rotten things you think about me, I don't use people. Right now there's only one woman I'm interested in spending the weekend with."

At the look in his eyes, the jumpiness in her stomach grew worse. "Travis, I—"

"And just because you won't give me the time of day doesn't mean I'll grab a good person like Donna and use her as a substitute. Even when she says she doesn't mind." He cupped the roll in his hand and leaned over the basket to take a bite. "Mmm," he murmured. "Mm-mmm."

Gwen gasped. "You *told* her you were interested in me?"

He swallowed. "Only when she wouldn't back off." He winked at her. "You might want to avoid her for a while. I don't think you're her favorite person at the moment."

Gwen set her cup and saucer down so she wouldn't drop it. Then she stood and began to pace. "Well, that's it. Now people will assume we're lovers."

"No, they won't. I told Donna you don't think much of me."

"And she told you I was crazy, right?"

"Pretty much." He polished off the cinnamon roll and licked his fingers. "Damn, but those are good. Do you think you could bring some out to the Rocking D once in a while this summer?"

She thought of the tortuous pleasure she would get from doing exactly that—staying for coffee and watching him eat those rolls with his usual gusto. The sensual side of Travis called to her so strongly that she wondered how she'd ever keep him at bay, although she had to. She really had to.

But she couldn't stop seeing Matty and Sebastian because Travis would be there at the ranch. And a gift of cinnamon rolls would be a nice thing to do for the newlyweds.

She threw up her hands. "I might as well. Everyone will expect me to spend a lot of time out there now, chasing after you. I'll be labeled as your summer romance."

"I don't see how you figure that." He picked up his cup and took a swallow of coffee. "Unless you've decided to be my summer romance when I wasn't paying attention."

"You still don't get it, do you? You told Donna you were interested in me. You are staying overnight in my house. No woman in this town will believe that I can resist Travis Evans under those circumstances. Everyone will assume that before the sun comes up, you will have won me over, whether it's true or not."

He gazed at her, a smile lurking in his eyes. "Are you saying I've ruined your reputation?"

"Are you kidding? Women would kill to be in my predicament. I'll bet some would rank spending the night with you above winning the lottery. You haven't ruined my reputation, you've made it. I'll be the envy of every single woman in Fremont County."

"Yeah?" He looked exceedingly pleased with himself. "I'll be damned."

"But before you get too puffed up, let me warn you that despite all that, maybe even because of it, I'm not going to bed with you. People can think whatever they want, but when everyone 'expects' me to do something, I tend to do the opposite. And you can check with my parents on that one."

He set his cup back in his saucer with a soft little click. "Okay. You've made yourself very plain." He fixed her with a long, penetrating look. "But let's make sure I've got the message. I turn you on, but you don't like the conditions I put on making love, so you'll take a pass. Does that about sum it up?"

She wrapped her arms around her body to keep it still. When he looked at her like that, she had no more willpower than a mushroom. "That pretty much says it all."

He leaned forward, rested his elbows on his knees and wove his fingers together. "Then I get it."

His fingers were so supple and sexy that she couldn't help looking at them with longing. She wouldn't ever know what those fingers could do to her body. But that was for the best.

He gazed at her steadily. "When you told me no at the wedding, I didn't believe you. When you told me no on the phone, I still didn't believe you. But you win, Gwen. I finally believe you. I won't try anything, tonight or anytime. You're safe from me. So you can relax on that score."

Relax? Her stomach was in knots as she struggled with regret. "Good," she said.

"Oh, it could have been." He sounded as sad as she felt. "It really could have been, Gwen."

Didn't she know it. Fairness prompted her to say one more thing. "Maybe you'd…want to call Donna tonight. About next weekend."

He smiled gently and shook his head. "I already explained that thing about substitutes."

"But—"

"I guess you still think I can switch myself from one woman to the next with no problem at all, but— surprise—I can't. Just because I don't plan to try and seduce you anymore doesn't mean I won't want to. It only means I'll control myself. I don't know how long I'll go on wanting you, but however long that is, I won't be dating anyone else. It wouldn't be fair to them."

"I…I see." And she did. Far too much. She saw that Travis had more moral fiber than she'd ever given him credit for. Maybe he didn't play by her rules, but he stuck by his own. That made him more honorable than most men she'd known.

He'd mentioned taking time to get over her before he dated someone else. She wondered if she'd ever get over him.

AS TRAVIS HELPED Gwen with the dishes, he did his damnedest to shut down his response to her. It was one of the toughest assignments he'd ever given himself.

He thought about retreating to his bedroom, but that seemed like the coward's way out and he'd never considered himself a coward. After the dishes were done, he borrowed a paperback mystery from her bookshelf. Now he was attempting to concentrate on the plot while sitting on her crushed-velvet sofa in the parlor while not five feet away she worked on her loom. She'd built a little fire in the small fireplace to take the chill off the room, so she said.

In his estimation, there was no chill in the room. Heat sizzled across the five feet separating them, and he was aware of every movement she made at the loom. He'd watched Matty weave a few times and knew the process had a steady rhythm to it. He hadn't realized that rhythm could be sexy.

As Gwen worked the treadles with her feet, his attention got snagged on the flex of her ankles, the bend in her knees, the subtle motion of her thighs…. He thought of nestling between those soft thighs and his mouth went dry. And each colorful thread was snugged into place with a soft thumping sound that made him think of…well, never mind what it made him think of.

It occurred to him that he'd never spent this kind of leisure time with a woman his own age since he hit puberty. Lovemaking, or leading up to it, or recovering from it had always been the primary activity connected with a lady friend.

Except for the heavy sexual tension in the room, he might have enjoyed the chance to be with Gwen on this quiet evening, each doing something different, yet sharing the same space. The idea intrigued him, except he was too aroused to know if he liked the concept. All he could think of was dragging Gwen off that stool and tearing her clothes off—starting his own kind of rhythm, weaving his own brand of excitement.

Whenever the pressure to do that became too intense, he went upstairs to check on Lizzie. He made quite a few trips upstairs.

He'd started up for maybe the sixth or seventh time when Lizzie started coughing. And this cough sounded different from the way she'd coughed during the day. There was a barking quality to it that he didn't like at all. He called to Gwen as he took the stairs two at a time.

She arrived in the room right after he did, which told him she'd been on her feet before he'd called her.

He scooped Lizzie up and turned to Gwen. "She's worse."

"She does sound a little croupy," Gwen admitted. "That can happen at night."

Travis fought panic. If anything happened to this kid, his life would be over. "Let's take her to the doc."

"We can do that," Gwen said, "but it's started raining out there."

"Raining?" He hadn't even noticed. That's how completely he'd been focusing on Gwen.

"It's getting sort of nasty. Could turn to sleet, I think. Let's try something before we take her out in a cold rain," Gwen said.

Travis thanked his lucky stars he wasn't out at the ranch alone with Lizzie. "What?"

"One of my guests had a kid with a cough like that. They turned on the hot water in the shower and closed themselves in there with the baby. The bathroom was almost like a sauna. It didn't do much for my wallpaper, but it worked wonders on that cough."

"Let's do it. I'll get you new wallpaper." He could feel Lizzie's cough vibrating through her little body. She was coughing so hard, he was afraid she'd shake something loose inside.

"I'll start the shower," Gwen said. Then she turned back to him. "It'll be hot and humid in there. You might want to strip her down to her diaper and take off your shirt."

"Got it." He laid Lizzie back in the crib and pulled off his shirt so fast the snaps popped like buckshot. If he hadn't been so worried, he'd have laughed. Gwen had just ordered him to take off his shirt. He'd been hoping for such a request for hours.

In seconds he had Lizzie undressed, and he carried her toward the bathroom.

Gwen came out and closed the door behind her. Her hair was damp and her blouse clung to her breasts. "It's steaming up pretty good in there. Go on in and I'll get some apple juice she can drink when you bring her out again."

"And if it doesn't help?"

"Then we'll bundle her up as best we can and go over to Doc Harrison's house. But I think this might work."

Travis looked into her eyes and drew confidence from her. "I don't want to take any chances."

"Don't worry. We won't."

His panic eased. He didn't put his trust in a lot of people, but putting his trust in Gwen felt good and right. Something shifted in the region of his heart, as if a barricade had toppled.

He gave her a swift kiss on the mouth. "That didn't

count as a pass," he said. "It's just my way of saying thank you." Then he carried a coughing Lizzie into the steam-filled bathroom and closed the door.

CHAPTER NINE

ALL THE WAY DOWNSTAIRS and into the kitchen, Gwen savored Travis's "thank-you" kiss. No matter how much her mouth tingled, she now believed him to be a man of his word, and she didn't think the kiss had been any kind of seductive gesture.

He'd simply been grateful for her presence and her suggestion of the steam bath for Elizabeth's cough. It would be entirely in character for a man like him to show his gratitude with a kiss. But Travis, being Travis, couldn't give a woman a brotherly peck. He only had one mode—full out.

She poured apple juice in one of Elizabeth's bottles and secured the nipple. No, Travis wasn't about to go back on his word to stay away from her. After all, he'd sat reading a book for two hours in the same room and hadn't made a single suspicious move. She'd obviously convinced him that she didn't want him to make love to her. Damn it.

No, not damn it. Good. She didn't want to be one of those women who claimed no responsibility for sex, who allowed herself to be "swept away," and then pretended she'd been seduced against her will and was simply a victim of a man's relentless sex drive. That was operating from weakness and Gwen considered it unworthy of a modern woman.

She started back up the stairs. She might be a modern woman, but she'd had an old-fashioned reaction to Travis when he'd appeared bare-chested in the hall carrying Elizabeth a short while ago. Advertisers had been making hay recently with the image of a well-muscled father holding his tiny baby, and Gwen had thought the campaigns were overdone and trite.

But her entire take on the subject had changed when she'd emerged from the misty bathroom to discover Travis approaching with Elizabeth. She'd never seen him without a shirt before, never realized that he was truly a work of art. She'd been totally unprepared for his powerful biceps and well-developed pecs. And he had exactly the right amount of chest hair to suit her, enough to provide a tactile thrill against bare breasts, but not so much that a girl would feel as if she was making love to a furry beast.

At the sight of Travis bare-chested, she'd been swamped with unknown and unfamiliar instincts heating her blood and heightening her senses. She'd longed to bury her nose against his throat and breathe in his scent, to rake his flesh with her teeth. To stake her claim. To mate.

Ridiculous fantasies, she told herself now as she stood on the landing and watched light and steam filter from under the bathroom door. Travis had no intention of being anyone's mate. Obviously her instincts were leading her astray.

Elizabeth's barking cough came again, but it sounded looser. Gwen was no expert, but she thought the steam was having an effect. She tapped lightly on the door. "How's it going?"

"I think it's helping her," Travis called above the

sound of the shower and Elizabeth's coughing. "Although your wallpaper doesn't look too good. How long do you think we should stay in here?"

"At least a few more minutes. Until the coughing slows down some more. I don't care about the wallpaper, but what about you? Are you growing webbed feet?"

In response he croaked like a frog, and she laughed. "I'll take a turn next. I brought up the apple juice."

"Good. Where will you be?"

Gwen enjoyed the feeling of being needed, if only temporarily. "I'll stay in her bedroom and wait for you."

"Okay. Don't go far."

"I won't." It was *very* nice to be needed. She walked into Elizabeth's room and switched on a bedside lamp Then she crossed to the window and looked out.

Sure enough, the rain had turned to sleet. Summer would come eventually to the Rockies, but it hadn't arrived yet. Elizabeth shouldn't be taken out in this weather unless absolutely necessary, she decided. The cold sleet would be hard enough on her, but the streets would be treacherous, making it risky to drive even the few blocks to Doc Harrison's house.

She and Travis could handle this.

She walked over to the crib and took Elizabeth's sock monkey out. Then she set the bottle of apple juice on the dresser, went over to the double canopy bed and sat down to stare into the monkey's button eyes. Matty had bought the stuffed animal at Coogan's the day after Elizabeth had been left on Sebastian's doorstep, and it had become the baby's favorite toy.

Gwen remembered the light in Matty's eyes when she'd described Sebastian using the monkey like a puppet when he played with Elizabeth. Matty said her heart melted every time she watched Sebastian interact with Elizabeth, and now Gwen found herself in the same predicament watching Travis care for the baby. Only Gwen didn't want her heart to melt.

From the bathroom came the squeak of a faucet handle, and the sound of running water ceased. Travis must have decided Elizabeth could take a break from the steam treatment. Gwen hoped he'd think to wrap the baby in a towel when he brought her out, so she wouldn't get chilled.

"What do you think, Bruce?" Gwen propped the monkey on her lap. "Are we handling this the way Matty and Sebastian would want us to?"

"I think so," Travis said from the doorway.

Gwen looked up. He was still shirtless, of course. His skin was damp and drops of condensed steam clung to his chest. The steam had turned his hair into a cap of ringlets, making him look even sexier, if such a thing was possible. Her heart warmed as she saw that he'd bundled Elizabeth in a towel like a little papoose, with only her face sticking out. He was such a good daddy.

The baby coughed once, sticking her little tongue out in the process, but the alarming bark was nearly gone.

Travis wiped her nose with a tissue he pulled from the pocket of his jeans. "I think she's better than she was," he said, "and I think she's ready for some apple juice."

Gwen put down the monkey and held out her arms. "I'll take her. Are you cold? Maybe you should grab a towel for yourself." *Please get a towel for yourself.*

"I will. Here you go." He settled Elizabeth in her arms, which required only minimal contact between them, the brush of his bare arm against her sleeve, a whisper of his male scent when he moved. His erect nipple passed within two inches of her mouth.

Although he didn't make a big deal out of being close to her while he was half-naked, Gwen nearly went out of her mind with the urge to kiss and nibble every inch of that tempting chest. Then she made the colossal mistake of looking into his golden eyes. Framed by lashes spiked with moisture from the steam bath, they glowed with banked passion. She gulped.

She *so* wanted this man. How sweet it would be to lift her mouth for his kiss, to beg him to make love to her until neither of them could see straight.

His gaze warmed a fraction more. Clearly he wanted her, too. All he needed was a word from her, and…

"The juice is on the dresser," she said.

"Right." He turned away from her and picked up the bottle. "Here you go," he said as he handed it to her.

"Thanks." She offered the bottle to Elizabeth, who took it greedily.

Travis cleared his throat. "That's a good sign, isn't it? Being so eager for it?" He coughed. "I meant Lizzie, with the bottle…."

"I'm sure it's a good sign." Gwen swallowed hard. If she didn't show any embarrassment over his comment, there didn't have to be any.

"Yeah, a real good sign."

"An excellent sign." She sneaked a peek at him.

He stood watching her, not the baby, and the fire in his eyes was unmistakable. But the minute her gaze met his, he glanced away. "Weather's nasty out."

"Yes, nasty." She looked quickly back at Elizabeth. "Good thing she seems to be getting better."

"Yep, sure is."

"I'll take a turn in the sauna after she finishes her bottle," Gwen said. "Then maybe she'll sleep for a while."

"That would be good."

"Yes." Good for Elizabeth, dangerous for her, Gwen thought. When Elizabeth was asleep, she and Travis had way too much time on their hands. She became aware of his breathing in the stillness of the room. She wanted him to put something on, damn it, but to ask would give her away.

And she dared not raise her glance again. Instead she blurted out the next thing that came into her head. "Have you ever noticed that apple juice is the same color as beer?" She closed her eyes in mortification. What an idiotic thing to say. Better to endure the thick silence than babble like an imbecile.

"I can't say I ever did." He sounded as if he was seriously considering the subject. "But now that you mention it, I'll stay alert when I'm on apple juice detail, so we don't accidentally get Lizzie ploughed."

Now that she'd started this ridiculous conversational thread she decided to keep it going. "I didn't think to offer you a beer with dinner. I have some in the refrigerator, though, if you'd like to have—"

"Thanks, but I decided to forgo booze this week. No point in taking a chance of being even slightly fuzz-brained while I'm in charge of the kid, especially now, when she's sick."

"That's…that's very responsible of you."

"You sound surprised." There was an edge of irritation to his voice.

She glanced up. "Sorry. It's just that—"

"A guy like me couldn't be expected to give up his quota of beer for the week?" A mix of anger and sexual awareness lit his gaze, and he looked like an avenging god standing there. "As if a few long-necks mean a damn to me compared to Lizzie's welfare. I guess you haven't figured out yet that I'd do anything for this kid."

Gwen took a deep breath. "I apologize. I have figured that out. But you're making me nervous. I'd appreciate it if you'd go put on a shirt."

He looked confused for a minute. "A shirt?" Then understanding obviously dawned. "Oh. A *shirt.*"

"Please."

He nodded. "Be right back." He started out of the room.

"Take your time. I can handle Elizabeth for a while." *But I can't handle you.*

Travis walked into his room and picked up the shirt he'd thrown across the bed. He moved slowly, taking his time as Gwen had suggested. They both needed time apart to cool off.

Doggone it, he didn't know how he was going to survive this. He'd never been in a situation like this one, where both parties wanted to make love but one of them, namely the woman, had reservations. Women had never had reservations about him before.

That was what made Gwen so special, he realized. She didn't allow herself to be ruled by her desires. *And neither did he.* The thought amazed him, but once it had popped into his head, he knew it was true. Being around Lizzie had stirred up all sorts of desires he'd tried to bury, like the urge to get married and have a family, the urge to have a place of his own and not be on the move so much, the urge to grow old with one, special woman who was *not* his mother.

But he was smart enough to know that his mother wouldn't mix well with another woman. She was as demanding as a spoiled saddle horse, as bossy as the oldest mare in the herd, as territorial as a mama cougar.

Travis's father had always given Luann everything she wanted, and the result was that she required Travis's undivided attention when he was around. She claimed to love the secluded cabin in Utah, and had said she'd never consider moving.

His commitment to his father left him with no choice but to forget marriage for the time being, and maybe for good.

Gwen wanted a husband, and he envied the lucky son-of-a-bitch who would have that privilege. She'd make somebody one hell of a wife, one hell of a lover, one hell of a mother to their children. He couldn't think about that too much or he might go a little crazy.

He was tucking in his shirt when he heard Lizzie start to cough again. He hurried into the other bedroom and nearly collided with Gwen.

"She started up again after I changed her diaper," she said. "I'm taking her back into the steam."

His stomach began to churn with anxiety as he listened to Lizzie's barking cough. "What can I do?"

"Make us some coffee," Gwen said. "I have a feeling we'll be up most of the night with her."

"Maybe it's time to call Doc Harrison."

"And take her out on those slick roads?"

He hesitated. "We could ask him to come here."

"We could, and we will, if the steam treatments stop working. But I've watched parents go through this when they've been unlucky enough to have a kid get sick on vacation here at Hawthorne House. They've told me it's usually a matter of accepting that you'll have a sleepless night and keeping watch. Waiting it out, basically."

"I hate her being sick. I can deal with anything else, but this is the pits."

"I know." Gwen's smile was determined. "Welcome to parenthood."

He made a face. "I'll bet this is the part that makes you old and gray before your time. I'll go make the coffee." He headed down the stairs. Behind him the bathroom door closed and the water came on.

Lizzie would help keep him in check where Gwen was concerned, he thought as he started making the coffee, but he'd trade a thousand frustrating nights with Gwen in exchange for Lizzie being well. If she turned even slightly worse, he was calling Doc Harrison and telling him to get his butt over here.

TRAVIS NEVER DID call the doctor, although he came close two or three times. But finally, about four in the morning, Lizzie seemed to be over the hump. She felt cooler to his now-experienced touch, and her cough didn't come nearly as often. Best of all, it was a normal cough, and not the harsh croupy one he'd learned to hate the sound of.

"Let's see what happens if we put her down for a while." Gwen carried a drowsy Lizzie over to the crib and laid her gently on her tummy.

The baby's eyelids fluttered and closed. Her breathing seemed almost normal.

"Thank God," Travis murmured as he stood by the crib. His nerves were strung tight with worry and too much caffeine.

"I think we made it," Gwen said. "Let's sneak out and see if she stays asleep."

"Go ahead. I'm gonna watch a little longer and make

sure she doesn't start up again." He'd lost count of the number of times they'd left the room and started down the stairs, only to turn right around when Lizzie had started coughing. They'd taken turns with the steam in the bathroom, and the wallpaper seams had all begun to curl from the constant moisture.

Travis felt a little like a swamp creature, himself, although he'd been careful to put his shirt back on each time after Gwen had reminded him about it. She'd stayed dressed, of course, and each time she'd come out of the steamy bathroom with her blouse plastered to her breasts, he'd had to turn away and get control of himself.

"Do you want any more coffee?" she whispered softly from the doorway.

"God, no. I think I'll be awake for a week as it is."

"I could brew some chamomile tea."

He glanced at her standing in the doorway, wanting to help, and gratitude softened his response. "Thanks, but I'm not really into the herbal tea scene."

She smiled. "Hot chocolate?"

"Maybe." God, she was beautiful. The steam had taken all the curl out of her hair, and it spilled over her shoulders and down to the sweet rise of her breasts in one smooth river of black. He knew what he wanted from her, and it sure wasn't hot chocolate. "Let's see if she stays asleep."

"I'll be downstairs."

He watched her go, his body aching with the need to hold her. He'd just have to get over it.

WITH EVERY STEP Gwen took down the stairs away from Travis, she became more sure that she would make love to him. That is, if he would have her, and she thought there was a good chance he would.

Watching his tireless dedication to Elizabeth through the long hours of the night had worn away the last of her resistance and replaced it with admiration. She was lucky enough to have a rare and wonderful man under her roof, and she'd be a fool to miss the opportunity he offered.

He'd told her he couldn't give her more than pleasure. She no longer believed him. She'd seen the depth of his character tonight, his capacity for patience, courage…and love. If he could give of himself to a child, he could do the same with a woman, the right woman.

Gwen believed she was the right woman. People so often gave to others what they wished for themselves. Because she'd been with Travis through this harrowing crisis with the baby, she knew something about Travis that no other woman did. She knew what he wished for, even if he didn't know it himself.

Carefully she prepared the hot chocolate…and waited.

IF HE HAD any sense, he'd stay upstairs, Travis thought. He could lie on that frilly canopy bed for a while. Even if he was too wired to sleep, he could try and get some rest. Ha. Rest was out of the question with Gwen in the house.

As of this moment, making love to her seemed like the only thing in the world worth doing. He wondered if that was a normal reaction parents had after going through a night of worry over a kid. What a comfort that would be, to turn to each other and celebrate making it through the ordeal.

He thought they had made it through. For the first

time since yesterday Lizzie's cheeks weren't flushed deep rose. Instead they were a soft, healthy pink. He stood by the crib listening to her steady breathing and the knot in his gut loosened. Yes, she was better, really better. Earlier he'd only been hoping she was better, but now he knew, in the same way he knew when he'd finally made the exact right adjustment on the carburetor of his truck.

He'd had to go through this whole night constantly gauging her condition to become an expert, but now he was one. He knew something about taking care of Lizzie that Matty and Sebastian didn't know. That made him feel pretty damn good. Wonderful, in fact.

His step was light as he walked down the stairs and into the kitchen.

Gwen stood at the stove, her back to him as she stirred what smelled like hot chocolate in a pan on the stove. Steam rose from the pan.

"Lizzie's better," he announced happily. "I'm sure of it."

Gwen switched off the burner and turned, a smile on her face.

Her smile knocked him for a loop, and he couldn't have explained why if somebody had held a gun to his head. All he knew was that he wanted her so much it was making him dizzy. He didn't dare say anything as he waited for the feeling to pass. Maybe he'd hurt women before, like she'd said, but he damned sure wasn't going to hurt her.

Her lips moved, but he couldn't hear her with the buzzing in his ears. She walked toward him with the most amazing light in her eyes, and then she laid both hands flat against his chest.

His voice sounded hoarse, as if he'd been the one who'd been sick. "Gwen, I don't think you'd better—"

"I do." She slid her hands around his neck and kissed him.

CHAPTER TEN

HE WAS IRRESISTIBLE. Gwen could no more have stopped herself from walking over and kissing Travis than she could have stopped herself from breathing. As he stood there glowing with happiness because the little baby they'd spent the night tending was finally better, his uncomplicated joy captured her as nothing else could have.

She'd barely touched her mouth to his before he took her by the shoulders and eased her away from him. "Hey," he muttered, his breath coming fast. "Watch that. I know you feel happy about this. So do I, but—"

"I feel grateful," she said in a husky voice.

"Yeah, me, too. But the thing is, I'm not in very good control of myself right now."

"I feel *very* grateful." She was desperate to be near him, to touch the essence that was Travis. She tried to close the distance between them.

His grip tightened as he kept her from moving closer, and his voice roughened. "I know. I'm grateful, too, but if you kiss me, stuff's gonna happen."

"Yes." She focused on the point where his fingers clutched her shoulders and imagined his touch over her entire naked body. Oh, yes.

His gaze grew hot. "Damn it, Gwen, this isn't a game."

"No."

He searched her face, as if trying to understand. "You want to…"

"Yes."

"Why?"

She trembled with desire. "I told you. I'm grateful. Grateful that such a good man is standing in my kitchen."

Conflicting emotions burned in his eyes—passion and restraint fighting it out. "I'm not a good man. You were right. I use pleasure to get women to agree to my rules. It's not fair."

She took a long, shuddering breath. "You'll give me more than just pleasure."

Wariness crept into his golden gaze. "I can't—"

"Yes, you will." She looked past his hesitation and found raw hunger, the kind only she could satisfy. "And I won't ask for promises, but I know who you are, Travis. I know what you need."

He closed his eyes and groaned softly. "You don't know. Don't do this. You'll get hurt."

"After watching you with Lizzie tonight, I'm willing to take that chance." She cupped his beard-stubbled face in both hands. "Come to bed with me," she whispered.

His body shuddered in reaction as he stood, eyes closed, head bowed. Finally he released her shoulders to cup his hands over hers. Then he brought her palm up to his mouth and kissed her tenderly there.

Her pulse raced as she waited for his answer, although she was sure what it would be. He was, after all, a highly sexed man. And he'd finally heard the invitation he'd been wanting since the wedding. He wouldn't be able to resist her any more than she could resist him. And she would show him what love could be.

But when he opened his eyes, his gaze was bleak and his voice was tight. "No." He cleared his throat. "I can't believe I'm saying this, but no." Giving her hands a squeeze he released her and stepped back.

The unexpected rejection cut through her, leaving her breathless with pain. She should turn away while she could still maintain some composure. "Why?"

"Because I care about you too much."

She saw the light burning in his eyes and knew he'd told her the truth, a truth that wiped away her pain. A truth that gave her hope. "I see."

He backed toward the door leading into the hall. "This is for the best."

"Maybe it is." She pressed her lips together to keep from smiling.

"I'll…go on upstairs, then."

She nodded.

"Are you…are you okay?"

She nodded again. "Fine." Then she realized that sounded too carefree. "Disappointed, but I'm sure I'll get over it."

"Good." He looked positively miserable as he turned and walked down the hall. His steps as he climbed the stairs sounded like the tread of a doomed man.

Which he was, she thought with a grin as she hurried into her bedroom. A quick shower, some scented lotion, a dab of cologne at various strategic spots, and she was ready. A red silk robe that would slide off her shoulders and pool at her feet provided the dramatic touch she was looking for. Then she dug through her vanity for the foil packages a guest had left behind and slipped them in the pocket of her robe.

Her skin flushed with anticipation, she turned off the lights and started up the stairs.

LISTENING TO the shower going downstairs, Travis suffered the agony of imagining Gwen with water rushing over her sweet body. He tried to think of other things to distract himself.

He'd mentally ridden every mile of barbed-wire fence on both Matty's and Sebastian's spreads. Staring out through the lace curtains covering the double-hung bedroom window, he'd watched the raindrops hit the glass and relived last year's roundup, complete with the cold rain that had made the experience one of his least favorites in the Rockies.

But thinking of the rain brought him back around to the shower running downstairs, and Gwen standing naked under it. Sure enough, he started wondering what color her nipples were. From her Native American ancestry he imagined them dusky-rose against her honey-shaded skin.

If the shower was warm and the pressure light, they'd be petal soft and supple to the touch, velvety under a man's fingers. But if she'd adjusted the spray to pelt her breasts and cooled the temperature of the water to draw the heat of desire from her body, her nipples would be taut and nubby, ready for the curl of a man's tongue and the nip of a man's teeth.

He licked dry lips and wished…oh, hell. Now he was lying in her tidy little guest room with an erection so hard he could chip stone with it. He'd never be able to sleep in that condition, but then he hadn't much expected to sleep, anyway. Getting out of that kitchen without grabbing Gwen had been the biggest achievement of his sorry life. Once finding the strength to do that, he now had to meet the challenge of staying where he was until daybreak.

He had no business going downstairs for many reasons, but one compelling one was the lack of birth control. Because he'd promised not to touch her if she'd let him stay with Lizzie, he hadn't brought any with him when he'd come back to Hawthorne House from the ranch. She probably hadn't thought of preventing pregnancy when she invited him to share her bed. He hadn't thought of it, either, but he did now.

Of course, they could have made love in other ways, bypassing the need for condoms and still staying safe. He could imagine how she'd taste, and how her mouth would feel on him. Oh, they could have a fine time, even without birth control. But that was neither here nor there, because he was staying upstairs. He most certainly was.

Daybreak. He could last until then. Once the sun came up he could cart Lizzie over to Doc Harrison's for another quick check before he took her back out to the ranch. He could handle things on his own, now that the immediate danger was past. Yep, all he had to do was make it to daybreak.

And he would make it, somehow. Sure he would. Staying up here and out of her bed was the right thing to do for Gwen, and for himself, too. Making love to her would have landed them both in hot water. He already felt a mental connection to her that was different from what he'd felt for any other woman. Add a sexual relationship and no telling what sort of mess he'd get into.

He turned away from the window and shifted to his back. The smooth sheet caressed his stiffened penis. Damn. Maybe he shouldn't have stripped all the way down before climbing into this bed, but he'd always preferred sleeping in the raw and had followed his usual pattern. He hadn't been alone in bed with an erection since he was fifteen.

And he'd had a method for taking care of the situation when he was fifteen, he thought with a grimace. He'd hoped not to be reduced to such measures ever again, but this problem was bordering on painful. A cold shower was out for him. He didn't want to take the chance of waking Lizzie by running water so close to her room.

Ah, he was in agony. The family jewels ached almost as much as if he'd been kicked. And no telling how long the condition would last. He couldn't very well walk into Doc Harrison's office in such a state, that was for sure.

Unfortunately, only one solution seemed available to give him relief, and he felt like a teenager having to resort to it, but he had no choice. With a sigh of resignation he threw back the covers and wrapped his fingers around the solid shaft. Squeezing the sensitive tip, he moaned. He would have rather had Gwen's soft hand caressing him right there instead of his own callused one, but the price was too high.

He closed his eyes and tried to imagine Gwen there with him. As he started a slow stroke upward, the loose board on the stairs creaked.

He stopped in mid-motion, his heart hammering. She was probably coming up to check on the baby. He lay there, his jaw clenched, his penis hot and straining in his grip as he waited to hear the stair creak again, signaling that she'd gone back to her room.

Instead the door edged open.

A night light in the hall threw her into silhouette, but he knew the bed was still in deep shadow. She wouldn't be able to see him until her eyes adjusted to the darkness.

Her scent beckoned to him, an erotic combination of perfumed soap, her cologne, and aroused woman. His body twitched in response. Slowly he unclenched his fingers from around his shaft and eased his hand to his side. He dared not move much. Maybe she was only checking to make sure he was asleep. Maybe…

Then he almost stopped breathing. Gliding as quietly as a ghost, she stepped into the room and closed the door silently behind her. Bare feet whispered over the Oriental carpet as she crossed to the bed, bringing that wonderful aroma with her.

"Are you asleep?" she whispered.

If he hadn't been so damned aroused he might have laughed at that. He wondered if he'd even be able to speak around the knot in his vocal cords. "No." He sounded like a rusty hinge. "Is…Lizzie okay?"

"Yes."

"Good." In the dim light from the window he could make out that she wore some sort of soft bathrobe that tied around the waist. He could only think of one reason why she'd come into his room, and God help him, he no longer had the strength to send her away.

"I can't see you very well," she said.

"That's good." He decided to wait and not make a move, in case he was wrong.

"Why?" she asked softly.

"You'd probably be shocked."

Her voice dropped to a low, sensual purr. "Because you're lying there naked?"

"There's that." His body hummed and throbbed, demanding release.

Her breathing quickened. "And...hard?"

"That, too."

She untied her robe and lifted it from her shoulders. "Maybe I can help." As she lowered her arms, the robe drifted to the floor.

He swallowed. Even in the dim light from the window, he could tell she was magnificent. Her breasts were as full as he'd imagined and her nipples tipped up slightly, as if in invitation to his eager mouth. Her narrow waist flared to graceful hips and thighs perfectly made to cradle a man...or birth a child. And that was exactly the kind of notion that would get him in trouble.

"That is if you'll let me help," she added, her tone sultry. "Or are you going to send me away in some noble gesture?"

"No one's that noble, Gwen."

She stepped close to the bed and gazed down at him. "I want the light."

"So do I." He propped himself up on one elbow and reached for the bedside lamp switch.

"Wait." She rounded the bed and walked to the window.

He kept his thumb on the switch as she reached up to pull down the rolled shade. When she raised her arm, he sucked in a breath at the beauty of her in profile against the silver light from the window. Then she pulled the shade and he shoved his thumb against the switch, blinking furiously so he wouldn't miss that first, revealing moment.

"Oo. Bright light." She brought her hand up to her eyes to protect them.

"Ah, Gwen." He sighed with pleasure as his gaze traveled from the curve of her throat down the valley between her breasts, over the sweet indentation of her navel, and finally to the dark curls covering her sex.

She peeked through her fingers at him, and a slow smile curved her full mouth. "Ah, *Travis*." She lowered her hand and glanced boldly at his arousal. "Were you expecting me?"

"No. Wishful thinking." His breathing grew ragged. "Listen, you need to know that I don't have any—"

"I do. In the pocket of my robe."

He gazed at her and shook his head in wonder. "I must be dreaming."

"Sometimes dreams come true." She put a knee on the bed and leaned toward him. Her breasts swayed gently as she moved.

"I've never dreamed anything this terrific."

"I know. Me, either." She leaned down to brush her lips against his.

"If this is a dream—" he paused and slid a hand under her hair, spreading his fingers to cup the back of her head "—don't wake me."

"I only plan to love you," she murmured. Then she settled her lips against his.

Her kiss nearly made him erupt. He had no idea a woman could suggest so much with a kiss, but Gwen was telling him with the movement of her lips and tongue exactly what was on her mind. He groaned and thrust his tongue deep, telling her exactly what was on his.

She drew back a fraction, and her sweet breath feathered his mouth as she whispered the word *soon*. He sure hoped so. They'd spent hours in mental foreplay, and he was beyond ready.

He cupped the weight of her breast, and a tremor of need shook him. "Lie back," he urged softly. "I want—"

"Not yet." She wrapped her fingers around his shaft, as he'd imagined her doing only moments ago, when he'd been alone.

And just like that, she was in complete charge. He had all he could do to keep sane as she stroked him with loving care. *Loving.* It was the only word that stayed in his fevered mind as she leaned down to caress him with her tongue, her lips, her breath, even the silken strands of her hair.

He didn't think he could last…and yet he wanted this to go on forever. He'd never felt so cherished by a lover before, so aware of the gift…or the giver. He groaned her name and bunched her hair in his fist as he fought for control. When he thought he'd lose the battle, she paused, as if knowing she dare not push him any further.

"There." Her voice was soft and rich with satisfaction.

Gulping for air, he opened his fist and let her hair slide through his fingers as she moved up beside him. He looked into her dark eyes. He'd seen passion many times in a lover's gaze. He'd seen urgency and need. He'd never seen unconditional love. Until now.

He could almost hear the crash of barriers coming down as he drank in the emotion like a man dying of thirst. The drive to possess this woman rose in him, making him quiver with the force of it. He needed to be cradled by those soft thighs, to be deep within her loving, giving body.

Understanding flickered in her eyes and her lips parted slightly, symbolically. A red haze blurred his vision. He'd never wanted a woman this much. Never. He rolled her to her back and moved between her thighs.

She murmured something, but desire had deafened him to everything but satisfying this incredible need for her. For Gwen. For her warm body, her heat, her moist, silken sheath to enfold him. He prepared to thrust deep.

"Travis!" she whispered hoarsely, pushing at his chest. "Wait."

And only then did he realize what he'd been about to do.

Muttering a soft oath, he drew back. "Gwen, I'm sorry." He leaned his forehead against hers, his breathing ragged. "I don't know what I was thinking."

Her voice was low and heavy with desire. "Don't you?"

He lifted his head to look into her eyes. He could drown in those deep brown eyes. And he wanted to sink into her, now, without any barriers between them. He must be going crazy. "What…do you mean?"

"You want a baby."

"No." He ran from the truth as fast as he could go. "I want you. And I lost control."

She gazed at him with those knowing, passion-filled eyes.

He took a shaky breath. "But I'm back in control."

"Are you?"

She was getting way too close to his secrets, he decided. Time to distract her, and with luck, himself. "Oh, yes. Back in control." He leaned down and placed a kiss in the hollow of her throat. He'd been meaning to make this journey, anyway. Now was the time.

Easing farther down on the bed, he scooped the weight of her breast into his cupped hand and flicked his tongue over her nipple. Ah, heaven. When he drew her into his mouth, her whimper of delight told him she might not object to a little of the attention she'd lavished on him.

Loving her was sweet torture. Every inch of her skin begged to be explored, to be licked and nuzzled and kissed. Again, and yet again. But every new exploration ratcheted his own tension up another notch.

Still, it was only fair that he should steal her sanity the way she'd stolen his, and he loved knowing he was doing that. Her quivering sighs became sharp gasps, and when at last he parted her thighs to taste her womanhood, she whispered his name and trembled uncontrollably in his arms. And he knew that he'd been granted a privilege, being allowed to touch her this way.

Only the luckiest man in the world would be allowed to bestow this intimate, erotic kiss and listen to her soft moans as he moved his tongue in a gentle, insistent rhythm. He was that man. And he wanted… yes, he wanted to be that man forever. And he could not be.

Frustration poured through his mind like lava, bringing greater urgency to his caress. He'd meant to excite, to tease, to stop short of taking her over the edge. Now he didn't want to stop. He needed her to surrender everything now, when she was most vulnerable, most open to the caress of his lips and tongue, as if that would seal some sort of pact.

It made no logical sense, but logic wasn't what drove him. She thrashed under him and at last arched upward, pleading for release.

Fiercely he gave it, absorbing her shudders. His body throbbed in response and nearly followed her into the whirlwind. She was his. *His.*

She muffled her cries with a pillow as she bucked in

his arms. Finally she grew still and sagged weakly in his arms. He eased her back against the mattress.

He had no idea how he found the condoms in the pocket of her robe on the floor, or how he managed to put one on while he was shaking so violently, but somehow he managed. She lay limp and unresisting beneath him, looking up at him with those incredible eyes.

Feeling bathed in the glow of that gaze, he slid both hands under her bottom, lifted and thrust deep. Once, twice, three times, and he exploded. And then he closed his eyes, needing, for that moment, to hide.

Because she was right. He wanted a child. With her. Only with her.

CHAPTER ELEVEN

GWEN WOKE in the dim room and noticed daylight edging the shade covering the window. The bed was empty.

For one terrible moment she was afraid Travis might have packed up Elizabeth and left, but then laughter filtered up the stairs—deep, masculine enjoyment and baby giggles. And the aroma of coffee filled the house. Gwen stretched and smiled. Still here.

She got out of bed and put on the robe that Travis had left draped across a chair. Nice of him to take time to pick up her clothes, she thought. He'd be a handy man to have around. And she believed he would be around. Only hours before, when he'd been about to make love to her, when he'd been so aroused he'd forgotten all about using protection, he'd given her *The Look*.

Gwen had waited since puberty for a look like that from the male of the species, and now that a man had given her one, she wasn't letting him blather on about staying single. When a man gave a woman *The Look*, he didn't really want to continue his bachelor life, no matter how much he insisted that he did.

She ran her fingers through her hair and headed downstairs, eager to see Travis and Elizabeth again. Yet when she came to the loose board on the stair, she stepped over it so she wouldn't make noise. She wasn't really sneaking up on Travis, she told herself.

Well, okay, she was sneaking up on him. He might try to present his carefree bachelor mask to her this morning, even though she'd seen the real Travis when they were making love. He was always real when he interacted with Elizabeth, and glimpsing him that way would give Gwen the courage to say what needed to be said.

She padded quietly to the doorway of the kitchen and pecked in. Travis had pulled on jeans and a shirt before coming downstairs, but his feet were bare. He sat in one of the oak kitchen chairs with his back to her.

Such a broad, beautiful back, she thought. Powerful and strong. Yet the nape of his neck looked so vulnerable, with the tender way his hair wanted to curl right there. His barber must have a tricky time trimming that part. She longed to put her lips against that spot, to swirl her tongue in the same pattern that the hair grew.

Travis had obviously been into the cinnamon rolls, judging from the crumb-filled pan on the table next to him. Beside it sat an empty bottle of Elizabeth's formula and a box of tissues. He had the baby propped on his left thigh and Barney the purple dinosaur propped on his right.

Apparently he was talking for the dinosaur. "You scared the spit out of us last night, Lizzie," Travis said in a Barney voice as he waggled the dinosaur's head. "Sounded like a toad in the riverbed, girl. Ribbit, ribbit."

The baby laughed and held out both chubby hands toward the dinosaur. Then she coughed, but it was a mild cough, nothing like the night before.

"Whoops, snot alert," Travis said. He set the dinosaur on the floor and grabbed a tissue from the box.

Elizabeth strained backward against his arm, obviously trying to avoid the tissue. Gwen imagined her little pink nose was still sore.

"Gotta do this, Lizzie." Travis cupped her head and held her still while he wiped very carefully. "Otherwise you'll have green slime running down your face, and that's not gonna attract the guys, let me tell you."

Gwen smiled, but his tenderness and gentle voice had begun to affect her in more potent ways, making her skin tingle and her body quicken. She became very aware of her nakedness under the red silk as her erect nipples pushed against the material.

Travis would notice that right away. She might feel confident of the eventual outcome of their relationship, but she didn't want to be quite that obvious first thing in the morning.

She backed away from the doorway to collect herself and ran into the spindly-legged antique table she kept in the hall. The crystal dish of potpourri on top crashed to the floor and broke, scattering dried rose petals everywhere.

Embarrassed beyond belief, Gwen dropped carefully to her knees and picked up the two biggest pieces of the dish.

"Gwen? Are you okay?"

She glanced up to find him standing in the kitchen doorway, Elizabeth in his arms. Despite her embarrassment, she couldn't help enjoying the picture he made. He hadn't shaved yet, and he looked wonderfully domestic and sexy with that baby in his arms, like a daddy who had gallantly taken on the child care to give mommy more time to sleep. Oh, he would do just fine.

"I'm okay. I just bumped into the table," she said. "It's probably a dumb place to have a table like that,

anyway. I think I'll put it somewhere else from now on."
She stood, hoping he'd think she'd bumped into the
darn thing on the way into the kitchen.

He surveyed the situation and quite obviously noticed
that she was positioned between him and the mess,
which meant she must have hit the table going backward.
His cocksure grin flashed. "Spying on me, were you?"

"Not exactly." Heat suffused her cheeks.

He turned to the baby. "Count on it, Lizzie. She was
spying. Can't say as I blame her. She's really hot for
me."

Elizabeth crowed and bounced in his arms.

Gwen automatically bristled at his cavalier attitude,
the very one she'd been afraid he'd show up with this
morning. Eventually he'd be wonderful, but he still had
a ways to go. "I'm surprised you and that ego of yours
can even fit through a doorway, Evans."

"Am I wrong?"

She looked into his eyes, those golden eyes that had
mesmerized her so completely a few hours ago. The
gleam of male satisfaction was firmly in place. Before
they'd made love, she wouldn't have looked beyond his
bravado. But this morning she gazed at him a little longer
and found, buried under that bluster, the shadow of un-
certainty, the hunger he so rarely allowed anyone to see.

She knew how she was supposed to respond in order
to play the game by his rules. She should laugh and
assure him that he wasn't bad for a broken-down saddle
tramp. Instead she gave him a long, steady look. "No,
you're not wrong," she said softly. "I'm crazy about you."

The cocky grin slipped a little.

"I'll be even more specific than that," she continued.
"I think we're meant for each other."

That wiped the smile completely off his face. "Hold on, Gwen. Don't go getting serious on me."

"Too late. I'm in for the long haul."

He stared at her, his jaw slack.

"And if you're honest with yourself, so are you. We belong together, Travis."

"Gwen, just because we had a great time in that bed upstairs doesn't mean that—"

Elizabeth grabbed his nose in her tiny fingers and twisted.

He winced and firmly removed her hand. Then he shook it gently. "Hey, Lizzie. I've already got one woman here trying to put a ring through my nose. Don't you start."

Gwen kept a tight rein on her temper. "I'm not basing this conclusion on good sex alone."

"Great sex," he corrected, glancing at her as he hoisted the baby higher up on his shoulder. "But that still doesn't mean it's white-lace-and-promises time. I warned you I wasn't into that. And don't forget that you came to my room, not the other way around. I didn't talk you into a damn thing."

"My memory of our time in bed together is perfectly good." She made sure he was looking at her before she ran her tongue deliberately over her lips. "How's yours?"

His eyes darkened. Then his gaze traveled from her mouth to her breasts and lingered there. By the time he looked into her eyes again, his breathing was ragged. "Time to change the munchkin's diaper," he said hoarsely.

She felt no sense of triumph that she could sway him with the power of suggestion. After all, he affected her as strongly as she affected him. The only difference was that she had admitted what that meant to both of them. He was still fighting it.

"Let me sweep the hall before you walk through," she said. "I don't want you to cut your feet on a piece of glass."

"Thanks." He stepped aside and she moved past him, the silk robe swishing against her legs as she walked. She heard him gulp.

After dumping the broken halves of the dish in the garbage, she took out a broom and dustpan from the cleaning closet and walked past him again to sweep the hall.

Elizabeth gurgled and cooed in his arms, but he stayed darkly silent. Gwen was sure he was watching her every movement. And if the front of her robe happened to gape open a bit while she was leaning over to sweep the rose petals into the dust pan, she couldn't help that.

"All clear," she said at last. "While you're changing her, I think I'll go take a shower."

"Fine."

She sneaked a peek at him as he stalked out, and noticed the denim crotch of his jeans was bulging. Well, good, because she wanted him just as much.

But it wasn't only about sex, she thought as she went into her suite of rooms and took off the bathrobe. She tossed it on her bed, went into her Victorian bathroom and turned the porcelain knobs to start her shower.

She hadn't gone to Travis's room last night just because she'd wanted him sexually, although that had been part of it. She'd gone because she'd finally seen the warm and caring person under that playboy exterior he was so proud of. She'd gone because the man Travis had shown himself to be through the long night of nursing Elizabeth was a man worth loving.

He hadn't disappointed her. She'd never felt more

complete than she had in Travis's arms. From his response, she knew he felt the same way. But something was keeping him from honoring that part of himself that could love, honor and cherish a woman for a lifetime. Gwen intended to find out what that something was.

In the meantime, she'd freshen up with a shower. Although she sometimes indulged in a long soak in her claw-foot tub, she'd also installed a shower head over it and hung a curtain around it for those occasions when she didn't have time for a bath.

Now was one of those times. She wound her hair on top of her head and secured it with a butterfly clip. Then she climbed into the tub, pulled the curtain into place and stepped under the warm spray. She didn't intend to linger, but the spray felt good on her skin, and she stood and let it pulse down on her. She should get going, she told herself. She needed a cup of coffee and a little breakfast. She needed—

The shower curtain whooshed back.

"Travis!" Before she could react, he wrapped his arms around her waist and lifted her out of the tub in one swift motion.

"You're driving me crazy," he muttered in her ear as he pressed his naked, aroused body up against her slick backside.

Hot desire roared through her and she started to turn toward him, but he held her fast, cupping her breast with one hand as he slid the other boldly between her thighs.

"Where's—" She gasped as he found the sensitive nub buried deep in her curls. "Where's the baby?"

His voice rasped in her ear. "She's fine. She's in the crib, playing with Bruce."

His probing fingers had reduced her to a liquid state already, but she wasn't sure they should be doing this, with Elizabeth still awake upstairs. She tried to say that, tried to ignore the ache building in her womb, the trembling in her thighs. If he hadn't been holding her up, she would have crumpled to the floor, weak with passion. "Travis, I don't think—"

"Don't worry," he said gruffly. He continued to caress her intimately as he guided her to her knees on the fluffy rose-colored bath rug. "This won't take long."

Her heart raced as his mouth touched her damp shoulder and his teeth nipped her skin. His stroked her with knowing fingers, bringing her close, very close. And as he wooed her with his touch, he pressed his chest against her back, urging her down on all fours. He meant to take her like that, she realized, maybe so he could satisfy his lust without looking into her eyes, without allowing her to look into his. This time he didn't want her to see the emotions there.

Her mind told her to protest, but her body and soul craved the joining that he silently promised, the chance to have him deep inside her again. She welcomed his first thrust with a shudder of delight.

He groaned and thrust again. And again. His body quivered against hers with each penetration, and the heavy sound of his breathing filled the small room.

"Coward," she taunted fiercely, even as she yearned for each deliberate stroke. Her body tightened, reached, lifted.

"Witch," he said with a gasp as he drove deep.

Contractions swept through her, forcing a cry from her throat.

He increased the pace, his thighs slapping hers as the wild friction prolonged the intensity beyond anything she'd ever known. At last, when she thought he'd drive her insane with pleasure, he pushed deep, his body pulsing with release as he gasped out her name.

As he quieted, he gradually eased them both down so she lay in the circle of his body, spoon fashion, with her head pillowed on his outstretched arm.

He tenderly kissed the nape of her neck.

With that single gesture, he made her feel cherished. "I know I mean something to you," she said softly. "More than just a summer fling. I can't be wrong about that."

He smoothed a hand over the curve of her shoulder. His voice was husky. "You're not wrong. You've turned everything upside down for me. But the thing is, I can't get hooked up with you…or anyone."

She took a shaky breath. "Why not?"

He didn't respond.

"I think I deserve to know."

"Maybe you do."

"Will you tell me?"

He eased away from her. "I'll think about it." With a final kiss on her shoulder, he got up and left the bathroom.

Eyes closed, she lay on the soft rug, her body richly satisfied, her mind in turmoil. He hadn't said he *wouldn't* commit to her. He'd said he *couldn't*. And that sounded like a more serious hurdle than she'd anticipated.

JUST LIKE he'd been afraid of, the situation was out of control. As Travis dressed and got Lizzie ready to haul her over to Doc Harrison's for a checkup, he thought how desperate he'd been when he'd gone downstairs to satisfy his unbelievable hunger for Gwen. He'd never felt like that, like some caveman who was ready to drag his mate off by her hair. It was a damn good thing Gwen had wanted to make love, because he trembled to think what he would have done if she'd refused him.

But she hadn't refused him, because she loved him. He knew it and she knew it. What's more, he was beginning to believe he was in love, too, for the first time in his life. The sexual craving, heavy-duty though it might be, wasn't his major clue, either. No, the other major clue was the kind of man he became when he was with her—a better man, a kinder man, a man he liked looking at when he shaved in the morning.

Gwen wasn't so much interested in what she could get as what she could give, and that was a novelty he didn't have much experience with. No question about it, she'd knocked him for a loop. And now he had to decide whether to tell her about his mother.

He put on his suede jacket, bundled Lizzie up and carried her downstairs. Gwen was in the kitchen making soup, and it smelled terrific. She had on a green velvet lounging outfit—pants and a long-tailed shirt. Her hair was piled on top of her head. He wanted to take down her hair and strip off her clothes.

She glanced up from the pot simmering on the stove and stopped stirring the contents. There was a question in her dark eyes.

He picked up the infant seat he'd left on one of the kitchen chairs. "I'm taking Lizzie to Doc Harrison's, to be on the safe side."

She lifted the spoon out of the pot and laid it on a spoon rest before turning toward him. "Will you be back?" Her voice cracked slightly. Obviously the answer was very important to her.

Oh, yes. He couldn't stay away, and that was what had him tied in knots. If the doc agreed that Lizzie was better, he had no excuse to stay with Gwen another night, but that's all he could think about. "We'll be back."

The tense lines around her eyes relaxed. "Good. We need to talk."

"I know." He felt Lizzie slipping and hoisted her up more firmly against his shoulder. The baby gurgled and grabbed for his ear. With one hand holding the infant seat and the other holding the infant, he couldn't do anything about it while she twisted the lobe of his ear in her baby fingers.

"Hey, Elizabeth, don't be so rough." Gwen stepped closer, reached up and unclenched the baby's fingers. Then she offered her own finger for Lizzie to hold, and there they were, all linked together.

He breathed in Gwen's scent and grew dizzy from wanting her. When he spoke, his voice was tight. "As long as I'm going out, do you need anything?"

Pink tinged her cheeks, and she had that look in her eyes, the one that made him feel about ten feet tall. "Only for you to come back," she said.

"I will. This won't take long."

Her color deepened, and he realized he'd said exactly the same thing right before he'd made love to her beside her claw-foot tub. Damn, he was aroused in no time thinking of the way she'd opened to him, the way she'd cried out, the way he'd felt at the moment of climax.

He looked into her eyes and was sure she was reliving it, too, by the fire in her gaze and the quickening of her breath. He cleared his throat. "I need to go. Lizzie's getting hot."

Gwen smiled at that and slipped her finger out of the baby's grip. "I'll bet."

"See you soon." He left the kitchen while he could

still walk. What a mess, he thought as he went out the front door into the rain-dampened morning. Gwen was the ruler of her pretty Victorian house, and his mother ruled the cabin tucked into the forest in Utah. Unfortunately, he couldn't imagine either of them giving up their kingdoms.

CHAPTER TWELVE

ONCE TRAVIS WAS GONE Gwen pulled on a light trench coat and went for a walk around her tidy little neighborhood. She'd been cooped up too long in the house and the fresh air would help her think. The minute she stepped out on her front porch and breathed in the pine scent of the blue spruce in her front yard, she knew she'd made the right decision.

The morning breeze was brisk but the sun warmed the wet grass and the sidewalk was already beginning to dry. Everywhere she looked were signs of spring—trees budding, birds chirping and tulip and daffodil bulbs sending shoots up through the damp earth in the neat flower beds that trimmed nearly every home. Snow might still drape the Sangre de Cristo Mountains, but the valley would soon overflow with blooming color.

No doubt about it, she loved this place. She'd made it a point to meet her neighbors so that she could call out a greeting whenever she saw them. At Christmas she took home-baked goodies to each of the houses on her block, and Halloween meant giving all her little friends treats as they proudly showed off their costumes.

She'd grieved with elderly Mrs. Jackson over her dearly departed cat, and given weaving lessons to ten-year-old Lisa Henry. She'd baby-sat for the Johnsons when the young couple had desperately needed a night away, and she'd taken soup to Ethel Sweetwater when she'd come down with the flu. Her neighbors automatically included her in family celebrations and happily spread the word about her bed and breakfast, bringing her more guests every year.

For the first time Gwen began to wonder how loving Travis might change all that. He had a winter home in Utah, but he traveled to Colorado every summer to work for Matty. Now he'd be working for Matty and Sebastian. Assuming she could overcome whatever obstacle was keeping him from a commitment, would he expect her to live in Utah and only spend summers here, like a tourist? Could she uproot herself after so carefully and painstakingly making the little town of Huerfano her home?

Huerfano meant *orphan* in Spanish according to her brother, who'd said it was a melancholy name for a town. Gwen had always liked it. She thought of this place as a haven for anyone who felt orphaned, which she had, in a way, despite having parents. To her, an orphan was someone who had no real home, no place where they belonged, and until she'd moved to Huerfano, she'd felt like that.

She hoped that Travis's place in Utah wasn't anything special to him. With luck it was a typical bachelor's hangout, with no real character. He liked her house. She could tell by the way he'd made himself so completely at home.

And at home with the lady of the house, too. She still felt a thrill of shock and desire whenever she thought about him coming into her bathroom like that. She doubted those sorts or things happened much among her conservative neighbors. But that kind of daring was one of the things she loved about Travis, one of the reasons she hadn't been able to get excited about a more conventional man.

Oh, Travis excited her, all right. When she turned the corner and saw his black truck parked in front of her house already, her skin flushed and her heart started beating faster. She hadn't expected him back so soon. She hoped he'd been so eager, he couldn't help but rush to her side.

He sat on the porch in her wicker rocker, holding Elizabeth on his lap and rocking slowly back and forth. He'd shoved his Stetson to the back of his head and unbuttoned his suede jacket. Even surrounded by white wicker and flowered cushions, he looked incredibly masculine, incredibly sexy. Elizabeth seemed drowsy, but she wasn't asleep.

"Sorry," Gwen called as she hurried toward the porch. "I took a little walk to work the kinks out. I didn't think you'd beat me home."

"You have kinks?" He watched her come toward him with that hot, penetrating look that melted her bones.

"Um, not really." She felt herself blushing. He must have thought she'd strained something during their morning lovemaking. "It was just an expression. I'm sorry I made you wait, though."

"No problem. We haven't been here long. But I think Lizzie's ready for her noontime bottle and a nap."

Gwen's pulse quickened. A nap for the baby could mean playtime for the adults. She had no doubt Travis was thinking exactly the same thing, especially after his comment about kinks. "What did Doc Harrison say about her cold?"

"We have it on the run." Travis smiled. "He was real

pleased with how we got her through this. He says that he thinks her teething will be no sweat for us, now that we've weathered this cold."

"Teething?" Surprised, Gwen studied the baby. "So soon?"

"She'll be getting teeth before we know it, he said." A note of pride crept into his voice as he looked down at Elizabeth. "She's advanced for her age. She'll be an early crawler, he said."

Gwen was afraid he was setting himself up for heartbreak by making the assumption that Elizabeth would be around in a few weeks when she started teething, and later, when she started crawling. She hated to burst his bubble, but she thought someone should keep him rooted in reality.

"Jessica could show up between now and then," she reminded him gently.

Travis glanced up, and his eyes glinted with determination. "So what? She walked out on this kid."

"She probably had a good reason."

"She'd better hope to hell she did. Sebastian and I have talked about this, and unless she had a damned good reason, she's gonna have a legal fight on her hands if she expects to waltz back in and take this kid away. I have rights, too, assuming I'm Lizzie's father, which I'm sure I am."

"You'd want custody?" Hope blazed bright as she considered that Travis might be thinking of settling down.

The light went out of his eyes. "No, probably not."

"But you just said—"

"I'd want Sebastian and Matty to have her, though, and they'd let me see her all I wanted. It would be almost like having her with me."

So he wasn't thinking of settling down. Glancing away while she battled her emotions, she took the key from her pocket and fit it into the lock. "Let's go in. I'll fix us some lunch while you give Elizabeth her bottle."

Travis stood and followed Gwen into the house. He'd hated seeing the disappointment on her face when he'd told her he wouldn't seek custody of Lizzie. The truth of the matter was that he'd love to have custody, but it wouldn't work. He couldn't be dragging the little girl to Utah for the winter and back to Colorado again for the summer. In Utah his mother could help with her, and would probably love it, but he wouldn't leave Lizzie there for the summer and be away from her all that time.

She needed a mother and a father, full-time, and that's what Sebastian and Matty could give her. They were ready and willing to do that, although part of Sebastian's urge came from his stubborn belief that *he* was Lizzie's father. Any fool could look at the baby and know that wasn't the case. She was Travis all over.

He was positive he'd crawled early, too. He'd done everything early, he thought with a grin as he remembered the incident with Cindy Rexford in the hayloft the summer he turned fifteen.

"Are we gonna have some of that soup?" he called out to Gwen as he took Lizzie upstairs to get rid of her outdoor clothes and his jacket.

"Not for lunch," Gwen called back. "It needs to simmer longer."

Travis paused on the stairs. "Leftover lasagna?"

"Sure."

As he continued up the stairs, he could almost taste that lasagna. Man, that woman could cook. And after lunch, when Lizzie had gone to sleep, then he and Gwen could snuggle up and…of course he was forgetting about the talk they needed to have. He would like to put that off, but he didn't think Gwen would let him do that.

He wished life could stay the way it was right now, with the three of them sharing this house and living so easily together. He didn't know about Gwen, but for him this was paradise. He had his baby near, the most delicious food he'd ever tasted, and a woman who satisfied him completely. What more could a man want? To have it go on forever, he thought with a sigh.

He brought Lizzie down for her bottle and discovered Gwen had it waiting on the table. "Thank you," he said. One more example of what it was like to have a woman like Gwen around, he thought. He sat down and fed Lizzie while he watched Gwen move around the kitchen getting lunch ready.

The room smelled like heaven with soup on the stove and lasagna warming in the oven. When he noticed the loaf of bread she was cutting didn't have any store wrapper on it, he realized she'd probably baked that, too.

"You're amazing," he said.

She paused in the act of slicing the bread and glanced at him. "Not really."

"Really. How many other women these days bake bread and do all this cooking?"

She resumed slicing the bread. "They don't because they've found better things to do. They run companies and discover medical cures or get elected to office. Or they run a ranch, like Matty. I'm outdated."

"Bull. And besides, you run a bed and breakfast. I'll bet a lot of people go broke trying that, but you seem to be doing great."

"Thanks for saying so."

He was surprised by how grateful she sounded, as if she didn't really think much of her contribution to the world. He thought her contribution was just about perfect. "You know, all those women who are company presidents and scientists and lawyers and God knows what else need a cozy place to rest and recover from all that stress. They need places like this and people like you."

She wrapped the bread in foil and popped it in the oven. "I hadn't thought of it like that."

"Well, think of it." He felt good, being able to say something that might make her see herself in a better light. She'd done that for him. He noticed that she had a little smile on her face as she set the table for lunch, and he liked to believe he'd helped put it there.

When he'd finished giving Lizzie her bottle, he made sure he got a good burp out of her. Then he stood. "She's really sleepy. I'll go change her and put her down before we eat."

Gwen's glance was almost shy. "Okay."

His body tightened with desire. The aroma of the lasagna made his mouth water, but he could always eat that later. Gwen was a hell of a lot more tempting right now. Maybe they wouldn't make it through lunch, after all.

He hurried upstairs and had Lizzie changed and down for her nap in record time. Before he went back downstairs he reached in the pocket of his jacket, took out the box he'd tucked in there and retrieved a couple of foil packets. The trip to Doc Harrison's had taken no time at all. He'd been able to swing by Sloan Drug on the way back to Gwen's house.

Gwen had the lasagna dished out by the time he walked into the kitchen, and she was putting the bread into a straw basket lined with flowered material. Everything she did had style, he thought. Even the smallest things. And especially the way she made love.

He looked at the lunch she'd gone to so much trouble to fix for them. Then he looked at her. He had no trouble making the choice, but the man he was trying to be would offer her one. "Gwen."

She glanced up from the bread basket.

"We could, um, keep lunch warm in the oven."

She gave him a long, serious look that didn't bode well for his chances. "We could, but we won't," she said. "While we eat, I want you to tell me what's keeping you from settling down with a wife and children."

He'd half expected her to ask him at the next opportunity, but he'd sure like to stall this discussion. "We could be wasting precious time talking. No telling how long Lizzie will sleep."

She walked over to the table, the breadbasket in her hand. "It's not a waste of time." Her gaze held his. "Our future depends on it."

His stomach lurched, and suddenly he wasn't hungry anymore. He gripped the back of the kitchen chair. "We don't have a future," he said. "That's what I've been trying to tell you. I'm a bad deal. We can enjoy a couple of days here, but then maybe we should just go our separate ways." His stomach hurt even more as he said that. He wasn't sure he could live through losing Gwen, but he couldn't think of any other option.

"You don't want that any more than I do. I can see it in your eyes."

"What I want and what I can have are two different things."

She slammed the breadbasket down on the table so hard the bread popped right out of it. "Dammit all, Travis, why is that?"

He swallowed. "Because I promised my dad before he died that I'd take care of my mother. For the rest of her life."

She stared at him as if he'd grown two heads, and then she started to smile. "That's all?" she said. "That's *it?*"

"That's enough." He might have figured she'd react this way. Most people would if they hadn't met Luann Evans. "You don't know my mother. She's high-maintenance. She—"

"Hold it right there." Gwen came around the table and cupped his face in both hands. "You are not going to put our happiness on hold because your mother needs you. No way." Her eyes glowed with purpose.

He'd never seen her look more beautiful. But she didn't understand a damned thing about this situation. "I can't leave her. I won't leave her. Not even for you, Gwen."

"I'm not asking you to do that," she murmured, edging up against him so he had no choice but to let go of the chair and grab her. "You can bring her here."

He laughed. "Oh, sure. Right. I'm sure that would work."

"Why wouldn't it? This is a big house. She could have her own room upstairs, unless she has trouble with stairs. In that case we could—"

"She doesn't have trouble with stairs." The velvet outfit Gwen had on sure felt good when he wrapped his arms around her.

"So she's not handicapped, then. That's wonderful.

I think she'd like the room in the back. It's bigger, and we might even be able to put in a small half-bath for her."

"You don't get it." He closed his eyes as she began moving sensuously against him, the velvet rubbing against the material of his shirt, the fullness of her breasts luring him. Much more of that and he wouldn't be able to think straight. "She wouldn't have trouble with the stairs, but she would have trouble with you," he said.

"Me? Why?"

His hands automatically cupped her behind and began a gentle kneading motion as he gazed into her eyes. Ah, she felt so good, looked so good, smelled so good.

"Why, Travis?"

He tried to remember what she'd asked him. Oh, yeah. Why his mother would have trouble with her. "Because she's used to being the boss in her house, and so are you."

"It's a big house." She ran her fingers through his hair. "We could work it out."

He loved her touch. Needed it. "And besides, she's used to having me all to herself. I'm the only kid. She's spoiled rotten, if you must know." He discovered her velvet pants had an elastic waist and he slipped his hands inside, encountering silk panties. His erection strained against his jeans. "But I promised my dad, and I'm keeping that promise."

"Of course you are." She cupped the back of his head and urged him down toward her full, delicious mouth. "But you can do that here, with me."

"I don't think so." He could think of lots of things he'd like to do here with her, but co-existing with his mother wasn't on the list. Gwen was living in a dream world. But that didn't mean he didn't want to kiss her. That didn't mean he didn't want to make love to her until they were both wrung out and as limp as Lizzie's sock monkey.

"You're giving your mother too much power," she whispered, her breath soft against his mouth.

"You don't understand. She's—"

"Kiss me, Travis. And kiss me good."

He didn't need to be asked twice. With a groan he took the bounty she offered. She was so lush, so sweet, yet so bold. He wondered if kissing her would always remind him of that first time, when she'd used her mouth so generously to give him the most incredible pleasure of his life. He thrust his tongue deep, remembering.

He kissed her until they were both breathless and working at each other's clothes. He had the fastening on her bra undone and she'd pulled the snaps of his shirt open by the time they looked at each other and smiled.

"The lasagna's getting cold," she said.

"That's about the only thing that is." He slid his hands under her shirt and caressed her full breasts. "I'll bet your lasagna's good cold."

She pulled his shirt from the waistband of his jeans. "Want to find out?"

"Absolutely."

She ran her hands up his bare chest. "Travis, I want you to bring your mother here for a trial visit."

He shook his head. "You don't know what you're saying. It would be a disaster." He shivered as she leaned forward and kissed his nipples. "Do that again," he murmured.

"It wouldn't be a disaster." She ran her tongue over each tight nipple.

His breath caught. He liked that little maneuver. Liked it very much. There was so much they had yet to learn about each other. It would take a lifetime. "It would be a disaster," he said.

She stepped out of his arms, took both of his hands in hers, and began backing toward the door to her suite. "Come into my bedroom," she said softly, "and we can discuss it."

He gazed at her flushed face, her lips red from his kisses and her thick hair falling from its arrangement on top of her hair. He pictured taking that hair all the way down and burying his face in it. And that was just for starters. "Lady, I'd discuss inviting Godzilla for a trial visit if we can talk about it in your bedroom."

CHAPTER THIRTEEN

CLOTHES WERE A damn nuisance, Travis decided as he stood beside Gwen's four-poster struggling with her outfit while she helped him get rid of his. The only good part of the undressing was when he stopped to kiss whatever part of her body was currently available, but mostly he wanted to remove every stitch as quickly as possible so he could get down to business.

He used to be the king of the slow seduction, peeling a woman's clothes off inch by tantalizing inch, teasing her with the long unveiling. It seemed like a stupid game he didn't have time for now. This was for real.

While he pulled off his last sock, Gwen turned and threw back the comforter on the bed, filling the room with the delicate scent of lavender. Then she climbed in. He followed, and promptly sank into what felt like a giant marshmallow.

"What the heck?" Without quite meaning to, he rolled on top of her and nearly lost her in the billowy mattress.

She laughed as she wrapped her arms around him. "Feather bed. Extra thick, extra soft."

"No kidding. Put another one of these things on top of us and we could be shipped anywhere without getting broken." When he tried to lever himself up on his outstretched arms, his hands sank in past his wrists. "A guy could have trouble getting any traction on this thing," he warned, waggling his eyebrows at her.

She smiled up at him. "I'm confident you'll find a way."

"Guess I'll have to keep myself steady as best I can." He leaned down and nuzzled her breasts. "Ah. Here's an outcropping I can latch onto for balance." He captured a nipple in his mouth and drew it in.

She sighed and arched upward. "That works."

Oh, it sure did. He began to get the hang of maneuvering in the fluffy mattress, and they were definitely *in* it and not *on* it. As he felt more cradled and less smothered, he began thinking he could get used to making love this way. As long as he had Gwen, he'd learn to make love standing on his head, if that was the only available option.

Her bedroom was dappled with sun filtered through the lace curtains over her windows, and he made the most of this daylight chance to love her with his eyes as well as his touch. Her skin was golden and smooth, and he had to pay close attention, deliciously close attention, before he found the small birthmark on her left breast, over her heart. The freckle on the inside of her right thigh took even more effort to locate, but once he found it, he decided to linger and explore the territory thoroughly.

She writhed beneath him, bringing his need to a frenzied pitch with her eagerness. "Please," she cried, breathing hard. "Now, Travis."

"Hope I can make it back into position," he said as the mattress billowed with his movements. "Roadblocks," he said, managing a grin even though his heart was pumping a mile a minute. "Al- ways…road…" His grin faded as he absorbed the sweet invitation of her body beneath his and the glow in her eyes as she shifted, opening her thighs. His body quivered in anticipation when he realized how easily he could slip right into her, how easy it would be to forget birth control and love this woman the way she should be loved.

Damn, he was crazy about her. The idea of making her pregnant with his child kept swirling through his mind. He was pretty sure he'd accidentally fathered Lizzie, and now he understood how sad that was, when the most complete joy he could imagine would be creating a child on purpose with a woman he loved. *The* woman he loved. This woman.

He managed to reach the condom on the bedside table. "I want you like you wouldn't believe," he said, panting. "But you'll have to help. If I try to balance on this mattress while I put this thing on, I'm liable to kill us both."

She took the package immediately, tore it open and tossed the wrapping away. Then she did the most arousing thing he'd ever experienced. Holding his gaze through the entire process, she reached down and carefully, expertly sheathed him without once losing eye contact. She did the whole thing by feel. By the time she'd finished, he was a lit fuse.

"Now," she murmured, lifting her hips as she continued to look into his eyes.

"Yes, now." He pushed home, glorying in her soft cry of pleasure and the way her face seemed lit from within. This was good. So good.

He marveled at how easy it was to make love when you were holding the right woman. No thought of technique. Only the wonder of sinking deep, followed by the warm friction of retreat, all the while anticipating the fun waiting for him on the next forward thrust. He and Gwen moved with such togetherness that he didn't know if he matched her beat or she matched his. Or if they'd created this special rhythm together.

All he knew was that he'd found something rare, something he would never find again with any other woman. She urged him on, faster, faster, faster. He watched her eyes widen and her breathing grow ragged. Her gaze burned into his as she dug her fingers into his hips.

"Kiss me now," she said, gasping. "So I don't wake the baby."

His heart bursting with love for her, he leaned down and took her cries of release into his mouth, and then he let her absorb his. His body rocked with the force of his climax, jolted as if he'd been hit by lightning, and he kissed her so hard he felt the imprint of her teeth against his mouth.

When their cries softened to whimpers, he lifted his mouth from hers and kissed her gently. Then he sank against her soft breasts while his body continued to celebrate with little rocket bursts of sensation.

She stroked his hair and took a shaky breath. "End of discussion," she murmured.

"Discussion?" He could barely move, let alone think.

"Can you live without this?"

The answer came before he could censor it. "No."

"Neither can I." She took another shaky breath. "So you have to bring your mother here. We have to try it."

He supposed they did. The joy he'd experienced here in this bed with Gwen was a miracle. He closed his eyes and prayed there were more where that came from. "Okay. We'll try it."

SEVERAL DAYS LATER Gwen's stomach churned with nervousness as she gazed across the kitchen table at Matty. "Good Lord, what have I done?"

"The right thing," Matty assured her, reaching over to squeeze her hand. She'd packed up Elizabeth and driven into town to spend the afternoon with Gwen while she waited for Travis and his mother to arrive. Mother and son had left Utah the day before and had spent the night in Durango. They were due any minute.

Gwen desperately needed the moral support Matty was providing, even though the plan had been entirely her idea. But she'd discovered that once Travis had committed to it, he was hell-bent to see it through. He said they had to find out if it was a workable plan, or if, as he predicted, it was the worst idea of the new millennium.

He'd reminded her that Matty and Sebastian would begin running cattle soon and he'd be needed for that, so if they were going to entertain his mother, it had to be right away. The minute Matty and Sebastian had returned from their honeymoon, Travis had driven to Utah to invite his mother to spend a week at Hawthorne House. Gwen didn't know what he'd said to convince her, but she'd agreed.

And Gwen had the horrible feeling she'd bitten off more than she could chew. "Maybe I should have held off for a few months, until fall."

Matty put down her coffee cup. "Why? Strike while the iron is hot, I say."

"Ga-ga!" shouted Elizabeth from her position on Matty's lap.

Matty smiled down at the baby. "See? Even Elizabeth agrees with me." She glanced back across the table at Gwen. "You have to try to make this work with Travis, and there's no time like the present to get started." She grinned. "Speaking from experience, the honeymoon alone is worth all the aggravation these guys put us through."

"I'm happy you had a great time." Gwen was also glad she and Travis hadn't called them when the baby got sick, for many reasons. Sure as the world, Matty and Sebastian would have cut short their honeymoon, and Travis and Gwen would never have discovered each other.

"Great doesn't even begin to describe it," Matty said. "Except for the one day we checked out private detectives, we did nothing but play."

"You both needed that. You work so hard." She took a drink of her coffee and decided she should make a new pot, so it would be fresh when Luann Evans arrived. She stood. "Excuse me. I'm going to make coffee."

"This is only ten minutes old, Gwen."

"I'm making fresh coffee." She ignored Matty's sigh and walked over to the counter. "You know I have mixed emotions about putting a detective on Jessica's trail." She ground the beans swiftly and poured them into the coffee filter. "In a way, considering she might have conceived Elizabeth with Travis, I'd rather not drag her back here and have to deal with her. I know that's selfish, but—"

"If it is, then I'm guilty of the same thing. Don't forget it might have been Sebastian she slept with."

"Do you really think so?" Gwen couldn't imagine Sebastian in that role at all.

"I think it's possible. I found out he gets pretty wild and crazy when he's had a few drinks. I'd never seen that side of him, but in Denver the hotel gave us a bottle of champagne, which we polished off, and Sebastian really…well, um…"

Gwen turned to stare at her friend. "Matty! You're blushing!" She loved it. If she'd ever been worried that Sebastian was too tame for Matty, she could forget that concern right now. She added the water to the pot and started it perking before she returned to the table and sat down. "Are you going to tell me about it?"

"Nope." Matty fanned her red face with her hand. "Let's just say that I think it's entirely possible that this baby belongs to Sebastian."

"My goodness." Gwen couldn't stop grinning. "Still waters run deep, I guess. Okay, so we don't know whose kid she is, at this point."

"No, and that's just it. I think we have to get it settled. We can't have those two guys wrangling over this baby forever. It might work as a TV sitcom, but in real life, it sucks." Matty took another sip of her coffee. "Which reminds me, how are you planning to explain Elizabeth to Travis's mother?"

That problem sobered Gwen up real quick. "I've thought about that."

"I can imagine."

"Travis and I considered having him tell her about the baby on the way over, but then we were afraid that would put her in a bad mood before she ever got here. I mean, how can she be happy about Elizabeth? Either the baby's proof that her son got drunk and acted irresponsibly, or Elizabeth's not even her granddaughter. But that's the only way to present it to her. We're not going to lie, because if Elizabeth is Travis's baby, then Luann will be a part of her life."

"True." Matty gave Elizabeth a spoon to play with

and the little girl banged it on Matty's arm. "I sure hope Luann is flexible."

"Travis gave me the impression she's very *in*-flexible." Gwen's stomach began to knot. She watched Elizabeth sucking on the spoon and pushed back her chair. "I think I'll polish the silver."

"Gwen, sit down. The silver doesn't need polishing."

"Maybe not. But you know what? I think I forgot to dust the windowsills." She started to get up again.

"For heaven's sake, sit down. Do you want your future mother-in-law to find you with a feather duster in your hand? That sets a terrible precedent, if you ask me. Might as well put on an apron and a little cap to go with it, because you'll be cast in the role of maid for the rest of your association with her."

Gwen sighed and leaned her head in her hands. "Maybe she's not as bad as Travis makes her out to be."

"I'm sure she's not."

Gwen lifted her head to look at Matty. "But after the way he's talked, I can't help picturing some six-foot-tall, overbearing, demanding, obnoxious bully of a woman."

"She's six feet tall?"

"Well, Travis never exactly said, but—"

"Anybody home?" called a deep male voice.

Gwen's heart lurched into a faster rhythm and her mouth went dry. She clutched her coffee cup in both hands and stared at Matty. "Oh, God. They're here."

"Hang tough," Matty murmured. "You're the best thing that ever happened to her son, and don't you forget it."

An unfamiliar female voice floated in from the porch. "These wild colors on the outside make it look like a cathouse, son."

Gwen glanced at Matty.

Matty raised her eyebrows and squared her shoulders. "It does *not,*" she said under her breath to Gwen.

"I like it, Mom," Travis said, his voice getting closer. "It's cheerful. Hey, Gwen, where are you?"

He'd risen to her defense. Gwen loved him more at that moment than she ever had before. "Coming!" she called. She gave Matty a shaky smile and stood, smoothing her hair and straightening the skirt of her dress. "Do I look like a Madam?" she asked Matty.

"Of course not!"

"Then here goes nothing." Heart pounding, she walked into the hall.

She nearly collided with Travis.

"Hey, there." He caught her by the shoulders and gave her one quick glance of approval. "Nice." But he didn't kiss her, Gwen noticed. He turned. "Mom, I'd like you to meet Gwen Hawthorne. Gwen, this is my mother, Luann Evans."

The hallway was cool, but Gwen felt sweat trickle down her back. She widened her mouth in what she hoped was a smile and not a grimace as she braced herself for the Amazon woman she expected to be filling the hallway with her bulk.

But Luann Evans was *tiny.* The front door stood open, blocked by a large suitcase, and the light coming from it cast her in shadow, but she couldn't be more than five feet tall, and probably wore a size two dress. Her suitcase was bigger than she was.

Gwen controlled the desire to laugh. Travis jumped through hoops for this little bitty thing? She stepped forward and her eyes adjusted to the dim light of the hall.

Luann wore her gray hair cropped short and obviously didn't believe in hair dye or makeup to disguise her fifty-something years. She wore jeans and a sweatshirt, and her eyes were the same tawny gold as Travis's.

Gwen decided this would be a piece of cake. She stretched out her hand. "Mrs. Evans, it's a pleasure."

Luann grasped her hand, and her grip was extremely firm. Amazingly firm and strong, for such a small woman. "Call me Luann."

"All right." Gwen smiled. Yes, this would be just fine. Travis had exaggerated the problem.

Luann released Gwen's hand. "And we might as well get this out in the open right now. Are you sleeping with my son?"

Gwen's mouth dropped open. She glanced at Travis, who had suddenly bolted toward the door, abandoning her.

"Let me get this suitcase upstairs for you, Mom," he said. "Would you like to freshen up? Your bathroom's upstairs, right next to your bedroom, and I'm sure you'll love it. The wallpaper's curling a bit, but that will be fixed soon. Gwen has those cute little soaps you like, the ones with the pictures that stay in the soap clear through."

"Never mind about my bedroom and little soaps and wallpaper, son." Luann didn't take her gaze from Gwen's. "I'm more concerned with your sleeping arrangements at the moment."

Gwen felt heat climbing into her cheeks. She waited to see if Travis would step forward and say something, but he lingered by the suitcase, as if ready to take his cue from her.

Apparently he hadn't made his relationship with her crystal clear to his mother. But she could hardly blame him. The idea was to win Luann over, not throw their sexuality in her face. Still, she'd vowed to be honest with this woman from the first, so now was not the time to tell a lie, even a socially acceptable, little white one.

She cleared her throat and gathered her courage. "Yes, Luann, I am sleeping with your son."

Luann nodded.

Gwen let out her breath in grateful relief. The woman had accepted the situation gracefully. One hurdle crossed.

"I'd like you to stop doing that," Luann said.

"What?" This time Gwen heard Travis echo her question.

He came forward. "Listen, Mom, I don't think that's any of your—"

"I'm a guest in your home, Gwen," Luann said, still looking directly at her. "This is an old house. I don't want to have to put up with any thumping and bumping in the night. It's unseemly for a mother to hear those kinds of goings-on."

Score one for Luann, Gwen thought. She *was* a guest, and no telling how much sound carried from downstairs. Now that Gwen thought about it, she remembered being privy to a few thumps and bumps coming from upstairs over the years of running the bed and breakfast. Couples came for a getaway, after all.

Of course she and Travis would have been very careful. In fact, they might have been so intimidated they might have stayed celibate the entire week, although Gwen wasn't sure they could have stood that. But what could she do, assure Luann that she and Travis would be quiet when they made love?

"Uh, you have a point, Luann," Gwen said. "I'm sure Travis will be happy to sleep upstairs in the bedroom next to yours during the week of your visit."

Travis definitely *didn't* look happy. His scowl could

have curdled milk. Gwen glanced at him with a small smile. She was inventive. They'd loan his mother one of their trucks and suggest she explore the town. Or Gwen would bribe Matty to invite Luann to the ranch for lunch. They'd get her out of the house one way or another, at least for a couple of hours.

But if all went well and Luann agreed to move here and live with them, Gwen would have the downstairs suite soundproofed. There was no way she'd spend years sneaking around to make love to Travis.

Luann looked as pleased as Travis looked displeased. "Thank you for honoring an old lady's wishes," she said with a queenly nod of her head.

From the kitchen doorway came the distinctive sound of someone blowing a raspberry. Gwen turned to find Matty standing there holding Elizabeth. Gwen had been so absorbed in dealing with Luann that she'd completely forgotten Matty and Elizabeth were in the kitchen.

Elizabeth looked at them, stuck her little tongue out and blew again, spraying spit everywhere.

"My thoughts, exactly," Travis muttered.

Luann brightened. "What a darling baby!" She glanced at Matty. "Are you her mother?"

"Uh, no," Gwen cut in. "Luann, this is my friend Matty Lang. Matty, this is Travis's mother."

"Nice to meet you," Matty said without much inflection.

Gwen could tell Matty was still ticked about the cathouse remark. Plus she'd probably overheard the whole song and dance about who was sleeping where and had decided she wasn't a fan of Travis's mother. But Gwen wasn't ready to make a negative judgment yet. After all, her own mother wasn't a very warm and fuzzy person, either. Plus her mother was never around these days.

And at least Luann liked babies. She was gazing adoringly at Elizabeth, as if she could hardly wait to get her hands on the little munchkin.

"So," Luann said, clasping her hands in front of her, "who does this sweet child belong to, may I ask?"

Gwen decided she'd handled the first bombshell, and Travis could handle this one. She gave him a pointed look.

He shifted his weight and adjusted the tilt of his Stetson. "Actually, Mom, there's a good chance this baby's mine."

CHAPTER FOURTEEN

TRAVIS HAD NEVER THOUGHT much about the concept of heaven and hell before, but now he knew exactly what each was like. Heaven was like the time he'd spent with Gwen after Lizzie had recovered from her cold. But the past four days with his mother in the house had definitely been hell.

She'd decided that he was some sort of sex fiend who'd impregnated one woman and now was cavorting mindlessly with another one. Except there would be no cavorting on his mother's watch. Nosiree. She refused to let him out of her sight, and she was constantly finding things for him to do for her, like hauling her to the store for this or that, and driving her around to see the sights. She wouldn't take the truck herself and do that, oh, no. She wanted Travis.

And Gwen kept encouraging him to humor his mother. They wanted his mother to like Colorado, Gwen said, so the more he showed her a good time, the more likely she'd agree to move here. Maybe so, but he doubted it, and he was so desperate to make love to Gwen that he was considering luring her out in the backyard some night, chilly and uncomfortable though that would be.

He wasn't even sure Gwen would agree to a plan like

that. She seemed to think they shouldn't try to trick his mother, either, and that they should honor their promise to her not to fool around while she was in the house. Gwen seemed to think that if they demonstrated their consideration, his mother would eventually thaw and give them both her blessing. In a pig's eye.

The only bright spot was that Luann seemed to have fallen hard for Lizzie. Travis wasn't surprised his mother loved the baby. Everyone did. Funny, though, how his mother could lecture him for hours about his unforgivable mistake in getting Jessica pregnant and still go all gaga when Matty brought Lizzie around for a visit.

Gwen had put great store by that, and on the fact that Luann seemed interested in all Gwen's domestic projects. Today Gwen was giving Luann a weaving lesson and he'd felt in the way, so he'd driven out to help Sebastian repair a section of fence before the cattle arrived the following week.

It felt good to saddle up and ride out with Sebastian, and if this thing with his mother hadn't been driving him nuts, he'd be looking forward to the summer. He'd be looking forward to his whole damn life, come to think of it.

"I can hardly wait until Elizabeth's old enough to ride," Sebastian said as they trotted their horses along the fence line of the south pasture.

"Me, either. Once she can sit up by herself, I thought I'd put her on in front of me and take her for a little walk, just around the corral." Travis liked that mental picture of Lizzie and him tucked into the saddle, cruising around on a warm summer day, with Gwen looking on, so proud. He sighed. There was only one dang fly in the ointment. His mother.

Sebastian glanced over at him. "From that frown on your puss I take it you're thinking about the situation with your mother."

"Yep."

"Gwen's gonna get her to come around. Don't give up yet."

Travis shook is head. "I've known my mother longer than any of you. There's no way she'll move into another woman's house and play second fiddle for the rest of her life. No way. Gwen's catering to her now, making her feel like she's in charge of our lives, but that couldn't go on if she was really living with us. Nope, in the end she'll refuse to cooperate. I can feel it coming."

"I think you underestimate Gwen. I—" Sebastian paused as his cell phone buzzed.

Travis jumped. "Every time I hear that damn thing I think it's a rattler."

"I know." Travis reached back and took the phone out of his saddlebag. "But I can't leave Matty with no way to contact me. Not with the baby to think of. And Jessica." He punched a button on the phone. "Hello?"

Travis kicked his big bay into a canter, to give Sebastian some privacy for his conversation. Probably just lovey-dovey talk between Sebastian and Matty. The two of them couldn't stand being apart, but they couldn't take the baby out on every ranch chore. This time Matty had stayed behind.

But seconds later Sebastian called out to Travis. "How'd you like to spend some quality time with Gwen?"

Travis pulled the gelding to a skidding stop and turned in the saddle. "You mean *quality* time?"

Sebastian winked. "That's what I'm talking about, cowboy."

"But how? My mother—"

"Matty's taken pity on you and come up with a plan," Sebastian said as he drew alongside Travis and reined in his horse. "Are you up for that?"

Travis laughed. "I am so up for that."

"I thought so." Sebastian put the phone back to his ear. "It's a go. Yeah. I'm sure he'll be forever grateful. Love you, too. Bye." He pushed the disconnect button and put the phone back in his saddlebag.

"How's she going to work this?" Travis asked.

"She'll call Hawthorne House and beg for Gwen and Luann's help. She'll say she needs Gwen to follow her into Hennessy's Garage because she has to drop off her truck to be worked on, and then she needs to do some yarn shopping and desperately wants Gwen's advice. She'd take the baby, except that Elizabeth has been fussing lately, probably because a tooth is about to come through. She'll ask Luann to baby-sit."

Travis stared at Sebastian. "But she doesn't really want Gwen to follow her to the garage or help pick out yarn, right?"

Sebastian grinned. "I knew you were smarter than you looked."

Travis tried not to let his eagerness show, but it was no use. "Hot damn. How long before I should head back to the house?"

Sebastian clucked to his horse and set off down the fence line. "Matty says give her an hour to set everything in motion. If she runs into any snags, she'll call us, but she's seen the way Luann looks at that baby. The woman is dying to have that kid to herself. She'll probably be so happy about that prospect that she won't smell a rat."

Travis kept his gelding even with Sebastian's. "Is Matty going to tell Gwen the plan? Because Gwen has been insisting we have to play this straight, you know. She doesn't want to chance getting my mother riled up."

"Yeah, and Matty thinks Gwen might have some moral objection at first, which Matty thinks is silly. So she's not saying a word until they get to the garage and Luann's already settled in with the baby at the ranch house. Then Matty's gonna tell Gwen to hightail it home because there's a hot cowboy waiting for her. At that point she thinks Gwen will go along with the program."

Travis couldn't stop smiling. "Did I ever tell you that you're married to a very terrific lady?"

"Once or twice. Now shake a leg. We need to mend as much fence as we can before you leave. All this romance is playing hell with the ranching business."

GWEN THOUGHT it was a little strange that Matty had picked this particular day to get her truck fixed. It had been shifting poorly ever since she'd nearly stripped the gears back when she was spaced out on wedding plans, but she'd never indicated that fixing the truck was a top priority, especially considering that she could use Sebastian's Bronco whenever she needed a vehicle. Still, Gwen wasn't about to deny a friend a favor, and Luann had been overjoyed at the prospect of baby-sitting for Elizabeth.

So Gwen dutifully followed Matty to Hennessy's Garage and sat in her purple truck waiting for Matty to come out of the small office attached to the double-bay garage. She rolled the window down and breathed in the flower-scented air. Spring had arrived in Huerfano, and even Hennessy's had a little window box of daffodils blooming merrily away.

Eventually Matty came out, but instead of climbing in the truck with Gwen, she walked around to the driver's side.

"Is something wrong?" Gwen asked.

Matty smiled and tucked her thumbs in the pockets of her jeans. "Nope. I just came to tell you that I won't need your help after all. Jake Hennessy's going to loan me his Jeep to do my errands, so you're welcome to go home if you like."

Gwen felt a flash of irritation. This was so unlike Matty, roping her into something unnecessary, especially when her life was so complicated already these days. "What about Luann? Shouldn't I go to the ranch and help her with Elizabeth?"

Matty gazed at her, that same little smile on her face. "No, I think you should go home and spend some time with Travis."

Gwen's irritation rose to the surface. "Travis isn't there! As you well know. He's out riding fence with Sebastian." Gwen hesitated as Matty continued to give her that knowing look. "Isn't he?"

Matty slowly shook her head. "He's at Hawthorne House, waiting for you."

Gwen gasped as she finally understood what was going on. "You set this whole thing up, didn't you?"

"Somebody had to beat Luann Evans at her own game, and it sure didn't look like you had the heart for it. Now you don't have to follow through, of course. If it bothers your conscience too much, I'll tell Jake I don't need the loan of his vehicle, after all. But if you can see your way clear to cooperate, I figure you and Travis have about two hours to kill."

Excitement built quickly, and her voice quivered when she spoke. "But when I took Luann out to your place, I saw Travis's truck parked over by the barn."

Matty nodded. "And a little more than two hours from now, it'll be parked there again. Don't worry. Luann's not going to leave that baby to go prowling around the barn checking on whether Travis's truck is still there."

Gwen began to smile. "No, I guess she won't."

"Go on, now. You're wasting time."

Gwen reached for the ignition key, her hand shaking from anticipation. "Matty, I already feel guilty about fooling Travis's mother like this."

"A little guilt adds some spice to the experience, don't you think?"

Gwen looked at her friend and laughed. "Guess I'm about to find out."

"Have fun."

Gwen lifted her hand in farewell and pulled out into the street. She had to force herself to drive the speed limit through the little town as she pictured Travis waiting for her. She'd caught the looks of frustration he'd thrown her way in the past few days. A man like Travis didn't take well to frustration.

For that matter, Gwen hadn't weathered the dry spell very well, either. She'd slept poorly and had increasingly erotic dreams whenever she did manage to fall asleep. But thanks to Matty's devious plans, she would feel Travis's arms around her again, experience the sweet urgency of his mouth, the driving force of his... Gwen slammed on her brakes. She'd nearly missed a stop sign.

She concentrated on the road after that, but when she turned down her street and saw Travis's black truck in front of Hawthorne House, her hands began to shake. She'd never been such a basket case over a man, and the intensity of her emotions frightened her a little. If Luann refused to consider moving to Colorado... Gwen shoved the thought aside. Luann would agree to move. She had to. Gwen couldn't imagine life without Travis.

She parked behind Travis's truck and hurried up the walk. The minute she started up the steps, the front door opened. He'd been watching for her.

He stood back from the door, holding it open for her. He'd never looked sexier. His voice rumbled low in his chest. "Get in here, woman."

Heart pounding, she crossed the porch and stepped through the door.

He grabbed her, kicking the door shut with his foot as he pushed her up against the wall. She'd never in her wildest dreams imagined being flattened against this flower-sprigged wallpaper and kissed until she couldn't breathe. When Travis began taking off her slacks, she figured out that more than kissing would happen in this hallway, barely inside her front door.

Desire flooded through her, drenching her completely. She fumbled with his belt, unfastening it as he wrenched her zipper down and shoved his hand inside her panties. Without hesitation he pushed his fingers inside her, as if he expected to find her exactly as she was, hot and wet. She gripped the waistband of his jeans and whimpered with pleasure.

He lifted his mouth a fraction from hers, and he was panting. "Finish your job. Condom's in my left shirt pocket." He pressed the heel of his hand against her damp curls.

"Oh, my. *Travis*."

"I thought you'd never get here." His mouth came down on hers again as he stroked her with one hand and used the other to shove down her slacks and panties. She arched against the movement of his fingers, but she managed to unzip his jeans. Jeans and belt hit the hardwood floor with a clunk as she pulled down his briefs, freeing his erection.

"Hurry," he mumbled against her lips. *"Please, hurry."*

He was making her so crazy she couldn't remember which was his left shirt pocket and she groped around in the wrong one for the condom. When he growled low in his throat, she switched pockets and found the condom. It seemed to take forever, but at last she had it on.

He drew back slightly, and his breath was hot on her mouth. "Brace…your hands on my…shoulders," he said, gasping.

She gripped his shoulders. He cupped her bottom and lifted her up against the wall. Her slacks and panties slipped down her legs to the floor just before he thrust into her with a soft cry of triumph.

His fullness inside her brought tears of happiness to her eyes. She had missed him so much. She wrapped her legs around his hips in welcome.

She held on, her back flat against the wall as he gripped her bottom and surged into her with enough force to shake the wall. A picture hanging on the parlor side clattered to the floor. Travis didn't even pause.

Nor did she want him to. The pressure built to an exquisite pitch, and then, with one swift upward thrust, he set her free. Laughing with joy, tears streaming down her face, she came apart. With a guttural sound of satisfaction, he followed her, his body shuddering against hers as he held her tight against the wall and leaned his forehead against hers.

Gradually his breathing slowed, but he still held her firmly, still stayed deep inside her as he lifted his head to look into her eyes. "I love you," he said quietly.

Fresh tears filled her eyes. "You've never said."

"Ah, but you had to know."

She nodded. "I knew. But I still needed to hear it."

"Sorry it took so long." He gave her a crooked smile. "I wouldn't mind hearing it from you, either."

"Oh, Travis, of course I love you." She'd told him so many times in her imagination that it came as a shock that she'd never said the words out loud.

His gaze heated. "That sure sounds good, especially considering the week we're having." He kissed her tenderly, then drew back with a sigh. "I don't think my mother will agree to move here."

She didn't want this moment to be spoiled by gloom and doom. "Don't give up yet."

"Okay, but even if she doesn't, I will." He looked into her eyes. "I will, Gwen. I want you to marry me."

Her throat tightened as she realized the sacrifice he was willing to make, the guilt he was willing to endure, for her. "Of course I want that, too, but I can't ask you to go back on your promise," she said softly.

"You didn't ask. I'm telling you what I'm prepared to do."

"But—"

He silenced her with a kiss, a kiss that soon became sensual and suggestive. His lips slid down to her throat. "Let's not talk about it now," he murmured against her skin. "We have some catching up to do."

Her pulse quickened. "I thought...we just did."

His tongue dipped into the hollow of her throat and he chuckled. "Oh, sweetheart, that was only to take the edge off. Now we can get down to some serious loving."

Although she'd felt thoroughly loved a moment ago, Gwen felt the passion rise in her again. "Which room would you like to try next?"

He eased her to her feet. "I had the parlor in mind. That fainting couch has possibilities. Oh, and Gwen?"

"Yes?"

"I'm moving back to your bedroom tonight."

GWEN TRIED to talk him out of moving into her bedroom. She thought they had a better chance of winning Luann over if they went along with her wishes and didn't openly sleep together during this trial visit. But making love to her after four days of celibacy seemed to have flipped a switch in Travis. He was no longer interested in compromise.

He made no effort to hide the fact he was moving back to Gwen's room, and every night he reached for her, as if to prove he could make love to her whether his mother approved or not. Gwen couldn't resist him, even when she suspected his reasons weren't entirely pure. Still, although it wasn't easy to do, she kept their lovemaking extremely quiet.

Luann couldn't have been bothered by any noise from their bedroom activities, Gwen knew, yet Travis's mother seemed to have picked up the gauntlet he'd thrown down. In the last days of her stay her jaw seemed to tighten with a secret resolution. Gwen was afraid she'd resolved not to give Travis and Gwen her blessing, let alone agree to live with them in Colorado.

Gwen watched the widening rift between mother and son with anxiety. She couldn't imagine Travis would be happy if he became estranged from his mother, despite his big talk, and Luann would be downright miserable. She apparently had nobody besides Travis.

Gwen found herself compensating by urging Luann to relax instead of helping around the house, as she'd done the first four days of the week. Gwen even let some of her own chores go and took Luann into Canon City for lunch one day, and out to Matty's for lunch and a chance to play with Elizabeth another day.

Her efforts didn't do much to loosen the set of Luann's jaw.

Travis probably knew they were headed for disaster, but he wouldn't discuss it with Gwen during any of the private times they had together. So they stumbled through until Luann's last night at Hawthorne House. Travis had decided that during dinner they'd announce their plans to marry and ask Luann if she'd be willing to move permanently to Colorado.

Gwen worked most of the day on the meal, and because she wanted Luann to feel special, she'd politely refused her offer of help. Instead she'd suggested Travis take her on a day trip to the Royal Gorge. They both returned from the outing in such a sour mood that Gwen wondered if she'd done the right thing sending them off together.

While they both went to wash up, she put the finishing touches on the table, lit the candles and adjusted the bouquet of flowers she'd bought for the centerpiece. She knew the beef was tender, the vegetables steamed perfectly, the salad crisp, the dressing imaginative, but she'd never been so nervous about the outcome of a meal in her life.

Travis and his mother arrived at the table at the same time.

"Smells great," Travis said. He walked over to Gwen, pulled her close and kissed her full on the mouth. "I missed you."

Gwen blushed and drew back from his embrace, a question in her eyes. Despite his defiant move back to Gwen's bedroom, he'd never been so blatantly affectionate with Gwen in front of his mother. "I missed you, too," she said.

"Don't mind me," Luann said, pulling out a chair. "I can dish myself. Unless you need this table for something else. In which case I'll just take my plate to my room. No problem."

Gwen extricated herself from Travis's arms. "Luann, we didn't mean to offend you. We—"

"Love each other," Travis finished for her. "We love each other, Mom, and we're going to get married. Soon."

Luann gazed at him, and her eyes grew bright. "It's no more than I expected. Been acting like a couple of rabbits."

Gwen opened her mouth to protest, but she noticed that the brightness in Luann's eyes came from a delicate sheen of tears. The woman was about to cry. Oh, dear. "We want you to come and live with us," she said quickly.

Luann pushed back her chair and stood. "I'd sooner hang by my teeth from the Royal Gorge Bridge." Then she left the room.

Gwen started to go after her. "Luann, please don't—"

Travis caught her arm. "Let her go," he said in a tense, angry voice. "I *knew* she'd be like this!"

Gwen turned to look at him. "You set her up to be like this, by kissing me right in front of her."

"There is no reason I shouldn't!"

"Maybe not eventually, but right here in the beginning, it looked to me like you were goading her. And it sure worked. I'm going up there to try and straighten things out."

His grip tightened on her arm. "Don't you dare go up there and beg her."

Gwen gazed at him. "Why not? Why not beg her to reconsider? What have we got to lose?"

"Our pride!"

"To hell with our pride!" She shook her arm from his grasp. "I'm going to talk to her."

"It won't do any good, I tell you!" His eyes blazed with anger. "She's going to cut off her nose to spite her face. If she can't have me all to herself, then she doesn't want me at all. I knew she'd be that way, and by God, she didn't disappoint me. Well, I'm finished with her. She's run my life long enough!"

Gwen was surprised at the force of his anger. "I can't see the harm in trying to reason with her. Maybe she just needs time to think about this. I think we should leave the door open, so that she can—"

"Don't you understand? This is the *first thing* I've ever asked her to do for me. The *first thing*. And she can't even consider it. What kind of mother would be that way?"

Slowly Gwen began to understand. Travis had learned a few lessons in parenting recently thanks to Elizabeth, and he was freshly acquainted with the fact that parenting involved sacrifice. It had been gnawing at him that his mother didn't seem the type to sacrifice for him. Once upon a time he might have thought she loved him too much. Now he was afraid she didn't love him at all.

But Gwen didn't believe that for a minute. She'd seen the look on Luann's face each time Travis walked into a room. "Let me talk to her, Travis. I think we just don't appreciate how hard this must be for her, but I—"

"Don't even think about trying to sweet-talk her into staying. Not now. Not with that reaction. I don't want her here."

Gwen was losing patience with his stubbornness. "You can't mean that."

"I mean it! Damn it, I mean exactly that! And I'm sick to death of debating it with you. I'm going for a drive." He left the room. Moments later she heard the front door slam and then his truck roared to life.

Gwen gazed at the flickering candles and the little vase of roses in the middle of the table. The scene she'd worked so hard to create began to blur as tears dripped silently down her cheeks.

CHAPTER FIFTEEN

BY THE TIME Travis pulled up in front of the log-style ranch house at the Rocking D he'd cooled down some, but he was still furious with his mother. He used to take it for granted that he had to organize his life around her, because that's what his father had taught him to do.

But he'd watched Matty and Sebastian rearrange their whole lives for Lizzie. Hell, he'd rearranged his whole life, too. Without asking, he knew Gwen was prepared to do the same for Lizzie or other children they might have. It was what parents did.

In the past week he'd come to realize that his mother had no right to control his life the way she'd been doing. He'd still look out for her as he'd promised, but on his own terms. If she wouldn't move to Colorado, then he'd hire somebody to help her get through the long Utah winter. She wouldn't like that, but he didn't much care. She'd had things her way long enough.

He crossed the wide front porch and rapped on the front door of the ranch house. He had a strong need to see his baby girl.

Sebastian came to the door chewing a mouthful of food. He swallowed. "Hey, Travis. Where's the rest of the gang?"

"Still in town. Sorry. I guess I interrupted your dinner."

"No problem." Sebastian looked curious as hell but he didn't ask any questions. "We just got a call I'm sure you'll be interested in hearing about. Come on in."

Travis stepped into the rustic living room with its huge rock fireplace and comfortable furniture. He took off his Stetson. "Jessica?"

"No, but it has to do with her. Hey, Matty," he called as he headed for the dining room. "Look who's here."

Matty sat in a dining chair making an attempt to eat while she gave Lizzie a bottle. "What a coincidence. Hi, Travis. We were just talking about you."

"Yeah, Sebastian said something about a phone call." Travis took a seat next to Matty and hung his hat on the back of his chair. "Why don't you let me give her the rest of that bottle so you can finish your dinner?"

"I'll accept that offer." Matty eased the bottle away from Lizzie and set it on the table before lifting the baby and transferring her to Travis's lap. "Oof. This girl is getting heavy."

Travis settled the baby in his lap and felt a surge of happiness at having her in his arms again. "She's growing up, that's all. She'll have a tooth soon, won't you, princess?"

Lizzie drooled and waved a fist at him.

"I know, I know. You want to finish your chow. Then we'll talk." He poked the bottle back in her eager mouth.

"Have you eaten?" Matty asked. "I'd be glad to fix you a plate."

Travis thought of the beautiful dinner Gwen had spent all day preparing and felt really sad that it had all gone to waste. He'd make it up to her. "That's okay," he said, gazing down at Lizzie as he gave her the bottle. His baby was getting prettier every day. He couldn't wait to see that first pearly tooth. "I'm not hungry, but I'd take a cup of coffee, if you have it."

"I'll get you one," Sebastian said. "Matty, tell him who called."

Travis looked up at her. "Yeah, who called?"

"Boone."

"He did?" Travis was pleased. Boone Connor was a hell of a nice guy, and Travis was always glad when summer came and the big blacksmith returned to the Rocking D from his hometown in New Mexico. "He must be about ready to head up here, huh? He needs to shoe the horses before—"

"He didn't call about shoeing horses," Matty said. She glanced down at the baby in Travis's lap.

Travis followed her gaze and a feeling of dread washed over him. Boone had been there that night in Aspen, too. Sebastian had said something about the call having to do with Jessica. Slowly his gaze rose to meet Matty's and his arm tightened instinctively around Lizzie. "Don't tell me he got a letter."

"Okay," Sebastian said as he set the mug of hot coffee in front of Travis. "Then I'll tell you. He got a letter."

"No way." Travis's stomach clenched. "This late?"

Sebastian sat down across from Travis. "He's been traveling all over with that horse-shoeing business and the letter just now caught up with him. He's headed up here."

Panic surged through Travis's heart. This was his baby. His. Once he married Gwen, he'd be in a position to have custody. Matty and Sebastian could have visiting rights, of course. Generous visiting rights. "You're not going to tell me he thinks he's Lizzie's father. In that case we're talking Immaculate Conception. I think Boone's still a virgin."

"You'd better not say that to Boone. Remember how he was drinking and carrying on that night about feeling betrayed because his old girlfriend was getting married?"

"Yeah, and I think he lost that girl because he was too slow out of the gate. Next to the word *shy* in the dictionary is a picture of Boone Connor."

"He's not that bad," Sebastian protested. "Hell, I'm shy around women, myself."

Travis shook his head. "Boone's shy. You're clueless. There's a difference."

"A big difference," Matty said, laughing.

Travis leaned toward Sebastian. "I'd believe you were Lizzie's dad before I'd believe Boone was, and I don't believe you're even in the running."

"Watch it," Sebastian said.

Matty pushed back her plate. "You guys may not think it's true, but Boone is absolutely sure he slept with Jessica, first because drinking makes him act out of character and he drank a lot that night, and second because he was so broken up over his old girlfriend."

"Well, that's just bull!" Travis said.

Lizzie jerked in surprise at his loud tone.

"Whoops." Travis cuddled her closer. "Sorry, sweetheart. Daddy didn't mean to scare you."

"Careful how you throw that word around," Sebastian said with a slight edge to his voice.

"If the shoe fits," Travis said casually.

Sebastian glowered at him. "It fits me like a glove, as a matter of fact. I—"

"Boys!" Matty held up both hands. "I will not sit here

and listen to another one of these idiotic arguments. I tremble to think what it's going to be like when Boone shows up. I might have to go stay with Gwen." She glanced at Travis. "And speaking of Gwen, where is she? And Luann? Isn't this your mother's last night here?"

Travis's chest grew tight and he kept his gaze on Elizabeth. "Yep."

"Uh…her last night, but you're here, not over there," Matty said. "I detect a problem."

"Oh, Matty, you're always detecting problems," Sebastian said. "Everything's fine, right, buddy?"

"Sure." Travis watched Lizzie drain the last of her bottle. He set it on the table and lifted the baby to his shoulder. "Couldn't be better."

"Oh, don't risk your shirt, Travis," Matty said quickly. "She's drooling like the dickens these days, and she'll mess up that black material. Sebastian, why don't you take Elizabeth? I think she needs to be changed." She glanced pointedly at Sebastian.

"Maybe Travis would like to change her," Sebastian said. "He hardly ever gets—"

"*Sebastian.*"

"On the other hand, I'd be more than happy to do it." He took the baby from Travis. "Come on, little one. Let's go find Bruce."

As he left, Matty leaned closer to Travis. "What happened?"

"Gwen asked her to move in permanently to Hawthorne House, and she said she'd rather hang by her teeth from the Royal Gorge Bridge."

"Oh, Travis." Sympathy shadowed Matty's blue eyes. "Did you try to talk to her about it?"

"Nope. And don't be telling me I should." A bitter taste returned to his mouth. "I've been dancing to that lady's tune for a long time, and if she's not willing to sacrifice a little bit for me, then I'm through with her."

Matty didn't say anything for a minute. Finally she spoke. "How'd Gwen take it?"

Travis sighed. "I'm sure she's upset. She wanted to try and talk my mother into changing her mind, but damn it, I don't want my mother there if she has to be dragged into it. She'll make me pay if that's the way it goes. Gwen doesn't get that."

"Did you fight with Gwen?"

"No. Yes." He looked away from Matty's direct gaze. "Sort of. But I'm sure she knows I'm not mad at her, just at my mother."

Matty reached over and squeezed his hand. Then she stood. "I'm going to drive into town and see Gwen."

Travis glanced up at her. "You're not thinking you'll talk my mother into staying, are you? Because I don't want you doing that. Not you or Gwen."

She patted his shoulder. "I won't try to talk your mother into staying. I just think Gwen could use a friend right now."

"She made a beautiful dinner," Travis said. "And we didn't get to eat it." Because he'd kissed Gwen and forced the issue, he thought sadly. But it would have come out the same in the end. His mother was insanely jealous, and she didn't want her perfect little life disturbed for anything or anyone.

"Tell Sebastian I'll be back in a couple of hours," Matty said. "And try not to get into a wrestling match with him over this kid while I'm gone."

DINNER WAS TUCKED into plastic containers in the refrigerator by the time Gwen opened the door and found Matty standing there.

"Got dessert?" Matty said with a grin.

"Oh, God, Matty. Travis must have driven to your place and told you what happened."

"He did."

Gwen hugged her friend tightly. "Thank you for coming. I've never been so glad to see anybody in my life."

Matty laughed and hung her jacket on the coat tree in the hall. "Oh, I wouldn't go that far. I'm sure you were more glad to see Travis earlier this week."

Gwen felt her cheeks warm as she remembered exactly what had gone on in the hall, right about where she and Matty were standing at this very moment. "It's a different kind of glad," she said.

"Let's hope so." Matty chuckled as she headed back toward the kitchen. "So, what did you make for dessert?"

"That better-than-sex chocolate cake you gave me the recipe for."

Matty groaned. "I knew it was calling me. Is it gone yet?"

"Gone? Why would it be gone?"

Matty sat at the kitchen table in her regular seat. "If I'd been the one dealing with this horse hockey, I probably would've eaten the whole thing by now."

Gwen smiled at her friend. "You're so good for me. I feel about a hundred percent better, already."

"Don't mention it. You've come through for me a time or two. So, where's Luann?"

"Upstairs in her room." Gwen looked up at the

ceiling and grimaced. "She probably won't come down until she's ready to leave in the morning."

"I see. Well, first off I need to tell you that Boone Connor called and he got a letter asking him to be a godfather, too. He's on his way, ready to do his duty by this little girl he thinks is his."

Gwen sank onto a chair in amazement. "You're kidding."

"Don't I wish. Jessica has created a real mess. I'd love to get my hands on that woman."

Gwen shook her head. "Three men, all thinking they did the deed. Jessica had better show up fast."

"The detective is working on it, but Jessica's slippery. So anyway, I thought you should know about that little development."

"Thanks. I'm sure you told Travis." Gwen could just imagine Travis's reaction. He was becoming very possessive about the baby.

"I told him. He doesn't believe for one minute that Boone's the father, and neither does Sebastian. And I can guarantee Boone will fall in love with Elizabeth just the way the other two have. It'll be a circus around here." Matty looked hopefully over at the counter. "Um, are you gonna give me some cake?"

"You bet." Gwen didn't often forget her hostess duties, and she stood immediately, irritated with herself for being so absentminded after Matty had specifically indicated she wanted some dessert. Gwen crossed quickly to the counter and lifted the dome top from her cake platter.

"Sweet Lord in Heaven, that is a sight for sore eyes," Matty said worshipfully. "You're gonna make some man a hell of a wife. Shoot, I wish you'd be *my* wife.

With Sebastian for my husband and you for my wife, I'd be in high cotton."

Gwen laughed, but her heart wasn't in it. She cut a generous slice of cake for Matty. "You know, it's not going to work, me marrying Travis if he has this big rift with his mother. He thinks he can break off his relationship with her and just go on, but I know he can't. He loves her. And she loves him. I don't know what to do." She set the cake, a napkin and a fork down in front of Matty before taking a seat across from her.

Matty looked at her in surprise. "Where's your piece?"

"I'm not hungry."

"For *this?*" Matty hooted. "*No*body's not hungry for *this*. Get yourself some. It's therapy. And put the coffeepot on. We need to have us a brainstorming session."

Gwen sighed, but she got up and started the coffee brewing. Then she cut herself some cake and sat down at the table again. "It's no use. Travis doesn't want me to talk to his mother. And she leaves tomorrow, so there's really no time to change her mind, even if I thought I could sneak in a few conversations when Travis wasn't looking."

"We could both go up there right now, hold some cake just out of reach, and tell her she could have some if she'll be a good girl."

Gwen laughed. "That's better than anything I've come up with."

Matty took her first bite and rolled her eyes in ecstasy. She swallowed and cut another bite with her fork. "I swear, it would work. At least it would work on me. I'd clean the barn floor with a toothbrush if you promised me a piece of this cake at the end." She chewed and swallowed, then pointed at the cake with her fork. "I've made this, and it didn't taste half this good. You are one helluva cook."

"Thank you." Gwen took a bite of the cake, and it did taste pretty good. Chocolate was supposed to be a mood elevator. She took another bite.

"You could probably bring about world peace with this cake. I'm not kidding. You have a gift." Suddenly Matty paused, her fork in midair. "Maybe too much of a gift."

"Too much?"

Matty stared at Gwen. "God, that's it. I'm brilliant."

"I agree, but what brilliance are you guilty of this time?"

"No wonder Luann has a burr under her saddle. Tell me, did she expect you to wait on her hand and foot while she was here?"

"Not really. I wanted to do things for her." Gwen got up to pour them each a cup of coffee. "At first she insisted on helping out a little, but then, after Travis moved back into my bedroom I felt guilty about that, so I tried to make her stay even easier."

"So then you were doing it all."

"Pretty much." Gwen set a cup and saucer down by Matty's elbow. Then she brought over the sugar and poured cream into a favorite little flowered pitcher before putting that on the table, as well.

"Do you see that?" Matty pointed to the cream pitcher.

"Yeah, isn't it pretty? I found it in an antique shop in Colorado Springs, and I—"

"Not the pitcher, sweetie, the fact that you had to put the cream in it instead of plopping the carton down on the table, like I'd do! You have this perfectionistic tendency that is so adorable, unless we're talking about your potential mother-in-law, who suddenly feels completely outclassed."

Gwen's mouth dropped open as she stared at Matty. "Outclassed? By me? That's ridiculous."

"Is it? You had this place spit-shined before she arrived. Then I'm sure you tried to keep it that way while she was here. I'm sure you fixed perfect meals and arranged beautiful bouquets for the table."

Gwen continued to stare at her friend.

Matty pointed a finger at her. "Didn't you?"

"Of course! She was my guest, and a very important guest. I wanted her to feel happy here. Special. I wanted her to think I'd be good enough for her son!"

"Oh, she knows you are. The problem is, she's become extraneous. I'll bet the only time she felt really needed was that day I schemed to have her baby-sit Elizabeth. She actually looked happy that day. She even cleaned my kitchen while she was there, which only proves my point. Around here she felt useless." Matty shot Gwen a look of triumph.

"But she wouldn't be useless if she lived here!" Gwen couldn't believe that Matty was right. "Surely she could figure out that I'd love to have her help with the business, and with the children, when we have them, and with—"

"Not if she thinks you can do everything better than she can. And you've proven how efficient and capable you are, so what purpose would she serve? Besides that, you'll make her look bad in front of her son. No way will she subject herself to that kind of comparison."

Gwen dropped her head in her hands and groaned. "I tried to make everything perfect, and all I did was screw it up. Now it's all ruined, and Travis and his mother are fighting, and they're both incredibly stubborn."

"I've decided all men are stubborn. So Luann must have more testosterone than most of us."

Gwen lifted her head with a faint smile. "Because we're never stubborn."

"Never." Matty grinned.

"But Matty, what am I going to do? No way can I turn this around in the next twelve hours. No way."

"I don't think so either."

"So I'm doomed?"

"Nope. Ordinarily I wouldn't approve of doing something like this, but we have a state of emergency, here."

Gwen allowed herself a small bit of hope. "I'll consider anything."

"You're sure? Because I have a feeling this will be very hard for you."

Gwen thought of all that was at stake and didn't hesitate. "Anything. I will be eternally grateful, Matty, for whatever you can think of to do."

"Forget the eternal gratitude. Just keep me supplied with cake."

CHAPTER SIXTEEN

AN HOUR LATER Gwen lay in bed under piles of blankets waiting for Travis to arrive. He showed up right on schedule. She heard his key rattle in the front door lock and then his boots hit the floor in quick strides as he hurried back to the bedroom.

He hesitated in the doorway. "Gwen? Honey, what's the matter? Matty said you weren't feeling good."

"I feel terrible," she said. "Chilled to the bone, upset stomach, bones aching."

He crossed quickly to the bed and crouched beside her. He laid the back of his hand against her cheek. "You're burning up. Must be the flu. I'll call Doc Harrison."

"Don't you dare. There's nothing they can do for the flu, anyway, except tell you to rest and drink fluids."

"It could be something worse." Travis's eyes clouded with worry. "What if it isn't just the flu?"

Gwen felt a surge of guilt for putting him through this. Matty had been right that it wouldn't be easy. Gwen rationalized by telling herself she did feel sick— heartsick. Or she had, before Matty had given her a plan.

"I'm sure it's nothing serious," she said. "But, listen, don't get too close, okay? I don't want you to catch it. You have to drive to Utah tomorrow."

"Fat chance. I'll put my mother on a Greyhound before I'll leave you when you're sick. And I don't care about getting sick. I want to take care of you. Do you need anything? Some juice? A back rub?"

She thought he looked entirely too eager to administer the back rub. "Oh, Travis, that's so sweet." She gave him what she hoped was a sickly smile. "But I can take care of myself. It's the guests, Bill and Charlene Ingram, I'm worried about. They arrive day after tomorrow."

"I'll call them and tell them the visit's off. It'll be just you and me. And the germs."

"You can't reach Bill and Charlene now." At least that much was true. "They're already on the road and they weren't sure where they'd stop on the way here because this trip is supposed to be spontaneous, except for their weekend at Hawthorne House."

Travis made an impatient noise in his throat. "If they're so spontaneous then they can find another place to stay this weekend."

"Oh, Travis, we can't ask them to do that. It's their first wedding anniversary. They spent their honeymoon here a year ago. I have a small piece of their wedding cake in the freezer."

Travis gazed at her, frustration shining in his golden eyes. "Look, sweetheart, I would be willing to do whatever I can, but you know I'm a lousy cook, and I'm even worse at arranging flowers and setting out hand towels and all those little things you do to make the house nice for people. And you can't be doing it. You won't feel like it, probably, and besides, you might give this bug to them, which wouldn't be very neighborly."

Gwen moaned. "Oh, Travis, I hate this. The Ingrams

have been looking forward to their weekend for a whole year."

"I know, but stuff happens." He smoothed her forehead. "I'll help them find another place to stay. I'll call around."

"I wish I could think of another way. I wish…" She paused. "Travis, there is one solution. Oh, God, if only she'd be willing to help out."

"Who, Matty?"

"No, not Matty. She and Sebastian are going to buy cattle this weekend, remember? They're taking the baby."

"Yeah, that's right. I can't believe I forgot. So who were you thinking of?"

"Your mother."

"My *mother?*" He gave a short bark of laughter. "Oh, sure. That would work. Not. She can hardly wait to get out of here. I can't imagine her agreeing to hang around and cook and clean for your guests."

"You're probably right." Gwen sighed. "But it would solve everything if she'd just agree to stay a few more days. You could take care of me, and she could run the house temporarily."

Travis studied her. "You'd trust her to do that?"

"Of course I would." She'd never let him know how tough that was to say. Her little house was her domain, and she really wasn't looking forward to turning over the reins, but Matty had convinced her she had to if she ever expected to earn Luann's goodwill.

Travis rubbed his chin and looked thoughtful. "It would solve the problem, all the way around. When you're better, I could drive her home. No matter how mad she makes me, I wasn't looking forward to putting her on the bus. And a plane's no good, either. It'd only get her as far as Salt Lake City, and then she'd have to take a bus from there. She's not used to traveling alone."

"You'd be worried sick about her."

"Unfortunately." He grimaced. "I guess when it comes to her, my bark is worse than my bite."

"I thought as much." Gwen touched his hand. "At least ask her. If she turns you down, then we'll think of something else."

The muscles in his jaw tightened. "If she turns me down, I may put her on the bus after all."

LUANN DIDN'T TURN Travis down, and Gwen spent the next two days in bed trying not to go completely insane. She was bored out of her tree, which was bad enough, but even worse she had to lie there and listen to the sounds and scents of Luann cooking on her stove, washing her china, running her vacuum cleaner and dusting with her lemon polish. Matty had warned her she'd have trouble with that, and she definitely had trouble. The hardest pill to swallow was realizing that Luann seemed to be coping fine. Gwen wasn't indispensable.

Then she had to battle guilt again when Travis brought her a Ouija board as a "poor-me" present. But she had to smile at his choice. It was so Travis to bring her something to play with.

Immediately she suggested asking the Ouija board if he was Elizabeth's father. To her surprise he shook his head and told her she could ask the board anything else, but not that. His reluctance made her realize just how desperately he wanted the little baby to be his, and how ripe he was for a family of his own.

Although Travis looked in on her as much as possible

in between trips to the Rocking D, part of Gwen's care fell to Luann. The first day she brought Gwen a bowl of soup for lunch with businesslike efficiency, but didn't pause to chat. Gwen would have complimented her on the soup, but it was her own, not Luann's.

On the second day Luann brought in another bowl of Gwen's soup, but she loosened up enough to ask if the patient was feeling any better.

"I feel really weak," Gwen said. Matty had advised her to stay bedridden for at least three days, and perhaps four, if she could stand it. The flu was supposed to leave you weak, Matty had said, so that was to be Gwen's standard line.

"Well, don't worry about a thing. We're all ready for your company," Luann said with a touch of pride.

"That's great." Gwen was dying to ask if Luann had made sure they had enough eggs in the refrigerator, and whether or not she'd put fresh flowers in the bedroom. But she didn't ask. Matty had given her strict instructions not to bring up those kinds of questions, which would make Luann think she wasn't trusted to do the job properly.

"I really appreciate this, Luann," she said instead. "When you run a business all by yourself, you never count on getting sick."

"I suppose not."

"And although Travis would be more than willing to help, he's not much good in this situation."

A small smile appeared briefly. "No, that boy doesn't know potpourri from potato chips."

Gwen had thought of one other little glitch. "Uh, Luann, I should probably warn you that the couple coming this afternoon has only been married a year. I can't guarantee that they won't make some—"

"I'll put cotton in my ears at night," she said. "Well, you rest now. I have banana bread to bake."

Not long afterward the aroma of banana bread drifted into Gwen's bedroom, making her mouth water. She'd had to pretend that she didn't have much of an appetite, but she was starving to death. At this rate she really would be weak—weak from hunger.

She gauged how long the banana bread had been in the oven and figured out when it would be done. From the way Luann had handled herself in the kitchen before Gwen had mistakenly insisted she needed to relax, Gwen had a hunch she was a pretty good cook.

The ding of the kitchen timer coincided with the sound of Luann bustling around. Gwen recognized those sounds well—Luann had set the bread out to cool. God, but it smelled good.

Finally she couldn't stand it another minute. Trying to keep her voice sounding like a sick person's, she called out to Luann.

Luann came to the door of her bedroom. "Is anything wrong?"

"No, nothing's wrong. I just…that bread smells heavenly. My appetite seems to be returning a little. Could I possibly have a slice?"

The expression on Luann's face was worth every blessed minute Gwen had spent languishing in that bed. Travis's mother beamed. Gwen had never seen her look like that, and it transformed her from the taut-faced woman who'd arrived with Travis to the loving mother Gwen had hoped Luann was underneath.

"Would you like a little butter on it?" Luann asked. She'd never addressed Gwen in such a sweet tone.

"I would love a little butter on it."

"And maybe a cup of that cinnamon tea?"

"That sounds perfect."

"Be right back." Luann hurried out, her step light.

Gwen closed her eyes in gratitude. "Thank you, Matty," she whispered.

GWEN STAYED in her suite Friday night and Saturday morning while Travis and Luann entertained the Ingrams. Judging from the laughter and happy voices, things were going well. Before Travis left for the Rocking D on Saturday he brought in a bouquet of flowers.

"These are from Bill and Charlene," he said as he set the vase down by her bed. "They hope you get better soon."

"How nice of them." She glanced into his eyes. "Everything's going okay, isn't it?"

Travis scratched the back of his head. "Yeah," he said with some surprise. "Yeah, it is. Damned if I can figure it out, either. When I asked Mom the other night if she'd do you this favor she acted as if it would be a huge imposition. But if I didn't know better, I'd say she's having a good time."

Gwen thought she should get an Oscar for the way she responded. Instead of punching a fist in the air as she longed to do, she merely nodded. "She's a good sport to pitch in, and she's saved my butt, that's for darn sure."

Travis crouched down beside the bed and combed her hair back from her face. "Feeling any better?"

"I am." *You have no idea.* "But I don't think I should push it. Maybe tomorrow, after the Ingrams leave, I'll try getting out of bed for a while."

Travis gazed at her tenderly. "You've always been

such a can-do lady. I sure didn't want you to come down with the flu, but it makes me feel all macho and protective to know that you need help, sometimes, too. In some ways, that's been a nice feeling. Not that I want you to get sick again, ever," he added quickly.

Gwen was startled. "Don't tell me you thought I was invincible...?" She caught herself before she added the word *too*.

"I guess I did." He stroked her cheek with his thumb. "I knew how much I needed you, but I wasn't sure you really needed me."

"You're kidding."

He grinned, but his eyes remained serious. "Well, aside from the sex."

She pressed his hand against her cheek and her heart swelled with love for him. "Oh, Travis, sex is only part of it. I need you to talk with me, work beside me, laugh with me. Especially that last part. I thought you knew that."

"I didn't. Not really. But I do now," he said softly.

"I love you."

"I love you, too," he murmured. Then he stood and leaned over her to kiss her on the forehead. "Rest now. I want you to get well." He waggled his eyebrows at her. "And you might as well know my motives aren't pure, either."

"You want a fresh batch of cinnamon rolls?"

He laughed. "You know how much I love those things."

"Oh, I do."

"But on the list of what I'm hungry for, they run a very distant second." He winked and left the room.

Gwen lay there and battled extreme sexual frustration. Not only had she been forced to turn over her house to Luann, she'd had to pretend she wasn't interested in making love to Travis. One lusty response on her part and he'd have suspected she'd been pretending to have the flu.

She still wasn't sure how they'd made it through the times he'd helped her shower and wash her hair. He'd fought his arousal with such determination, and she'd felt like such a fraud. Yet apparently he'd benefitted from her fake illness as much as Luann had. Someday she'd tell him the truth about this weekend, but not yet, not when so much was still hanging in the balance.

Once the Ingrams were gone, Gwen planned to make a big deal about Luann's help during the crisis and drop some heavy hints about how much easier it would be to run a bed and breakfast if two women lived here. And it would be, Gwen admitted grudgingly, although she hadn't come to that conclusion without a struggle. Staying in this bed had taught her some things, too. She wondered if Matty had intended that it should.

Giving up control of her house had been one of the toughest things she'd ever done, but now she knew she could. And with luck, so did Luann.

Travis called late in the afternoon to say a waterline had sprung a leak at the ranch and fixing it would make him late getting home. The Ingrams had gone out for their anniversary dinner, and Gwen was still playing sick and eating small meals from a bed tray.

To Gwen's delight, Luann chose to eat her dinner in Gwen's bedroom. During the meal the older woman was positively chatty, talking easily about gardening, cleaning projects and recipes. Gwen couldn't believe the change. She also realized how much she appreciated this kind of conversation, one she could never have with her own mother. Even Matty wasn't into domestic topics that much, but Luann cared about the same things Gwen did. For the first time Gwen began to think of Luann as a bonus instead of a burden. It was a liberating thought.

Gwen wasn't sure how long Luann would have stayed to talk, but Travis came home, tired and hungry, and she hurried to the kitchen to heat up his food. Gwen half expected him to bring his plate into the bedroom, too, but instead she heard chairs scrape in the kitchen, as if he and his mother had sat down at the kitchen table.

For one unworthy moment Gwen felt jealous. Then the moment passed. After all, she'd been working toward this very goal, mending the rift between mother and son. If they were choosing to talk alone in the kitchen, then she'd accomplished her mission. But she was dying to know what they were talking about. And who.

She pulled her Ouija board out from under the bed and set it on her lap. With the plastic piece under her fingertips she silently asked who the conversation was about. Sure enough, it slid across the alphabet to spell out her name.

Damn, but she wanted to hear what they were saying! Yet she couldn't very well lurk at the door. If Travis came back in, she'd never make it back to the bed without him catching her. She put the board away and snuggled down into the covers.

Travis and Luann's voices were hushed, and she couldn't make out words at all. She'd just have to trust Travis to be diplomatic in his dealings with his mother, the way she'd had to trust Luann to take good care of her house guests. She heaved a sigh. Another lesson to learn.

Still she couldn't help straining to hear. Finally the attempt to make out words amidst the steady drone of voices had a hypnotic effect, and she must have dozed off, because the next thing she knew the bedside light snapped off and Travis crawled into bed with her.

She turned sleepily to give him a good-night kiss. He kissed her back and there was so much restrained energy in that kiss that her eyes popped open. "Travis? Is everything all right?"

His whole body seemed to hum as he gathered her close. His voice was rich and deep in her ear. "She wants to stay."

Gwen gasped and looked into his shadowed face. "She *does?*" She'd never in her wildest dreams imagined that Luann would capitulate of her own accord.

"She wants me to ask you if the offer is still open."

Gwen let out a whoop of triumph.

"Hey." Travis chuckled. "Don't get too excited. You might trigger a relapse."

Barely in time Gwen remembered her role. She coughed several times, as if the whoop had really taken the starch out of her.

"See?" Travis rubbed her back. "Look what you've done. Want some water?"

"No. No, thanks." Her body warmed to his touch. "Oh, Travis, how wonderful. I'm thrilled that she wants to stay."

"Me, too." He continued to stroke her back. "I hate to say this, but it's probably because you got sick."

"*Really.*"

"Yeah. She admitted to me tonight that until that happened, she didn't think there was a place for her here. But now she realizes what a drain this place can be on one woman. She can see that you really do need her if you're going to try and run a bed and breakfast and raise a family, too."

"And she's so right!" Gwen snuggled against him. His muscular body felt so good pressed against hers. He'd worn a T-shirt and briefs to bed, as he'd been doing the entire time she'd been pretending to be sick. She wanted the underwear off.

Travis sighed and held her close, resting his cheek against the top of her head in an almost brotherly fashion. She gritted her teeth.

"Thank God she came to her senses," he said. "I was trying to imagine our wedding without her there. It made me sort of sick to my stomach."

"And now she can help us plan it." Gwen envisioned the fun she and Luann would have making this an event to remember. And then would come the honeymoon. Gwen could hardly wait for that part.

"Oh, she wants to help plan it. But I warned her I'm looking for speed, here. Two weeks, tops."

"Two weeks?" She raised her head to look up at him. "That's not nearly enough time."

"With you two on the job? It's more than enough time, unless you think it'll be tough on you, just getting over being sick and all."

She rubbed her body against his. "That won't be a problem. I'm practically well."

"But not completely. Stop that."

She slipped a hand up under his T-shirt. "I think I'm well enough."

"I don't know about this, Gwen."

"I do." She felt his nipples tighten under her caressing palm. "And I'll bet you'd like to."

"Uh…it's possible." His breathing grew labored.

"Maybe we could try it, if we only use the missionary position and I'm very careful with you."

Her heart raced and her body moistened just thinking about making love in some position, any position at all. "I think we could risk it."

"Okay." His voice was husky. "Easy now." He rolled her slowly to her back and slid his hand under her sensible cotton nightgown. "After being sick for so long, you may be a little slow to…" He sucked in a breath as he encountered her moist heat. "Then again, maybe not." As he stroked her beneath the gown, his breathing grew ragged. "Maybe I should leave this on, so you don't catch a chill."

She wanted that nightgown gone. In fact, she'd be willing to burn it. "Let's take it off and then I'll put it back on, afterward."

"If you're sure."

"With it on, I might become overheated."

"Oh! I didn't think of that. Well, then we should take it off." He stopped caressing her long enough to work her nightgown carefully over her head. "Still okay?"

"Peachy. What about your clothes?" She reached for the elastic of his briefs.

"I'll do it." He slipped out of his briefs and took his T-shirt off over his head. "You're only supposed to lie there and enjoy."

"Yes, sir." She quivered with anticipation.

"You're shivering. Are you cold?"

"No. Yes. If you cover me with your body I'll stay warm."

"I can do that." He started to move over her. "Wait. I need to get a con—"

"I don't think you do."

He went very still. "I don't?"

"Didn't you say two weeks?"

"Or less."

"Then why bother with those silly things any more?"

A fine tremor passed through him. "Cover your eyes," he said at last. "I'm turning on the light."

"Okay." She put her hand over her eyes as he leaned over to switch on the lamp. Slowly she uncovered her eyes to find him looking down at her with more focus and intensity than ever before. "Why did you want the light?" she asked.

His gaze never leaving hers, he moved over her. "Because I want to be able to look into your eyes while I make you pregnant with our baby."

Desire swept through her. With a moan she grasped his hips and urged him forward.

He resisted her. "No. I'm taking this slow."

"You don't have to." She was wild to have him inside her. "I'm really okay now."

"I believe you. I'm taking it slow because I want to remember this moment for the rest of my life." And with that he gradually eased into her, the flame in his eyes growing brighter and brighter, until at last he was settled, deep and secure within her.

He gazed into her eyes. No doubt about it. He was giving her *The Look*. "Forever," he murmured.

Joyfully she took the promise into her heart. They would have a ceremony someday soon, with a minister and all of their loved ones, and she knew it would be beautiful and moving and important. But it would only be a formality.

Tonight they would exchange their vows.

She cupped his face in her hands. "Forever," she whispered.

* * * * *

BOONE'S BOUNTY

CHAPTER ONE

Snow.

Boone Connor sighed and switched on the wipers. Didn't it just figure he'd hit a late-season snowstorm on his way over Raton Pass. Damn. It was nearly June. The snow should be gone by now. But his luck had been running that way lately.

And this didn't promise to be one of those wimpy storms that sifted down from the clouds like cake flour and dusted the pine trees so they looked like a Christmas card. This wasn't the kind of snow that blew off the road like white sand. Nope. This was a serious, drifts-to-your-crotch, black-ice-on-the-curves kind of storm. His truck tires were already losing traction.

The roadblock didn't surprise him, but it sure frustrated the hell out of him. His old king-cab could make it through anything, and he sure was anxious about getting to the Rocking D to see that baby. *His* baby, most likely. The idea that he probably had a kid still made him dizzy. He couldn't quite believe the baby was real, and setting eyes on her would help anchor his thoughts.

But Smoky was about to throw a crimp in his plans, obviously.

Boone rolled down his window and snow blew in,

nipping his cheeks with cold. He ignored the discomfort and tipped up the brim of his Stetson so he could look the cop in the eye while he tried to make a case for getting past those orange and white barriers.

The patrolman, bundled to the teeth, looked up at Boone. "I'm afraid you'll have to turn back, sir." His breath fogged the air. "Road conditions are bad up ahead and getting worse by the minute."

"My truck's got four-wheel drive, Officer," Boone said, although he didn't expect that information to make any difference. "And I've driven this road hundreds of times. I need to get to Colorado right away."

"I understand that, sir." The patrolman didn't sound particularly understanding. He sounded as if he was sick to death of standing in the cold reciting this speech to unhappy folks. "But we can't let you take a chance on that road until the storm's over and the snowplow clears it. With luck we'll be able to let people through tomorrow morning."

"Hell."

"There's a little motel and café about three miles back," the patrolman added, stomping his booted feet.

Boone knew the place. He'd stopped there for coffee a few times, but hadn't bothered this trip because he'd been trying to outrun the snow. He'd never stayed at the motel. He mostly liked driving straight through until he got to where he was going. The motel wasn't very big, as he recalled. Ten or twelve units, maybe.

He glanced up at the patrolman. "How many people have you sent there?"

"A few. But I expect most of them drove on back to Santa Fe. The motel's clean, but not exactly the Plaza."

The patrolman glanced past Boone's truck. "I'll have to ask you to move your vehicle, sir. There's someone behind you."

Boone glanced in his rearview mirror and saw the small white sedan, its fog lights picking out the flakes and causing them to sparkle while the rest of the car was nearly invisible in the swirling snow. Now *that* vehicle had no business trying to maneuver down the road ahead, but Boone still thought he could make it with no sweat. Still, he knew a losing battle when he saw one. He put the truck in gear and swung it around to the other lane.

As he paused to roll up his window, he glanced over at the sedan. Its window slid down, and he caught a quick glimpse of the driver—young, blond and female. With her hair caught up in a funky ponytail on top of her head, she looked even younger than she probably was. His irritation with Smoky eased a little as he considered how vulnerable that woman would have been if no one had set up a roadblock to protect her from doing something stupid.

He heard her arguing hotly with the officer, and he shook his head in amazement. Yep, without that roadblock, she'd have done something real stupid. She'd have ended up a statistic for sure, off in a snowbank, frozen solid.

He rolled up his window and headed back down toward the motel, still marveling at how naive that woman was, thinking she'd drive that little bitty compact over a snow-choked mountain pass. Better to have the roadblock, even if it meant he'd get delayed, than to leave greenhorns like that free to take chances with their lives.

WHEN SHELBY MCFARLAND first saw the roadblock,
she panicked, sure that Mason Fowler had reported her
to the police. But no, the barricades were on account of
the weather. The patrolman wanted her to turn back.

But turning back meant possibly heading toward
Mason, who by now could be in hot pursuit. She abandoned her usual caution.

"You don't understand," she said to the officer
standing beside the car. "I *must* get through. The road
can't be that bad!"

"I'm afraid it is, ma'am. You wouldn't stand a chance
with this light vehicle." He leaned down and looked into
the car. "And I'm sure you wouldn't want to take any
risks with that little guy. You a Spurs fan, son?"

"Yep," Josh replied. "Bob, he is, too."

Shelby glanced over at Josh sitting in his car seat,
proudly wearing his San Antonio Spurs jersey. She
should have dressed him in something less identifiable,
but he loved that jersey. And of course, she couldn't risk
ending up marooned in a snowbank, not with Josh in
the car. What had she been thinking?

Josh stared in fascination at the patrolman. "Do you
gots a gun?" he asked.

"Yes, son, I do," the officer said solemnly.

"My daddy gots a gun," Josh said.

Shelby felt sick to her stomach. She didn't doubt
Mason had a gun, but the thought of Josh somehow
coming into contact with it scared the daylights out of
her. "How do you know that, sweetheart?"

"He showed me it."

Shelby closed her eyes briefly, as if that would block
out the ugly image. If she needed any more reasons to

keep this child away from Mason, there was a huge one. A gun and a three-year-old. She shuddered.

"I hope your daddy keeps that gun locked up good and tight," the patrolman said. "Guns are not toys."

"The policeman is absolutely right, Josh," Shelby said. "You must never touch a gun." And if she had anything to do with it, he'd never get the chance again. She glanced back at the officer. "I want to thank you for preventing me from doing something foolish. I wasn't thinking clearly a moment ago. Trying to go over that pass tonight would be suicide."

"Bob and me, we never seed any snow before," Josh offered.

The patrolman peered into the car. "You got a little dog in there named Bob?"

"No," Shelby said. "Bob is Josh's special friend, and he's very talented. He can make himself invisible."

"Ahhh." The patrolman nodded solemnly. Then he glanced at Shelby. "There's a motel and café back down the road about three miles. Maybe you could wait it out there."

Shelby didn't remember the place, but it sounded better than driving to Santa Fe. "How long will it be before the road's open, do you think?"

"Hard to say, ma'am. If I was you, I'd try to get a room for the night. They're not fancy, but they're clean."

Shelby took a shaky breath. She didn't know for sure that Mason was following her, but she had a bad feeling he was. All he would have had to do was ask her apartment manager where she'd gone. The manager had been on his way into the building just as she and Josh were leaving, and Josh had blurted out that they were going to Yellowstone to ride horsies. She hadn't remembered to tell Josh it was a secret.

Still, she had a head start on Mason, so the motel was probably a safe bet for tonight. Besides, it wasn't as if she had a lot of choice. "Okay," she said. "We'll try that. And thanks again."

"No problem. Just doing my job, ma'am. 'Bye, son."

"'Bye, Mister Policeman."

Shelby gave the officer a smile before rolling up the window. Then she waited for him to step aside before she guided the car around in a half circle. Fortunately no one else seemed to be coming up the road.

Three days ago—it seemed like three years—Mason had called to say he was coming over the next morning to take Josh to the zoo. Something about the arrogant way he'd announced his intentions instead of asking Shelby if that was okay put her on alert. He'd been dropping hints for weeks that if the courts didn't grant him custody, he'd take Josh anyway.

The longer she thought about his brusque tone during the call, the more she became convinced that Mason didn't intend to bring Josh back. So she'd rented a car, hoping that would throw Mason off a little, packed some clothes for her and Josh, and left town.

"Where're we goin', Shebby?" Josh asked. "Back home?"

"No, not home, Josh. But we can't keep going up the mountain road because there's too much snow. So we'll stay overnight in a motel and try again tomorrow morning, okay?"

"Okay, but when are we gonna get to Yellowstone? You *said,* Shebby. Bob wants to see geezers."

"*Geysers,* Josh."

"Yeah, those. And we're gonna ride horsies there, right?"

"That's the plan." She should change the plan, but Josh was so excited she didn't have the heart, at least not yet.

"Bob, he knows how to ride horsies real good. He's gonna teach me."

"Good thing Bob knows so much, huh?" Shelby said. Right about now she wished Josh's imaginary friend really existed, and that he was about six-five, weighed two-fifty and could bench-press his own weight.

"Bob, he knows *this* much." Josh spread his arms wide. "A whole bunch, is what Bob knows." He glanced at Shelby, as if he expected her to contradict him. "Right, Shebby?"

Shelby smiled. No matter how scary life got, she took heart from this little bundle of sunshine sitting in his car seat next to her. He was unsinkable. And so damned normal, with his love of basketball and his imaginary friend. A child psychologist might say the imaginary friend had made an appearance at this particular time because of what Josh had been through recently. That could be true, and if so, she was impressed with the way the little boy took care of his own needs.

She glanced over at Josh. "Right. Bob is awesome."

Josh nodded. "Awesome. When are we gonna see geezers?"

"Well, first we have to go all the way through Colorado, and then most of the way through Wyoming. But before we do that, we have to get over this mountain, and we can't do that until tomorrow morning."

"'Member that song about a mountain? The one we singed in school?"

"Sure. Want to sing it?"

"Yep." Josh launched into a close approximation of "She'll Be Comin' 'Round the Mountain."

Shelby joined in, helping him through the parts he'd forgotten. How she loved this little boy. Long ago, in spite of herself, she'd begun to think of him as her own child. He even looked like her—same blond hair, same blue eyes. Patricia hadn't ever seemed to have time for him, especially after she'd divorced Mason.

And during the breakup of Patricia's marriage, Shelby's parents had been so busy worrying about Patricia, their favorite child, that they hadn't seemed to have any concern left for Josh. And now all three of them were gone—her sister and both her parents.

Shelby's chest tightened as a nick of pain touched her heart, like the whisper of a very sharp knife that barely cuts the skin but is capable of dealing a killing blow. It was a warning sign that she needed to shut down her emotions, and fast. Ever since the boating accident four months ago that had claimed her parents and Patricia, Shelby had kept a tight rein on her feelings. She had Josh to think about.

Josh stopped singing as Shelby pulled into the parking lot of a small motel with a café nearby.

"Is this it?" he asked.

"This is it." Shelby surveyed the rambling building, which was in definite need of a paint job. Her parents would have turned up their noses at the accommodations, but Shelby was grateful for anything reasonably clean. Quite a few cars and trucks were gathered in the lot, and she hoped she wouldn't have any trouble getting a room.

And she definitely wanted one. Driving all the way back to Santa Fe was too risky. The lights shining through the café's windows made it look cozy in the gathering gloom brought on by the heavy snowfall. The thought of a hot cup of coffee beckoned to her, but she turned the wheel left and parked in front of the first unit of the motel where an orange neon sign in one corner of the window read Office. In the opposite corner was another neon sign in blue that said Vacancy.

Shelby sighed with relief.

"They don't gots no swimmin' pool," Josh said. "Bob was gonna go swimmin'."

Shelby laughed as she unbuckled her seat belt and reached in the back for their coats and hats. "Bob must be a member of the Polar Bear Club."

"Huh?" Josh giggled. "Bob's not a *bear*."

"The Polar Bear Club is a bunch of people who go swimming when it's really cold outside." Shelby helped him get out of the car seat and into his coat and hat. "So they call themselves Polar Bears."

"Do they gots white fur?"

"No, they wear bathing suits." She zipped up his jacket and decided she didn't need to fasten the chin strap on his hat for the quick trip inside. "Just like you do when you go swimming. Now stay right there, and I'll come around and get you out. If I carry you in, I won't have to bother putting your boots on."

"I can walk, y'know. I'm a big boy."

"I know." Shelby put on her own coat. "But the snow's started to drift out there."

"Bob wants to play in it."

"We'll see." But she knew she couldn't allow Josh

to play out in the snow in front of the motel. He'd be way too visible.

As she started to get out of the car, the sign in the window changed to No Vacancy. "Oh, no!"

"What, Shebby?"

"Uh, nothing, Josh. Sit tight. I'll be right there to get you." Grabbing her purse, she stepped into the snow, ignoring the icy dampness soaking her running shoes as she closed the car door and ran around to get Josh. She'd talk the motel owner into letting her spend the night somewhere in this building, even if it was on a cot in a broom closet. She'd sit up all night and let Josh have a mattress on the floor, if necessary. But they couldn't spend the night in the café, where Mason could come along and find them.

She slung the shoulder strap of her purse bandolier-style across her body before lifting Josh out of the car.

He turned his face up to the snow and laughed with delight. "It tickles!"

"I guess it does, at that." She hurried toward the office door.

"It tastes like Popsicles! I gots some on my tongue! See?"

"Oh, sweetheart, I can't right now. I will. Later I will." She hated not being able to enjoy Josh's first experience with snow. She hated this whole mess, in fact. A bolt of pure anger shot through her. Damn them, all of them, for not putting this little boy first in their lives. Damn them for taking her dad's high-speed boat out on such a foggy day. Damn them all for dying. Now Josh had no one but her. Somehow, she would have to be enough.

A buzzer sounded when she opened the office door. She hurried inside, adding her wet tracks to the ones already covering the carpet. A very tall cowboy stood at the scarred counter, his back to her while he filled out a registration form. He looked at least seven feet tall, but Shelby guessed part of that was due to the heels of his boots and the crown of his hat.

The desk clerk, an older man with glasses, peered around the cowboy. "I'm really sorry, but I just rented our last room." He pointed to the No Vacancy sign in the window. "We're full up."

"Surely there's somewhere you can put us," Shelby said. "I only need a cot for Josh. I can take the floor. We're desperate."

The cowboy laid down the pen he'd been using and turned to look at her.

The sheer size of him made her take an involuntary step back. Then she looked into his eyes, which were an incredible shade of green. But more than that, they were the kindest eyes she'd ever seen. Although she had no logical reason to feel better, she did.

"You forgot Bob." Josh clapped his cold hands against her cheeks and forced her head around so she had to look at him. "Bob, he needs someplace to sleep, y'know," Josh explained, his blue eyes earnest. He looked so cute, with his hat on crooked and the chin strap dangling down.

"I know," she whispered, giving him a quick kiss on the cheek.

"Well, that makes it really hard," the clerk said. "Even if I could figure out something, I'm afraid we don't allow pets."

"The dog'll probably be okay in the car for the night," the big cowboy said quietly. "You and the boy can take my room."

Shelby realized how close to the surface her emotions were when the offer made tears gather in her eyes. "Oh, I couldn't —"

"Bob, he's not a dog," Josh said. "He's my friend."

The cowboy frowned. "You left another kid out in the car? It's mighty cold out there for a—"

"No, it's not another kid," Shelby said. "Bob is—"

"Awesome!" Josh said.

"Yes, he is," Shelby said as she looked the cowboy in the eye and hoped he would get the message as quickly as the patrolman had. "He's so awesome that he can make himself invisible if he wants to." She lowered Josh to the floor and took off his hat. "As a matter of fact, Josh, I happen to know he can sleep anywhere, because he told me so. He could even sleep *under* your bed if he wanted to, and be perfectly comfy."

Josh's forehead crinkled in thought. "You're sure?"

"It's one of his special tricks." She glanced over at the cowboy to see if he was buying the story.

He was. His smile was gentle as he inclined his head just the faintest bit in her direction, letting her know he had Bob all figured out.

That soft, understanding smile made her insides quiver a little, reminding her of pleasures she hadn't enjoyed in quite a while. And it would be a while longer, considering how her life was going these days.

"Then it's settled," the cowboy said. "You, the boy and…Bob can have unit six."

"But what about you?" She desperately wanted the room, but she felt guilty taking him up on his offer.

"No problem."

She gazed into his ruggedly handsome face. If they were in a movie, she'd suggest sharing the room, platonically, of course. Her tummy quivered again. But this was no movie. She turned to the clerk. "Is there anything else? Maybe a large closet, or—"

"I'll be fine," the cowboy said. "Don't worry about a thing. The café's open twenty-four hours. I'll just stretch out in a booth and make myself at home."

"But—"

"Hey. I'm used to such things. If the weather wasn't so nasty, I wouldn't have even bothered with a motel. I'd have slept in my truck, which I've done a million times. So it's no big deal for me." His gaze rested on Josh. "I want to make sure that little cowpoke gets his rest."

Shelby's heart swelled with gratitude. Right when she needed a knight in shining armor, one had appeared. "I can't thank you enough," she said, her voice husky from the lump in her throat. And those damn pesky tears kept trying to well up in her eyes. She blinked them back. "You're a very nice man."

"Don't mention it." With a touch of his fingers to the brim of his hat, he walked past her out into the snow, leaving behind the scent of leather and denim.

"What a gentleman," she said, thinking how well it fit the tall cowboy. He was truly a *gentle man.*

"He is, at that," the clerk said. He was gazing after the cowboy with an expression of great respect. "Those booths are made of molded plastic. I'd hate to spend the night in one."

"I'll have to find a way to repay him," Shelby said as she fished in her purse for her wallet and took out her credit card. Belatedly she thought to glance at the registration form the cowboy had left on the counter. She caught the name Boone Connor printed boldly across the top line before the desk clerk whisked the form away and crumpled it up.

Boone. She smiled. What a perfect name for him. He'd definitely been a boon to her, that was for sure.

Josh tugged on the leg of her jeans. "Can Bob and me read those? They gots horsies."

Shelby glanced to where Josh pointed and saw some western magazines on a table. She looked up at the clerk. "Is it okay? He knows not to tear pages out or anything."

"Sure, it's okay." The desk clerk smiled down at Josh. "Go ahead and read the magazines, son."

Shelby watched Josh go over to the table, carefully choose a magazine, and climb up in a ratty overstuffed chair before he started slowly turning the pages and muttering to himself, pretending he was reading. Every once in a while he glanced beside him and pointed out something in the magazine. Obviously he was sharing the experience with Bob.

"He's a fine boy," the clerk said. "You must be a proud momma."

"Oh, I——" Shelby caught herself before she told the clerk she was not Josh's mother. It was an automatic response, one she'd become used to giving because she'd taken care of Josh so much.

She'd once calculated that she'd spent more time with him than Patricia had. That had turned out to be a blessing, all things considered. If Josh had been closer to his mother and his grandparents, he would have been more grief-stricken when they had disappeared from his life. As it was, he seemed sad and definitely a little confused, but not overwhelmed.

Shelby was obviously the most important person in

his world, but now was not the time to advertise the fact that Josh was her nephew, not her son. And besides, someday she hoped to be his mother, legally. If only Patricia had left a will, that wouldn't be so damned complicated, either.

She brushed the thoughts away and smiled at the clerk. "I am very proud of Josh," she said.

CHAPTER TWO

ALL SIX BOOTHS in the small café were full, but Boone had expected that. Later on, as people returned to their rooms, the place would empty out. Then he'd stake out a booth for the night.

He'd forgotten the bench seats were the hard plastic kind. Oh, well. He would have done the same thing, even if he'd remembered. He would have done the same thing if the seats had been made of barbed wire. A woman with a little kid needed a motel room more than he did. *A pretty woman.* He pushed the thought aside. He wasn't in the market for a pretty woman.

Taking a stool at the counter, he ordered a cup of coffee from the café's only waitress. Her name was Lucy according to the tag she wore, and she was definitely pregnant. She also looked worn-out, probably from handling a bigger crowd than usual.

"You live around here, Lucy?" he asked her as she poured him some coffee.

"Not too far away." She moved with precision that came from experience. "Why?"

Boone glanced out the window before looking back at her. "The way it's coming down out there, seems like you ought to head home while you still can."

She gave him a weary smile. "That's right nice of

you to think of that. As a matter of fact, I am leaving in about another hour, after we get these folks fed. The couple who owns this place said they could handle everything. No need for Mr. Sloan to hang around the motel office now that the rooms are all rented, so he's gonna come over here and help Mrs. Sloan so I can leave."

Boone nodded. "Good. You got four-wheel drive?"

"Yeah. My hubby's coming to pick me up in the Jeep." She looked down shyly at her belly. "He's sort of protective these days."

"He should be," Boone said.

Her cheeks turned a happy shade of pink. "I'm hoping for a boy, but Gary doesn't care what we have, so long as the baby's healthy. I—" She paused and broke eye contact as someone in a booth called her name. "Excuse me. Table two needs some looking after." She bustled out from behind the counter and hurried over to the booth in question.

Boone had the urge to take over for her so she could put her feet up until her husband arrived. Sure, some activity was good for a woman in her condition, but not this much. He'd make a damn poor waitress, though, and he doubted she'd let him help her, anyway. Leastways not after he'd broken a few dishes and mixed up a couple of orders.

So he sipped his coffee and thought about whether Jessica had worked too hard while she was pregnant with Elizabeth. She should have notified him right away when she found out she was pregnant. Thinking of her struggling through the pregnancy and birth by herself drove him crazy with guilt.

The coffee had warmed him up considerably, so he

took off his leather jacket and laid it across his lap.
Then he unsnapped the breast pocket of his shirt and
took out the note he'd gotten from Jessica. He'd read it
about a million times, yet he still needed to keep looking
at it to convince himself this wasn't some bad dream he
was having.

> Dear Boone,
> I'm counting on you to be a godfather to Eliza-
> beth until I can return for her. Your quiet strength
> is just what she needs right now. I've left her with
> Sebastian at the Rocking D. Believe me, I
> wouldn't do this if I weren't in desperate circum-
> stances.
>
> In deepest gratitude, Jessica

The letter was dated more than two months ago.
She'd gotten the zip code wrong, so that had delayed it
some, and then when it had finally arrived in Las
Cruces, he'd been on the road hunting up horseshoeing
jobs.

Still holding the letter, Boone rubbed his chin and
gazed out the window at the steady snow. Snow had
landed him in this fix in the first place. More than two
years ago he'd let his three best buddies—Sebastian
Daniels, Travis Evans and Nat Grady—talk him into a
skiing trip in Aspen. He didn't belong on skis any more
than a buffalo belonged on roller skates, but he'd gone
for Sebastian's sake. They'd all nearly gotten themselves killed in an avalanche while they were blunder-
ing around on the slopes.

Jessica Franklin had been working the front desk of
the ski lodge, and it was their dumb luck that they'd

struck up a friendship with her and she'd offered to go with them that day. Otherwise Nat would've been toast. Jessica had figured out where he was buried and had kept her head, directing the rest of them to help dig him out before he smothered.

"More coffee?" Lucy asked as she passed by again.

Boone glanced at his cup. It would be a long night, and he could probably use the caffeine. "Sure," he said, smiling at her. "And thanks."

"Anytime."

After she left, he resumed staring out the window, and his thoughts returned to his predicament. He wished he could think about something else, but he couldn't. If only he hadn't gone to the avalanche reunion party last year. He'd thought the idea was kind of morbid, but once again he'd gone along with the crowd.

Besides, he'd needed the distraction. Darlene had just announced that she was breaking up with him to marry that dork Chester Littlefield.

As it had turned out, Nat hadn't made it to the reunion party because of some prior commitment. That had left Boone, Jessica, Sebastian and Travis to celebrate. Boone didn't usually drink much. Over the years he'd seen what liquor could do to a man while watching his father's bouts with the bottle.

But that night, thinking about Darlene, he'd guzzled everything in sight. Sebastian and Travis had put away a fair amount themselves, but Jessica, being a good friend, had stayed sober so she could drive them back to their cabin and see that they all took some aspirin before they tumbled into bed.

And that was when Boone figured he'd stepped over the line and dragged Jessica into bed with him. Sober he'd never have considered such a thing. But drunk and depressed about Darlene, he might well have.

He was sure Jessica knew he hadn't meant to, that he didn't think of her like that. Hell, he'd probably called her Darlene in the middle of it all. So Jessica had shouldered the whole burden when she found out she was pregnant. But now she was in some kind of trouble and had asked him to be a "godfather."

Boone didn't buy that godfather label, not for a minute. He was the baby's father. When he'd called the Rocking D, he'd found out that Sebastian and Travis had gotten letters naming them as godfathers, too. But those other letters were a smokescreen. Sebastian was too honorable to have done such a thing, and Travis was too experienced to be caught like that. Besides, Jessica easily could have shoved those two guys away, considering they were drunk.

But even drunk, Boone had the strength of two men. Jessica wouldn't have been able to get away. He hoped to hell he hadn't hurt her. He'd spend the rest of his life trying to make it up to her for being a brute. And he would never touch another drop of alcohol as long as he lived.

"Mr. Connor?"

The soft voice brought him back to his surroundings. Turning from the window, he realized the blonde and her little boy were standing right next to him. Quickly he folded Jessica's letter, tucked it in his pocket and snapped the pocket closed. Then he stood.

"Sorry," the woman said. "You don't have to get up. I didn't mean to disturb you."

"No problem," he said. Women were constantly surprised by his manners, but he couldn't help that. His mother had taught him to stand in the presence of a lady, and he couldn't change that training now, even if he'd wanted to. "How did you know my name?"

Color tinged her cheeks. "I looked at the registration form before the clerk threw it away." She held out her hand. "My name is Shelby McFarland."

"Pleased to meet you, Shelby." He took her soft hand gently in his, careful not to put too much pressure into his handshake. She was so delicate, he imagined he could leave a bruise if he was the least bit enthusiastic.

He enjoyed the contact, though, enjoyed it more than was good for him. He liked looking into her blue eyes, too. He read basic goodness and honesty there, but she was wary, too, as if something was spooking her. He put that together with the way she'd argued with the Smoky about going up the hill and wondered if she was running from something...or someone.

"And this is Josh," she said, bringing the little boy forward. "Josh, can you shake Mr. Connor's hand?"

Josh nodded and stuck out his hand, but his eyes widened as he looked Boone up and down. "You're big as a *elephant*," he said.

"Josh!" Shelby reddened.

Boone laughed out loud. "Can't argue with the truth, son. I'm about as graceful as one, too." He glanced around. "I'm afraid all the booths are taken up, so if you're here to eat, you'll have to grab a couple of stools." The prospect of having her sit down beside him gave him a forbidden thrill. Then he thought of the note in his pocket and reminded himself of his reason for being on this road in the first place.

"Oh, we're not staying," she said.

He frowned. Surely she wasn't going back out in that snowstorm now that she had a roof over her head. And truth be told, he didn't appreciate having his generosity thrown back in his face.

She must have figured out he was ticked, because she put her hand lightly on his arm. "I mean we're not staying in the café," she said quickly. "We'll just get something to go. We're definitely staying in the room you so graciously gave up. That's what I wanted to talk to you about. I would like to do…something in return. Buying your dinner seems inadequate, but I can at least do that much."

Her touch on his arm felt like the nuzzle of a timid foal. And now that he looked closer, he could see that her whole body was poised for flight. She'd glanced over at the door several times. His curiosity grew.

"How 'bout a star?" Josh asked. "When I'm a good boy, like when I 'membered to pick up my room, you give'd me a star."

Shelby blushed. "Well, that's a good idea, Josh, but I'm not sure that Mr. Connor—"

"The name's Boone, and I'd love a star." He probably shouldn't have said that. No doubt about it, he was having trouble keeping his distance from these two.

"Uh, okay." She looked flustered, but she dug around in her purse and came up with a sheet of peel-and-stick gold stars. She peeled one off. "Where… where do you want it?"

Even if he was creating a problem for himself, he couldn't help loving this. "On my shirt's fine."

She looked him over, and finally stuck the star on the flap of his shirt pocket, smoothing it carefully without looking at him. Her cheeks were bright pink. "There," she said, glancing up. "There's your star."

"And a kiss!" Josh said.

Boone knew he should tell her to forget the kiss, but

he couldn't make himself say it. Only a fool would turn down a kiss from someone as adorable as Shelby, with her ponytail perched on her head and that sweet blush on her cheeks.

"A star and a kiss!" Josh insisted. "You *always* do that."

Apparently she decided that giving in quickly was better than making a bigger scene by protesting. Standing on tiptoe, she leaned over and gave Boone a quick peck on the cheek.

Her lips were soft and full, and her scent swirled around him. He fought the urge to close his eyes with pleasure. But he needed to keep the moment light, so he grinned at her. "Thanks. Now I've been fully rewarded."

"I do appreciate the room," she said shyly.

"You're most welcome. Listen, why not stay and eat here? Taking the food back to the room will be a real hassle in this weather." Well, hell. He seemed determined to dig himself into a hole. If he didn't watch it, he'd ask for her phone number next.

Fortunately for both of them, she didn't fall in with his plan. A wary look flashed in her eyes again, and she glanced away. Boone had the strangest feeling she was thinking of some story to explain why she couldn't stay in the café to eat dinner.

"Bob wants to stay," Josh said. "'Cause Bob gots to go potty."

Shelby looked down at him. "I'm sure it won't take long for them to whip up a couple of burgers and fries. Can Bob wait until we go back to the room?"

Josh held his crotch and peered up at her. "I gots to go, too," he whispered. "Real bad, Shebby."

Shebby. Boone heard it, plain as day. No way had the kid said *Mommy* just then. Shebby was probably his version of her name, Shelby. This wasn't her son. The word *kidnapper* flashed in his brain, but he just couldn't buy it.

She sighed and looked around until she located the sign for the rest rooms. "Okay." She glanced up at Boone. "If you'll excuse us, we'll—"

"Do I hafta go in where the ladies go?" Josh hung back, his gaze pleading.

"Yes." She took his hand firmly in hers.

Josh hung on her hand and tried to plant his feet. "But last time that lady was laughin' at me."

"She was laughing at the Cheerios, Josh, not at you. We don't have to use them this time if you don't want to. Now come on."

Boone had to ask. "Cheerios?"

Shelby glanced back at him. "I throw some in the bowl. It gives him a target."

Josh gazed up at Boone with a worried expression, as if he now expected Boone to laugh, too.

Boone bit down on the inside of his lip so he wouldn't. "Great idea," he said, although his voice was husky with the laugh he'd swallowed.

Josh's expression cleared and his smile came out like sunshine. He pointed a stubby finger at Boone. "Me and him could go."

Shelby shook her head and tugged on his hand. "No, I'm afraid not, Josh. Now come on."

"Please," Josh wailed, hanging back and dragging his feet. "I wanna be a big boy."

Boone's heart went out to him. He remembered a few trips to the ladies' room, himself, when he was a kid. He'd always been tall for his age, so a couple of women had given him the evil eye when his mother had insisted on taking him in with her. He'd hated every minute of it, although now he completely understood why she'd done that. The world had some sick people in it.

"I'd be glad to take him," Boone said. "I realize you don't really know me, but—"

"I know you," Josh said. "You gave us a room. Please, Shebby. Let me and him go."

Shelby paused. She looked exhausted, frustrated and scared. "Okay," she said at last. "If you're willing to do that, I appreciate it. While you're gone I'll put in our order. Can I get anything for you while I'm at it? I'd love to be able to buy you some dinner."

"No, thanks." Boone had decided that eating would be his main entertainment tonight, and he didn't want to rush it. "I'm not really hungry yet."

She seemed even more frustrated that she couldn't repay him with dinner, but Josh began hopping up and down, so she put the boy's hand in Boone's. "Thank you for everything," she said. "You've been a real godsend."

"Glad to help." He touched a hand to the brim of his hat, which coaxed a faint smile from her. Then he had to focus all his attention on keeping Josh's tiny hand in his. Such a small hand. Boone had to lean to the right to keep hold of it as Josh ran along beside him on the way to the rest rooms.

"Do you gots horsies?" Josh sounded breathless but determined to communicate. "'Cause me and Bob, we like horsies. We're gonna ride some in Yellowstone."

Boone realized the little guy was puffing because Boone's stride was too long. He shortened it. "I have two horses," he said. "One I keep with my friend Sebastian at the Rocking D, and the other one I keep at my folks' place in Las Cruces."

"Rocking D? What's a Rocking D?"

Boone pushed open the swinging door to the rest room. "A ranch."

"A *ranch?* You gots a *ranch,* like on TV?" Josh seemed beside himself with excitement, so beside himself that he'd obviously forgotten why he was in the rest room in the first place.

"Well, it's not my—"

"Can I come there? Can I?"

"We'll talk about that later. Right now you'd better tend to business."

"'Kay." Josh headed for a stall.

"You can do it here if you want," Boone said as he gestured toward a urinal. "I'll hold you up."

Josh turned back to him, his expression confused.

"Come on. I'll show you. This is how big guys do it." Boone demonstrated.

Josh watched in obvious fascination.

Boone zipped up and glanced over at Josh. "Ready to try?"

Josh nodded vigorously.

In the end, Boone decided it would work best if he crouched down and let Josh stand on his knees. The little boy chortled happily all through the process, as if it was the highlight of his day.

Boone realized he was having a great time. What fun it would be to show a kid like this around the Rocking D. Sebastian had that gentle gelding, Samson, who would be perfect for Josh to learn on. But that was a pipe dream, for sure. Boone didn't think Shelby would make a special detour to the Rocking D. She looked like a lady on a mission.

Besides, Boone had no business daydreaming about

taking her there. She would be too big a temptation. He'd already caught himself thinking about what sort of body was hidden by the bulky ski jacket she wore, and he was in no position to go down that road with any woman.

As Josh finished washing his hands, he started in again on the topic of visiting the ranch. "I never been to a ranch," he said. "Can I come? Me and Bob?"

"I imagine you have places to go and people to see," Boone said.

"Well, we're gonna see geezers in Yellowstone." Josh dropped the paper towel neatly in the waste container.

"You mean geysers?" Boone was impressed with the boy's neatness. Somebody had taught him well.

Josh nodded. "They go whoosh! Up in the air!" He threw his arms up to illustrate.

"Sounds like fun." Boone decided to do some fishing for information. "Are you going to meet your mommy up there?"

"I don't think so. My mommy's in heaven with the angels."

The casual statement slammed into Boone like a brick to the stomach, but Josh seemed completely at ease about it. Shelby probably wasn't a kidnapper, not that Boone had seriously thought she was. But she was nervous about something. "Then maybe your dad?"

"Nope." Josh started marching toward the door of the rest room. "My daddy's in S'Antonio."

"Really?" Boone held the door open for Josh.

"Yep." Josh walked through the door. "He gots a gun."

SHELBY HAD WATCHED Boone lead Josh away and no warning bells had sounded in her head. Boone inspired trust and a sense of security. She could feel it, and she was sure Josh could feel it, too.

Poor little guy hadn't had much in the way of male role models. His grandfather had never been particularly interested in kids, not even his own daughters when they were young. Mason had ignored Josh until he'd smelled money, and even with the lure of that money, Mason had a hard time pretending to be a loving dad.

No wonder Josh had latched onto Boone so quickly. Seeing the way Boone abbreviated his long stride to accommodate Josh's short one made Shelby's heart hitch.

Not all men brushed children aside the way her father had, she reminded herself. Patricia, the beauty, had eventually gained her father's admiration by going into the high-profile world of television broadcasting. He and Shelby's mother had been able to brag about Patricia, who eventually had her own local talk show. Shelby's modest desktop-publishing business and her more average looks hadn't been able to compete.

Shelby watched until Boone led Josh away through the swinging door of the men's room. Then she turned to catch the eye of the waitress working behind the counter. She noticed that her name was Lucy. Shelby's mother's name. Another sharp pain sliced through her before she could shut down her feelings.

The woman, who was visibly pregnant, came over toward Shelby. "Can I help you?"

"You sure can. Can I please get two hamburgers and two orders of fries to go?" Shelby knew it wasn't the most nutritious meal in the world, but she'd worry about getting some green veggies into Josh tomorrow, after they'd put some more miles between them and Mason.

"You and that little boy aren't going back out on the road, are you?" asked the waitress.

"No, thank goodness. We have a room at the motel, thanks to that gentleman who was just sitting here. He had the last room, but he gave it to us, instead."

The waitress's expression grew soft. "Isn't he the nicest man? He was worried about whether I had a way to get home."

"Apparently he's the kind who looks out for others," Shelby said. "It's good to know there are still guys out there like that."

"And he's pretty darned cute, too, did you notice?"

"I guess." Shelby thought about the gentle smile that had made her tingle. Oh, yes, she'd noticed. Besides his understanding green eyes, he also possessed a couple of other noteworthy features, like a very masculine-looking jaw and curly black hair. Her heart had raced when she'd leaned over to place a kiss on his suntanned cheek.

He was built well, too. Although some large men tended to look beefy and slightly out of shape, this one didn't seem to have a spare bit of flab on him. Nice tush, too. Watching him walk away with Josh had given her guilty pleasure.

"It's a wonder some woman hasn't snatched him up," the waitress said. "But he's not wearing a wedding ring. And he's the type who would, if he was married." She glanced pointedly down at the bare ring finger of Shelby's left hand.

Shelby stuffed her left hand into the pocket of her jacket. The waitress might think she could do a little matchmaking in between serving orders, but whether Boone Connor was married or not was of no consequence to Shelby. She couldn't think about such things under the current circumstances. Even ogling his cute tush meant she was allowing herself to be distracted from her goal of keeping Josh safe. That wasn't good.

She leaned closer to the waitress. "Listen, since he'll have to spend the night in the café, could I leave some money with you to pay for whatever food he eats? I'd like to find some way to repay him for being so kind."

"I'll be leaving soon, myself, but I suppose I could arrange that with Mrs. Sloan. Why don't you just stay and eat your dinner when he eats his? Then you could just pick up the check for everything."

Shelby trotted out the excuse she'd been about to give Boone. "Well, I would, but Josh has a program he wants to see on TV, so we need to get back to the room."

The waitress rolled her eyes as if to say that Shelby was crazy to let something like that stand in her way. "If you're sure."

"I'm sure." She pulled some bills out of her purse and gave them to the waitress. "That should cover ours and anything he has, don't you think?"

The waitress looked at the cash Shelby had given her and chuckled. "That's more than enough. I'll go put in your order."

Shelby positioned herself with her back to the counter so she could see the front door of the café. No one had come in for some time, and hardly anyone had left, either. The booths along the wall were still occupied. The place had taken on a party atmosphere, as if being stranded here together had made everyone friends.

Except her. A woman on the run didn't stop to make friends along the way. Too risky. Boone Connor had helped her out, and she was grateful. Under different circumstances, she would have liked to get to know him, but once she left this café tonight, she never expected to see him again.

She'd driven out of San Antonio without much of a plan except an instinctive urge to head for Yellowstone Park. But she couldn't stay in Yellowstone. She'd continue north to Canada.

Once out of the country, she'd find a good lawyer and assess her chances of legally keeping Josh. But she'd keep him, legally or illegally, because she knew one thing for sure. No matter what a judge might say, as long as she was alive Mason Fowler was never, ever getting custody of his son.

CHAPTER THREE

BOONE HATED TO ADMIT how much he missed Josh and Shelby once they'd left the café with their bags of food. But no way would Shelby stay to eat. Something was going on with her, and Boone was afraid he'd never find out what it was.

When he learned that she'd left money to pay for his food, he had half a mind to go over to her room and give it back. Then he recognized that he was only looking for an excuse to see her again, which was a fool's errand, for sure. He was the sort of guy who needed time to build a relationship, and after tonight, he and Shelby would probably never cross paths again. That was probably just as well.

Still, he couldn't let Shelby buy his dinner. It didn't seem right. So he asked Mrs. Sloan to put the money aside for Lucy, who could probably use some extra cash for that baby she'd be having soon.

By eleven the café had emptied out and Boone had his pick of booths, not that one looked any more comfortable than the other. He was on a first-name basis with Norma Sloan and her husband Eugene. The couple reminded him of Jack Sprat who could eat no fat and his wife who could eat no lean. They'd been more than kind, providing a pillow and a blanket to help him through the night.

About eleven-thirty, Norma sent Eugene into the café's back room to grab a catnap while she kept the coffeepot going. Who they were brewing coffee for was a mystery to Boone, because no other customers showed up. Boone crammed himself into his chosen booth and pulled his hat over his eyes.

When Eugene came out to relieve Norma at one in the morning, Boone unfolded himself from the booth. He didn't think he'd slept much, and he felt as if he'd been rode hard and put away wet. Stretching the stiffness from his spine, he walked over to the counter.

"Want some java, Boone?" Eugene asked around a yawn.

"No, thanks. But why don't you go on back to bed and let me take care of anybody who comes in? I doubt anybody will, anyway."

"That's a nice offer, but my conscience wouldn't let me." Eugene yawned again and poured himself a cup of coffee. "You're a customer, not my hired help."

"Speaking of that, who usually mans the counter when you're open all night? Don't tell me Lucy works graveyard."

"Nope." Eugene unwrapped a sweet roll as he talked. "We have another gal, Edna. She's older than Lucy and says she likes working nights. Prefers the peace and quiet. But I didn't want her on the road tonight, so I called and told her to stay home, that we'd handle it. That's what Norma and I always do when the weather gets like this. We'd rather stay up all night ourselves than worry about an employee skidding all over the road trying to get to work." He bit into the sweet roll. "Want one?"

"No, thanks." Boone turned to gaze out the window

at the snow still falling. "Then how about closing the place until morning?" He glanced back at Eugene. "Nobody but a crazy person is still on that road tonight."

Eugene smiled. "No can do. Staying open is a matter of pride with me. My daddy used to own this place, and when I took over he made me promise to keep the coffee going twenty-four hours a day. He said we'd never know how many lives we'd saved by giving people a place to pull off the road, get some coffee and a bite to eat, but he figured we'd saved our share."

"I'll bet you have, at that." Boone rubbed his chin and felt the stubble there. He'd grab a shave in the rest room before he left in the morning. "I've stopped here myself a few times, when I was feeling groggy. You might even have saved me."

"And there could be someone else out there battling his way through the storm, and the light from our sign could be a beacon in the night."

"Like a lighthouse," Boone said. He could understand Eugene's urge to save people. He had that sort of urge all the time. That's why he was sleeping in a booth tonight.

"Exactly," Eugene said. "A lighthouse. You sure you don't want some coffee and one of these rolls?"

Boone sighed. "Yeah, why not. I'm not having much luck sleeping, anyway." And he could tell Eugene wanted somebody to talk to. So he sat at the counter and swapped fishing stories with the guy for a good hour.

He talked so long and grew so tired that sleep sounded like a real possibility, even in a hard plastic booth. But before he could excuse himself from Eugene, the café door opened, bringing with it a blast of frigid air and blowing snow.

Boone swiveled on the stool to see if one of the

motel customers had decided to come over for a midnight snack. For one crazy moment he hoped it might even be Shelby. Instead it was someone he didn't recognize from the crowd that had filled the café earlier that night.

The man was built like a fireplug, short but solid. His ski jacket bulked him out even more, but Boone could tell from the fit of the guy's jeans that he probably worked out in some fancy gym to build up his muscles.

"Damn!" The man pulled off a black stocking cap as he stomped his feet on the mat just inside the café door. His hair was cropped close to his head, military-style. "It's a bitch out there!"

Boone usually reserved judgment on folks until they'd had a chance to prove themselves one way or the other, but for some reason this guy put him on edge. There was something hard and unyielding about him that showed in his voice, in his movements, even in the bristle of his haircut.

"I'll bet you could use a cup of coffee," Eugene said eagerly. "And there's some pie left, if you—"

"Black coffee," the man said.

Boone was relieved to see the man order something. For a minute he'd imagined the guy taking out a gun and demanding that Eugene empty the cash register. Staying open all night for weary travelers was one thing, but Boone wondered if Eugene and Norma had ever been left alone to face the wrong kind of customer. This fellow was probably harmless, but all in all Boone was glad to be here tonight, just in case.

"Where're y'all headed?" Boone asked as the guy sat down at the counter. Boone laid on the good-ol'-boy accent on purpose. That, combined with his size, tended to make people think he wasn't very smart, and then he found out things he might not have otherwise.

The man looked Boone over, his pale gray eyes clearly taking Boone's measure. "Nowhere, it appears. Damn storm."

"Yeah, it's holdin' folks up, all right," Boone said.

Eugene set the coffee in front of the man. "Sure I can't get you something to eat? A sandwich?"

"Nothing." The man took a swig of his coffee.

Eugene lifted the pot in Boone's direction and Boone nodded. He didn't need more coffee, but he wanted an excuse to sit at the counter a little longer and find out what this stranger was up to.

"How long before these pansy-ass cops let us through?" the man asked.

Boone decided to play along. "God knows. My truck could make it right now, no sweat, but you know these Smokies. Treat us all like a bunch of old women."

Eugene's eyebrows lifted, and Boone winked at him when the other guy wasn't looking. Eugene grinned and turned to put the coffeepot back on the burner.

"Ain't that the truth," the man muttered. "And then I couldn't rouse anybody at the motel office. Knocked so hard I about broke the door down. Those people must sleep like the dead."

Boone wondered why he'd try to beat down the door of a motel office that had a No Vacancy sign in the window. His sense of uneasiness grew.

Eugene turned to the man. "I'm sorry, but we don't have any rooms left."

"Oh, so you're the one in charge?" The man looked at Eugene with new interest.

"My wife and I run both the motel and the café. All

I can offer you is something to eat and drink, and a booth to stretch out in if you like."

"Actually, none of the above." The guy leaned forward. "I want to know if a woman and a little kid checked in after the barricades went up. She's blond, and he's about so high." He held his hand about three feet off the floor.

The pieces clicked into place for Boone. Shelby, arguing with the patrolman. Shelby, desperate for a room. A room to hide in. And Josh's innocent little voice as he announced, "My daddy gots a gun."

Boone glanced at Eugene and thought he saw the older man stiffen. He might have guessed what was going on, too. He could have noticed, like Boone had, that Josh didn't call Shelby Mommy. Kidnapping a kid from his legal guardian was serious stuff, if that's what Shelby had done. But if this guy was on the up-and-up, he would have asked the patrolman at the barricades to help him find Shelby and Josh.

Holding his breath, Boone waited for Eugene's answer. Even if Eugene refused to give the guy any information, the way he refused could tip the guy off that Shelby was here.

Eugene adjusted his glasses and paused. "Don't believe I've seen anybody matching that description," he said, smooth as butter.

Boone wanted to leap across the counter and kiss Eugene on both cheeks.

"I know the woman you're talking about," Norma said, coming out of the back room.

Boone's stomach tightened. If only Norma had stayed asleep.

"She came through about noon," Norma continued.

Now Boone had two people he wanted to hug. Not only was Norma covering for Shelby, she was misdirecting this guy.

"Yeah?" The man sat up straighter. "What did she look like?"

"Blond, pretty. The little boy was blond, too. They stopped in to get some food, but they took it to go because they wanted to get over the pass before the snow started."

The guy's fist hit the counter. "Damn it to hell." Then he sighed. "At least I guessed right on which road she'd take."

Norma gazed at him, her expression bland. "She must be important to you."

"Oh, she's important, all right," he replied with a sneer. "She took my kid."

"Goodness!" Norma sounded concerned, but her gaze had no warmth in it. "Have you notified the authorities?"

"Hell, the *authorities* couldn't find their ass with their own two hands. This is one slick chick."

Boone didn't think so. Shelby wasn't enough of a criminal to think of hiding her identity or Josh's. Fear was driving her, not cunning. She was running as fast as she could go and improvising a plan along the way. But he didn't think she was a match for this man.

Boone stood and stretched. Then he faked a yawn. "Well, folks, now that I've had my bedtime snack, I believe I'll go to my room and turn in."

Eugene covered his look of surprise quickly. "Might as well. They won't be opening that road until daybreak, maybe later."

The man looked at Boone. "You've been letting a bed go to waste? Hell, if you don't want it, I'll take it."

"Sorry." Boone clapped his Stetson on his head and pulled on his jacket. "I got here first." He gestured toward the booth where he'd left the pillow and blanket. "But the Sloans put out a blanket and a pillow in case anybody stumbled in during the night. I'm sure you're welcome to that."

The man eyed the setup and turned back to his coffee cup. "We'll see if I get that desperate," he said sourly.

Boone waved at Eugene and Norma and headed out the café door. Once outside he turned up his collar and held on to his hat as he ducked his head and trudged forward against the bitter wind. Snow sifted down inside his jacket and his bare hand grew numb. Once he warned Shelby about the man in the café, he wondered what the heck he was going to do with himself and whether he had enough gas to run the truck's heater all night.

SHELBY LAY in the double bed next to Josh listening to his steady breathing with a touch of envy. All he needed was a darkened room, a soft bed and his blue "blankie" clutched against his cheek.

How she'd love to escape into the world of childhood, if only for a little while, and feel safe again, safe enough to sleep. Her urge to head for Yellowstone had probably come from that same longing. She remembered staying in a little cabin with her mother and father and Patricia, all of the beds in one big room, like settlers on the prairie. They'd never been so cozy before or since.

There was nothing cozy about this room. The heater had a noisy fan, but it didn't block out the whistling of the wind through a crevice between the door and the frame or the rattling of a loose windowpane. After checking the lock at least twenty times, Shelby had dozed off, only to be awakened when she'd heard someone pounding on a door not far away.

Adrenaline had poured through her, but she hadn't wanted to wake Josh by leaping out of bed. By the time she'd eased over to the window, drawn back the curtain and peered out, the motel courtyard had been empty.

Now she worried about who had been pounding on a door in the middle of the night. She'd probably been foolish to take this well-traveled highway north toward Yellowstone. Early in Patricia's marriage to Mason, soon after Josh was born, Shelby had gone over to their house for dinner. She distinctly remembered reminiscing with Patricia about that Yellowstone trip. They'd talked about the fun stops along the way and how much the family vacation had meant to them.

If Mason remembered, he would know exactly what road to take to find her. She was terrible at this cloak-and-dagger stuff, and she really should give up on Yellowstone. Except it wasn't only Josh's excitement that was guiding her there. The thought of seeing the place again with Josh had become the only bright spot in her otherwise frightening world. She loved the way Josh insisted on calling the geysers "geezers." Maybe he'd mixed up the words when she'd mentioned one of the geysers was called Old Faithful.

The windowpane rattled again. Or was that a different sort of noise? She strained to hear over the whirr of the fan and the whistling of the wind. Then the noise came again. A rapid, soft tapping. On her door.

Her stomach lurched in fear and her heartbeat hammered in her ears as she crept quietly out of bed.

The tapping grew slightly louder, as if someone wanted to get her attention without alerting anyone else.

Easing back the curtain a tiny slit, she peered out. Then she gasped in surprise as she recognized Boone, his big shoulders hunched against the cold. Had he come to tell her they'd cleared the road?

Her vulnerability made her hesitate before opening the door. Then she shook off any doubts. After all, she'd received nothing but kindness from this man. Now that she'd become one of the hunted, she'd have to learn to trust her instincts if she planned to survive. Her instincts told her Boone wouldn't harm her or Josh.

Crossing to the door, she unlocked and opened it, belatedly remembering that she wore only a cotton nightgown. The cold took her breath away.

"I have to talk to you," Boone said. His face was in shadow. "Can I—"

"Come in, for heaven's sake," she whispered, stepping back. "It's freezing out." Once he was through the door she closed it, but the room temperature seemed to have dropped thirty degrees in that short time.

"Shebby?" Josh mumbled sleepily from the bed.

She hurried over to the bed and leaned down to tuck his blue blanket against his cheek. "Go back to sleep, sweetheart. It's only Boone."

"'Kay." And just like that, he snuggled back under the covers and dozed off.

Shelby was amazed. Boone and Josh had spent less than twenty minutes together all told, and Boone now had the little boy's complete trust. She straightened and turned. The room was almost totally dark, but she could make out the cowboy standing right where she'd left him by the door.

A thrill of awareness shot through her. Being alone in the dark with this virile man was the most exciting thing that had happened to her in a long while. He'd probably come over to give her a weather report or the latest information on the road, but for a moment she could fantasize that he'd come because he had a burning need to see her again.

"Do you mind talking in the dark?" she murmured as she walked back toward him. "I don't want to wake Josh."

"That's okay."

The closer she came to him, the more she felt the cold that had settled on his clothes, and it made her shiver. But she wasn't afraid. Maybe some of Josh's instinctive trust in Boone had rubbed off on her, because for the first time since she'd left San Antonio, she felt a little less alone.

She wrapped her arms around her body to ward off the chill and came to stand next to him. She had to move close, so she could keep her voice low. The scent of his aftershave teased her. "What is it?" she asked. "Is the road—"

"No, it's not the road," he said quietly. "Look, I don't mean to mess in your business, but there's a man in the café who might be looking for you and the boy."

She gasped and stepped back, her romantic notions shredded by one simple statement. Oh, God, no. Not right here. She'd lulled herself into believing the weather had protected her. Her stomach began to churn. But maybe Boone was wrong. "What...does he look like?"

"Short, stocky but solid, like he works out. He has a military buzz cut."

Nausea rose in her throat. She turned away and took several long, deep breaths until her stomach settled down a little.

"Do you know him?" Boone asked.

"I know him."

"Is he a threat to you?"

She gazed up into his shadowed face and decided to risk telling him the truth. "I suppose. I have his son."

Boone nodded, as if her honesty set well with him. "I figured. Josh told me his daddy has a gun."

Shelby glanced over her shoulder at the sleeping boy, but he didn't seem to have stirred. She lowered her voice. "Mason Fowler is a horrible person. He beat my sister and—"

He drew in a sharp breath. "Did he kill her? Josh said—"

"No," she whispered quickly. "Patricia divorced him two years ago. She...died in a boating accident with...my parents...four months ago." Shelby shuddered with the effort not to cry. She'd been able to stay strong until now, but this big cowboy was such a comforting presence that she was tempted to give in to her grief.

"I'm sorry." His voice was husky, tender.

"Me, too." She swallowed. "Anyway, Patricia didn't leave a will, so unfortunately Mason has more of a claim to Josh than I do. He's started the paperwork to get custody. I don't think the process is going fast enough for him. A couple of days ago, I felt sure he was ready to take Josh for an outing and just...keep him."

"So he wants the boy."

"Not really." She moved closer to Boone. She told herself it was so that he could hear her low-pitched explanation, but she also wished he'd wrap those strong arms around her. It was a dumb idea, and luckily for both of them, he didn't pick up on her body language.

"Mason wasn't the least interested in visitation rights after the divorce," she continued. "For two years he hardly saw Josh. Now he's pretending to be the perfect daddy. I'm convinced he's only after money. My parents did leave a will, and whoever gets Josh also gets the generous maintenance allowance my parents set up for him."

A growl of disapproval rumbled in Boone's chest, and even though Shelby couldn't see his face, she could feel the tension in his body. His righteous fury at hearing such news warmed her more than a blazing fire could have done.

It gave her the courage to ask the question she'd been dreading the answer to. "Does he guess I'm here somewhere?"

"I don't think so. Eugene said he'd never laid eyes on you and Norma said she'd seen you but you went through about lunchtime and were probably way down the road by now."

"Who are Eugene and Norma?"

"Sorry. The Sloans, the people who own the place."

Shelby stared up at him. "They lied for me? Why would they do that?"

"Protecting the privacy of a customer might be part of it, but I think it's also because they didn't take a shine to this Mason character any more than I did. They might have asked themselves why he's coming after you himself, instead of notifying the police. I wondered that, too."

"Because it's more his style. He'd rather intimidate me personally than trust that the law will be on his side. I have no doubt if he decides I'm in the way of his getting that money, he'll want to eliminate me completely. In some ways, I probably played right into his hands, running like this."

"What was your plan?"

She drew strength from the soft murmur of his voice in the darkness, and the woodsy, masculine scent of him eased her panic. "At first I could only think of getting Josh out of town, and I told him we'd go to Yellowstone. Once we were on the road, I realized we couldn't stay there, so I'd decided to continue north to Canada and get a lawyer up there to help me. But now, if Mason's right here…"

As the shivers started again, she wrapped her arms tighter around her body. "I don't know. Maybe he wanted me to do this. Maybe he's been goading me, hoping I'd take off. And the fact is, he *does* intimidate me. But I can't let him get Josh. I just can't."

Boone stood there in silence for a long time. Finally he blew out a breath. "I guess you'd better let me help you."

They were the sweetest words she'd heard in a long while, yet she couldn't imagine what this cowboy could do. "How?"

"Leave your rental car here and come with me to the Rocking D."

"Your…your ranch?"

"Not mine. It belongs to a good buddy of mine, Sebastian Daniels, and his new wife Matty. It's near Canon City, in a pretty little valley. You'll be safe there while you figure out what you want to do next."

"Oh, Boone, that's a wonderful offer." The idea filled her with such longing she could taste it, but she gathered her strength and pride, wrapping them around her like a cloak. "But I can't bring my troubles to roost at your friend's place, especially if he's a newlywed."

"You don't know Sebastian. If he found out I'd left a defenseless woman and a little boy—"

"I'm not defenseless." She refused to come across as a victim.

"You're not?"

"I took a self-defense class. I can take care of myself."

"Well, that's good," he said patiently. "That's real good. But it's kinda tough taking care of yourself when you have a little shaver to worry about."

She knew that. She just hadn't wanted to think about it. "You have a point there," she admitted reluctantly.

"Anyway, if Sebastian knew I'd left you to fend off some wife-beater by yourself, while taking care of the boy and all, he'd have my hide. Sebastian would want me to bring you to the Rocking D, once he understood the situation."

She struggled to keep a grip on the pride she'd been clinging to so fiercely. She needed a champion, needed one desperately. Two champions sounded like heaven, but she couldn't impose like that. "Sounds as if you and your friend are two in a million."

"Not by a long shot." He sounded embarrassed. "We're a couple of ornery cusses, if you must know. Travis, he's the charming one."

"Travis?"

"Travis Evans. You'll meet him, too. In fact, as long as we get out of here at a decent hour in the morning, you'll get to come to his wedding."

The conversation had taken on an unreal quality. "Boone, hold on a minute. You're planning on putting me, with all my problems, smack-dab in the middle of wedding festivities? You can't do that."

"Like I said, my friends would have a fit if I did anything different."

"Some friends you have, Boone." She was beginning to believe she'd stumbled onto the cowboy equivalent of the Knights of the Round Table. Still, taking advantage of such gallantry wasn't her style. "Listen, you're wonderful to offer, but I simply can't put you or your friends to that kind of trouble."

"Okay." His tone was patient. "What's your alternative?"

Good question. She thought of Mason lurking in the café, coiled like a rattlesnake ready to strike. She could watch for him to leave before she ventured out of the room in the morning, but that would mean being trapped without any way of getting food for Josh. Explaining that problem to Josh without telling him about Mason would be tricky.

She faced the fact that she had no plan unless someone offered to be her ally. Boone had offered. "I guess my biggest problem is how to get food to Josh if the road doesn't open right away in the morning," she said.

"I can help you with that."

"I would appreciate it." She was embarrassed by how constrained her position was. She tried for an attitude of independence and self-reliance. "Once Mason leaves, Josh and I can be on our way. Kind as your gesture is, we really wouldn't need to go with you."

He sighed. "Shelby, I've seen the guy. He's a tough customer, and he won't stay fooled forever. Sooner or later, he'll catch on and come back looking for you.

When he does, your self-defense courses aren't going to do you much good. If you really want to keep Josh out of his hands, you need help."

She knew he was right. Damn it, he was so right. She'd been foolish to think she could protect Josh by herself. Reckless and foolish. Humbled by her monumental ability to miscalculate, she finally understood that her pride could endanger Josh. Because she loved him far more than her stupid pride, she had no choice but to be indebted to Boone and his friends. "Okay," she said softly. "But I'll find a way to make it up to you. I'll—"

"No need," he said. "Don't even worry about it."

Of course she would. The debt already sat heavy in her chest. But Josh was more important than her own comfort zone right now. "What about my rental car?" she asked.

"You can call the office in Santa Fe and tell them you were afraid to drive it over the pass. That makes sense. You shouldn't drive it over the pass, at least not for a day or two. But you can say you found other transportation. They might charge you something extra if they have to come get it, but—"

"I don't care about that."

"Okay, then it's settled." He turned toward the door. "I'll come over here in the morning when I'm sure Mason's gone."

"Wait a minute." She'd been so caught up in her own problems that she hadn't thought about how Boone had engineered this visit to her room. "Mason's in the café, right?"

"Right."

"When you left, where did he think you were going?"

"To my room."

She gazed at him standing by the door. "But you don't have a room."

"He doesn't know that."

"You can't go back in the café now, can you?"

"No, but I'll be okay in my truck."

His willingness to sacrifice himself for someone he'd just met left her speechless. Finally she recovered enough to stop him before he opened the door. "You will not sleep in the truck, Boone. Share the bed with Josh. He doesn't take up much room. It's the least—"

"Not in this lifetime."

The steel in his words told her it was useless to argue the point. "Okay, then take the chair, or the floor. But you are not going out to that truck. If you do, then the deal's off. I won't go with you to the Rocking D."

"But…you don't know me."

She smiled at that. "Yes, I do. Stay with Josh and me for the rest of the night, Boone. I feel rotten enough about the trouble I'm causing you. Let me at least offer you shelter from this storm."

"You shouldn't feel bad. You're not the one causing the problem. Fowler is."

"Well, I do feel bad, and I wouldn't be able to sleep a wink knowing I sent you out to stay in your truck tonight."

He hesitated. "Well—"

"You'll be doing me a big favor." She pressed her advantage. His only weakness seemed to be his very soft heart. "I haven't been able to sleep hardly at all since I left San Antonio. I have a feeling with you here, I'll be able to finally relax."

"Then go on back to bed." Boone took off his jacket and hat before settling down in the room's only chair. "Don't be afraid to sleep. I'll keep you safe."

CHAPTER FOUR

BOONE SHIFTED his chair so that it blocked the door, just in case. Then he leaned back and closed his eyes, although he didn't expect to sleep. The room was too full of Shelby—her flowery scent, her soft breathing, her rustling movements as she turned over in bed.

His sexual urges were coming out of hibernation, and the timing sucked. For the first time in more than a year, he was seriously interested in a woman. But in spite of the lousy timing, he was somewhat reassured by the ache in his groin. After Darlene had dumped him, he'd felt more like a steer than a bull, except, apparently, when he'd downed a pint of good Irish whiskey and taken Jessica to bed. That hardly counted.

This counted. Nothing about Shelby reminded him of Darlene. Darlene was tall and big-boned, with brown eyes and hair. And damned impatient about getting a ring on her finger. He'd wanted to wait awhile to get married, so he could save enough money to give her a better style of life. At least that's what he'd assumed was his motivation. Sebastian had thought all along he was stalling because deep down he wasn't sure Darlene was the one.

No matter what the reason, his method of operation hadn't suited Darlene, and he'd lost her. Maybe she hadn't been the one, but she'd been a big part of his life for a good many years, and he still couldn't think of her without getting a lump in his throat.

Except now he could. Boone's eyes snapped open as he realized he'd been thinking about Darlene for several minutes, and his throat felt perfectly fine. Testing himself, he conjured up the pictures that usually sent him into deep depression—Darlene in a wedding dress, Darlene standing in front of the preacher with Chester Littlefield, Darlene and Chester in bed together.

The scenes that had once evoked such morbid curiosity and deep pain barely kept his attention now. Instead his thoughts were firmly anchored on Shelby. When he'd first seen her, he'd been fascinated with the way her hair spilled out of her perky ponytail, so silky and blond, reminding him of a corn tassel. The bounce of her hair when she moved had made him smile.

But tonight when she'd opened her door to him, he'd had no urge to smile. Instead his mouth had gone dry and his heart had begun to pound. In the light from the motel courtyard she'd looked like an angel, pure and untouched in her simple cotton nightgown with her hair falling gently to her shoulders.

Then his attention had settled on the swell of her breasts under the soft flannel, and he'd forgotten about angels and started thinking of naked bodies writhing on hot sheets. The urge to protect her had brought him to her door, but once there, he'd fought the equally powerful urge to claim her as his, to put her in an ivory tower away from the reach of other men. But within *his* easy reach.

Boone didn't generally believe in impulse, and he hadn't acted on it this time, either. Instead of pulling her into his arms and branding her with his kisses, a concept that made him tremble with temptation, he'd stood just inside the door while she went over to quiet the boy.

By the time she'd come back to stand in front of him, he'd had better control of himself. Marginally better. He'd still wanted to skim off her nightgown and make love to her until his name poured from her lips in a moan of delight. Totally uncharacteristic of him. His buddies would never believe he'd had such wild thoughts about a woman he'd just met.

But he did. She'd never know how hard he'd clenched his hands at his sides to keep from reaching for her, especially when she'd told him about her sister and her folks. She might have appreciated the comfort of a man's strong arms at that moment, but he hadn't trusted himself to keep his touch confined to comfort.

He'd have to be mighty careful in the next few days while he helped her sort out her problem. And no matter how much he might want to be, he couldn't be her solution. His first obligation was to Elizabeth and Jessica.

Shelby's breathing took on a slow, steady rhythm, and Boone dared to open his eyes and glance over to where she and Josh slept. The glowing red numbers on the bedside clock showed him it was after three in the morning. He really should try to sleep, too, but he couldn't stop looking at Shelby.

A sliver of light from a break in the curtains angled across the bed and shone on her golden hair. It touched the line of her jaw and moved across to pick out a narrow section of Josh's tousled curls.

The boy would help keep him straight, Boone thought. Without Josh in that bed, the impulse to climb in with her would be too great. But Josh was there.

Then, abruptly, both the red numbers on the clock and the light from the window winked out, and the heater fan whirled to a stop.

Boone muttered a curse. The storm had knocked out the power.

"Come back on, damn it," he muttered under his breath, but the world had fallen silent except for Shelby and Josh's quiet breathing. Boone figured these motel units were made of cardboard and chewing gum. He could already feel the chill seeping through the wall behind him, and soon the room would be very cold.

Putting on his jacket and shoving his hands in the pockets, he sat in the chair and waited. Still no heat. Eventually Shelby and Josh began moving restlessly in the bed and Boone knew the cold had penetrated the blankets.

He stood, walked over to the closet and took their coats off the hangers. He arranged the coats over them as best he could. Working carefully so Josh wouldn't wake up, Boone draped Josh's special blanket around the little boy's shoulders. Then he returned to the chair and hunched down into the sheepskin lining of his coat.

The temperature of the room fell a few more degrees and the restless movements from the bed continued. Finally Boone stood again, took off his jacket, and walked toward the bed. Josh had curled up as close to Shelby as he could get. They were both shivering. Boone was, too, but it wasn't as if he hadn't ever been cold in his life. He could stand a little shivering.

The toe of his boot caught the edge of the nightstand, making a clunking noise that must have awakened Shelby, because she turned over and mumbled his name sleepily.

He paused. "I'm here."

"Why is it so cold?"

"Power's out." He leaned down and draped his jacket over her and Josh. "It'll be morning soon. Try and get some rest."

She rose up on one elbow. "What are you doing, covering us with your jacket? You need it," she whispered urgently.

"I'm not cold," he lied.

"But I'm c-cold," Josh said, his teeth chattering. "S-so's B-bob."

Shelby gripped Boone's arm. "Take off your boots and get in here with us."

Panic gripped him. He wasn't sure he could trust himself. "I don't think that's a good—"

"Are you going to stand on ceremony when a little boy is shivering like this?"

"No." He had to risk it, for the boy's sake. "No, I'm not."

"Good." She released her hold on his arm. "Come on, Josh, move over closer to me. Boone's getting in on your side. The heat went out so we have to snuggle to stay warm."

Heart racing, Boone walked around the bed and sat on the edge so he could pull off his boots. The boy would be between them, he reminded himself. But this still felt way too risky.

"I *like* t-to snuggle," Josh said.

"I know you do," Shelby replied, her voice playful as she rustled under the sheets, obviously gathering Josh close to keep him warm. "You're my little snuggle-bunny."

In spite of his misgivings about getting in bed with Josh and Shelby, Boone had always yearned for a scenario exactly like this one. He'd counted on being a husband and a father by now. Darlene had taken away his plan to be a husband, and although he might be Elizabeth's father, nothing about that situation felt good to him. He took off his belt so the cold buckle wouldn't press against Josh.

"I love you, Shebby," Josh said, his voice muffled. "More'n all my Legos."

"I love you, too, sweetheart," she murmured. "More than all my Billy Joel albums."

"I love you more'n all my Tonka trucks."

"I love you more than my salt-and-pepper-shaker collection."

"Even the duck ones?"

"Even the duck ones," Shelby said.

"'Cause I quack you up, huh, Shebby?"

Boone chuckled.

"Exactly," Shelby said. "You totally quack me up."

From the way Josh giggled, Boone knew this must be a game they'd played many times over. He envied their closeness. Shelby and Josh had a good thing going. Mason Fowler had no business coming between them, no matter what his biological rights might be.

"Okay, I'm getting under the covers now," Boone said as he eased into bed next to Josh. The bed was a standard double, too short for him. With Shelby and Josh already in the bed, it was a tight fit.

Balancing on the edge of the mattress, he tried to find a place to put his sock-covered feet and brushed them against Shelby's bare calf. "Oops, sorry." He felt as if he'd touched an electric fence as the jolt of awareness traveled through him. He wondered if she wore anything at all under that nightgown. Probably not. He swallowed.

"Put your feet back over here," Shelby said. "Let me help you warm them up."

"That's okay. They'll warm up on their own." No way was he playing footsie with her under the covers. He laid his head on the pillow and figured if there was more light he'd be looking directly into Shelby's eyes. But as it was, he couldn't see much of anything.

Not being able to see sharpened his other senses, though. He breathed in her perfume mingled with the soapsuds scent of a little boy who'd had a bath only hours before. He tuned in to her breathing, and the rustle of sheets that telegraphed her every move. He scooted closer to Josh.

"You're a ice cube!" Josh shrank away from him.

"Help warm him up," Shelby said. "And then he'll keep you warm."

"Maybe this isn't such a good idea." Boone held himself away from Josh so his chilled clothes wouldn't get the little guy cold. He was about ready to fall on the floor.

"His shirt's cold, Shebby," Josh complained.

"Unsnap your shirt, Boone," Shelby said.

"What?"

"No, really. I read about this. Your skin is a lot warmer than your shirt. Actually the most efficient way for us to maximize body heat would be for everyone to cuddle without any clothes on at all."

Boone choked. "We're not doing that," he said in a raspy voice. He unsnapped his shirt though, because he knew she was right about the most efficient way to transfer body heat.

"No, of course we're not doing that," she said. "I'm just making a point."

"I wanna," Josh said brightly. He started wriggling on the bed.

"No, Josh." Shelby held him still. "Keep your pajamas on."

"Why?"

"Because it's not necessary to take them off. We'll be fine."

"But I would *like* it."

"I'm sure you would, you little streaker." She chuckled. "Josh grabs any opportunity at all to take his clothes off, don't you, buddy?"

"Yep."

All this talk about nakedness naturally led Boone to think of undressing Shelby, which wasn't helpful. But he smiled at the picture of Josh running bare-assed through the house. He'd forgotten how little kids loved to do that, and how much joy they took in the simplest of things. Their world could be uncomplicated and filled with wonder, so long as some adult didn't mess it up for them.

Without warning, Josh laid his small hand on Boone's chest. "Now you're warm," he said.

The trusting acceptance of that casual touch was deeply moving. "Good," Boone said.

"Let's cuddle," Josh said.

"We are cuddling," Boone said.

"Uh-uh. You gots to be closer."

Boone edged farther onto the mattress.

"You gots to put your arm around us," Josh said. "'Cause you're the biggest."

Boone wasn't too sure about the wisdom of wrapping his arm around Shelby and Josh. And Shelby had suddenly become very quiet over there. Maybe she was rethinking this, herself. He hesitated.

"Come *on*," Josh said, grabbing his arm. "Don'tcha know how to cuddle?"

He did know. In fact, he was hungry for the chance. With a sigh of resignation, he reached over Josh and slipped an arm around Shelby. As he drew them both into the shelter of his embrace, Shelby's breath caught.

So this bothers her some, too. Boone's ego welcomed the boost. Given a choice, he wouldn't have put either of them in this position, but with the power out, he had no choice. He closed his eyes and savored the pleasure of holding Shelby, even if they did have a three-year-old between them.

"Now you, Shebby," Josh said.

"Okay." Her voice sounded husky.

Boone nearly stopped breathing when she hesitantly brushed her hand across his rib cage. With the way he'd pulled his shirt open, she had no option but to slide her hand underneath it as she wrapped her arm partway around him.

He couldn't believe that such a small hand could have such a huge impact on his system. Sparks of excitement sent off a chain reaction throughout his body.

While Boone was still dealing with the sweet pressure of Shelby's handprint on his skin, Josh pressed his ear against Boone's chest, right over his heart. "It's beating," he said.

"I should hope so," Boone answered.

"Fast. Thumpity, thumpity, thumpity."

"I guess that's what the cold does to you," Boone said.

Then Josh turned and pressed his other ear against Shelby's chest. "You must be cold, too, Shebby."

"Mmm." Her hand stayed very, very still.

Light though her touch was, he felt the imprint of each of her fingers. He even imagined the spiral patterns of her fingerprints leaving a mark on his skin.

"I like this." Josh sounded sleepy.

"Good," Shelby said. "Now go to sleep."

"'Kay."

Boone loved the sound of Shelby's voice in the dark. He loved the warmth of her body inside the circle of his arm while the wind howled and battered at the windows and the snow covered the world in white. He loved the delicate pressure of her fingers against his back. Sure, sex was on his mind, but his body wasn't raging out of control. Mostly he felt incredibly right being here in this tiny bed with her and Josh, keeping them safe.

He'd known them for such a short time, and yet he felt as if he'd slipped into the most perfect spot in the universe. He hadn't thought he could sleep in such a cramped bed with such a tempting woman so close, but gradually contentment crept through him, lulling him into one of the deepest sleeps of his life.

"VROOOM! Vrrrrooom-vrooooom! Beep, beep!"

Shelby woke to the familiar sound of Josh playing toy cars on the floor beside her bed and the unfamiliar sensation of being cuddled spoon-fashion against a very big, very aroused male body. From the steady sound of Boone's breathing, she was sure he was still asleep.

But his sexual instincts were wide awake. His erection pressed against her bottom, and his arm shifted slightly so that his big hand cupped her breast. The contact felt… wonderful.

Daylight seeped in around the closed curtains and the bedside clock blinked rapidly, flashing twelve o'clock.

The heater fan whirred and clanked, so it was no real surprise that the room was warm once again. Power had been restored.

But Shelby was more interested in a different sort of power, the sexual kind issuing from the man cradling her body in his. Boone would be very embarrassed if he knew what he was doing, she thought with a soft smile. Apparently both of them had been so exhausted they hadn't awakened when Josh climbed out of bed. They'd simply shifted positions.

Shelby liked this position. In a minute she'd need to slide out from under Boone's arm and get out of bed before he realized how forward he'd been with her. But for now, she'd close her eyes, draw the sheet up to her chin and pretend to sleep a little while longer so that she could enjoy her fantasy.

She'd never quite admitted to herself that she had a fantasy man in mind, but during that childhood trip to Yellowstone she'd wandered away from the cabin and become lost. A cowboy on horseback had found her and returned her, scared and crying, to her family. He might not have been a very large man, but to a kid of seven, he had seemed enormous in his boots and ten-gallon hat.

Maybe that cowboy was one of the reasons she hadn't ever fallen in love enough to consider marrying. Maybe all along she'd been hoping to find her big, brave cowboy again. What a silly, girlish dream. And yet, lying here tucked against Boone, she didn't feel the least bit silly or girlish. In fact, if Josh weren't in the room, she'd stay right in this bed and see what happened when the big guy woke up.

He might be shy at first, and that fit right in with her

fantasy because it meant that he didn't have tons of experience with women. She suspected that when this man gave his heart, he gave it for keeps. He would be a tender and considerate lover, but if a woman knew how to push the right buttons, she'd bet that he'd turn into a real force of nature.

A picture of Boone filled with wild passion certainly got her juices flowing. Considering the size of the erection pressing against her, he might even be a little scary. Her heart beat faster with a mixture of excitement and trepidation. Ah, but he was also a gentle man. The combination of size, power and gentleness was nearly irresistible to her.

Beneath the hand he'd cupped over her breast, her nipple tightened. Okay, she needed to get out of this bed *now,* before she embarrassed herself, as well as Boone. Shifting her weight slightly, she took hold of his wrist and tried to move his arm away. It was like trying to lift a felled tree.

His arm didn't budge, but his fingers flexed against her breast.

She closed her eyes again, trembling slightly. His touch felt so good. She'd been so focused on Josh since—well, really since he'd been born—that she'd had no social life, let alone a man in her bed. The guy she'd been seeing when Josh was born hadn't been interested in babies and couldn't understand why she'd felt such a responsibility for her nephew. After she'd broken off that relationship, she hadn't bothered to cultivate another.

Under different circumstances, she wouldn't mind cultivating this one. But she couldn't get involved with Boone, not when she needed all her energy to keep Josh safe. With regret, she got a stronger grip on Boone's wrist and attempted to pull his arm away.

Still no dice. He moaned her name softly and pulled her in tighter, pressing the crotch of his jeans hard against her bottom. Her pulse raced as she wondered if he was only faking sleep. But no, his soft snoring told her he was truly zonked. At least the name he'd mumbled was hers. That gave her a great deal of satisfaction.

But he was too strong for her to budge him. She hadn't fully realized just how strong he was, and without his brain and conscience in gear, his basic needs had taken over, keeping her prisoner. She'd have to wake him up.

She shook his arm as best she could, considering it was wrapped around her like a steel band. "Boone. Wake up."

Josh scrambled to his feet and came to the edge of the bed to stare at her. "I woked up."

"I see that." She was glad the covers disguised the grip Boone had on her breast, although Josh wouldn't think anything of it. After all, a three-year-old didn't know anything about sex between a man and a woman.

"I goed potty and then I played trucks."

"Good for you. You're a big boy. Boone! Isn't Josh a big boy?"

"Huh?" Boone came awake with a start, released her breast as if it had burned his hand, and fell out of the far side of the bed with a terrific thud.

CHAPTER FIVE

BOONE HAD his boots on, his shirt snapped and his coat buttoned faster than his buddy Travis could rope and tie a calf, and Travis was known for his speed. "I'll check on breakfast," he said as he clapped his hat on his head and charged out the motel room door.

He hadn't dared look at Shelby, and one quick glance at Josh confirmed that the little boy was staring at him as if he'd just grown ears and a tail. Which he practically had.

Damn! How had he ended up plastered against Shelby's backside, clutching a handful of her breast? What had happened to the kid who was supposed to sleep between them and keep everything respectable and proper? Who told that boy he could get out of bed, anyway?

And that was another thing. Boone, the macho protector who had assigned himself the job of staying alert to the slightest danger threatening either the boy or the woman, hadn't even realized when Josh had left the bed. Boone had promised to keep watch. Some guardian he'd turned out to be.

He snorted in disgust at himself as he stomped through knee-high drifts toward the café. The sun was out and the sound of heavy machinery from down the road indicated the snowplows were working. Most of the cars and trucks that had been parked at the motel the night before were gone. Squinting up at the sun, Boone judged the time to be around nine in the morning. Late. Fowler should already be on his way to Colorado Springs.

Boone's face still felt hot with embarrassment, so he paused, leaned down and scooped up a handful of snow to pat over his cheeks. He used to think he couldn't trust himself when he drank. Now apparently he couldn't trust himself when he slept, either.

He'd been having a dynamite dream about Shelby, which must have been inspired by the way he was groping her in his sleep. He wondered how long he'd been doing it, how long she'd had to endure his fumblings while she tried to escape without making a big deal of it in front of Josh.

In those first groggy seconds of waking up, he'd been aware of two things—a full erection shoved right up against Shelby's soft bottom, and the weight of her breast cradled in his left hand. The pleasure of both sensations had lasted for the space of a breath. Then his brain had cleared enough to allow humiliation to come roaring through to destroy that pleasure completely.

An apology was definitely in order, but he couldn't picture himself trying that maneuver in front of Josh. No telling what Josh would think he was trying to apologize for. In Josh's world there was nothing wrong with people "snuggling" together.

Boone wondered what Shelby must be thinking right now and groaned aloud. Maybe she'd refuse to go with him to the Rocking D, figuring she'd take her chances on her own rather than trust her safety to a sex maniac.

Well, he couldn't force her to go with him, but he could make sure Fowler was gone before she set out, then follow her until she'd made it over the pass and onto dry pavement. But hell, he wanted her to go with him so he could guarantee she wouldn't run into Fowler. Somehow he had to convince her that he would never, ever lay a hand on her again.

He stomped the snow from his boots before walking into the café. A gray-haired woman he'd never seen before was behind the counter serving coffee to a couple of men in heavy coats seated on stools. The waitress was probably Edna, Boone decided, remembering the other employee Eugene had talked about. He saw no sign of either of the Sloans, and best of all, no sign of Fowler.

Sitting at the counter next to one of the men, he grabbed a menu from the aluminum holder in front of him. "Guess the road's open, huh?" he commented to the guy beside him.

"Sure is," the man said. "We came through about twenty minutes ago, and they got it cleared pretty good both north and southbound. I hear a few folks were stranded here last night."

"Yep." Boone studied the menu and tried to think what Josh and Shelby might like him to bring them for breakfast. He'd been so hell-bent on getting out of the room he hadn't stopped to ask. He rubbed his chin and reminded himself he needed to get his shaving kit out of the truck.

"Including you?"

"Yep. Say, what do you think a three-year-old boy eats for breakfast?"

The man chuckled. "That's anybody's guess. Mine used to like cold spaghetti."

"Or cold pizza," added the man next to him. "With the cheese congealed into this globby mess on top. My kid loved that for breakfast."

The waitress turned from the coffeemaker. Sure enough, her name was Edna. "Peanut-butter toast is your best bet," she said. "Unless he's allergic to peanuts."

Boone shook his head, dazed at the odds of lousing up such a simple thing as breakfast. "I'll try an order of peanut-butter toast for him," he said. "But I'll find out about the allergy thing before he eats it."

"Okay." Edna took her order pad from her apron and started writing. "This will be to go?"

"Yes. All of it. I'll need two large coffees, the toast, and…" Boone paused to scan the menu again. "Milk," he decided, figuring Josh could drink it and Shelby could use it for her coffee if she took her coffee with cream. He couldn't believe he'd fondled a woman's breast, yet he had no idea how she took her coffee, or even if she drank the stuff.

But her nipple had been tight. Tight and aroused. The tidbit of information must have been buried under layers of his own embarrassment, but when it surfaced, it was a revelation to him. Maybe she hadn't endured his touch, after all. Maybe she'd even liked it. Maybe she'd even *wanted* it.

Well.

"Anything besides the toast, coffee, and milk?" Edna asked.

"Huh?" Boone glanced up in confusion.

"On your order," Edna said, smiling a little. "Or should I get you some coffee first so you can function? I know how I am before my first cup in the morning."

"Uh, no!" He was afraid he was blushing. "I mean, I can finish up the order without a cup of coffee. Let's see—how about two orders of scrambled eggs, hash browns, bacon, and a couple of sweet rolls?"

Edna's smile broadened. "Working up an appetite, are you? Want any juice?"

"Yeah, juice. Orange. Three glasses. That should do it." He closed the menu with a decisive snap. As it turned out, he did have an appetite, now that the idea of returning to the room and facing Shelby wasn't quite so embarrassing. Maybe she'd been turned on, too. She might even have been the one who'd cuddled up to him, once Josh had climbed out of bed.

Both of them had been under a strain. If they'd needed a little human contact, they couldn't be blamed for that. He certainly didn't blame Shelby.

The two men paid for their coffee and left, wishing him a good trip. While his breakfast order was cooking, Boone paid a quick visit to the café's rest room. He looked like a goddamned derelict, he thought, grimacing at his reflection and trying to finger-comb his hair.

And he continued to think about Shelby's nipple. If her nipple had been like that, then maybe the rest of her had responded, too. She might have been lying there all warm and damp and ready.

He might never know, but he sure felt good thinking that she might have. And if things were different, if he didn't have Elizabeth and Jessica to consider, then he'd have devoted some effort to finding out how she reacted if he touched her like that again. As it was, he'd better not try it. He was in no position to start something he couldn't finish.

His order was packaged and ready when he returned to the counter. As he headed out the door of the café with two paper sacks, Eugene walked in. He looked tired, but he'd obviously taken the time to shave, shower and change clothes. Boone felt grungy in comparison. Once he'd taken care of breakfast, he really had to see about cleaning up. He wondered if he dared risk using the shower in Shelby's room, or if that was asking for more trouble.

"Hey, Boone," Eugene said. "Glad to see you made it through the night okay."

"Yeah, I, uh, did."

Eugene lowered his voice. "You went to warn that young woman when you left here last night, didn't you?"

"Yeah. That guy creeped me out."

"Me, too, but then I couldn't figure out where you were going to sleep. Did you spend the night in your truck?"

Boone shifted his weight from one foot to the other. "Actually, she—well, she needed someone to sort of guard her and the boy, so I stayed."

Eugene smiled. "Good." He glanced at the sacks Boone was holding. "Breakfast for all of you?"

"Yeah."

"Well, I won't keep you, then. But if it makes you feel any better, that fellow was one of the first ones out of here. He took off the minute the snowplow came through."

Boone nodded. "Did you happen to notice what he was driving?"

"Sure did. Black Land Rover. Fancy."

"That's good to know. Thanks. Listen, I'll be taking Shelby and Josh with me and she's going to leave her rental car here." He hoped Shelby hadn't reconsidered the plan because of what happened between them in bed. But he had to go on the assumption that she still wanted his help. "We'll call somebody to come up from Santa Fe to get the car, but I wanted you to know."

Eugene's smile deepened. "Sounds like you're doing a little rescue work yourself. Like that lighthouse thing you talked about last night. Or in your case, maybe it's more like a knight in shining armor."

"I'm going to try." After last night, Boone figured his armor was tarnished, but he still intended to keep Shelby and Josh safe.

Eugene gripped Boone's upper arm and gave it a squeeze. "You're a good man, Boone. Stop by any time you're on this road. I'll buy you a cup of coffee."

"Thanks." Boone returned Eugene's smile. "I'll look forward to that."

THE MINUTE Boone was out the door Shelby had got dressed in record time and then helped Josh into his clothes. After they were totally ready and nearly all packed, she'd neatly made the bed, thinking that would help Boone feel less awkward when he returned. She smoothed the spread so that it looked as if no one had slept there, let alone cuddled and fondled and enjoyed…oh, she had to stop thinking about that.

But no matter how hard she tried, she couldn't seem to put the thought of Boone's hand on her breast or the bulge of his erection out of her mind. When he knocked on the door, she was *still* thinking about it. She glanced out the window to make sure it was him, and the sight of his big, beautiful body made her palms sweat.

Josh had scrambled up to the chair to look out the window with her. "Boone's here!" he shouted and ran to the door to fumble with the lock. "He gots presents!"

"Food," Shelby said, going over to help him with the lock. Josh's eagerness broke her heart. She wondered how she'd ever console the little boy when he had to tell his new friend goodbye. "It's only breakfast, Josh."

Josh threw open the door. "Hi, Boone! Whatcha gots for me and you?"

Boone grinned at Josh as he walked through the door with the bags balanced in one arm and his free hand behind his back. "Wait'll you see," he said as Shelby closed the door behind him.

Josh started jumping up and down. "What, Boone? What, what, what?"

He crouched down in front of Josh and brought his hand forward. "A snowball."

Josh gasped in wonder and reached out a finger to poke at the glistening white ball. "Brrrr!" He glanced at Boone. "Can we throw it?"

"Sure. If Shelby will open the door again for a minute, you can throw it right outside."

Shelby followed instructions and opened the door. Now that the sun had come out, it wasn't nearly as cold, anyway.

"Go ahead, Josh," Boone coaxed. "Pick it up."

Josh made one attempt to hold the snowball and dropped it back in Boone's hand with a squeal.

"Just do it fast," Boone said.

"Aw*right*." Josh grabbed up the snowball and pitched it about three feet beyond the doorway. "I did it! I throwed a snowball, Shebby!" He danced up and down and waved his cold hand. "I throwed it out there. Right there. Can you see it?"

"I sure can."

"Bob wants to throw one."

"Oh, I forgot." Boone reached in the pocket of his coat

and took out an imaginary object. Here's Bob's snowball."

Josh peered down at Boone's palm. "Yup. There it is. Throw it, Bob."

"I'd better close the door now," Shelby said. "We're letting out the heat."

"Wait!" Josh said. "Bob gots to throw his."

"Okay. But tell Bob to hurry."

Josh studied the open doorway. "Okay. He throwed it."

"Then let's close the door." As she pushed it shut she dared to glance down at Boone still crouched on the floor. She discovered him gazing up at her. He was practically kneeling at her feet.

Silently he mouthed the words *I'm sorry.*

Her heart did a somersault. God, his eyes were green. "It's okay," she murmured softly. Then she took a deep breath and spoke normally. "Well, I guess we need to eat, huh?"

"Yeah, before it gets cold." He broke eye contact and levered himself to his feet. "I hope you don't mind about the snowball, but I thought maybe, if Josh had never played in the snow, he'd—"

"I wanna play in the snow!" Josh tugged on her hand and looked up at her with pleading blue eyes. "*Please,* Shebby? Can me and Bob *please* play in the snow?"

Boone stepped closer to her and lowered his voice. "It's all clear."

Shelby looked quickly at Boone and was once again drawn in by the beauty of his eyes. They reminded her of a summer meadow, lush and tempting. "You're sure?"

Boone nodded.

Shelby couldn't look away. Boone's gaze was so

warm, so full of life. Slowly Josh's pleading voice faded from her awareness as her attention drifted to Boone's mouth. She imagined at first it would settle tenderly over hers, but as he caught fire, his kiss would become more demanding. Then he'd move from kissing her lips to kissing other parts of her body, and…

"Shebby." Josh hung his whole weight from her hand, nearly pulling her over.

Dazed, she looked down at the little boy. "What is it, Josh?"

Josh spoke with great deliberation. "Can…me…and… Bob…play…in…the…snow?"

"Maybe for a little while. After we eat some breakfast."

"Whoopee!" He started running around the room. "Snow, snow, snow, snow."

"Okay, settle down." She caught him by the shoulder as he ran past.

"Might be a good idea at that," Boone said. "To play awhile after breakfast. He can work off some of that excess energy before he gets into the truck."

Josh stopped his wiggling and stared up at Boone. "What truck?"

"You and Shelby are going to ride with me to the Rocking D."

"The *ranch?*" Josh's eyes widened. "Where you gots *horsies?*"

"That's right."

Josh turned slowly and looked up at Shelby. "We really are?" he whispered, as if he couldn't believe such good fortune.

Her heart wrenched. Perhaps this was a terrible idea. The more time Josh spent with Boone, the harder their eventual separation would be. She should probably tell

Boone that she'd changed her mind. They'd drive the little rental car on through Colorado and into Wyoming, as she'd intended.

"Shelby."

The sound of her name spoken in Boone's deep, gentle voice sent shivers of pleasure up her spine. She glanced at him.

He cleared his throat. "I know what you're probably thinking. Listen, please don't let what happened last night…. Well, it won't ever happen again." He swallowed. "I swear to God it won't. You need to come to the Rocking D. Everything will work out better that way."

She wished they were alone so she could let him know that what had happened last night, or rather early this morning, hadn't bothered her a bit. Poor guy, he thought she was offended and that's why she was hesitating. She could hardly explain in front of Josh, especially considering that her main concern was for the little boy. She didn't want him to get his heart broken.

But neither could she send away a good man like Boone, letting him think he'd horrified her with his perfectly natural urges. They needed time to sort out this tangle, and a day or so at the Rocking D might be the answer for that.

Besides, given a little time, maybe she could figure out a way to keep some contact with Boone, for Josh's sake. Once she and Josh knew where the ranch was, they might be able to go back for a visit someday, after the mess with Mason Fowler had been handled. The thought cheered her. She'd like to reconnect with Boone once she was no longer on the run. Something might even come of it.

She looked down at Josh, who stood there with a

very worried expression on his face. "We'll go to the Rocking D for a day or so," she said. "Long enough for you to ride a horse, Josh."

Josh beamed as he looked from Shelby to Boone and back to Shelby again. "Me and Bob, we're gonna *love* it there," he said.

As she absorbed the happiness shining from the little boy's eyes, Shelby found tears gathering in hers. He so needed a wonderful man in his life, a man like Boone. Come to think of it, she wouldn't mind having a wonderful man like Boone in her life, either.

"Well, now," she said, forcing cheer into her voice as she quickly blinked away the tears. "We'd better get going. We have lots to do before we get on the road!"

CHAPTER SIX

SHELBY INSISTED Boone use her calling card to phone his friends at the Rocking D and explain the situation. Then she looked for an excuse to vacate the room while he shaved and showered, and came up with an errand she and Josh could run. They'd head for the café to get plastic bags to tape over their shoes so they could play in the snow more easily. She even mentioned she might stay for a cup of coffee or hot chocolate.

But even hot chocolate couldn't sway Josh. The little boy begged to stay with Boone, which showed how much he was beginning to attach himself to the big cowboy. Shelby could see the way Josh constantly watched Boone, looking for clues as to how a man behaved. Shelby finally gave in and left him there. After all, she was the only one who needed to get far away from the erotic pull of having a sexy man in her shower.

Norma Sloan was behind the counter when Shelby walked in, and she hauled out the café's lost-and-found box. The box produced mittens and boots that would work for Josh, and an old pair of boots, a stocking cap and some gloves for Shelby.

Caught up in the excitement of such unexpected treasures, Shelby forgot to stay for coffee. She remembered after she was out the door but decided not to worry about it. Boone probably took quick showers.

On the way back to the room, she noticed his truck for the first time. She identified it easily because his name was on it, painted on the side panel of the door. Boone Connor, Farrier. So he was a blacksmith. That fit him, she decided. The job seemed to be made for someone who was both strong and gentle.

She continued on to the room, eager to share her success, and opened the motel door without thinking to knock. "Hey, guys, you'll never believe what I—" She came to a screeching halt and almost dropped the boots at the breathtaking sight that greeted her through the open bathroom door. Boone, naked except for a towel knotted around his hips, was helping Josh pretend to shave. Tension curled deliciously within her.

Boone turned immediately, and a dull red crept over his cheeks. He'd probably meant to be dressed by now, but Josh had slowed him down. "Uh, don't worry," he mumbled. "I took the blade out."

"Oh. Okay." She hadn't gotten far enough in her thinking to be worried about that. She was too busy assimilating the picture Boone made. And salivating. She might have known his chest hair would be dark, curly and thick. And talk about a hard body. The blacksmithing job kept him very fit indeed. She grew warm just looking at all that muscle. Much more of this view and she'd be ready to attack him.

The bathroom mirror was still fogged, but he'd rubbed a clean spot so that Josh could see himself from where he was kneeling on the vanity, a towel tied around his neck to protect his clothes. While Boone steadied him with an arm around his waist, he carefully stroked the shaving cream from his face with Boone's razor.

"I'm shavin', Shebby!" Josh called out. "See me?"

"I see you." But she had a tough time concentrating on her nephew.

She should turn away, but she didn't have the will-power. Not only was he beautiful in body, but his sensitive treatment of Josh displayed a beautiful spirit, too. Pride radiated from Josh as he carefully worked the razor in obvious imitation of the way he'd watched Boone do it. He'd probably pestered Boone the whole time the big guy was in the shower, until Boone had finally given up and agreed to help him shave when he got out.

She imagined Boone in the shower. With no towel.... She almost groaned aloud. If Josh hadn't been here... But he was. He most certainly was.

Shelby wondered if Boone realized that Josh would now be his slave for life. In all his three years, Josh had never had a man take as much time for him as Boone had in the past few hours. Shelby had given him all the attention she could, but some things were beyond her. Teaching him how to shave was only one in a long list of male-oriented activities.

No doubt about it, she'd need to find a way to keep Boone a part of Josh's life. The two had taken to each other from the beginning.

Boone cleared his throat. "What did you find?" he asked, keeping his attention on Josh.

Bless his heart, he was trying to keep this moment from being awkward, for Josh's sake.

"Uh, boots." She held them up, even though he wasn't looking in her direction. Damn, but he was gorgeous. He'd already surpassed her fantasies about

big strong cowboys, and now he looked like the perfect
father, too. "Mrs. Sloan had a lost-and-found box under
the counter and these were in there. She also had mittens
for Josh and some gloves for me."

"Good." Boone gazed into the mirror. "How're you
coming, there, buddy?"

"Almost done." Josh had shaving cream everywhere—all over the towel and dabbed on the mirror and
the sink, even on Boone's chest, but he'd managed to
get most of it off his face.

"Looks good," Boone said. He reached over and
snagged a hand towel from the rack. He rubbed it over
his chest before handing it to Josh. "Wipe with this.
Then you can slap on some shaving lotion."

"Yeah." Josh nodded. "Shavin' lotion." He wiped his
face and peered at himself in the mirror. "All shaved."

"Okay. Down we go." Boone lifted Josh effortlessly
from the sink using only the arm he had wrapped around
the little boy's waist. He acted as if Josh were no heavier
than a feather.

Shelby knew better. She'd hefted Josh enough times
to know how much he weighed. She watched in fascination as Boone's back muscles flexed with the motion.
She'd give her entire salt-and-pepper-shaker collection
to feel those muscles move under her hand.

Boone untied the towel from around Josh's neck,
careful to keep his gaze on the boy and not let it stray
toward Shelby. "Now hold out your hands, like this."
Boone cupped his hands in front of him.

Josh mirrored him perfectly. Shelby thought what a
wonderful video this would have made. She'd left her
camera back in her apartment because it hadn't seemed
necessary under the circumstances. Now she was sorry,

although Boone would never have agreed to be filmed, now that she thought about it.

"I'm going to sprinkle some shaving lotion in your hands," Boone said, "but don't do anything yet. We'll slap it on together."

"*Okay.*" Josh gazed up at his idol with reverence.

Boone shook some lotion into his own hand. "First you rub your hands together like this," he said, demonstrating. "Then slap your cheeks like this." He patted his face briskly.

Josh clapped his hands against his cheeks and grinned. Then he ran over to Shelby. "Smell!"

She crouched down, put her nose against Josh's cheek and took a deep sniff. "Mmm, good," she said. "Good enough to eat." She nibbled his ear.

"Don't bite on me!" Josh said, giggling.

"I can't help it," Shelby said. "You smell so good." Now if only Boone would let her do the same thing, her world would be complete.

Instead he closed the bathroom door. "I'll be out in a minute," he called. "You two can start putting on your boots."

Shelby glanced at the closed door and sighed. The show was over.

MASON FOWLER calculated that he had some heavy-duty driving to do before he could hope to catch up with that bitch Shelby. She'd probably stopped for the night somewhere around Colorado Springs, but by now she'd be back on the road, hell-bent for Wyoming. Good thing her apartment manager had told him about Yellowstone. If he had anything to do with it, she'd never make it that far.

She was a sentimental little twit, and not all that

smart about covering her tracks. As if a rental car would throw him off. All he had to do was look for a Texas plate on a compact sedan and see if she and Josh were in it. He figured she was about two or three hours ahead of him, but he'd make that up. She wasn't the type to speed and he made good use of his fuzz-buster.

Once he found her, he'd force her off the road and take the kid. Any court in the country would back him on that one. Aunt kidnaps man's only son, man goes berserk and chases woman until he gets his kid back. Aunt loses custody. She'd played right into his hands, exactly as he'd hoped she would if he crowded her long enough.

The only thing he hadn't counted on was the snowstorm. But the folks at the café had been real helpful. At least he knew for sure she was on this road, which had to mean she was going for the Yellowstone experience, back to her childhood. Dumb broad.

He'd about puked the night she'd raved on to him and Patty about that Yellowstone vacation. She'd loved having the whole family in one room, like some *Little House on the Prairie* fairy tale. Nobody had ever taken him on a pansy-ass vacation like that when he was a kid. Good thing, too, because he would have hated it. Only real reason for going out in the woods was to shoot yourself a bull elk.

His stomach began to pinch and he realized he'd better stop for some food. He started watching the billboards. Nothing but damned fast-food chains. He hated big business. Big business and big government, the scourge of the independent spirit in this country. Then he saw a small billboard for the Shooting Star Café. Falling Star was probably more like it—some poor guy trying to make ends meet while he shoveled most of his income to Uncle Sam. Mason decided to stop there and get something to go.

Even the star on the billboard needed some paint. They should have done it in that reflective gold. Maybe he'd suggest that when he got there. A little gold paint wouldn't cost much. Maybe…

Oh, shit. The gold star. The goddamned gold star on the pocket of that big cowboy in the café.

Swerving to the shoulder of the road, Fowler slammed on the brakes. Then he sat there cussing himself, that cowboy and his idiot sister-in-law. She'd been there, at the motel, all night long. The motel was out of rooms, the cowboy had said. He'd been sitting there at two in the morning, not using his. It had seemed weird at the time, but lots of things seemed weird at two in the morning.

Fowler slammed his fist against the steering wheel. That bitch was forever putting little gold stars on Josh for some stupid reason or other. Sure as the world that shit-kicking cowboy had given up his room to her and she'd rewarded him with a goddamned gold star. Fowler had sat there looking at the guy and for some reason that stupid little star on his pocket hadn't registered.

But it registered now. He looked for a break in traffic, cut across the highway, barreled the Land Rover through the weeds on the median and headed back the way he'd come. So the café owners had lied to him. He'd have to decide what to do about that, too. But first he had to find that little bitch and get his son. Nobody was going to stand in his way. Nobody.

JOSH WANTED a big snowman, taller than Shelby, so Boone decided Josh should have a snowman. Boone hadn't built all that many, himself, growing up as he had in Las Cruces, so he completely understood how Josh felt about making Frosty. Got snow, gotta have a snowman.

Shelby seemed to be having a good time, too, and Boone enjoyed watching her relax and play in the snow. He wondered if she'd noticed how many times they'd accidentally touched or brushed against each other during the snowman project.

Boone had sure noticed. The whole time they'd been working his mind had been filled with the thought of pushing her gently down in the snow and covering her body with his. He'd never been so obsessed with sex in his life.

Towards the end of the project, Eugene Sloan got into the act, coming out with an old battered hat and a carrot for the snowman's nose.

Making the head was Josh's job, and after Shelby helped him roll a snowball big enough, Boone lifted it on top. Then Boone held Josh while he positioned stones for eyes and a mouth, the carrot for the nose, and crammed the hat over the snowman's head.

Eugene watched the final decorations with a smile on his narrow face. "Mighty fine work, folks."

From his perch in Boone's arms, Josh stared in fascination at the completed snowman. "Will he come alive now?" he asked hopefully.

"Hard to say," Boone replied. "I've heard sometimes that happens after dark. I'm afraid we won't be here to see that."

"I'll check it out for you, young man," Eugene said.

Josh nodded. "Good. 'Cause he might come alive. He gots a hat and that makes snowmens come alive."

"You folks have time for a cup of coffee or hot chocolate before you go?" Eugene asked. "On the house."

"Hot chocolate!" Josh bounced in Boone's arms. "Bob wants some, too!"

Boone thought of the miles they had yet to drive. He'd cleaned the snow off his truck, but they still needed to transfer Shelby and Josh's belongings into it. Sebastian was expecting him to roll in before nightfall, and they should leave soon in order to make it by then.

"We need to get a move on," he said, lowering Josh to the ground, "but why don't you give me your keys, Shelby? Then you and Josh can go on in and have something warm to drink while I load your stuff into the truck."

She glanced at him. "Why don't you give me *your* keys and I'll move everything while you and Josh go in and have something warm to drink."

Eugene laughed. "I can see a Mexican standoff coming. Let me take that boy in for some hot chocolate while you two get your loading done. Then Norma will fix you two coffees to go. How's that?"

Shelby smiled. "That would be wonderful, but I hate to put you to the trouble."

"No trouble. Helping folks out is what gets us out of bed of a morning."

"Well—"

"Can I, Shebby?" Josh tugged on her hand. "Can I, please?"

Boone understood Shelby's hesitation. He was a little reluctant to let Josh out of his sight, too. He still believed Mason could come back.

"All right," Shelby said finally. "We won't be long," she added, glancing at Eugene.

"Take your time." Eugene held his hand out to Josh. "Come on, son."

"Bob needs some, too."

"We'll make sure Bob gets some," Eugene said. "Let's go see if Norma has some marshmallows to put on top."

"Yum!" Josh hurried off, hand in hand with Eugene. Shelby gazed after them, her expression uneasy.

Boone longed to wrap a comforting arm around her shoulders, but he didn't dare. "He'll be okay," he said.

"I'm sure he'll be fine." She sighed. "It's just that ever since the accident I've kept really close tabs on him. Preschool in the mornings has been the only time he's been out of my sight, and all the teachers there had strict instructions not to let anyone take him out of school for any reason."

"I'm sure Fowler's well down the road by now." Or so he hoped.

She turned to him, her blue eyes serious. "You're probably right. But let's not leave Josh in that café any longer than necessary."

"Go on in with him, Shelby. I can handle this."

She smiled. "Oh, no, you don't. Open up that big truck of yours and I'll be there with our stuff before you know it." She started toward the rental car.

"Oh, no, *you* don't." He fell into step beside her, his boots crunching on the snow. "I'll help you carry. I'm betting that the back seat is piled high."

"You'd win that bet. I wasn't sure how long we'd be gone, so I threw in everything I could think of that Josh might want. His whole toy box, practically. I hope you have room."

"No problem. We can put some in the back of the king cab with him and some in the camper." He held out his arms. "Load me up."

Shelby laughed as she unlocked the back door of

the small sedan. "Gonna pull the big-strong-man routine, are you?"

"A guy has to go with whatever works. Big-strong-man works for me."

"You'll get no argument from me on that. I think big-strong-man is what you do best."

They were flirting with each other, he thought, and they both knew it. He shouldn't be doing that, and soon he'd have to tell her why. He'd hoped to put it off for a while longer, because he'd selfishly enjoyed the spark between them.

She piled toys into his arms—trucks and cars of various sizes, colorful boxes full of games and puzzles, and a whole zoo of stuffed animals. In the process she kept bumping and nudging him, and he didn't think it was accidental. He longed to drop the whole pile and pull her into his arms. He figured she wouldn't mind if he did.

His urges were getting out of hand, so he pretended interest in the toys. "Looks like this kid knows how to have fun."

"Materialistically, he's in good shape." She added more toys to the pile. "My parents used to give me money, lots of money, and ask me to buy the Santa Claus presents."

Boone rested his chin on top of his stack to keep it from toppling. "A grandma who doesn't want to buy presents for a grandkid?" He couldn't picture such a thing. His mother had gone wild buying things for his nieces and nephews.

Shelby gathered an armload of things and kicked the door shut with her foot. "Past tense," she said tightly.

He closed his eyes. Damn. Well, that sure took care of the sexual tension in a hurry. "Sorry," he said.

"Hey, you can't be expected to remember." She started toward his truck. "Even I don't always remember. Ever since the accident, there are times I've been absolutely sure I'll wake up and it'll all be a bad dream."

Boone followed her. He felt helpless and inadequate because he couldn't think of anything to say or do that would ease her pain. In his experience, the only thing that worked at a time like this was simple human contact. More than anything else, Shelby needed to be held. And he was not the man for the job.

When they arrived at his truck, she rested her pile on the hood and turned to him. "Keys?"

Whoops. He should have taken his keys out of his pocket before she loaded him to the chin with toys. "They're, uh, in the right front pocket of my jeans." He felt the heat of a blush rising from his neck to his cheeks, but it was more from guilt than embarrassment. He wanted her to get those keys, wanted her hand sliding into his pocket. He was truly a pig.

She smiled and walked toward him, the teasing, flirty light back in her eyes. "If you were any other man, I'd say you engineered that on purpose."

"I swear I didn't." Not consciously, at least.

"I believe you. Hold still and I'll get the keys." She walked behind him, which allowed her to shove her hand into his pocket the same way he would do it.

The process seemed to take forever. And although the sensation should have been exactly the same as if he'd been digging the keys out himself, it wasn't even close. And he was getting turned on. Very turned on.

"Got 'em." She stepped around in front of him and dangled the keys from her hand. "Now, wasn't that fun?"

His breath caught at the hunger in her eyes. If he tried to kiss her now, she wouldn't stop him. Oh, Lord. "Maybe a little too much fun," he said.

She gazed at him. "Boone, are you attracted to me?" she asked softly.

He swallowed and knew he had to come clean. Especially when she was looking at him like that, with eyes as clear and blue as a mountain lake. "Yep. Unfortunately."

"Unfortunately?" The sparkle faded from her eyes. "Is that because you'd rather not get involved with a woman in my crazy situation?"

"It's not your situation. It's mine."

Her eyes clouded. "Good grief. I should have guessed. You have a girlfriend."

"No, not exactly." He took a deep breath. "But I have…a baby girl."

Her jaw dropped.

He could imagine what she was thinking, and how her glorious picture of him had just shifted to something a lot less flattering. He hated having her think less of him, but truth was truth. "It's complicated. I just found out a few days ago, and I need…that is, I'm not sure what her mother will need…"

"Of course. You don't owe me any explanation whatsoever," she said quickly. "Forget I said anything. Your private life is none of my business." Avoiding his gaze, she held up the keys. "Which one?"

"The one with the round end." He felt completely miserable. "Listen, I do owe you an explanation after what happened last night. You probably think I'm some sex fiend."

"I most certainly do not." She unlocked the door and

started fumbling with the catch that would release the front passenger seat and give him access to the back. "You're human, that's all. There's no crime in that. And you've been more than kind to Josh and me. How foolish of me to start imagining that you—oh, hell! Why can't I figure out this stupid seat?" And she started to cry.

To hell with whether he was the right guy to hold her or not. She needed a shoulder. "Move over," he said.

Turning, she leaned against the truck and covered her face with her hands. "Oh, God." Her body quivered with each muffled sob.

He dumped the armful of toys in the front seat, turned and coaxed her into his arms. "Come here, Shelby."

With a wail of despair she wrapped her arms around him and buried her face against the leather of his jacket.

He held her close, murmuring words of comfort as he stroked her back. Damn, she was tiny. The top of her head, even including the stocking cap she wore, only came to his breastbone. In order to kiss her he'd have to stand her on a box. Not that he intended to kiss her. He'd love to, but it wouldn't be right.

His job was to hold a frightened woman while she cried. She felt so small in his arms that he might have been comforting a kid. Except he knew better. Her breast had felt lush and full in his hand, her bottom nicely rounded and inviting against his groin. It was crazy, considering how different they were in size, but she fit more perfectly into his arms right now than any woman ever had. He could stand here holding her forever.

Slowly her sobs grew weaker and farther apart. At

last she sniffed and rested quietly against him. "I don't suppose you have a handkerchief?"

"Sure." He continued to hold her close with one arm while he reached in his back pocket, pulled out a clean red bandanna and handed it to her.

She took it with a watery chuckle. "This is too perfect. The cowboy who saved me at Yellowstone gave me a red bandanna, too." She blew her nose.

Instantly he was jealous. "What cowboy?"

"When I was seven and on a family vacation, I got lost, and this cowboy was out riding and found me. That probably explains why I have this thing for cowboys."

"Oh." So he was only a generic attraction. His grip on her loosened.

In contrast, hers tightened up. "That came out wrong." She gazed up at him, her nose red and her eyelashes still spiked with tears. "I might have noticed you because you're a cowboy, but now that I know you as a person, I like you because of who you are, not what you are." She managed a smile. "Thank you for letting me get your leather jacket all wet. You're the best, Boone."

He was still stuck back on her earlier comment. "Do you go out with a lot of cowboys, then?"

She looked confused. "Why would you think that?"

"You said you had a *thing* for cowboys."

"Oh." She toyed with a button on his jacket. "That sounds really bad, doesn't it? Like I hang out at country-western bars and pick up anything in a Stetson. The truth is, I haven't gone out, period, not since Josh was born, and I've never dated a cowboy. It's just that you showed up right when I was in trouble, sort of like in

Yellowstone when I was seven and that other cowboy showed up. It made me realize I've always sort of…" She glanced away, her cheeks turning rosy. "Never mind. I talk too much. We need to get the truck loaded." She tried to step back.

He held her captive. "Tell me."

"It's silly. And it has nothing to do with you."

"Tell me anyway." How he loved holding her. Absolutely loved it.

"Okay, but I'm warning you, it'll sound dumb." She took a deep breath and looked up at him again. "I think, subconsciously, I've been wishing my cowboy would come along some day, and sweep me off my feet. Like some girls dream about their Prince Charming. I realize after meeting you that I've been dreaming about my cowboy, who would lift me up to his saddle and we'd ride off into the sunset together. I even wonder if I was headed up to Yellowstone to find him. Well, not him, exactly. He'd be older than dirt by now. But someone like him. Stupid, huh?"

He gazed down at her, a lump in his throat. If he didn't have a baby and obligations waiting for him at the Rocking D, he would kiss Shelby this very minute. He wouldn't need a box. She was so light he'd be able to lift her up. She could wrap her legs around his hips and they could kiss all day like that. And he would sweep her away.

Shelby nodded. "Don't worry, you won't hurt my feelings if you think that's a juvenile fantasy. I know it's not very adult to still believe in fairy tales. I'm working on that."

"No." He shook his head. "Don't work on it. Don't change yourself, Shelby. It's a good dream."

"But it's still just a dream," she said. "I need to focus on reality at the moment."

"I wish you didn't have to. Damn it, I wish I could be your—"

She laid a finger against his lips, silencing him. "It's okay," she whispered.

This time, when she stepped out of his arms, he let her go.

CHAPTER SEVEN

Mason was at a disadvantage trying to watch oncoming traffic for a glimpse of Shelby and Josh, and he hated being at a disadvantage. There was a good chance he'd pass them without knowing it in the split second he'd have to figure out who was in each car. And he felt like a fool for believing the story he'd been fed. He was usually more suspicious of people than that, but those local yokels hadn't seemed smart enough to trick anybody.

When he'd nearly reached the motel without spotting them, he decided he'd have to start his search by getting some straight information from that lying little motel owner about what kind of car the bitch was driving and exactly when she'd left the motel. The scrawny little guy and his overweight wife should be easy enough to intimidate. After all, they were pretty isolated on this lonely stretch of road.

First he'd cruise past the place, though, and get the lay of the land. With luck, no other customers would be around to interfere with the questioning process. If the motel owner knew what was good for him, he'd cooperate. Mason was so damned hungry his stomach hurt. That, on top of being lied to, had put him in a really bad mood.

The first thing he saw as he drove past the place was

a big old king cab sitting in the café parking lot. He vaguely remembered it had been there when he'd left. The second thing he saw nearly made him swerve off the road. That dumb-ass cowboy was standing beside the truck, and unless Mason missed his guess, the little lady in his arms was Shelby.

His heart beat faster. Yep, it was her, all right. He'd seen her in that ski jacket a few times. The two of them seemed oblivious to the world. So *that's* how things were.

She must be mighty grateful to that cowboy. Mason could just imagine how she'd shown her gratitude. He ground his teeth together. Patricia had been a runaround like that, too, ready to trade her sexual favors for whatever she wanted. He'd never trusted her around other guys, not from day one. Well, she'd got what she deserved, and now he intended to get what he deserved.

Josh was nowhere in sight, and Mason wondered if there was any chance he could snatch the kid while these two were pawing each other. Obviously he needed to do a little reconnaissance work.

He continued south until the road curved to the right and he could no longer see the motel in his rearview mirror. Parking carefully on the snowy shoulder, he left the motor running and grabbed his binoculars. The large snowbanks left by the plows gave him good cover while he hiked back to where he could see the motel parking lot.

Damned snow might as well be good for something. In fact, a snowdrift made a perfect bunker, hiding him from passing cars as he crouched down and peered through his binoculars.

What a charming couple. Made him want to hurl, just watching them. He searched the area for Josh and saw no sign of the little brat. But he was somewhere around, sure as the world, probably pestering the café owner for candy or cookies. Mason had that covered. He'd stowed a ton of candy in the Land Rover. Candy was cheap and it usually worked to keep the kid quiet.

The cowboy and Shelby managed to tear themselves away from each other, and Mason watched closely, trying to figure out what was going on. When he realized what they were doing as they loaded things into the big truck, he cursed a blue streak. Damned cowboy was *taking her with him.*

Mason's plan was shot to hell. He could do fine against the bitch, but the cowboy put a whole new spin on things. The guy might be dumb as a post, but he was big. He probably thought of himself as some frigging Sir Galahad, ready to defend Shelby to the death.

The courts would excuse a man for pushing around the woman who'd kidnapped his son. But with the cowboy around, that wouldn't be easy, and although Mason could always use his .45 Magnum to take the big guy out, he'd have a tough time making it look like self-defense.

Maybe, if he studied the situation, he could engineer another accident to get rid of both Shelby and this John Wayne type. He probably couldn't top the genius of that boating accident, though. Even Shelby, who hated his guts, didn't suspect a thing. That had been one slick operation.

Mason kept his binoculars pointed toward the café, and eventually the scrawny motel owner and his fat wife appeared with Josh. A sickening farewell party followed—hugs all around, until it pained Mason to watch them slobber all over each other. That was one thing he'd liked about Patricia's old man and old lady,

besides the obvious advantage that they'd been filthy
rich. They hadn't gone in for all this hugging shit. To
Mason's way of thinking, a hug was wasted energy
unless it counted as foreplay. He'd hug a babe any day
of the week if she looked like she'd put out.

Finally the cowboy buckled Josh into the back seat
and helped Shelby into the front. Couldn't let her climb
in. Oh, no, he had to get his hands on her and lift her
in. Mason swore eloquently. He'd bet the farm those
two had been doing the horizontal hula while he'd been
crammed into a hard plastic booth trying to get some
shut-eye. Somebody would have to pay for that.

Unfortunately it wouldn't be the café owner and his
wife. Mason didn't have time to play with them now.
Maybe another trip. Right now he had to get his butt
back to the Land Rover and follow that truck to
wherever it was going.

The happy little threesome would never guess he
was behind them, either. Patricia never had, in all the
times he'd followed her back when she'd pretended to
be his ever-faithful wife. Too bad he'd never caught her
with one of her lovers, or the divorce settlement would
have looked a hell of a lot different. Yeah, he'd been
shafted then, but he'd even the score this time. All he
had to do was get that kid of his and he'd be on Easy
Street.

"WHEN WE GONNA get there?"

"Oh, Josh." Shelby groaned as the question that had
been asked at least a hundred times in the four hours
they'd been on the road came sailing up from the back
seat yet again.

"Not too much longer," Boone said. His calm tone

betrayed no irritation whatsoever. He acted as if Josh's query was brand-new, interesting and worthy of a reasonable answer. "Maybe a couple of hours. Maybe less, depending on the road conditions."

Shelby had decided Boone Connor was a saint. Nothing else explained his incredible patience with a squirmy three-year-old who'd talked nonstop, it seemed, from the time they'd left the café.

"How long's *that?*" Josh asked.

"Plenty of time for a little nap," Shelby suggested hopefully.

"Naps are for babies," Josh said. "I'm a big boy. Me and Bob, we're gonna ride horsies when we get there. Right, Boone?"

"Tomorrow morning," Boone said. "Don't forget it'll be almost dark when we get there tonight."

"And my snowman could be comin' alive."

"Could be."

"Is Mr. Sloan gonna call us if he comes alive?"

"He might."

"Me and Bob, we can ride horsies in the dark. We gots flashlights."

"Ah, but the horses will be sleeping," Boone said. "All tucked into their warm stalls for the night. You wouldn't want to wake them up, would you?"

"No," Josh said. "But can we see 'em sleeping? Me and Bob, we'd be very, very, very, very quiet." He started whispering. *"Very, very, very quiet."*

"Then maybe we can go down to the barn," Boone said.

"Yay! Yay, yay, yay!" Josh started singing. "We're going to the ba-arn, we're going to the ba-arn, and see the horsies slee-ping." Then he paused. "Now how long is it?"

Shelby sighed. "How about if I read you another book?"

"Nope."

"We'll count cars," Boone said. "And see who wins. I'll take red. Shelby, what color do you want?"

"Green." She flashed him a grateful smile. She'd only taken one car trip with her family, and she wasn't very experienced at coming up with games to play on the road, but Boone seemed to know exactly how to handle Josh's boredom.

"I want black!" Josh said. "Like Batman gots!"

"Oh, how about yellow, Josh?" Shelby said. "You like yellow, don't you?" Although it was silly of her, she'd rather not have Josh pointing out all the black cars on the road. Mason's Land Rover was black, and even though Shelby was convinced he was far away, black vehicles still gave her the willies. She'd rather not have Josh sing out every time he saw one.

"I want black," Josh insisted.

"Then black it is," Shelby said, not wanting to argue about it.

The game was a success, giving Josh a chance to show his hero Boone that he knew his colors and his numbers. Shelby and Josh were tied at six each, with Boone trailing with four.

"Seven!" Josh shouted.

"Where?" A chill went down Shelby's spine as it had each time Josh had pointed out a car, until she was able to see it and make sure it wasn't a Land Rover. She craned her neck. "I don't see a black car."

"I seed it. Seven."

"I don't see it, either, buddy," Boone said. "Was it going the other way?"

"It was up there." Josh pointed up toward Boone's rearview mirror.

Shelby had a sick feeling in the pit of her stomach as she turned and looked back down the road behind them. "I still don't see it."

"It's gone," Josh said. "But it counts, right?"

"Sure, it counts." Shelby continued with the game, but she kept glancing in the rearview mirror, looking for that black car Josh had seen. She pictured a big Cadillac driven by a retired couple who were cruising along under the speed limit. Or an old junker limping down the road as best it could. Anything but a Land Rover.

Eventually she realized Josh had stopped counting the cars. She glanced back and saw that he'd fallen asleep. "He's finally conked out," she murmured to Boone. "You've been extremely tolerant."

Boone smiled. "He's just a normal kid. That's kind of amazing, all things considered."

"I know. I give thanks every day that he hasn't been warped by what he's been through."

"I'll bet you're the one who can take credit for that, Shelby."

She shrugged. "I think it's Josh. He was born with a sunny disposition, and even if life knocks him down, he smiles and gets right back up." She clenched her hands together in her lap. "At least he has so far. If Mason gets ahold of him, I'm not sure how long that resiliency will last."

"You were worried about that mysterious black car Josh saw, weren't you?"

"Yeah." She took a deep breath and blew it out. "Mason drives a black Land Rover."

"I know. Eugene told me."

Shelby felt an overwhelming attack of conscience. "Boone, you have no business getting involved in this. I should never have agreed to it. What if Mason isn't on his way up to Wyoming? What if he somehow figured out what we've done, and that was his Land Rover Josh saw in the rearview mirror?"

"All the more reason for you to be with me."

"But don't you see?" Shelby gazed at the determined clench of Boone's jaw. He was too noble for his own good. "You don't deserve to be sucked into whatever scenario Mason has in mind. He's a violent man, and I don't know what he might do. You shouldn't put yourself in harm's way for somebody you don't even know."

He sent her a long look. "The fact is, I would do the same for a stranger. But I don't think of you as a stranger. Maybe that's how you think of me, though."

"No. No, I don't." She gazed back at him, instantly filled with remorse. She'd hurt his feelings, which was the last thing on earth she wanted to do. "I think of you as a friend," she said. "An incredibly generous friend. And that's why I'm concerned about you getting involved. I'm not in the habit of dragging my friends into nasty situations. I really thought Mason would head down the road to Wyoming and you'd never have to deal with him. Now I'm not so sure."

"Just concentrate on Josh," Boone said gently. "Do what's best for that little boy, and you'll be making the right decision."

She had no doubt that meant sticking close to Boone. "Even if I impose horribly on you in the process?"

"I'll let you know if you're imposing on me," he said. "So far you're not even close."

"You're too good." She shook her head in wonder. "You must have been raised in a warm and loving family, to have such a generous heart."

"Warm and loving, so long as my dad was sober. If he was drunk, all hell broke lose and the smart ones ducked for cover."

Shelby took a moment to digest that information. Somehow she'd imagined Boone with a golden childhood, light years away from her cold and isolated upbringing. "That must have been rough, growing up like that," she said softly.

He grimaced. "Sometimes. And you'd think I'd have learned how the bottle changes a man. But no, I had to get myself plastered and prove I could be an idiot under the influence, too."

"Oh, Boone, I can't picture you doing anything bad, drunk or sober."

"How about having sex and not using any protection?"

"People get carried away sometimes." The thought of Boone getting carried away thrilled her to her toes. "I can imagine how that might happen. You're so—" She stopped herself before she said something really embarrassing.

"I'm lower than a snake, is what I am. Jessica was only trying to be kind to me, and I repaid her by making her pregnant. I don't blame her for not telling me once she found out. She probably wasn't sure she wanted me around the baby."

Shelby laid her hand on Boone's arm. He was trembling. "Listen, I don't know this woman or her thought processes, but I do know you. I would trust you with any child, of any age. She should, too."

"Then why did she name Sebastian and Travis as

godfathers?" He gripped the steering wheel so hard his knuckles grew white. "Because she wanted them to keep an eye on me when she couldn't be there to do it, that's why."

"She's not at the ranch?"

"Not right now."

"Where is she?" Shelby was woman enough to admit being relieved that Jessica wouldn't be there when they arrived. She'd been bracing herself for meeting the woman who had carried Boone's child. She hadn't been looking forward to it.

"She has some sort of problem, and she didn't want the baby to be part of it. She dropped Elizabeth off at the Rocking D two months ago."

"*Two months?* How old is this baby?"

"She'd be four months now, going on five."

"She hasn't seen her baby in more than two months?" Even Patricia wouldn't have pulled something like that, Shelby thought, and Patricia had definitely foisted Josh on Shelby at every opportunity.

"No, but she calls every once in awhile, Sebastian said. Short calls, asking if Elizabeth's okay. Something must have really scared her and made her think the baby would be in danger if they stuck together."

"Well, that I can understand." Thinking back, Shelby now realized that some of Patricia's "neglect" might have been a way to keep Josh out of harm's way. But not all of it. Patricia had once admitted Mason tricked her into getting pregnant to get another hold over her. She'd never really wanted a child.

"Sebastian and Travis have hired a private detective to find Jessica," Boone said. "When we get there I'm going to take over that expense and do whatever else I can."

"I'm amazed you didn't hightail it up there two months ago."

"I would have. Jessica wrote letters asking all three of us—me, Sebastian and Travis—to be Elizabeth's godfathers, but my letter got delayed."

"Wait a minute." Shelby was having a hard time sorting this out. "She didn't specifically name you as the father?"

"No, but I know it's me, even if I don't remember exactly what happened that night."

Shelby gazed at him. "You mean you don't remember…the, um, act itself?"

A ruddy stain crept up his neck. "Nope. And that's pitiful. Shows you what drink can do to a man."

"Well, I don't have a lot of experience in this area, but I always thought that the more a man drank, the less he could…perform, so to speak."

"But I'm Irish."

Shelby laughed. "Sorry," she said, quickly composing herself. "I know this isn't a laughing matter. But I don't see what being Irish has to do with it."

"An Irishman can do anything drunk that he can do sober. He just might not remember it afterwards."

"I see." Shelby couldn't help smiling at Boone's sturdy belief in his inherited abilities. She could see that arguing with him wouldn't do any good, but she also wondered if he was truly this baby's father. Her heart grew a little lighter with the knowledge that he might not be.

"At any rate, don't go thinking I'm doing all this for you and Josh. I'm doing it for me, too."

"How do you figure?"

He glanced her way, and his green eyes were troubled. "By helping you, I can try to convince myself I'm not such a bad guy, after all."

"Boone." She squeezed his arm. Touching him gave her such pleasure that she felt guilty using comfort as an excuse. "You are not a bad guy. You are so not a bad guy."

"Thanks, Shelby." He sighed. "All I know is, I have to do right by Jessica, if she can forgive me, and that little baby of mine."

"I'm sure you will." Shelby longed to ask Boone exactly what he meant by that, but she didn't want to pry into something that was really none of her business. Still, she might make it her business, if she could determine one critical point in this situation. The most important thing about Jessica, from Shelby's viewpoint, was whether or not Boone was in love with her.

CHAPTER EIGHT

THE CLOSER Boone got to the Rocking D, the more his thoughts seemed like a bed of hot coals. One concern would flare up and he'd worry about that for a while until another one began to flicker and glow, drawing his attention. For one thing, he worried about whether Elizabeth would like the set of blocks he'd brought her. He would have rather made his own set, but he hadn't had the time.

Then he worried about whether Elizabeth would like *him*. She'd had more than two months to get used to Sebastian. As for Travis—well, Travis would have won her over in five minutes. Travis had a gift that way. But Boone was afraid he'd scare her with his size and his big hands.

When Boone wasn't thinking about Elizabeth and how that mess would turn out, he worried about whether he could keep Josh from ending up with Mason Fowler. He was as committed to that cause now as Shelby.

Like Shelby, he had an uneasy suspicion that Fowler might be tailing them. Boone had spent a fair share of time checking the rearview mirror, but he hadn't noticed a black Land Rover. A couple of times while going up a hill he'd thought maybe a vehicle behind them could have been the Land Rover, but it had been too far away to be sure, and he hadn't wanted to worry Shelby.

Taking her and Josh to the Rocking D was the one thing Boone was positive about, the one thing that didn't worry him at all. From the Rocking D, with Sebastian and Travis as potential backups, Boone believed he had his best chance to defend the woman and the boy. Out here on the road wasn't a good place to make a stand.

Fowler struck him as a survivalist type who might have practiced the art of following a vehicle without being seen. The guy probably had more than one gun and maybe even an assault rifle. But if he needed to have custody of Josh in order to get any money, he wouldn't be mowing anybody down with his firepower.

He might have wanted Shelby to run. Boone had thought about that some, too, after Shelby had mentioned the possibility. Fowler might have decided that in order to cinch his chances of getting the kid, he had to make Shelby look bad. So he'd scared her into taking off. Then he could look like a frantic father if he chased her down and took his kid back.

But he hadn't counted on Boone.

Shelby would be safe from Mason at the Rocking D. Boone hoped she'd be safe from him. The thought of making love to her never left his mind for long. Riding in the truck together for most of the day hadn't helped. But they wouldn't have much opportunity to be alone with so many people around the ranch. He was counting on that to keep him honest.

"It's black as pitch out here," Shelby said as they traveled down the dirt road that led to the turnoff to the ranch. "How do you know where you're going?"

"Habit," Boone said. He kept his voice low so he wouldn't wake Josh, who was still asleep in his car seat. "I've based my horseshoeing operation at the Rocking D every summer for the past nine years."

"So that's how long you've known your friend, the one who owns the ranch?"

"Yep." He loved Shelby's voice. It had a musical sound to it, and her slight Texas accent made her sound sexy, no matter what she said.

"How'd you meet him?" she asked.

"I came to the ranch drumming up business. I was living out of my camper, and Sebastian and his wife were scraping by at the time. Sebastian offered me a place to stay if I'd cut him a deal on the shoes every year. That's how it started."

"Wait a minute. Didn't you tell me Sebastian's a newlywed?"

"Yeah. He and his first wife got a divorce about three years back. He just married his neighbor, Matty."

"Okay. Sebastian and Matty." Shelby paused as if committing the names to memory. "What do they look like?"

"Matty's small and blond, like you." *But not stacked like you are,* he thought, but decided that wouldn't be a good thing to mention. "She's the no-nonsense type. Can rope and ride as well as a man. Sebastian's hair is…brown, I guess. He's built pretty solid, but he's not as tall as me."

"Got it," Shelby said. "And what about your other friend? What does he do?"

"Travis? He used to be Matty's head wrangler, but now he works for both Matty and Sebastian, I guess."

"Didn't you say he was getting married tomorrow?"

"Yeah." Boone chuckled. "Never thought I'd see the day, either. He's quite a lady's man. Good dancer, quick with a joke. He used to walk around saying, 'So many women, so little time.' But according to Sebastian, he really fell hard for Gwen Hawthorne." Boone hadn't considered it before, but he was glad Travis had a woman. That way he wouldn't make a play for Shelby.

"And what does Gwen look like?"

"Near as I remember, she's tall with dark hair. Looks sort of like an Indian princess. I think maybe there's some Cheyenne in her background. She runs a bed-and-breakfast in Huerfano."

"That little town we just went through, right?"

"Yep."

"I liked it," Shelby said. "The way people are fixing up those turn-of-the-century houses is nice."

"Gwen's place, Hawthorne House, is one of those. Skiing and tourism saved Huerfano," Boone said. "Used to be a booming mining town, but the mines played out. The ranches around here couldn't keep a town going, but tourists can."

"I've never thought of living in a small town before, but if I get custody of Josh—"

"You mean *when* you get custody of Josh," Boone said. Any other possibility would be obscene.

"Okay, *when* I get custody of Josh." She sighed and leaned her head against the seat. "You have no idea what it means to me, having you on my side, Boone. I haven't felt as if I had anybody on my side ever since the accident."

He glanced over at her. In the faint light from the dash she looked beautiful, but pale and vulnerable, too. She needed him, and how he longed to be everything she needed, in every way. But he couldn't. "Don't you have a lawyer?"

"Yeah, my parents' lawyer. He loves to paint the 'worst case scenario' as he puts it, which involves Mason winning full custody and me only getting limited visiting rights. He seems to relish reminding me that judges are usually fathers and will quite possibly side with Mason in this case. My parents picked a real crepe hanger for a lawyer. He's a cold fish, just like they—" She turned to him, her eyes wide. "Forget I said that. My God, they just *died.* I have no right to—"

"Sure you do," he said gently. He reached over and took her hand, thinking that any person would do the same. Taking her hand wasn't a sexual thing. The problem was that once he had her hand in his, he wanted to bring it to his lips. He wanted to pull the truck over to the side of the road and kiss her. Really kiss her.

But he didn't.

"My parents didn't know any better." Shelby held tight to his hand. "Somebody, maybe my grandparents, taught them that money and prestige were everything. They taught Patricia the same thing."

"But not you." He rubbed a thumb over the delicate bones in the back of her hand and wondered if a big guy like him could make love to her without doing damage. Of course, he'd never find out.

"I've always been the different one in the family," Shelby said. "I never quite fitted in, never liked getting all dressed up and going to fancy parties, never wanted a career in the limelight. Maybe that was because I wasn't the pretty one, but—"

"Are you crazy?"

She turned toward him. "You mean because I blew a chance to be part of high society?"

"Not that! You just said you weren't the pretty one!

You're—" He suddenly realized he'd gotten loud and was about to tell her she was beautiful, gorgeous, sexy. "You're very pretty," he said quietly, grateful for the darkened interior of the truck so she wouldn't see the hunger in his eyes.

"Shebby's *bootiful*," Josh said from the back seat.

"Listen to the kid," Boone murmured, wishing he could speak as freely as the three-year-old about his feelings for Shelby. "He knows what he's talking about."

"You're both embarrassing me." She eased her hand out of Boone's grasp.

The minute Shelby took her hand from his, Boone felt disconnected from an important energy source. He longed to feel that power surge again, and he had to stop himself from reclaiming her hand. Uh-oh. He was starting to need Shelby McFarland.

Shelby turned toward the back seat. "How long have you been awake back there?"

"I dunno. I heared you talking. When are we gonna get there? Me and Bob, we gots to go potty."

Boone spotted the entrance to the ranch looming up ahead. "How about if we're almost there? How's that?"

"We're there? Really there?"

"See those two poles with another pole across the top?" Boone asked.

"Yep!"

"That's the main gate. There's a sign hanging down from the top pole. You might not be able to read it in the dark, but it says Rocking D Ranch, and it has Sebastian's brand on either side."

"Brand? What's that?"

"His special sign. He stamps it on all the cows that

he owns, and on a few other things around the ranch, too." Boone decided not to get into the details of branding cows. Truth be told, Boone had never much liked the process, himself, which was why he was a blacksmith and not a cattleman.

"What's it look like?" Josh asked.

"It's a letter D sitting sideways on top of a curved line, like the rocker on a rocking chair. The whole thing looks kind of like a cradle."

Josh thought about that for a while. "I know my ABCs," he announced. "Wanna hear?"

"Sure." Boone welcomed the distraction. Up ahead was Elizabeth, his little baby girl. His stomach clenched.

Josh began to sing the alphabet song, but he only got to the letter M before he interrupted himself. "Lights!" he chortled. "I see a house!"

Shelby let out a long breath. "Oh, Boone, what a lovely place. You didn't tell me it was made of peeled logs. And a stone chimney with smoke coming out. Could anything be more welcoming?"

"It's a nice house," Boone said as he parked behind Travis's shiny black rig. He was so nervous he thought he might be sick. Thank God he had Shelby and Josh with him. They helped calm him down a little.

"It's a *great* house," Josh said.

Boone unbuckled his seat belt. "Sebastian planted those aspens in the front." He noticed the aspens were taller than last year. He'd missed this place, but the rush of homecoming he always felt was overshadowed by a bad case of nerves. "You can't see the mountains too well when it's this dark, but Sebastian gets a real pretty view from here."

"I can see them," Shelby said. "Just barely."

"Me, too!" Josh exclaimed.

"I can hardly wait for morning," Shelby added, "so I can see everything better. Josh, this is a little bit like Yellowstone, with the mountains and the trees and everything."

"Do you gots geezers?" Josh asked.

"No, afraid not." Boone smiled, despite his nervousness. "But you could ask Sebastian about it. Tell him you're looking for geezers." Boone liked to kid Sebastian about his age. He'd just turned thirty-five, which made him the oldest of the bunch, and nobody ever let him forget it, either.

"Where's the horsies?" Josh asked.

"Down in the barn." Boone opened his door and drew in a lungful of cool, clean air scented with pine. "We'll go take a look in a little while, after you go potty and get some chow into you."

"Can't we see 'em *now?* Bob wants to see 'em now."

"No, Josh," Shelby said. "It wouldn't be polite to rush down there. We need to go in and meet Boone's friends first."

Boone rounded the truck and helped Shelby down. He wished he could just hold on to her for a little while. He knew holding Shelby would steady him.

She rested her hands on his arms. "Are you okay?"

"Sure."

"But you're shaking."

"Nervous about the baby, I guess."

She squeezed his arms. "It'll be fine, Boone. I—"

"Gots to go *pot-ty,*" Josh sang out from the back seat.

"Let's get him out," Boone said. He'd barely lifted

the little boy to the ground when a commotion came
from the house. He turned as people and dogs erupted
out of the front door. They surged across the porch and
down the steps toward Boone's truck.

"They gots doggies, too!" Josh cried in delight.

"Big doggies," Shelby said as she scooped Josh up
in her arms.

"Hey, Boone!" Sebastian was in the lead, a huge
smile on his face. "Where you been, boy? Can't believe
a little snow would slow you down!"

"I tried to talk my way through it." Boone clasped
Sebastian's hand as Fleafarm, Sebastian's mixed breed,
and Sadie, Matty's Great Dane, danced happily around
him, panting and barking.

Boone's glance moved to Matty close on Sebastian's
heels, and Travis and Gwen calling out greetings as
they brought up the rear. Nobody was holding a baby.
Elizabeth must be taking a nap or something. He was
relieved. He'd have a little more time to prepare himself.

"I'd like you all to meet Shelby McFarland," Boone
said. He quite naturally put an arm around her shoulders to guide her forward and it sure felt right, as if he
was bringing his sweetheart home to meet his friends.
Which of course he wasn't, and he'd do well to
remember that. "And this here's Josh," he added.

"Pleased to meet you," Sebastian said, his smile wide
but his gaze assessing.

"Thank you for having us on such short notice and
in the midst of all your activities," Shelby said.

"Wouldn't have it any other way," Sebastian said.
Then he glanced back over his shoulder. "Matty? There
you are." He scooped her in next to him. "This is my
wife, Matty," he said with obvious pride.

"Welcome to the Rocking D, Josh and Shelby," Matty said. Her smile was as bright as her husband's, but she gave Shelby and Josh the once-over, too. Then she glanced at Boone. "Do I get a hug, big guy?"

"You bet." Boone embraced her warmly. "Congratulations, Matty. Wish I'd been here for the ceremony."

"Yeah, yeah, yeah. Break it up, break it up." Travis appeared and clapped Boone on the shoulder. "At least you're here for mine." He tipped his Stetson in Shelby's direction. "Though I can see why you might want to dawdle and keep this beautiful woman to yourself. Pleased to meet you, Shelby. You, too, Josh." He caught Gwen by the hand and pulled her close. "You remember this lovely lady, right, Boone?"

"Sure do." Boone touched the brim of his hat. "Good to see you, Gwen. And this here's Shelby and Josh."

"I'm glad to meet both of you," Gwen said. Her expression was friendly, but as openly curious as Matty and Sebastian's had been. "How was your trip?"

"Good, thanks to Boone," Shelby said, glancing at him. "He kept Josh entertained the whole way."

"We counted cars," Josh said. "And I winned. But now me and Bob gots to go potty."

"I'll bet you do." Matty stepped forward and put her arm around Shelby. "Let's get you both inside," she said, guiding them toward the porch. "The guys can bring the stuff in."

"You're probably both starving, too." Gwen fell into step on the other side of Shelby and the dogs pranced at her heels. "And you might even be able to use a glass of wine, Shelby."

"Sounds wonderful," Shelby said.

"You gots lemonade?" Josh asked.

"I think we can find some," Matty said.

Boone watched them hustle Shelby and Josh into the house and felt displaced. He was glad they'd welcomed them into the group and were taking such good care of them, but damn it, he'd gotten used to the job.

"Who's Bob?" Sebastian glanced around the yard.

"Josh's imaginary friend," Boone said, gazing after them. "The way Josh talks, you'd think he really existed. We always have to make sure we include Bob in everything."

"We?" Travis asked. "Sounds cozy."

Boone whipped around to face him and knew he was blushing. "I didn't mean it like that. It's just that we've all been together since last night, and I—"

"Easy, big fella." Sebastian rested a hand on Boone's shoulder. "She's a nice girl. I can see why you're interested."

"I'm *not* interested. I'm only helping her out!"

"That's not the way it looks from where I'm standing," Travis said. "I say you're interested. And so's she."

"That's ridiculous," Boone said. "I can't be interested, and you know it."

"I do? What, you took a vow of celibacy I don't know about?"

"Yeah," Sebastian said. "Darlene's out of the picture, so why can't you be interested?"

Boone stared at both of them. "Don't be dense. Because of Jessica. And the baby."

Sebastian and Travis exchanged a look. Then Sebastian turned to Boone. "You're not assuming you're Elizabeth's father, are you?"

"Of course I'm assuming it. Which means I have an obligation to Jessica."

Travis laughed and shook his head. "I can't believe this."

"It's not funny!"

Sebastian grinned. "Yeah, it is. Travis and I have dealt with the same damned thing you're putting yourself through. Both of us almost missed a chance for happiness with the women we love because we convinced ourselves we had an obligation to Jessica."

Boone squared his shoulders. "In the first place, I'm not even close to being in love with Shelby." He felt a twinge of guilt. He was lying to his two best friends. "Second of all, you don't have an obligation to Jessica, because you're not the baby's father. But I am, so I do."

Travis sighed and glanced at Sebastian. "Well, maybe he's going to have to find out the hard way, like we did. It'd be nice to think a man was willing to take his best friends' advice, but that's obviously not the case. I think we're flapping our gums for nothing, Sebastian."

"Could be."

"Look, you two, there is nothing going on between Shelby and me," Boone said. Another twinge of guilt.

"Oh, there is most definitely something going on," Sebastian said. "The question is whether you're going to be smart enough to take advantage of the fact. Come on, let's get your gear out of the truck, or my chicken dinner is going to be overcooked before we're ready to eat it."

CHAPTER NINE

THE INSIDE of the ranch house was so cozy, Shelby sighed with delight. Matty took their coats and directed them to the bathroom down the hall. Then she and Gwen left to organize drinks for everyone, including wine for Shelby and lemonade for Josh.

On her way through the living room, Shelby took appreciative notice of everything. The furniture was the kind that could withstand dogs and children and big men wearing dusty jeans. A wing chair and an old rocker flanked a wear-polished leather sofa, and a sturdy wooden coffee table sat in front of it.

The house not only looked comfortable, it smelled that way, too—a homey combination of cedar crackling in the fireplace, chicken in the oven and sweet peas in a jug on the coffee table.

So this is what a real home feels like. Shelby contrasted it with her parents' showplace in San Antonio. After growing up in a formal atmosphere, Shelby had known what she didn't want. Seeing this rustic, comfortable room, she finally knew what she did want.

A light was on in a bedroom at the end of the hall, and Shelby heard a baby coo, followed by the low murmur of a woman's voice. Shelby's stomach rolled. *Jessica.*

She hustled Josh into the bathroom, flipped on the light

and closed the door. Then she leaned against it and fought for breath. Suddenly this perfect house wasn't so perfect anymore. She felt like crying. For a few precious minutes she'd imagined herself fitting into this world of Boone's, and she'd loved the feeling. But if Jessica had arrived, that could only mean one thing. She was here to see Boone. And Boone would have no more time for Shelby.

"Shebby?" Josh stared up at her.

She gazed down at the little boy and quickly whipped her priorities into order. This whole trip wasn't about her, it was about Josh. If Boone stopped paying attention to him because of Jessica and the baby, he'd be devastated. She'd have to be ready to compensate, as she always had.

"You look like you been runnin'," Josh said.

"It's the altitude," she said, taking a deep breath.

"You gots a bad altitude?"

She couldn't help smiling. "*Al*titude," she said. "That means we're up in the mountains, which is a higher altitude than down in San Antonio. There's less oxygen up here, so that sometimes makes it a little harder to catch your breath."

"What's ox-gin?"

"Something in the air that helps you breathe. Come on, Josh, we'd better tend to business, here." She walked over and put up the toilet seat.

"It's *wood*, Shebby."

"Oak. Yes, it is." She started to help him pull down his sweats and underpants.

"I'll do it." He shoved her gently aside. "Boone showed me how to get my wee-wee out. Look. I don't gots to take my pants off. They gots a hole. See?"

"I see. Good for you." She swallowed a lump in her

throat. How much longer would Boone be available to coach Josh in the art of being a boy? Maybe the end had already come.

BOONE, Sebastian and Travis trooped into the house. Travis had insisted on taking all Josh's toys and Sebastian had Shelby and Josh's suitcases, so Boone had been left to carry only his duffel. Since nothing had been said about the baby, Boone finally decided he'd have to ask. "Where's Elizabeth?"

"Still back with Luann, I guess," Sebastian said over his shoulder. He glanced at Matty who had just come in the living room with a tray of drinks. "Where do you want us to put everything?"

"Luann?" Boone set his duffel down, not sure where he'd be sleeping yet. "What'd you do, hire a nanny?" He'd veto that quick. He didn't want his baby taken care of by strangers.

"Luann's my mother," Travis said. "Cool toys we have here, Sebastian. We can have ourselves some fun with—"

"Your *mother?*" Boone interrupted. "You never said anything about a mother. Where's she been all this time?"

"In Utah." Travis's answer was nonchalant. "I see drinks are being served. Let's unload this stuff and party. Matty? What goes where?"

Matty set down the tray on the coffee table. "I thought we'd put—"

"Wait a minute," Boone said. "Do you mean to tell me, Travis, that when you went to Utah every winter, and we thought you were off playing with ski bunnies for six months, you were going to stay with your *mother?*"

"That's it," Sebastian put in before Travis could answer. "Hotshot pulled the wool over our eyes. Every winter he'd go home and take care of his mommy, like the good boy he is."

"Hey, there *were* a few ski bunnies!" Travis protested as well as he could, considering his chin was anchoring the pile of toys in his arms. "You're ruining my rep, here!"

Gwen came into the room with a bowl of chips and another of salsa. "You're getting married tomorrow. You don't need your rep anymore."

"I was a legend in Utah," Travis muttered. "No single woman was safe. That's my story and I'm sticking to it."

Matty chuckled. "Getting bridegroom jitters, Travis?"

"Not me. Just want to make sure the record's straight. Now, much as I'd love to stand around discussing my love life, these toys are heavier than they look. Where do they go?"

"I thought we'd put Josh back in with Elizabeth and I made up the daybed in Sebastian's office for Shelby."

Shelby and Josh reappeared at that moment. Josh went immediately to the rag rug by the fireplace where both dogs had plopped down. He began murmuring happily to them and rubbing their heads.

Shelby, however, glanced in obvious dismay at the load Travis and Sebastian were bringing in. "Boy, that's sure a pile of stuff. I promise we're not moving in, although you'd certainly think so."

Boone took a closer look at Shelby. Something about her had changed. When they'd first arrived, she'd seemed so happy to be here, but at the moment she didn't seem happy at all. He tried to catch her eye, but she seemed to be avoiding his gaze.

"Kids need a lot of things," Matty said. "Don't worry about it."

"See?" Boone said. "I told you it wouldn't be a problem."

Still Shelby wouldn't look at him. "I feel as if I've invaded your home," she said to Matty.

"Welcome invasion, if you ask me," Travis said. "Lizzie's toys were getting boring." He started down the hall. "I'll tell Mom to get a move on. She's probably fussing over every little ribbon, trying to make Lizzie perfect for her new audience."

Shelby's head snapped around and she stared down the hall after Travis. "Did he say *mom?*"

"Yeah, he did," Sebastian said as he passed her carrying her suitcase and Josh's. "Luann's been in there for the past hour dolling Elizabeth up."

Shelby turned to gaze at Boone with a smile, and the haunted look was gone from her eyes. "Travis's mom."

"Yeah." Boone didn't know what had caused Shelby to relax again, but he was glad she had. "I guess she's moved here from Utah. I didn't know—"

"Oh, that's wonderful," Shelby said in a breathless rush. Her smile widened. "Absolutely wonderful."

"I guess so." He thought it was okay, and probably nice for Travis, but he couldn't figure out why Shelby was so excited about the prospect. Still, he was glad she looked normal again.

Matty glanced over at him. "Is the couch okay for now?"

"Sure." He had no problem giving up his usual bed in Sebastian's office to Shelby.

Shelby's happy smile faded. "Oh, dear. I'll bet you usually sleep on that daybed, don't you?"

He shrugged. "Doesn't matter."

"I don't want to take your bed."

Josh glanced up from petting the dogs. "Let's all sleep together!" he said. "Like last night! We can cuddle."

Shelby sent Boone a horrified look. He became aware that Matty and Gwen were studying him, and he could feel the heat climbing up from his collar.

"It wasn't the way it sounds," Shelby said quickly, filling the silence. "Boone was sleeping in the chair, but the heat went out, and Josh was getting cold, so Boone came in with us, for more body heat, and…" Her voice trailed off, and now *her* cheeks were pink, too.

Boone felt responsible for her being embarrassed. If he hadn't groped her in bed this morning, she'd probably be able to tell the story without blushing. As it was, Matty and Gwen had apparently figured out something was going on, judging from their smug expressions. They probably had the same idea Sebastian and Travis did, that Boone was coupled up with Shelby. For everybody's sake, he needed to squash that notion.

"You know, maybe I'll sleep in the barn," he said.

"We don't have dormitory rules here," Matty said, her blue eyes sparkling. "You can sleep wherever you want, Boone."

"I wanna sleep in the barn!" Josh scrambled to his feet and ran over to Boone to gaze up at him. "Can I sleep in the barn with you and the horsies?"

"Actually, Josh," Matty said, "I really was hoping you'd be willing to sleep in Elizabeth's room. She's so little, and she gets lonesome in there. She needs a big strong boy to keep her company."

"She does?"

"Ready or not," Travis called as he came back down the hall. "He-rrre's Lizzie!"

Boone had been so absorbed in trying to help Shelby out of an embarrassing moment, he'd forgotten the baby was coming. He turned toward the hallway, his gut clenching.

A gray-haired, wiry woman dressed in jeans and a sweatshirt walked in holding…an angel. Boone stared, speechless with wonder at the vision in pink ruffles. She had little pink ribbons tied in her soft brown hair, and little pink booties on her feet. Her creamy skin and tiny pink mouth looked too perfect to be real.

She turned her head and looked right at Boone.

He gazed into those eyes, so like his father's blue-gray ones. She stared at him with such seriousness, such complete attention, almost as if she *knew* him. His doubts faded away. Elizabeth was his.

"Hey, Lizzie." Travis walked over toward the baby. "Show Boone what you can do. Come on, like I taught you."

The baby stuck out her little tongue and blew a juicy raspberry at him.

The males in the room, including Josh, all laughed.

"Atta girl!" Grinning, Travis scooped her out of his mother's arms. "Awesome."

"Honestly, Travis," Luann said. "Teaching that sweet little girl tricks like that. You ought to be ashamed of yourself. And it doesn't help that you boys laugh at her, either. You're setting a bad example." She glanced pointedly at Josh.

Travis seemed unfazed. "I figure Lizzie will need that trick someday. Mom, I'd like you to meet Boone Connor, the blacksmith for the Rocking D and some of the other ranches around the valley. And this pretty lady is Shelby McFarland, who rode up here with Boone. And the little guy is Josh. Folks, this slightly square but basically lovable woman is my mom, Luann Evans."

Boone tipped his hat to Luann. "Pleased to meet you, ma'am." He held Luann's gaze for as long as necessary to be polite, but quickly his attention returned to Travis holding that baby. The little girl reminded him of cotton candy, all pink and sweet-smelling. Sure, she was drooling a bit, but that only made her cuter. He wanted to hold her, but he was afraid he'd goof it up.

"I'm glad to meet you, too, Mrs. Evans." Shelby stood and shepherded Josh over toward Travis's mother. "Josh, can you shake the nice lady's hand?"

"Yep. But I wish I had a hat, like Boone. Then I could touch my hat 'stead of shaking hands."

Distracted as he was by watching Elizabeth, Boone took note of the comment and promised himself he'd see about a hat for Josh in the next couple of days. If the boy was going to ride a horse, then he needed a hat. Maybe boots, too.

"Please call me Luann," Travis's mother said as she leaned down to shake Josh's hand.

"Are you a gramma?" Josh asked.

Josh's innocent question was met with silence, and Boone realized that was probably a touchy subject, considering the battle to claim this baby. As he tried to think how to smooth over the moment, everyone started talking at once. Travis insisted that his mother was indeed a gramma, while Sebastian said the jury was still out on that, although he appreciated all Luann had done. Gwen said at the very least Luann was an honorary gramma, and Matty added that Elizabeth needed all the grammas she could get, so why not?

"My gramma's in heaven," Josh said. The announcement splashed like a bucket of water over the heated discussion, and everybody stopped arguing immediately as they all turned to gaze sympathetically at the little boy.

Everyone except Boone. He looked at Shelby, to see how the comment was affecting her. She met his gaze, and his heart ached as he watched the emotions raging in her blue eyes. Then she swallowed, and sent him a shaky smile. She wanted to let him know she was okay. It was all he could do to keep from crossing the room and taking her in his arms.

Of all the others in the room, Luann recovered herself first. She crouched down in front of Josh, and her voice was gentle. "In that case, how about if you call me Gramma Luann?"

Boone decided then and there that Luann Evans was all right.

"'Kay," Josh said hesitantly. "But do I gots to wear a tie?"

"A tie?" Luann glanced questioningly at Shelby.

"He means a necktie," Shelby cleared her throat. "My…mother liked him to dress up when he went anywhere with them."

Boone's heart squeezed. Poor little shaver, expected to dress up at this young age, just as Shelby had been forced to do when she was a kid. He didn't like to think ill of the dead, but he had a hard time thinking well of Shelby's parents, from what he'd heard so far.

"No, Josh," Luann said. "You don't have to wear a tie. Are you hungry?"

"Yep. Kinda hungry. They gots chips over there."

"I see those, but I was thinking of something like peanut-butter toast."

"I *love* that. Bob, he loves it, too."

Luann studied Josh for a moment and then she smiled. "I'll bet Bob is your special friend."

Boone exchanged another quick glance with Shelby, and this time her smile was brighter. Boone gave her a discreet thumbs-up sign. He was damned impressed that Luann had tuned into the Bob thing so fast. He could see the advantages of having an experienced mother around. Maybe that's why Shelby had been so excited when she'd found out Travis's mother was here.

Josh's eyes lit up. "Yep, he is my special friend! How'd you know?"

"Well, because Travis had a special friend when he was about your age. He always dressed in orange and pink, and his name was—"

"Mom."

Boone couldn't believe that Travis, the ever-cool studman, was blushing. Sebastian was doing his level best to keep from laughing, and Gwen and Matty seemed to suddenly find the pattern in the rag rug very interesting.

"Well, never mind," Luann said, glancing at her son with a grin. "I'll tell you all about it in the kitchen. Let's go make some peanut-butter toast for you and Bob." She stood and held out her hand.

Josh looked from Luann's outstretched hand to the baby girl in Travis's arms. "Can that baby come, too?"

No, Boone thought. *Not until I've had a chance to—*

"I think that's an excellent idea," Luann said. "Then you two can get acquainted."

"Can she play trucks?" Josh asked, clearly fascinated by the baby.

"Not yet," Luann said. "But she loves peekaboo."

"I can play that!" Josh's eyes shone with eagerness.

"It's settled, then." Luann retrieved Elizabeth from Travis, and with the baby propped on her hip and Josh holding her other hand, she walked back to the kitchen.

"Maybe she likes pirate ships," Josh chattered as he skipped along. "I gots a pirate ship, too. And little people. Me and Bob, we play pirates a lot."

Both dogs lifted their heads, lumbered to their feet and followed the three into the kitchen.

"Bless your mother, Travis," Shelby said after they'd left.

"Oh, she's a peach, that mother of mine." He crossed his eyes.

Gwen sidled over to him, a wicked gleam in her eyes. "So, Travis, what was your special friend's name, the one who dressed so tastefully in orange and pink?"

"Never mind."

"Yeah, Travis," Sebastian said. "You're just full of surprises these days. But did your mom get mixed up? If you went to all the trouble of making up a friend, it would have to be a girl, wouldn't it?"

Travis hooked his thumbs in his belt loops. "You know what? I have no idea what my mother was talking about. You'll have to forgive her. She's getting senile."

"Don't give me that. Your mother's sharp as a tack," Sebastian said.

Matty started lifting drinks from the tray on the coffee table. "I for one think it's charming that you had a little imaginary friend dressed in orange and pink, Travis. Now who wants something? Shelby, here's your wine, and another glass for Gwen. I have a draft for each of the guys, and—"

"Thanks," Boone said, "but I'm not having any beer."

"Oh, sure," Travis said. "An Irishman who won't bend an elbow at the bar. Since when?"

"Since the day I found out about Elizabeth."

Sebastian picked up his mug of beer and glanced at Boone, his gray eyes lit with challenge. "And that would be because..?"

Boone lowered his voice. "Don't get me wrong. Now that Elizabeth's here, I'm glad she was born and everything. But it shouldn't have happened in the first place. If I hadn't been drinking, it wouldn't have."

"Oh, I think it would have," Travis said easily. "Because once I'm bound on a course, you wouldn't have talked me out of it, even if you had been sober."

"You're making a powerful assumption, Travis," Sebastian said with an edge to his voice. "Let's not forget where Jessica decided to leave Elizabeth in the first place."

"You were closest!" Travis said. "Doesn't mean a thing!"

Matty sighed. "I guess we'd better hide the table knives, Gwen. It's starting again."

"Exactly what we figured would happen when Boone arrived," Gwen said. "The arguments will triple."

"There's nothing to argue about," Travis insisted stubbornly. "Lizzie's my kid."

"She's mine," Sebastian said. "She has the Daniels nose."

"She has my father's eyes!" Boone said.

Shelby set down her wineglass on the coffee table. "Since I'm the new kid on the block, somebody needs to fill me in before I get terminally confused."

Everyone seemed ready to offer an explanation to Shelby except Boone, who decided he'd be too embarrassed to explain it all, especially considering he'd been the one who'd actually committed the shameful deed. The others might like to think they did, but Boone knew in his heart who had.

Finally Matty called for order and sat next to Shelby on the sofa. "I'll tell it." She looked over at Shelby. "Bear with me. This gets confusing. Two years ago this April, these three guys plus another friend, Nat Grady, were in an avalanche in Aspen."

Boone was amazed by the look of terror on Shelby's face as she glanced up at him. The idea that he'd been in danger seemed to hit her hard. He kind of liked that.

"Jessica Franklin was working at the ski lodge then, and she'd agreed to go out skiing with the guys, because she realized they were totally inept."

"Hey!" Sebastian said. "We weren't so bad."

Matty didn't even acknowledge the protest with a glance. "They stunk," she said. "Jessica's probably the only reason they survived. Nat was completely buried in the avalanche, but Jessica knew what to do. She figured out where he was and directed the operation while the guys dug him out."

"Wow," Shelby said.

"It was pretty dramatic, all right," Matty said. "Anyway, the next year the guys and Jessica decided to have an avalanche reunion party, only at the last minute Nat couldn't make it, so it was just the three guys and Jessica."

"Yeah," Boone asked. "Has anybody heard anything from Nat since he went over to that place in the Middle East—what was the name of it?"

"I can't ever remember," Sebastian said. "I think they changed the name a couple of times, at least, after they overthrew the dictator. But no, he's been totally out of touch. Matty thought she saw him on the news the other night when they had footage of some Americans who were over there working with the refugees, specifically the kids."

"I know he's doing a good thing over there," Boone said, "but I wish he'd come back home."

"Yeah, me, too," Travis said. "He borrowed my best sheepskin vest to wear over there. If I'd have known he'd be gone this long, I would have told him to buy his own damn vest."

Gwen rolled her eyes. "I'm so sure it's the vest you're worried about."

"Well, I'd rather not get it back with bullet holes in it," Travis said.

"I wish he'd come back so he could help Matty and me do the paperwork for combining our two spreads," Sebastian said. "And we've been talking about selling a few acres of hers. I wouldn't trust that to any broker but Nat."

Boone nodded. "Better wait'll he comes back."

"Yeah, you'd better wait," Travis agreed.

"I hope I don't have to wait that long to hear the end of the story," Shelby said.

"The rest goes fast," Matty said. "The guys all got ploughed, and Jessica didn't. She seems to have a guardian-angel thing going. She drove them all back to their rented cabin and tucked them in. Nine months later, Elizabeth was born, and two months after that, Jessica left her on Sebastian's front porch with a note asking him to be her godfather, because she was in desperate trouble and couldn't take care of her for a while. He, of course, assumed he'd done the deed while he was drunk. The thing is, she also sent a note like that to Travis and Boone, and they both assume the same thing."

Boone couldn't keep quiet any longer. "The notes to Travis and Sebastian were just a smoke screen. I'm the guy."

Travis turned to him. "Says who?"

"Yeah." Sebastian set his beer mug on the mantel. "How do you figure, Boone?"

Heat warmed his cheeks, and he couldn't look at Shelby. He'd rather not admit this in front of her, but it needed to be said. "Because I'm the strongest, the only one she couldn't have gotten away from, even if I was drunk."

"Oh, yeah?" Travis set his beer mug on a lamp table. "Maybe she didn't *want* to get away from me. Maybe—"

"Maybe we should have some dinner." Matty stood. "Life always looks less complicated on a full stomach."

Shelby stood and gazed around at the three cowboys. "So you three are *fighting* about who gets to claim Elizabeth?"

"You've got it," Matty said.

"Most men would be ducking out the back door in a case like this," Shelby said.

Gwen glanced at her. "If you stick around awhile, you'll soon discover that these aren't most men."

"I guess not," Shelby said. She looked into Boone's eyes. "No, I guess not."

He gazed back at her. He'd expected her to be disgusted with him for forcing a woman to have sex. Instead admiration shone from her blue eyes. Maybe she didn't really believe that he was the one.

"I am Elizabeth's father," he said quietly, looking into her eyes so she'd know he was telling the truth. He didn't want her spinning any daydreams about him.

"Like hell you are," Sebastian grumbled.

"Time to eat!" Matty said brightly, and led the way into the dining room.

CHAPTER TEN

SHELBY WAS SEATED next to Boone, which she suspected Matty had done on purpose. With all the people at the table, it was close quarters, and her knee was in constant contact with Boone's thigh. They bumped elbows more times than she could count, and her shoulder brushed his if she moved even slightly in his direction. Once, as he reached for the dish she was passing him, his forearm grazed her breast. She felt it clear to her toes, and she knew from the flush on his cheeks that he was completely aware of the intimate contact.

As if that weren't enough to start her engine running, everyone at the table treated them as a couple. Their names were linked often in the course of the conversation, and everyone kept giving them knowing looks. Surely they wouldn't do that if they knew Boone was in love with Jessica, Shelby thought. Maybe, just maybe, Jessica and the baby weren't such an insurmountable obstacle after all.

Holding Elizabeth during the meal was a privilege, apparently, and everyone vied for the chance to do it except Boone, Shelby noticed. He was the only one who held back, although she could plainly see that he wanted to. She'd decided the next time she had Elizabeth, she'd simply hand the baby over to Boone.

Near the end of the meal she was about ready to

ask Luann for a turn with the baby when Sebastian raised his glass. "I have a more schmaltzy speech planned for tomorrow, but that doesn't mean we can't toast the happy couple tonight. Long life and happiness, Travis and Gwen."

"Same here," Boone said, raising his water glass. His arm brushed Shelby's in the process, but it had happened so many times they'd both stopped apologizing for bumping each other.

He'd still refused to have a drop of liquor. Later the men were planning a modified bachelor party at the Buckskin, a saloon in Huerfano, and Boone had vowed he'd stick to soft drinks there, too.

Shelby raised her wineglass. "I'm thrilled to be here, tickled pink for you, and I have no idea what I'll wear to the wedding."

Matty laughed. "I'll loan you something." She lifted her water glass. "Here's to Travis and Gwen, the surprise match of the year."

"And a darn good one." Luann touched her wineglass to Matty's. "Right, Elizabeth?"

From her perch on Luann's lap, the baby chortled happily.

Josh, who was sitting on two telephone books so he'd be the right height for the table, held up his milk glass in imitation of the grown-ups. "Yippee!" he said.

"I think that sums it up," Sebastian said with a smile. "Yippee, you two."

Everyone had clinked glasses and taken sips by the time Travis looked over at Matty. "What's with the water, Matilda? I just now noticed you haven't had any wine all night. Don't tell me Boone's new program is catching on?"

"Oh, I felt like having water tonight," Matty said a little too casually.

"But this is a celebration!" Travis said. "You've always been a celebrating kind of gal, Matty."

Matty exchanged a quick glance with Sebastian. Even Shelby, who hadn't been around long, could tell the two had a secret.

Gwen must have caught the look, because she squealed and leaped up to run around the table. "You're pregnant!" she cried, hugging Matty fiercely.

"I didn't want to steal your thunder." Matty looked teary-eyed and happy. "This is supposed to be your time in the spotlight."

"Nonsense." Gwen dabbed at her eyes. "Oh, Matty, this is wonderful."

Shelby felt a stab of envy. She'd loved being an aunt and stand-in mom for Josh. Having a baby of her own would be heaven, especially with the right sort of man.... She glanced sideways at Boone, who was looking a little wistful himself. Right sort of man, wrong sort of circumstances. Ah, but how his solid presence next to her made her ache with longing.

"Preggers?" Travis drew everyone's attention as he scowled at Sebastian. "You knew this outstanding fact and you didn't tell Boone and me, your best friends in the whole world?"

"Second best." Sebastian smiled at his wife. "You've been downgraded. Matty's my best friend now."

Travis clutched his breast. "I'm cut to the quick. How about you, Boone?"

"We've been betrayed." Boone barely contained a grin. "I think this calls for strong measures."

Watching him, Shelby felt warmth flood through

her. Boone was sexier than any man had a right to be. Circumstances or no circumstances, she'd love to know what a kiss from Boone would feel like. She wondered what he'd do if she took the initiative, sometime when they were alone. In this house, that might be never.

"Strong measures, indeed," Travis agreed. He pushed back his chair.

"Hold it, guys," Sebastian said. "Matty made me promise not to tell anybody. It's all her fault."

"Now he's hiding behind a woman's skirts," Boone said. He pushed back his chair and stood, flexing his hands. "Can't get much more cowardly than that, right, Travis?"

"Not much, Boone."

Shelby couldn't help but look at those strong fingers and remember how they'd felt cradling her breast.

"Time to teach Sebastian a little lesson," Boone said.

Josh's eyes grew round. "What're you gonna do?" His voice trembled.

Boone immediately turned and gave the little boy a smile of reassurance. "Nothing bad, Josh. Don't be afraid. We'll just roll him in a snowbank. I noticed there were still a couple down by the barn. It's a tradition around here when a guy gets his wife pregnant."

"A tradition that's about two minutes old." Sebastian's chair scraped on the wooden floor as he stood and faced his friends with a cocky grin. "*If* you can get it off the ground, which I doubt."

"If you break any dishes getting him outside," Matty warned, "I'll have all of your hides."

"You notice she didn't beg for us to spare you," Travis said, laughing. "So much for your best friend, Sebastian, old buddy. Loyalty ain't what it used to be."

"You know I never allowed roughhousing indoors, Travis Edward!" Luann said.

"Then I guess we'll have to take him outside," Travis said. "Ready, Boone?"

"Ready when you are, studman."

"Then let's get the new poppa."

Shelby was amazed that in the ensuing struggle only one glass was overturned and some silverware clattered to the floor. Travis and Boone managed to carry Sebastian out the back door without breaking a single dish.

The physical struggle excited Shelby more than she cared to admit, though. She watched Boone wrestle with Sebastian and wanted that sort of contact for herself. Boy, did she want it.

Matty was on her feet the minute they slammed out the back door. "We can watch from the kitchen window."

Shelby helped Josh out of his chair. "Do they do this kind of thing often?" she asked as she went with Matty, Gwen and Luann into the kitchen.

Matty chuckled. "To be honest? Yes. At the slightest excuse."

"This is more than a slight excuse." Gwen hugged Matty again. "How could you even think of keeping this a secret until after the wedding?"

"I had my time to be fussed over," Matty said. "I want this to be yours."

"Don't worry. This news will only add to the celebration."

Whoops and shouts of laughter, sprinkled with a few rich curse words floated back up to the house from the area down by the barn where the men wrestled in a small patch of snow lit by a dusk-to-dawn light.

Matty, Gwen, Luann and Shelby crowded around the window over the kitchen sink, each of them trying to get a glimpse of what was going on. Shelby lifted Josh up so he could see, and Luann held Elizabeth.

"Look at those crazy idiots," Gwen said with a chuckle. "You'd think they were all about five years old."

"I'm three years old," Josh announced proudly. "I builded a snowman. He's comin' alive. Can I build another one, Shebby? They gots some snow here."

"Maybe tomorrow," Shelby said. Then she remembered the wedding. "If there's time. When's the ceremony, Gwen?"

"Not until seven," Gwen said. "That'll give my brother time to fly in from Boston, and then, too, we wanted to have candlelight."

"I'll bet it'll be beautiful."

"It will," Matty said, "as long as all the guys don't end up with black eyes and broken noses. I wonder if we should break up the happy party down there before that happens. When they horse around like this, they sometimes forget and actually do damage to each other by mistake."

"Horsies!" Josh said, latching onto Matty's statement. "I wanna see the horsies sleepin'!"

"That's right," Shelby said. "Boone did promise to take Josh down to the barn before bedtime so he could at least look at the horses."

"I wanna go," Josh said. "And Bob, he does, too."

"We're not going to disappoint Josh or Bob," Luann said. "Gwen, if you'll take Elizabeth, I'll go with Josh down to the barn and on the way I'll tell those big lugs to knock it off before they end up looking like prize-fighters in the wedding pictures tomorrow."

"I'd like to go, too," Shelby said eagerly before she stopped to think. Then she glanced at the pots and pans on the stove and remembered there were a ton of dishes to do. "On second thought, never mind. I can see the horses tomorrow."

"Spoken like a typical woman," Matty said with a chuckle. "Go on down to the barn, Shelby. Gwen and I can handle this mess in no time flat."

Shelby shook her head. "Nope. That's not fair. A bride-to-be shouldn't be ruining her nails with dishes, and then there's the baby to worry about, too. Let me either take care of her or do some dishes. I want to repay a little of your generosity in having me stay with you."

Gwen laughed. "You want to do something? You can help us make the table favors for the reception after the guys head for the Buckskin. That should be tedious enough to drive us all crazy. Now get going, all three— excuse me, I mean all *four* of you, before Travis busts his nose and has to breathe through his mouth while he's saying his vows."

Shelby tried to stick to her guns, but Matty and Gwen were formidable when they joined forces. Moments later Shelby, Josh and Luann had bundled up against the cold and were headed down toward the barn. Shelby held one of Josh's hands and Luann held the other while Josh chattered away. Luann had agreed to hold Bob's hand, and she promised Josh that Bob was keeping up just fine.

Ahead of them the three men rolled on the cold ground in a tangle of arms and legs, their laughter punctuated with colorful swearing as their breath clouded the cold air.

"You boys watch your language, now," Luann called out. "I don't want this child picking up any of those words."

"What child?" Boone asked, glancing up. Then he grunted as Sebastian used the moment to ram an elbow into his ribs.

"You three stop this nonsense immediately," Luann said, her voice ringing with authority. "You should all know better. Look at you. Half-frozen and your clothes a sight."

The men all stopped wrestling and looked shamefacedly at Luann. Shelby had to press her lips together to keep from laughing. They'd all been acting like five-year-olds, and now they even wore the expression of five-year-olds caught being naughty. Each of them would make about two of Luann, but she was obviously the one in charge at the moment.

"I guess you got a point, Mom." Travis stood slowly and began brushing himself off as he surveyed his two partners in crime. "Looks like we ripped your sleeve, there, Sebastian."

"Yep." Sebastian sat up and glanced at it. "Matty'll have a fit."

Boone got up and held out a hand to help Sebastian to his feet. "Blame it on me, buddy. She'll probably go easier on me than she would on you." He glanced sheepishly at Josh. "How're you doin', Josh?"

"Shebby says I'm not s'posed to fight."

"And she's absolutely right," Boone said as he tucked his damp shirttail into his mud-smeared jeans. "We weren't really fighting. Just funnin'."

Shelby took in the heaving chest, the tousled hair, the mangled clothes, and it was all she could do not to sigh with longing. He was so damned earthy, so completely physical. She could eat him up with a spoon.

"But you ripped his *shirt*." Josh mimicked Luann's indignation perfectly. "And you gots mud all over."

"Yeah, and I'll probably need to buy him a new shirt and help Matty with the laundry," Boone said, looking guilty. "See, that's what I get."

"Yep," Josh said as if satisfied that Boone understood his transgressions. "That's what you get. We're gonna see the horsies sleepin'."

Boone looked even more guilty. "Oh, yeah. I said I'd take you, didn't I?"

"You're welcome to come along," Luann said crisply. "If you can behave yourself."

"Yeah, come along!" Josh let go of Shelby and Luann and ran over to gaze up at Boone. "Please?"

"Uh, okay." He glanced warily at Luann. "If you're sure."

"I'm sure," Luann said, her voice softening a little.

"Okay." Josh held out his hand. "Let's go."

"Wait a sec. I need to clean off my hand." Boone searched for a place on his jeans that wasn't covered with mud and finally found one large enough to wipe his hand on. "My hand's going to be cold, now," he warned as he leaned down to take Josh's.

"Then Bob and me, we'll warm you up! Like last night."

Shelby glanced at Luann with an apologetic smile. "I think we've been replaced," she said in a low voice.

Josh looked over his shoulder. "Come on, Gramma Luann. Come on, Shebby. Let's go see the horsies!"

"Not replaced," Luann said. "Included. That boy needs Boone like a plant needs sunlight."

"I know. I'm just worried—"

"My advice is to let him soak it up while he can," Luann said. "Now let's go see the horses."

Boone hadn't figured on Shelby and Josh coming down to the barn and catching him making a fool of himself wrestling with Sebastian. Had he known that would happen, he probably would have thought twice. He could see how Josh looked up to him, and he took that responsibility seriously.

He also didn't relish looking like a fool in front of Shelby. But she was part of the reason he'd gone along with Travis's idea to roll Sebastian in the snowbank. Sitting next to her at dinner and rubbing up against her every five seconds had worked him into quite a state. Wrestling with the guys was a good way to work off some steam, before he lost control and did something stupid with Shelby.

"Hey, Boone!" Travis called after them. "All three of us may be sleeping in the barn tonight, so throw some clean hay into a stall while you're at it, buddy."

"Uh-huh," Boone called back. "I suppose you'd like a mint on your pillow, too, hotshot?"

Travis laughed as he started up to the house beside Sebastian, who was limping slightly. "Fresh flowers would be a nice touch," he bellowed over his shoulder.

"You gots flowers?" Josh asked as Boone let go of his hand to slide the bolt open on the barn door. "Shebby loves flowers."

"Then maybe we should get her some pretty soon," Boone said. He wondered when Shelby had last had somebody bring her flowers. And she deserved them, for all she'd been through. He mentally added another item to his shopping list for the time when he took Josh into town for a hat and boots. Probably the day after the wedding.

Getting Shelby flowers might not be the wisest thing to do, because he wasn't in a position to ask her out or anything, but still, he'd love seeing the look on her face when he gave them to her. And she really did deserve some.

Boone led the way into the warmth and darkness of the barn and felt a thrill of sexual awareness, knowing Shelby was close behind him. City kids made out in the back seats of cars, but country kids, which Boone had been, usually learned about sex in the privacy of a barn. He'd lost his virginity to Darlene in a soft bed of hay.

"Smells good in here," Josh whispered, his voice trembling with excitement.

"Yep. I think so, too." Boone turned on a small battery-operated light Sebastian had mounted on the wall inside the door. It would allow them to see, just barely, without exciting the horses and making them think it was feeding time.

Boone glanced back at Luann and Shelby. "Can you two see okay?"

"I'm fine," Shelby said.

"Me, too," Luann added. "Come here, Josh. Let me hold you up so you can look over the stall doors."

"Boone can hold me," Josh said.

Boone eased the door closed to keep the barn warm. "I would, Josh, but I'm kinda dirty. Shelby probably wouldn't want you to get any mud on you."

"Oh, I'll bet Shelby won't mind too much," Luann said.

"No, of course not," Shelby said.

So Boone picked Josh up, trying to keep him away

from the worst of the mud while they started down the row of stalls. Boone whispered the names of the horses as they came to each stall, and all four of them stood and gazed into the shadowy depths at the horse lying or standing quietly inside. Luck was with them, and Samson roused himself enough to come to the stall door.

Josh held his breath and leaned down to carefully stroke Samson's nose. "See you tomorrow, Samson," he murmured. "Now, go sleepy-bye."

Josh didn't want to leave Samson's stall, but Boone knew it must be getting close to Josh's bedtime, so he coaxed him away and continued the tour. Gradually Josh relaxed in his arms, and eventually began to yawn, even though he was obviously fighting sleep so he could stay in the barn.

His head drooped closer and closer to Boone's shoulder, until at last it rested there. Boone discovered he absolutely loved the feeling of the little guy falling asleep in his arms.

"Somebody's out like a light," Luann said in a low tone. "Why don't you let Shelby or me carry him up to the house, Boone?"

"I'll do it," Boone said.

"That won't work very well," Luann said. "You're going to have to strip down before you go in that house."

"Good point." He wondered how Sebastian and Travis had handled that problem. Stripping down outside in this weather would be cold as hell. And Matty had been cleaning for days getting ready for the wedding, so she wouldn't take kindly to people traipsing through her house with mud on their clothes.

"Tell you what," Luann said. "You stay here where

it's warm. Shelby and I will take Josh up to the house, and one of us will bring you some clean clothes. I'm sure you've got a sink or a hose or something in this barn, so you can wash up a little. How's that?"

"Okay." It sounded much better than what Sebastian and Travis must have been put through, so he decided to grab the opportunity.

"Here," Shelby said, moving close to Boone. "Let me take Josh."

Gradually Boone transferred Josh to Shelby, which involved more touching, plus he got a good whiff of her cologne. He must not have blown off as much steam during the wrestling match as he'd hoped, because he was right back in a state of agitation. Worse yet, the dim light in the barn reminded him of the night before, when he'd been in bed with Shelby and wrapped himself around her in his sleep. The potent image grabbed him in a very specific area and started working on him.

"Got him," Shelby whispered. "Thanks, Boone."

"No problem," he lied, his voice husky. Major problem. He wanted her so much he could hardly breathe. He wondered if Travis's wedding tomorrow was putting ideas in his head, or maybe even Matty's announcement tonight had started him thinking about babies and how much fun it would be to make one. Whatever it was, Shelby had become an incredibly strong temptation, one he had to resist. Somehow.

"Okay," Luann said as she started toward the door of the barn. "One of us will be back down in a jiffy with fresh clothes."

Boone stared after them. He knew who would be the safest person to bring him some clothes. It was not the person he wanted to bring them.

CHAPTER ELEVEN

BOONE CONVINCED himself that Luann would be the logical choice to bring him his clothes. Shelby would be busy tucking Josh into bed. So it seemed safe to take off his mud-encrusted shirt and use the big utility sink Sebastian had installed near the front door of the barn to wash off at least part of the grit.

The water was cold, but not too bad. After cleaning his hands, arms and neck, he stuck his head under the faucet to rinse the mud out of his hair. Then he found an old but clean towel on a nearby shelf and rubbed it over his head. As he thought about that wrestling match, he began to grin.

Carrying Sebastian outside and throwing him in the snowbank might not have been the most mature thing to do, but it had been fun. After growing up with two sisters he'd always treated with great care, it was a relief to let go and have some fun with a couple of friends who gave as good as they got.

Although he might be bigger and a little stronger than Sebastian and Travis, they both had some moves that made them worthy wrestling opponents. Yeah, rolling around in the snow and working off his excess energy had felt great, especially after being cooped up in the truck for so many hours with a woman he wasn't supposed to want, a woman he couldn't stop craving.

The barn door creaked open, and he turned, expecting Luann.

Instead, Shelby stood in the pale light from the battery lamp with a bundle of his clothes in her arms. She nudged the door closed with her foot. "I…I had to guess what you might want me to bring," she said.

"Anything." He cleared his throat. "Anything's fine." His heart began to race. So she had decided to bring his clothes. He wondered if she knew how dangerous a move she'd just made. They'd never been really, truly alone until this moment. Surely she'd thought of that before she'd set out for the barn. Or maybe she had no idea he was on fire for her.

She'd caught him half-naked this morning, too. He'd been embarrassed then, but now…now he was too far gone for embarrassment. Long agonizing hours of wanting her had worn him down, and he was crazy to hold her warm body close.

With his shirt gone they were one step closer to what he'd been thinking about all day. One more tempting step. And that was why, if he had thought she'd bring his clothes instead of Luann, he would have left his shirt on.

She walked toward him and held out the clothes. "I, um, brought underwear, too." Even the weak light from the lamp picked up the bloom in her cheeks. "I wasn't sure if the snow got down in…well, I wanted you to have that option of changing your…"

Her explanation ran out of steam as she gazed at him, her lips parted, her breathing unsteady. Her ski jacket was open in front, as if she'd unzipped it in the house while she gathered his clothes and then hurried down here without bothering to zip it up again.

Or maybe she'd left it open on purpose. Maybe there

wasn't a single innocent thing about this trip to the barn. He swallowed. "Thanks." He took the clothes and his hand brushed hers. His heart nearly stopped. Her skin was so warm. So soft. She would feel like that everywhere. Oh, God.

"I like your friends so much, Boone," she went on, chattering as if standing here in the semidarkness was no big deal. As if they weren't moments away from a major decision. "Here I've burst in on the wedding festivities and yet they're making me feel completely welcome, as if having me and Josh around is no trouble."

He forced himself to say something, anything. "I'm sure they're glad to have you." He could barely see straight from wanting to touch her again. But he knew damned well touching Shelby would be like the potato-chip ad. He wouldn't be able to stop with just one.

"They act as if they are glad. Luann asked if she could put Josh to bed because it had been so long since she'd tucked a little boy in and she missed it so. Isn't that sweet?"

"Yeah. Luann's great." He sounded hoarse, as if he had a cold coming on. But it was heat, not cold that was running through him right now. He was a fool to keep playing with fire, to stand here half-naked talking to Shelby, but he couldn't seem to walk away from the blaze. "And she caught onto the Bob thing real quick." He didn't want to talk about Luann. *Touch me, Shelby.*

"I know. And when she asked Josh to call her Gramma Luann, I could have kissed her."

He nearly groaned. Sure enough, now he couldn't stop looking at her mouth. She had a world-class mouth—full lips shaped like an archer's bow, framing perfect white teeth. Kissing her would be better than winning the lottery. "Guess I should change my clothes and get on up to the house." But for some reason, instead of stepping back from her, which would let her know she should leave, he moved a little closer.

"I'm not sure I brought the right things." She seemed to be edging closer to him, too.

He watched the movement of her lips as she spoke, and he lost track of what she was saying as he imagined fitting his mouth to hers and exploring all that perfection with his tongue. Then he would thrust deep, to let her know what was really on his mind, and she would mold herself against him. And this was a woman with the curves to do it right.

"Maybe you should check through them before I leave."

He had no idea what she was talking about. "Check through what?"

"Your clothes." Her gaze held his, and her voice was breathy and soft. "In case you want me to take something back and bring you something else."

His nostrils flared as he breathed in her scent, and his groin tightened. There was a soft sheen on her lips, as if she'd run her tongue over them before coming into the barn. "I'm not fussy…about clothes," he said. *Only about the women I kiss.*

"You're sure?" Her eyes darkened.

The lack of light had probably made her eyes do that, he told himself. "These will be fine," he said. But she might be aroused. If she was, he should ignore it. Like hell he would, when he was trembling with the need to hold her. He gazed into those eyes, searching for heat to match his own. There. Maybe. Yes…no…

She laid her hand on the pile of clothes he held in his arms. "Because if you want something else…"

She'd leaned in close enough that he felt her warm breath on his chest. His nipples tightened. He wanted something else all right, something he had no right to ask for. "Shelby—"

"Boone Connor, if you don't kiss me in the next two seconds I'm going to explode."

He dropped the clothes and swept her up in his arms with a groan of surrender. Contact. At last. "This is a mistake," he murmured. They were the last coherent words he spoke as he found her mouth and lost his mind.

She was so light, no heavier than a child in his arms. Yet this was no child he was kissing. Her mouth was a woman's mouth, hot and eager. He'd meant to explore, maybe even to tease, but she parted those full lips and gave him an invitation he couldn't refuse. Her moan of delight when he pushed inside echoed throughout his body and settled heavily between his thighs.

He had to hunch down to keep his contact with her, and at first the wonder of her mouth and the openness of her response kept him so occupied he didn't mind. But a crick was developing in his neck, and besides, he wanted those full breasts right up against his chest.

He slipped an arm under her bottom to lift her so that her hungry mouth was level with his, and she wrapped her legs around his hips, exactly as he'd once imagined she would. *Ah, yes. There.* He felt the sensuous give of her breasts as he drew her in close.

But not close enough for her, it seemed. His pulse rate skyrocketed as she wrapped her legs even tighter around him, crushed her breasts against his bare chest and tilted her head back, inviting him deeper into her mouth. *Oh, Shelby.*

With a growl of need, he took what she offered and more, possessing her mouth with a frenzy that wasn't like him at all. He squeezed her so tight it was a wonder either of them could breathe. He'd thought of himself as gentle, deliberate, cautious. Not this time. Not with this woman.

She urged him on, and as his kisses became more intense she wrapped her legs tighter around him, putting sweet pressure right where he needed it. *Yes. Like that.* In a million years he wouldn't have imagined this much passion lurked within her. He didn't think women daydreamed about sex the way men did.

But Shelby acted as if she'd spent the past day building up as much frustration as he had. She began to rock against him, causing a maddening, wonderful friction against his chest…and lower, where his erection strained. As the tension ratcheted upward, she made little noises deep in her throat. Wild, needy sounds that shattered what little self-control he had left.

He backed her against the sink, propping her on the curved edge so his hands would be free. Free to reach inside the coat she'd left unzipped, free to pull her shirt from the waist of her jeans and reach up underneath to unfasten her bra. And all the while he drowned his conscience in the whirlpool of her kiss.

When he cupped her bare breasts her skin was hot as a furnace, and his caressing thumbs found her nipples already hard, thrusting eagerly against the pad of his thumb. His desire expanded. Now he wouldn't be satisfied until he took a warm, puckered nipple into his mouth, swirled the tip against his tongue, sucked and nibbled and licked until she became as wild with lust as he was.

Yet as he imagined tasting her breasts, he knew that wouldn't be enough. Maybe nothing would ever be enough, when it came to Shelby. He hadn't known he could ache like this, or that she would match him in her desperation.

Knowing she was as filled with repressed desire as he was made him want more, dare more. He gave up the heart-stopping pleasure of fondling her breasts so that he could tug off her coat. His blood surged when he realized she was helping him, wiggling out of the coat, pulling off her shirt.

Of course he shouldn't be doing this, but he couldn't stop and she wasn't about to stop him. This grinding need had been born when he'd woken this morning with her curled against his hot, hard penis. And it had never left. The need had been there underneath his thoughts about Fowler, his worry about Elizabeth, his joking with his friends. At last his need for her had burst free, and he was helpless before it.

He dragged his mouth from hers and supported her with an arm around her waist as she whipped the shirt off over her head, flinging it to the floor. Her bra followed.

Eyes hot, she held his gaze. Her mouth was swollen from his kisses, her skin pink from the scrape of his beard. As her breath came in quick little gasps, she braced a hand on each side of the sink...and arched her back.

"Oh, Lord." His heart beat so fast he thought he might need an ambulance soon. But he'd die a happy man, having seen such glory.

He'd been in a rush to rip away her clothes, but now

her beauty, evident even in the dim light, awed him. He hesitated, afraid to touch her creamy breasts for fear of marring them. Her small frame made them even more spectacular, more lush and exotic. His breath caught as he stared in admiration.

"My heart is pounding like a rabbit's," she murmured. "Touch me there, Boone. I want you to feel my heart going like sixties."

He slowly laid a hand over her heart and his fingers curved naturally, cradling her fullness. Her heartbeat tapped against his palm, a secret code spelling out her desire. A miracle, that a beautiful creature like this wanted him so much. He flexed his fingers, kneading gently. Her nipple quivered, lifted, tempting him. A sweet raspberry of a nipple centered on the areola, ripe and ready to be plucked. His mouth grew moist.

Yet still he hesitated, gazing at his big, work-scarred hand cupping the satisfying weight of her breast. He thought of how his calloused fingers and his beard might scrape her tender skin. "My hands are so rough," he whispered. "And my beard, too. I'll give you a rash. I'll—"

"I want your rough hands," she said breathlessly. "I want your hungry mouth and your rough beard. I've spent the whole blessed day wishing you'd touch me like this."

He looked into her eyes. "I've been going insane."

"Oh, so have I," she whispered. "So have I. Take what you need. Give me what I need. Please."

And at last, he did. Gently at first. Carefully. Until passion built to a flood within him, washing away restraint. Then he feasted like a wild man, mindless to everything but pleasure, heedless of all else but her soft moans and choked words of encouragement.

And now he wanted more. Another time, another place he might have held back, chained by his own reluctance to trespass. But his life was spinning out of control, opportunities slipping away. Shelby was here, offering him these few stolen moments, this chance at forbidden pleasure. Her ripe body roused a demon within him, one that had no limits and would not be denied.

He'd made no conscious decision to unfasten her jeans, and he barely remembered working them and her panties over her hips, lifting her up like a rag doll in the process. It was merely a necessary step toward his goal.

And now he had what he wanted, as he crouched in front of her, his hands splayed across her bare bottom. All he knew was that she didn't stop him. She wasn't going to stop him. His blood ran hot in his veins.

Slowly, deliberately, he tasted. She gasped and quivered in his arms. Breathing in the primitive scent of aroused woman, he savored the rich nectar of her response on his tongue, and his mind filled with a red haze of passion. A low, urgent groan rose from her throat. He took his prize.

Ah, she was sweet. And so willing, so ready for whatever he wanted. And he wanted. He trembled with wanting. He battled images of rising to his feet, ripping open his jeans and taking her completely. She was so open, so wet.

As he pushed her higher, the pressure to be deep inside her became almost beyond bearing. But he would bear it. She had endured so much. He would give her this. She was nearly there. Triumph welled within him. Yes, he would give her this.

As she climaxed, she bucked and quaked in his grip.

Her muted cries of release thrilled him more than shouts of ecstasy, and he was overcome with a fierce possessiveness. Despite the painful ache in his groin, her satisfaction eased the sharp edge of his desire and made way for tenderness.

He kissed her moist curls. Then he guided her to his lap, trailing kisses over her belly, her ribs, her breasts, her throat. At last they were once more face-to-face.

Resting her hands on his shoulders, she gazed at him, her eyes filled with wonder.

He cupped her face in one hand and brushed his thumb over her cheek. The expression on her face made the torture in his groin well worth it. He'd never been so bold with a woman he'd known such a short time. They'd come a long way, considering that two days ago neither of them had known the other existed. And it was probable this was as far as they'd ever go.

He took a breath. "I'm afraid I got...carried away. Something let loose in me, I guess. Like a dam breaking."

She nodded. "I know. I walked...down here to see..." She paused and took a breath, herself. "To see if I could get you to kiss me."

A smile tugged at his mouth. "You broke the dam."

"Sure did," she murmured. "Blew it to smithereens. That was some kiss."

And now he knew what else he had to say. Not the loving promises and pledges that he longed to make. No, he had to protect her from those, which would only hurt her. He would give her warnings, delivered with a smile that he hoped would take the sting out. "That might be the only one I can ever give you," he said. "I thought I'd make it count."

"You certainly did." She bracketed his face in her

hands, and she seemed to want to ignore the first part of his statement. "But it was a one-sided kiss, Boone."

"It's better that way." And it was, he knew. Letting her go after what they'd just shared wouldn't be easy, but once he'd known the joy of burying himself deep inside her, letting her go would be impossible.

"Better because you get to stay in control and I don't?"

"Maybe." He took a deep breath. "But I wouldn't say I've been totally in control. I really didn't mean to…"

"And I didn't mean to let you." She combed her fingers through his damp hair as her gaze searched his. "But I did," she murmured. "So where are we now, Boone?"

"Probably in a hell of a mess. Nothing's changed for me."

"Nothing?"

"Not really." He sighed at her look of disappointment. "I know that's not what you'd like to hear. But the truth is, I wanted you before. The only difference is that now I know what I'll be missing."

Her jaw firmed under his grip and her eyes gleamed in the dim light. "Not by a long shot. This is the tip of the iceberg, mister."

"I was afraid of that." The ache that he thought he had under control began building again. To distract himself, he looked around for the clothes she'd tossed on the floor. He reached over and picked up her bra. Holding that lacy confection did nothing to ease his discomfort. He shook it to get any bits of straw out and handed it to her.

"My cue to make tracks?" she asked.

"People will start to wonder where you are."

"They know where I am. I get the impression they approve." She slipped the bra on and arched her back to fasten it from behind.

"I'm sure they do. But I have to handle this situation my way." He shouldn't watch her fasten her bra, not if he wanted to keep his sanity. Glancing around, he located her shirt and picked that up, too. "The way I see it, the more we get involved with each other, the tougher it'll be when you go back to San Antonio and I have to stay here to deal with Elizabeth and Jessica."

She remained silent, not disagreeing, but not agreeing, either.

Shaking out her shirt, he gave it to her. "Don't pin your hopes on me, Shelby. I'm not your fantasy cowboy. I have two people depending on me. They have a prior claim, and I mean to honor that."

She put her arms in the sleeves and pulled the shirt over her head. Then she gazed at him. "Boone, could it be possible, just slightly possible, that Elizabeth is not your child?"

"She's mine," he said, surprised at how much the question irritated him. One look into the baby's eyes and he was ready to fight for the title of daddy. "But even if she's not, Jessica asked me to be her godfather for the time being. So either way, I have an obligation to Elizabeth. And to Jessica." Wrapping his arms around Shelby, he lifted her up as he rose to his feet. He made sure she'd regained her balance before he loosened his grip.

"I see." She'd fastened her jeans and reached for her coat before she spoke again. "You probably think I'm shameless, coming down here tonight. Especially when you've made it clear that you don't want to get involved with me."

He caught her chin and made her look at him. "I am involved with you. I can't help myself. Everything that happened just now, I wanted as much as you, maybe more. I think you're a beautiful, sexy woman. But the timing stinks."

She nodded and put on her coat.

Her resolute expression tore at his heart. She'd had to stuff her feelings about her parents and sister getting killed in order to be strong for Josh. Now he was asking her to stuff her feelings about him, too. "I wish I could be what you need," he said, knowing how lame that must sound to someone who'd fought the inner battles Shelby had.

She took a long, shaky breath and shoved her hands in her pockets. Then she gave him a bold once-over, tilting her head in a cocky, devil-may-care way. "You might not be Mister Right, but you make a fantastic Mister Right Now. I had a great time."

His heart broke. He didn't want to be the cause of her putting on a brave front, but he was. "Me, too," he said softly.

"Tip of the iceberg," she said, turning on her heel. "You might want to remember that."

"I probably will." Like for the rest of his life.

She paused, her back to him. "I don't know what this Jessica person is doing running all over the countryside, when a man like you is waiting right here, willing and ready to protect and take care of her. She must be ten kinds of a fool." Then, her head held high, she left the barn.

After she left, Boone paced the length of the barn a few times until his body cooled down. Gradually the full impact of his behavior settled on his conscience, and finally he sat on a bale of hay and dropped his head in his hands.

For reasons that escaped him, Shelby still had him on some sort of pedestal. She ought to have him run out of town on a rail.

All his life he'd thought of himself as a gentleman, a guy who treated women with every consideration. Darlene had even complained that he was too *much* of a gentleman, but he'd explained that was the way he was made. He had such respect for her and all women that he had to be polite, even when making love.

What a crock. Given the right circumstances, he could be an animal. He could get drunk and make a good friend pregnant without her consent. Then, as if that wasn't bad enough, he could meet a stranger and within twenty-four hours have her stripped and moaning in his arms.

And in spite of the fact that he knew that it was wrong, wrong, wrong, he wanted to do it all again. He couldn't imagine a sweeter fate than to be locked in a bedroom with Shelby for about two weeks.

But even so, he was prepared to abandon her, telling her she had to be sacrificed to his noble principles. Ha. He had no stinkin' principles, at least when it came to one short, well-endowed blonde.

He'd damn well better get some, though, and fast. Shelby didn't deserve to be treated like that. From now on, he wasn't laying a hand on her. He was never touching that silky skin again. That warm, creamy skin…that tender mouth…those plump, tasty breasts…

He groaned. Life used to be so simple.

CHAPTER TWELVE

IF ANYBODY NOTICED Shelby's rumpled condition when she came back from the barn, they were polite enough not to mention it. She managed to escape to the bathroom and repair the damage to her appearance while Matty, Gwen and Luann hauled out the supplies for making the party favors.

The damage to her heart would require a little more than a comb and some makeup, though. There was no doubt Boone wanted her physically. She'd gotten a whole lot more than she'd bargained for tonight. But no matter how wonderful he'd made her feel, his lust wasn't enough to satisfy her. She wanted everything Boone had to offer, and it seemed he was saving himself for Jessica.

Frustrated as she felt, she couldn't blame him for that. He thought he and Jessica were the parents of a child. If so, then he'd made love to her, and Boone wasn't the sort of man to take that lightly. At this very moment he might be trying to think himself into falling in love with Jessica, to justify what had happened. And while his thoughts were centered on another woman, he couldn't very well let Shelby into his heart. Unfortunately he'd already found his way into hers.

By the time Boone came into the house, Sebastian

and Travis were ready to head for the bachelor party at the Buckskin and the four women had begun assembling the favors at the dining-room table. Travis and Sebastian both came over to kiss their sweethearts goodbye.

Travis gave his mother a peck on the cheek, too. He dislodged her red granny glasses in the process, and although she pretended to be impatient with his gusto, Shelby could tell she was thrilled with the attention.

Shelby was the only one of the four who went kiss-free, and she was painfully aware of Boone's slightest movement as he waited for the others to say their goodbyes. Her skin flushed when she thought of the fevered kisses they'd so recently shared. And if she wasn't careful, she'd get caught giving him soulful glances.

Determined not to look like Miss Lonelyhearts, she aimed a brilliant smile in his general direction. "Have a great time!" she said cheerfully.

"How can he have a great time if he's drinking root beer?" Travis walked over and hooked an arm around Boone's neck as if to put him in a hammerlock.

Boone braced himself, looking as immovable as a bronze statue.

After Travis realized he couldn't knock his friend off balance, he gave up the effort with a grin. "It's not bad enough that he can usually beat me at arm wrestling even when he's drunk. Now that he's turned into a damned teetotaler I'll never win again."

"Somebody has to drive," Boone said. "I'm sure as hell not letting you have the keys, bridegroom."

Even the sound of Boone's voice made Shelby's whole body tingle. She'd have to get control of herself.

"None of you has to drive," Gwen said. "I think the

three of you should crash at Hawthorne House tonight. That's walking distance from the Buckskin."

"*Walking* distance?" Sebastian looked offended. "You must have us confused with yuppie city slickers. We're big he-man cowboy types. We drive our manly trucks or we ride our manly steeds. We don't *walk.*"

"Oh." Gwen grinned. "Excuse me. Then maybe you'd like me to pick you studly dudes up when I come back into town?"

"No need," Boone said. "I'll be fine to drive. And I'm supposed to bring Travis back here, right?"

"If you're sure you're all not going to stay at Hawthorne House," Gwen said.

Sebastian adjusted the tilt on his Stetson. "Nope. Thanks for the invite, but we're coming back here."

"Okay," Gwen said. "Then, yes, please bring Travis back with you. Luann and I can get more done in the morning if he's not around."

"Fine talk," Travis grumbled. "This is your new husband you're talking about."

"Exactly," Luann added. "And it's traditional for the bride and groom to be separated the night before the wedding."

"Got it," Boone said. "See you all later. Come on, you party animals. Let's go."

See you all later. Shelby had been included in the crowd. No special look, no special words for her alone. It was as if the moments in the barn had been a fantasy.

"You *used* to be a party animal," Travis complained. "I don't know how one little ol' long-neck will compromise your honor." He continued his lament as they went out the front door. "Or two little ol' long-necks. Or—" The door closed after them.

Shelby went back to wrapping favors, her heart aching. She believed that Boone wouldn't drink tonight, but she almost wished he would. Maybe alcohol would unlock some of the secrets of his heart.

"I hope they'll be okay," Gwen said as Boone's truck pulled away.

"They will." Matty tied her blond hair back in a scrunchie before she continued wrapping chocolate kisses. "Boone won't have anything to drink. He and Sebastian both have a stubborn streak a mile wide."

"I like Boone," Luann said. "He seems solid and trustworthy."

"He is," Shelby said. "And I'm very grateful that he decided to help me and Josh."

"He plays his cards pretty close to his chest, though," Matty said. "Far as I know, he's only been in love once, and that didn't turn out well."

Jessica? Shelby couldn't ignore the possibility. Maybe Boone was in love with Jessica, but she didn't return his love. That would make him feel especially guilty about the baby. And he hadn't seen Jessica in more than a year. He was probably frustrated, both sexually and emotionally. Of course he'd react the way he had in the barn tonight. Maybe he would have reacted that way with any woman.

The phone rang, and Matty went to answer it.

A lump of misery clogged Shelby's throat, but this was supposed to be a joyous time for the other women at the table. From years of self-discipline, Shelby was able to swallow the lump in her throat and begin asking Gwen and Luann questions about the decorations for the wedding. Gwen would be a beautiful bride. Shelby imagined how perfectly a white wedding gown would contrast with her dark hair and eyes and the golden tone of her skin.

The last wedding Shelby had attended had been her sister's lavish extravaganza. Patricia had been married with plenty of glamour, but not a tenth of the joy Shelby knew would surround Gwen and Travis's ceremony. Poor, doomed Patricia. At least if Shelby found herself feeling weepy tomorrow she wouldn't be the only one in tears. Happy tears and sad tears probably looked about the same on the outside.

In the midst of Gwen's description of how she and Luann had decorated the bed-and-breakfast and the surrounding Victorian garden for the reception, Matty returned.

"It was Jessica on the phone." Matty sounded weary.

Anger and jealousy coursed through Shelby. "What did she want?"

"The same. To know that Elizabeth's okay. That's all she ever asks and then she gets off the phone immediately. I could hear traffic in the background. I'm sure she was using a pay phone somewhere." Matty sat down again and picked up a chocolate kiss.

"But where?" Luann asked.

"Who knows?" Matty sighed and threw the piece of candy back in the pile. "I'm getting damned sick of this, you know? I think we hired a dud of a detective. He's turned up practically nothing, except to tell us she's been traveling all over the place, which we knew, anyway. She's always one step ahead of him. Maybe Sebastian and I should fire him and try somebody else."

"It is getting ridiculous," Gwen agreed. "We need to know which one of these guys is the father so we can all get on with our lives."

Shelby would be in favor of that, too. "Have you ever asked her about that when she calls?"

"We've tried," Matty said. "That's the point in the conversation where she hangs up. She doesn't want us to know who Elizabeth's father is, apparently. Or she's not willing to say on the phone. I did tell her just now that Boone is here, to get her reaction."

Shelby tried to keep the anxiety out of her voice. "And?"

"She just said 'good.' Then when I tried to ask if Boone was the baby's father, she hung up, like she always does."

Shelby began wrapping kisses again. So Jessica was happy that Boone was here. Maybe that meant she would be coming back. Maybe she'd decided she loved him, after all. She might have been waiting for him to arrive. "Boone really thinks he's Elizabeth's father," she said.

"Which makes him absolutely no different from the other two," Gwen said. "Travis and Sebastian are driving Matty and me nuts with their squabbling about it. I think you should consider hiring a new detective, Matty, or at least have a long talk with the one you've got."

"I'd vote for that." Luann took off her granny glasses and gazed at Matty and Gwen. "I'll always think of Elizabeth as my granddaughter, but I'd like to know if it's official or not."

"We'd all like to know," Matty said. "I think you'd like to know, too, wouldn't you, Shelby?" she added softly.

Shelby glanced up and her cheeks felt hot, but she looked bravely into Matty's blue eyes. Sebastian's wife missed nothing. "Well, sure, for Boone's sake," she said.

"And what about your own?" Matty asked.

"Uh, I think it would be premature to—"

"Hey." Gwen joined the discussion, reaching over to put her hand on Shelby's arm. "Don't feel like the Lone Ranger, hon. Matty and I have been where you are. It's hell when you're falling in love with a guy who won't commit because of some phantom woman who's running all over the countryside."

Shelby's cheeks warmed even more. "Oh, no. I'm not—"

Gwen squeezed her arm. "Sure you are. It's written all over your face when you look at that big cowboy. Right, Matty?"

"I'm afraid so."

Shelby was mortified. "Do you think he can tell?"

"Are you kidding?" Luann unwrapped a candy and popped it in her mouth. "He's a man, sweetie. You'd have to splash it across a billboard."

"I don't really want him to find out," Shelby said. "He already has so much to worry about, and I—"

"And you have a lot to worry about, too," Matty said. "Don't be too easy on the guy, or too hard on yourself. As Luann pointed out, he's a man. He probably has no idea what's good for him."

Gwen laughed. "Talk about stating the obvious. Of course he doesn't."

Matty picked up a piece of candy and stared at it for a while. Then she glanced at Gwen. "Maybe after you and Travis head off for your honeymoon, Sebastian and I can make a quick trip to Denver and talk to the folks at the agency." She looked across the table at Shelby. "Luann's going to be busy running the bed-and-breakfast for Gwen. How would you feel about baby-sitting for a couple of days? You and Boone?"

CHAOTIC THOUGHTS kept Shelby from sleeping very well that night. She had the definite feeling that Matty was matchmaking. Still, she tried not to dwell on the possibility that she and Boone would be able to spend more time alone together if Sebastian and Matty went to Denver and left them to watch the two kids. Sebastian might not even agree to the trip.

But he did. The next morning he and Travis were both at the breakfast table nursing a hangover when Matty informed them of Jessica's call. After Sebastian muttered a soft curse and massaged his temples, Matty proposed the quick trip to Denver. Then she suggested leaving Shelby and Boone in charge of the two children and the ranch while they were gone.

Sebastian looked at his wife and they seemed to exchange a signal of some sort. "Maybe that's a good idea," he said.

Elizabeth, who was in a playpen in the corner of the kitchen, picked that moment to start fussing. Sebastian winced and closed his eyes. Josh had appointed himself in charge of the baby's happiness, and he clambered out of his chair to go check on her. In the process he knocked over his milk.

He stared at the milk, crestfallen. "Whoopsy-daisy," he said.

Shelby grabbed a sponge and started mopping. "That's okay, Josh."

"It was a accident!"

"Sure it was," Matty said, coming over to the table and smiling at Josh. "Go ahead and see about Elizabeth, honey. She likes it when you talk to her."

As Josh trotted over and began singing the ABC

song to Elizabeth, Sebastian ran a hand over his face and sighed. "Yeah, Denver might be a very good idea."

"Denver?" Boone asked as he came in the back door. For the second night in a row, he'd bedded down in the barn.

Travis had spent the night, or what was left of it after the men had come home, on the living-room sofa. Bleary-eyed, he glanced over at Boone. "It seems they're appointing you and Shelby to baby-sit while they go to Denver and find out what's up with the private detective, who isn't finding diddly-squat."

"Oh."

Shelby concentrated on mopping up the milk and didn't look at him. As usual, his presence made her feel as if someone had touched her with a live electrical wire. She wondered if he was thinking the same thing that she was. In order to make sure she and the kids were safe, he'd have to sleep in the house instead of the barn. Matty had figured that out, of course.

"I guess that would be okay," Boone said.

His soft, gentle voice skipped along her nerves and her knees grew weak. They would be alone in this house together for at least one night and maybe two. Well, alone except for the children. Children who slept at night. If Boone was in love with Jessica, then Shelby should probably stay away from him, even if he did end up sleeping right down the hall. Of course, he might not stay away from her....

"That security system Jim installed for the house is top-of-the-line," Sebastian said. "So you don't have to worry about—" He glanced significantly over at Josh. "You know what," he added.

"*Tell* me about that precious security system," Travis

said. "I was afraid you and me were gonna end up sleeping on the porch last night when you were too ploughed to remember the code."

Sebastian eyed Travis across the table. "Oh, yeah? I distinctly heard you suggesting that we sleep out in the yard. You wanted to sleep under the stars like men, you said, to symbolize your last night of freedom. You were fried to your tonsils, hotshot."

"Was not."

"Were too."

Boone poured himself some coffee and sat down at the table. "Let me put it this way. The guys at the Buckskin will never forget the Daniels and Evans version of the theme song from *Bonanza.*"

Sebastian frowned at Travis. "We didn't sing that last night, did we?"

"Nah," Travis said. "Ol' Boone's just making that up to harass us."

Boone chuckled. "You did more than sing it. There was a considerable amount of bumping and grinding going on."

Sebastian gave him a deadpan stare. "I refuse to believe that."

"Okay." Boone shrugged and took a drink of his coffee. "Just don't be surprised if guys come up to you at the reception and ask how things are going out at the Ponderosa."

Matty laughed and pushed back her chair. "And I thought I was the boot-scootin' champion around here. Boone, would you like some breakfast? I can't seem to interest these two in my cooking, but you look like a man who could put away some bacon and eggs."

Travis groaned. "Just don't pass them under my nose."

"I'd love some breakfast," Boone said. "And if these cowboys can't take the heat, they can get out of the kitchen. What's the plan for today?"

Matty took a carton of eggs out of the refrigerator. "Shelby and I need to run into town for some reception goodies and take them over to Hawthorne House," she said. "If you three guys can handle it, I'd like you to watch the kids until we get back, which will be later this afternoon."

"Perfect," Boone said. "Then I can take Josh riding."

Josh leaped up from where he'd been crouching next to the playpen and ran over to Boone's chair. "Bob, too?"

Boone ruffled the little boy's hair. "Yeah, Bob, too."

The look he gave Josh made Shelby's heart turn over. Matty and Gwen were right. She was falling in love with Boone Connor.

AROUND THREE that afternoon, Shelby followed Matty through the front door of the ranch house. They were greeted with the sound of male voices raised in heated debate. Shelby figured out the noise was coming from Elizabeth's room after she heard a few baby chortles mixed in with the argument in progress.

"You didn't tell him to wipe from front to back, hotshot!" Sebastian said.

"That's because I was so busy keeping you from knocking over the baby oil!" Travis said. "You keep elbowing your way in there, because of course *nobody* does this as good as you, and now—"

"Will you two cowpokes back the heck off?" Boone sounded more impatient than Shelby had ever heard him. "No wonder I can't get the hang of this! It's as crowded as a bucking chute in here. And where's the blasted diaper?"

"I gots it!" Josh piped up. "Whoops. The tape comed off. It was a accident!"

Matty turned to Shelby and grinned. "It figures. Chaos."

"Oh, *man.*" Sebastian's complaint floated down the hall. "This is the bad kind of diaper. Who bought these losers, as if I didn't know?"

"*I* did," Travis said, "and you can quit your bellyaching, because they're more absorbent. The kind *you* buy leak like a sieve. See? Right here it says—"

"My kind does not leak, and this kind has bad tape!"

"So you're starting me out with substandard equipment?" Boone asked. "What kind of outfit are you saddle tramps running, anyway?"

Shelby put her hand over her mouth to stifle a giggle.

"Come on." Matty beckoned to her and crept toward the hall. "This should be worth the price of admission."

Shelby followed Matty as the diaper argument continued. When she peered in the room, she had to press her lips together to keep from laughing out loud. Their backs to the door, all three cowboys jostled for position around the changing table, completely blocking any view of the baby. Josh bounced around behind them, jumping up every few seconds as he tried to see what was going on.

"No, don't do it that way," Sebastian said. "Here. Let me—"

"Get your mitts off her." Boone batted Sebastian's hand away.

"She likes it if you make faces at her while you're changing her," Travis said. "Don't you, Lizzy?"

"Don't be distracting her, Travis!" Boone said. "I've just about got this thingamajig—"

"She likes my singing better," Sebastian said.

"Don't you wish!" Travis said. "Watch this. Stick out your tongue, Lizzy. Like this. Thata-girl."

"She also likes her monkey Bruce." Sebastian waggled the sock monkey over the changing table. "Here's Brucey, Elizabeth!"

"Will you *move over?*" Boone sounded as if he was at the end of his rope. "There! Got the diaper on, no thanks to you morons. Now what are we putting on her?"

"I don't gots diapers anymore!" Josh proclaimed, hopping up and down. "I'm a big boy. Can I throw the diaper away? Can I? I wanna slam-dunk it."

Sebastian reached up to a shelf above the changing table where baby clothes were folded in neat stacks. "Put this on her." He shoved a red-and-white-ruffled outfit at Boone.

"No, not that." Travis took down something else. "This yellow terry job. We gotta feed her, don't forget, before the women get home. Matty won't like it if we get that ruffled thing all gucked up."

"I wanna slam-dunk the diaper," Josh repeated, leaping up and down.

"Speaking of the women," Sebastian said, "I sure do like Shelby, Boone."

Shelby's smile faded and she tensed.

"Me, too," Travis said.

"Me, too!" Josh announced.

"I like her, too," Boone said quietly, "but—"

"But nothing, man," Travis said. "Don't be an idiot."

Shelby's face grew hot, but when Matty quietly put a hand on her arm and tried to draw her back down the hall, she resisted. She wanted to know what Boone had to say about her when she wasn't around, although of course they'd all be careful, with Josh right there.

"Travis is right for once," Sebastian said. "And for some reason she seems to like you, too, even considering you're as stubborn as they come. Are you going to be dumb enough to louse this up?"

Shelby held her breath as her heart hammered in anticipation of Boone's answer.

"Yeah, I probably am," Boone said.

Shelby's heart dropped to her toes. This time, when Matty tugged on her arm, she retreated with her, battling tears all the way.

When they were halfway back down the hall, Matty gave her a quick hug. "Hang in there," she murmured. "He'll come around."

Shelby didn't trust herself to speak, so she nodded.

"Come on, let's break up that party," Matty said softly. Then she raised her voice. "Hey, guys, we're home!" She started back down the hall, and unless Shelby wanted to look like a coward, she had no choice but to follow.

Sebastian spun around toward the doorway, the ruffled outfit still in one hand. "Matty!" He glanced guiltily at Shelby. "When did you two get back?"

"Just now," Matty said.

"Shebby!" Josh ran toward Shelby and threw his arms around her legs. "We rided the horsies!" He gazed up at her, his face alight with happiness. "Me and Bob and Boone! We went round and round and round and—"

"Sounds great." Forcing a smile, she leaned down to give him a hug.

"Time's getting short," Matty said to Sebastian. "Maybe you guys should go get cleaned up and into your duds while Shelby and I feed the kids."

"Yes, ma'am," Sebastian said. "Come on, bride-groom. You, too, Boone."

Boone hoisted Elizabeth into his arms and turned to Matty, but instead of holding the baby out so Matty could take her, he kept her close against his chest.

Heartsick, Shelby took in the sight of Boone holding that sweet little girl. He glanced over at Shelby and his eyes shone with a gentle light as he stroked Elizabeth's downy hair with one big hand. His whole manner had changed from tentative to possessive. Shelby realized that while she'd been in town with Matty, Boone had staked his claim to his daughter. And it looked as if he had no room left in his heart for Shelby.

He turned toward Matty. "If it's all the same to you," he said, "I'd like to feed her."

CHAPTER THIRTEEN

CANDLELIGHT WEDDINGS sure made a church look cozy, Boone thought as he stood next to Sebastian at the altar. While the minister, Pete McDowell, talked about the holy state of matrimony, Boone congratulated himself on making it to Colorado in time. He wouldn't have wanted to miss seeing Travis and Gwen hitched, and besides, he balanced out the wedding party.

Gwen had decided to challenge tradition and had asked Luann to stand up with her, along with Matty. That way Luann could hold Elizabeth, which had seemed the best way to get the baby into the ceremony. Elizabeth was becoming quite a handful, and she might have tried to climb out of the buggy they'd used for Matty and Sebastian's wedding. If Boone hadn't been around, Luann would have had to walk back down the aisle by herself.

He still had trouble believing that Travis was really tying the knot. Apparently the women in the congregation had trouble believing it, too. Boone saw many a young lady sniffling into her handkerchief, and Boone didn't think they were crying for joy.

Boone's gaze moved over the crowd and came to rest again on the face that held the most interest for him tonight. Shelby sat on the end of a pew, near enough to a flickering candle that the light sparkled on the tears she bravely blinked away. He hadn't considered how tough this celebration would be on her. She was still grieving for her family, and the warm, happy scene probably reminded her of how alone she was except for the little boy snuggled next to her, his hair slicked back and his eyes wide. Boone's chest grew tight and his arms ached with the urge to comfort her.

Matty had loaned Shelby a pale blue dress, and when she'd come out into the ranch-house living room wearing it, Boone had been so dazzled he hadn't been able to think of anything to say. Josh had told her she looked "like a princess." She'd glanced uncertainly at Boone, as if wanting his opinion. "You look nice" had been the best he could do. Lame, totally lame.

But maybe it was good that he hadn't paid her much of a compliment. He had no business getting her hopes up about him. He'd made a huge mistake with that incident in the barn and now this baby-sitting assignment was going to be a real test of his ability to stay away from her.

All he wanted to do was help and protect her, but instead he seemed to be making her miserable. Correction—he was making them *both* miserable, because after those moments in the barn, all he could think about was holding her like that again.

As Pete McDowell moved into the vows portion of the ceremony, Boone glanced over at Gwen. He didn't know much about women's clothes, but he could tell she'd gone for the old-fashioned look, with lots of ivory lace and little pearls everywhere. It was an impressive outfit, but the rapture on her face completely outshone the dress and veil.

Boone's heart twisted as he realized it was the kind of expression he longed to see on Shelby's face. Lord help him, he wanted to be standing at this altar with Shelby. And because of Elizabeth, he had no right.

FOR JOSH'S SAKE, Shelby kept a tight grip on her emotions during the ceremony. When the tears came, she whisked them quickly away. Concentrating on Boone helped keep her strong. His tux was too small, which only emphasized what a giant of a man he was. He appeared gorgeously serious and forbidding standing up there. Unshakable. Ah, but he wasn't. She'd seen him come undone.

No one observing Boone looking so dignified in his elegant tie and tails would ever guess what he'd been doing with her twenty-four hours ago. Her body warmed to the memory of how he'd kissed her…everywhere. In spite of what he'd said to his friends this afternoon, he hadn't been so cavalier when he held her in his arms. In fact, she'd caused this rock of a man to go a little crazy. She'd hold on to that knowledge.

Boone might never belong to her, but she got under his skin, and that was nice to know. He'd been thinking about her, she could tell. His gaze had touched hers more than once. Knowing him, he was probably wrestling with the question of how he'd get through babysitting without giving in to temptation.

She was sure he didn't want to succumb, because his moral code was a few notches above that of most men. Shelby didn't want him to go against that code if he would think less of himself as a result, but oh, how she longed for a night of loving Boone.

Judging from the experience in the barn, she could

probably override his control and seduce him. But she'd seen how he beat himself up over the possibility that he'd inappropriately made love to Jessica. No matter how satisfying loving Boone might be, Shelby didn't want to add another burden to his conscience. Boone was the sort to carry that burden to his grave. So it was settled. They wouldn't make love while Matty and Sebastian were gone.

Boone glanced in her direction again, and his green eyes glowed with an intensity that threatened to melt all her good intentions.

"Shebby," Josh whispered. "Gwen and Travis are kissing in front of all the peoples!"

"That's because they're married now, sweetheart," Shelby murmured, still holding Boone's gaze. Was it only sexual desire she saw there, or something more lasting?

Then the minister presented the newly married couple, and the congregation burst into applause. Boone looked away, and Shelby decided wishful thinking was making her imagine things. Boone might want her, but he wasn't happy about it.

FATE HAD SMILED on him, Mason decided as he slipped quietly out of the yard adjacent to Hawthorne House where the wedding reception was in full swing. Thanks to his excellent reconnaissance skills, he'd found out exactly what he needed to know by listening in on a few conversations.

He left the music and laughter and twinkling lights behind as he started the trek back to his campsite outside of town. Let the wedding guests enjoy themselves. The fun and games would be over soon enough.

Beginning tomorrow night, Shelby and the kid would be alone at the ranch except for one big, dumb cowboy and a little baby. With the element of surprise, Mason figured he could get his kid back. Maybe in the process he'd even put a nice little scare into Shelby, so she'd understand who she was messing with.

This whole operation was right on track. With Huerfano being a tourist town, he'd been able to locate a campground where he could keep a low profile. Although the wedding had seemed like a nuisance at first, he'd quickly realized he could use the time during the ceremony to check out the security system at the ranch.

It was nothing he couldn't get around. His crummy part-time job selling home-security systems had come in handy, after all. He might not have sold anything, but he'd learned a hell of a lot about how most systems worked.

He was good at this kind of mission, though, damn good. He'd have made a fine Navy SEAL, too, if the brass hadn't had it in for him. Once he got his hands on the kid and he was assured of a steady supply of money, he'd give up the security-systems racket and see what he could find that would make better use of his skills, something that would be fun.

There had to be people out there who would pay for his natural talent in espionage, people with deep pockets who didn't care to advertise in the Help Wanted section of the newspaper. A couple of his buddies had hinted they had contacts, but he'd never felt he had the financial freedom to try a risky new venture like that. But now—now anything was possible.

LATE THE FOLLOWING afternoon Shelby stirred a pot of beef stew in between setting the table for dinner and glancing out the window to catch a glimpse of Boone. He was doing the evening chores with Elizabeth in a carrier strapped to his back. Josh and both dogs stayed right at his heels.

Matty and Sebastian had left about lunchtime for Denver, and Boone had started immediately on the long-overdue job of shoeing Sebastian and Matty's horses. Shelby had kept Elizabeth and Josh up at the house, figuring they shouldn't be underfoot while Boone was working.

As dinnertime approached, though, Boone had returned from the barn and volunteered to take both kids so she could fix the meal without being constantly interrupted. It was a kind gesture, but Shelby could tell from the way he was interacting with both Elizabeth and Josh that he relished being with them.

She watched him now as he crouched down to look at some treasure Josh had found. It was probably only a stone that had caught the little boy's eye, but Boone examined it as if Josh had discovered the Hope diamond. Both dogs came over to look, too, wagging their tails and trying to lick Josh's face.

Then from her perch in the carrier Elizabeth made a grab for Boone's hat. He ended up taking it off and putting it on Josh, who wore it as if he'd been crowned King of England, even though it came down over his ears and he could barely see out from under the brim.

The faint scent of scorched stew pulled Shelby away from the window. She turned down the flame under the burner and vowed to pay more attention to her job, but her mind was filled with images of Boone, Elizabeth and Josh. Her own experience didn't give her much of a yardstick concerning family men, but even she could see that Boone would make a wonderful husband and father.

Minutes later Boone, Josh and Elizabeth came through the back door, followed by Fleafarm and Sadie. Once Boone was inside, he turned and set the security alarm. Shelby didn't know much about alarms, but this seemed like a good one. She doubted it was necessary, though. It was hard to believe Mason had tracked her to this remote ranch, but with the alarm, the dogs and Boone, she felt quite safe.

"Look, Shebby!" Josh held out his treasure, a baseball-sized rock flecked with bits of gold. "Iron pie-bite!"

"Py*rite*," Boone corrected gently.

"Yep," Josh said happily. "Looks like gold, huh? Me and Bob found it. Maybe they really gots gold around here!"

Shelby admired the sparkling rock. "You never know. It sure is pretty, though. Better go put it in a safe place in your room. Then go wash your hands. We're ready to eat."

"'Kay!" Josh started out of the kitchen, his free hand clapped over Boone's hat to keep it from falling off.

"And maybe you'd better give that hat back," Shelby said.

Josh turned and peered up from under the wide brim. "Do I hafta?"

"Tell you what, Josh," Boone said. "You can wear it until you go to bed tonight. Then tomorrow we'll take a run into town and find one that fits you a little better."

"This one fits real good," Josh insisted.

"It's not bad," Boone said, obviously trying not to smile, "but I think we can do better. And besides, you need boots. We'll pick those up tomorrow, too."

Josh grinned. "O*kay!*" He started to run out of the room.

"Walk," Shelby called after him. Then she turned to Boone. "Let me take that little papoose so you can go wash up, too."

"Thanks." He turned his back and hunkered down slightly so she could lift the baby out of the carrier. "Dinner smells good."

"It's a pretty simple meal—one of Josh's favorites." She tried to ignore the excitement that always stirred in her when he stood this close.

"I like simple food the best." Boone moved his arm back right at the moment Shelby leaned forward to lift Elizabeth out, and he nudged her breast. "Sorry."

"No problem." Her breast tingled, and the feeling began to spread.

Boone moved away the minute she had Elizabeth free. He took off the carrier and propped it in the corner. He made a good show of looking nonchalant as he walked to the stove and lifted the lid on the beef stew. "Yum. I was practically raised on this stuff."

Then what this world needs is more beef stew, if it produces hunks like you, she thought. "I sure wasn't raised on it," she said. She propped Elizabeth in her high chair. "We had a cook who fixed nothing but gourmet, and I used to dread meals as a kid. I faked stomach flu whenever we had escargots. I don't want to put Josh through that." She fastened the high-chair tray securely in place.

When she looked up she caught Boone silently watching her, his gaze on the top button of her blouse. His glance moved to her face, and his green eyes were hot. The tension crackling between them nearly made her forget what else he'd been doing when she'd looked up. Then she realized he'd been massaging his shoulder, as if he had an injury of some kind.

"Are you okay?" she asked.

He broke eye contact. "Sure. Fine. Listen, why don't I check on Josh?" He left the room before she could question him further.

As she spooned up cereal and scooped it into Elizabeth's rosebud mouth, Shelby could hear Josh and Boone laughing and talking in the bathroom. She wondered how Josh would ever manage when he had to leave Boone.

The two of them apparently found a lot to talk about, and Shelby was nearly finished feeding Elizabeth when Boone returned carrying Josh piggyback.

"Boone told me about hats." Josh bounced along happily. "They gots beaver hats, and straw hats, but when you buy one, you gots to fix it so it gots *style*. Right, Boone?"

"Right."

Elizabeth chortled and held out her cereal-smeared hands toward Boone.

"My turn, Lizzie," Josh said, with a trace of possessiveness. "You gots your turn. Put me up higher, Boone! On your shoulders, okay?"

"Sure." Boone lifted Josh up and settled him over his shoulders.

If Shelby hadn't been watching so closely, she might have missed Boone's wince of pain. "You're hurt," she said.

"Nah. How do you like it up there, pardner?"

"I'm king of the whole wide world!" Josh said.

Shelby gave Elizabeth's face and hands a quick wipe

and glanced back at Josh. "Time to get down, buckaroo," she said with a smile. "Dinner's ready."

"Aww." Josh stuck out his lower lip.

"Better listen to the lady," Boone said. "When it comes to chow-time, she's the boss." He set Josh back on his feet and repositioned the oversized hat. "Take a seat, cowboy. I'll help Shelby dish up."

"We'll see about that, Boone." Shelby stood, determined to find out if Boone was injured. "First, I want you to take off your shirt."

"What?" He stared at her.

"Go on, take it off. You said you're not hurt. Prove it to me."

He looked uncomfortable. "It's nothing. A little kick, is all. Then the carrier rubbed on the spot. But I'll be fine."

"I'm sure you will. Let me see."

Josh scrambled off his chair. "*I* wanna see."

"Hey, it's really nothing," Boone said. "Let's forget it."

She folded her arms and waited.

His green eyes grew soft and smoky. "Please."

She was no match for a look like that. When he gave her that kind of look she wanted to wrap her arms around him and lift her mouth for his kiss. She unfolded her arms and blew out a breath. "Okay, you win. Let's eat."

BOONE HOPED Shelby had forgotten about his shoulder in all the hubbub of dinner and starting the kids toward bed. While she read Josh a story, Boone let the dogs out for one last run. Standing on the porch waiting for them to come back, he assessed his shoulder by prodding it with the tips of his fingers.

He had a good-sized bruise there, and if he'd been alone, he would have taken time to put some ice on it. But doing that would bring attention to his injury. The bruise might upset Josh, for one thing. But the real danger was in letting Shelby get involved in nursing him.

The dogs loped back up to the porch and he went inside. The little kick of excitement in his stomach had to be ignored, he told himself. Nothing would happen between him and Shelby tonight. Absolutely nothing.

She didn't mention his shoulder again as they finished putting the kids to bed. He couldn't believe how much he loved taking care of Josh and Elizabeth, and how natural it seemed to be doing these chores with Shelby. The four of them were a great fit, with Josh taking the role of Elizabeth's older brother, and Elizabeth apparently happy to have Josh sleeping in the same room with her.

Josh needed a little calming down, but he agreed to go to bed once Boone reminded him that the sooner he went to sleep, the sooner morning would come and they could drive into town to shop for his hat and boots. Boone thought he was probably as excited about the prospect as Josh.

As a reminder of coming attractions, Boone left his hat on Josh's bedpost. After collecting good-night kisses from Boone and Shelby, Josh finally went to sleep clutching his "gold" rock in his hand.

Boone went out into the hallway and Shelby followed, closing the door partway after her.

"He's been in seventh heaven the past few days," she murmured. "Thank you for all the time you've given him."

"I've had fun." Boone glanced back at her. "He's a

great kid." *And he's the perfect chaperone.* Boone felt the privacy of the narrow hallway closing in on him, creating feelings he had no business having about the woman so temptingly near. He wanted to push her against the wall, kiss her senseless, unbutton her blouse, her jeans....

This was the moment he'd been dreading, when the two of them had no distractions. The light in the hallway was dim, but he could still see her expression far too well. She was looking at him with way too much tenderness.

"I wonder what's on the tube tonight?" he said abruptly. He hardly ever watched TV, but suddenly it seemed like the best idea going. "Let's go see." He started down the hall toward the living room.

She caught his arm. "Boone, let me look at your shoulder."

He tensed as the pressure of her fingers sizzled along his nerve endings. He squelched the urge to jerk his arm away, although that might be the safest move. Trying for a cool attitude in spite of his blazing hormones, he looked down at her. "Never mind about the shoulder," he said. "I'm fine."

Her gaze was soft. The rest of her would be, too. So very, very soft. "I don't believe you," she said.

"You have to." His voice sounded like tires on gravel.

"Why?" She left her hand right where it was, lightly holding on to his arm.

Her touch felt like a branding iron, burning through the cotton of his shirt to singe the hair on his arms. He gritted his teeth against the urges washing over him, the need to once again explore her mouth, her breasts, the warm, moist place between her thighs. "Because I'm not taking off my shirt."

She swallowed. "If you think I'm trying to seduce you, I'm not. I'm just worried that you're hurt and you won't take care of yourself properly. I checked and there's a first-aid kit in the bathroom. I could—"

"I don't think so."

She gulped, but her chin lifted with determination and that crazy little ponytail she liked to wear on top of her head wiggled. "Boone, don't be stubborn. I wouldn't—"

"No, but I would." In a heartbeat. He could have her clothes off in ten seconds flat.

Wordlessly she gazed at him, a pulse beating in her throat.

His chest tightened with the effort not to pull her into his arms. "Move…move your hand. Please."

Her eyes still locked with his, she released her grip on his arm.

"Thank you." Summoning all his strength, he turned toward the living room.

"Are you in love with her?"

He paused. She must mean Jessica. He sensed that if he lied and said he was, that she would back off and they'd both be saved.

"It's okay if you are," she said in a small voice. "And I don't think any less of you for what happened in the barn. I'm sure when a man is…frustrated, his control can snap. I was available. And you're only human."

He groaned and leaned a hand against the wall. He didn't want her thinking he'd only used her as a sexual outlet.

"I wonder if she realizes how lucky she is," Shelby whispered. "Well, good night, Boone. And please put something on that shoulder before you go to bed."

"I don't love Jessica." The words just came out. He

hadn't even realized what he'd been about to say, only that he couldn't let her believe herself only a handy convenience for him.

"You...don't?"

He shook his head, still not trusting himself to look at her. "That's why what I did, getting her pregnant, was so wrong."

"You really don't love her?" Shelby's voice came from right beside him. "Or are you just saying that because she doesn't love you back?"

He straightened and faced her. If only he had the strength to let her believe all the hogwash she'd made up about his situation, he'd spare himself and her a lot of grief. But then she'd think that whole episode in the barn had nothing to do with her, and everything to do with him missing the lady in his life. He couldn't have Shelby, who meant so much to him, thinking something like that.

Shelby's eyes glowed with feeling. "I can't imagine why she wouldn't love you back. You're everything any woman could want."

He wished he could be worthy of her high opinion. Looking at her angel's face, he could barely breathe, let alone talk. But he had to try. "Jessica and I are just friends. We've never been more than friends."

"But...Matty said..." She hesitated.

His face grew hot at the idea Matty had been talking about him to Shelby. Still, he had to know. "Matty said what?"

"That there was someone, someone you cared about, and it didn't turn out well."

"There was." And at the moment he couldn't imagine why he'd ever pined away for Darlene. She didn't hold a candle to Shelby.

"So are you still in love with *her?*"

"No." Amazingly, it was true. And he'd be happier about it if he hadn't jumped from the frying pan into the fire.

"Then you're not in love with anybody?"

He gazed down at her, his heart pounding. "I didn't say that."

CHAPTER FOURTEEN

SHELBY FELT UNSTEADY and shivery. A surge of heat followed, then shivers shook her again as Boone's reply echoed in her head. He was looking at her now with the same intensity he had during the wedding ceremony. Possibilities she'd never allowed herself to dream of seemed suddenly within reach.

But this wasn't the most forthcoming man in the world. She had to be courageous and risk rejection in order to make sure she understood him. "What are you saying, Boone?"

"I don't have a damn right to say anything." But his eyes still blazed with green fire.

The message in those eyes seemed blatantly clear. She began to quiver with anticipation. Embarrassed by how shaky she felt, she put both hands behind her back and leaned her shoulders against the wall, pretending to be casual but desperately needing the wall for support. "I'm not sure I understand what you mean."

"Shelby." His voice sounded strained. "Don't do that."

"Do what?"

"Lean like that." His gaze lingered on her breasts, and his breathing grew ragged.

She realized that her attempt to be casual had resulted in her breasts thrusting out and up in what looked like an invitation to touch. She hadn't done it deliberately, but as she noticed his agitation and the bulge in his jeans, her shakes began to disappear.

In the process she discovered something very wicked about herself. Now that he'd said he wasn't in love with someone else and had come close to admitting he might be in love with her, she was ready to play on his weakness for her body.

Her careful, deep breath strained the buttons on her blouse. "Why, does it bother you?"

He looked like a man about to break. "You know it does. And I can't—I have nothing to offer you."

"Except what you gave me the other night in the barn?"

The heat in his eyes increased by several degrees. "Damn it. Don't remind me of that."

"Do I have to remind you?" she asked in a low voice. "Or is it what you think about constantly?"

He stepped closer. "I think about it constantly," he said. Flattening his palms against the wall, he stared down at her. His warm breath feathered her face. "Constantly."

Her heartbeat sounded a deep and frantic rhythm in her ears. "Me, too," she whispered.

"Tell me to go away, Shelby." His attention became fixed on her mouth. "For God's sake, don't look so ready to be kissed. You're driving me crazy, you know that?"

"I know." Meeting the challenge in his eyes, she moistened her lips, parted them, teased him with a sultry look. "Drive me crazy, too, Boone. One more time."

"I have to kiss you. But that's it. Nothing else."

She started to put her arms around his neck.

"No," he whispered, leaning down. "Don't touch me.

Just let me kiss you. One kiss." His palms still braced against the wall, he leaned down and touched his mouth to hers. He began with slow, sensuous nibbles, as if her lips were a sugary treat he wanted to make last a long time.

"Your mouth is so...ripe," he murmured. He raked her bottom lip gently between his teeth. "I want to gobble you up."

"I want you to. I want you to kiss me all over."

His quiet moan spoke of his frustration. "I can't risk that again. But I can do this." As if he had forever, he outlined her entire mouth with languorous flicks of his tongue. And although his only point of contact was her mouth, he did indeed drive her crazy. He was making love to her mouth, she realized, and this was foreplay.

When she was gasping, nearly begging for a more full-bodied kiss, he gradually dipped his tongue deeper and settled his lips more firmly over hers. Her heart thundered as he stroked the inside of her mouth. The motion blended with memory, as her body recalled the satisfaction he'd brought her once before with that wonderful tongue. The throbbing core of her moistened in readiness.

As his tongue continued to caress her, the rhythmic sensation spiraled downward. An insistent tension coiled ever tighter between her thighs. Clenching her fists at her sides, she moaned and opened her mouth wider, wanting to be ravished. He continued to caress only her hot mouth as he plunged deep, his breath coming fast.

Her nipples tightened and thrust against her blouse. She wanted him to cup and stroke her there, yet still he kept his palms flat against the wall. The ache pulsed ever stronger between her thighs. She wanted him there, as well—caressing, kissing, thrusting. At last the force of her need tricked her, guiding her to imagine him touching her everywhere, and there, especially *there*. As he kissed her with passionate abandon, she arched away from the wall. Her shuddering climax took her by storm.

He caught her in his strong arms before she crumpled to the floor. "Shelby," he murmured against her cheek as he gathered her up and carried her toward her room. "Oh, Shelby, sweetheart."

She struggled for breath. "Come to bed with me," she begged.

His voice rasped in the stillness. "It's not...a good idea."

"Do it anyway."

He carried her into her bedroom. "No. I—" In the dark he tripped against Sebastian's office chair and sent it rolling across the floor. It was a testament to his strength that he stayed upright and didn't drop her. "I'm leaving you here. Lock the door." He deposited her on the daybed.

Sitting up immediately, she reached over and snagged his belt buckle before he could turn away. "Oh, no, you don't."

"Let go, Shelby." He sounded as if he might strangle on the words as he fought a desperate battle between desire and conscience.

She didn't let go. She'd made it this far past his natural barriers, and retreat wasn't an option. He wouldn't have birth control with him, so she had to find another way to show him what he would be missing if he walked out that door. Grasping the tab on his zipper, she pulled it firmly down.

He clearly hadn't expected her to be so bold, judging from his quick gasp. Before he could recover enough to grab her wrists and stop her, she slipped her hand inside and stroked the solid length of him.

He groaned and tried to manacle her wrists in his long fingers. "No," he whispered.

"Yes. Let me love you," she murmured. She pulled her hand away and her searching fingers found the opening in his briefs, caressing the hot, smooth skin of his erect penis. "Please. Let me love you before you go."

"It's not right." But his protest was weaker, the grip on her one wrist not nearly so tight.

Had there been more light in the room, he never would have let her touch him like this, she thought. Instinctively she knew he wasn't a man who freely opened himself to such intimacies. Yet here, in the dark, after the amazing kiss they'd shared, his defenses were down. He might, just might, give in to the fantasy.

"You've been so good to me," she said softly. "Let me make you feel good, too."

The moan deep in his throat could have been either protest or permission. She took it for permission. Slowly she eased her hand inside his briefs and grasped him gently. He was so large her fingers couldn't complete the circle.

Heart pounding from the discovery of his incredible girth, she explored his length and grew dizzy imagining so much man deep inside her. She would know that thrill, too, but first she needed to stake her claim.

The sound of his rapid breathing filled the small room, brushed by a faint glow of light from the hall, as she nudged his erection free of the cotton material. With a sigh of surrender he released her wrist. Triumph surged through her as she took him in both hands.

She could feel the blood pounding through the impressive length beneath her fingers. As she ran her hands slowly upward, his penis twitched in reaction. Then, as she eased her grip and slid her hands back down, she leaned forward and kissed the moist tip. His whole body trembled, like the quaking of a giant tree about to topple to the forest floor.

A sense of power encouraged her to taunt him even more. She swirled her tongue in a lazy motion around the slight ridge just below the tip, and he trembled again. Then she placed her mouth against the velvet surface, and in a pace designed to drive him wild, she began to draw him in.

He gasped for breath. And gradually, tentatively, his big hands cupped the back of her head, his thumbs resting against her temples. Whether his touch was meant to restrain or encourage her, she wasn't sure. But when he applied a slight pressure she knew that Boone, who never asked for anything, was asking now. His pride and shyness were being consumed by fiery need.

She could not take all of him, and he seemed to hang on to enough of his sanity to know that. But his passiveness slipped away as he began to thrust gently yet eagerly into her mouth. With a broken cry his fingers tightened against her scalp, and the salty rush of his climax flavored her tongue.

BOONE SANK to his knees in front of Shelby. He longed to shower her with diamonds, yet all he could give was a kiss filled with awe and tenderness. The taste of him remained on her lips, and he was humbled once again by her generosity. And still aroused. He'd never have guessed that this angelic woman would be so daring with a man. The room was filled with the erotic scent of passion, his and hers.

She wanted him still. He could tell from the way she opened to his kiss. And he, too, wanted more, wanted to find out if she would become a wild creature when he pushed deep inside her. She was so small. He would have to be careful with her—if she would let him be careful. Already his penis was stirring at the thought of being enclosed by that hot, tight little body.

Lifting his mouth from hers, he tilted her head back and gazed into her shadowed eyes. His voice was husky with an emotion he hadn't expected to feel again for a long time, if ever. "We're not finished, are we?"

"No," she murmured.

He brushed his thumbs across her cheeks. "Nothing's changed. I still have a duty to Jessica. And the baby."

"You do," she agreed, her voice low and rich with desire. "But everything's changed."

He took a shaky breath. "Maybe."

"If you don't know it yet—" she pressed her forefinger against his bottom lip before sliding it smoothly into his mouth "—you will when you're deep inside me."

The surge of lust came like a blow to the gut. No matter what had just happened between them, he wanted her so fiercely that he nearly pushed her to the mattress then and there.

But before he could decide his next move, Josh's small voice carried down the hall.

"Shebby?" he called plaintively. "Bob, he had a bad dream."

"I'd better go," she said.

He stood and zipped his pants. Then he stepped aside to let her pass.

She rose on tiptoe and gave him a quick kiss. "I'll be back."

Such a simple statement, but it made his heart thunder. "Do you want me to see if I can find some con—"

"*Yes.*" Tucking in her blouse, she hurried out the door.

Moments later, as he searched Sebastian and Matty's bathroom cupboards, he listened to the muted sounds of Shelby talking to Josh. His heart wrenched as he faced the truth. Both of them had become so much a part of him that he might not survive without them. But what if Jessica wanted marriage? After what he'd done, he couldn't refuse her anything.

Well, if Jessica wanted marriage, he'd give it to her. And if that happened, he would never hold Shelby in his arms again.

Jessica could return anytime. Tomorrow, in fact. Matty had said she'd sounded happy to know that he was at the ranch. Tonight could be all he and Shelby would ever have.

He found the condoms. Carrying the box, he made a last tour of the house, shutting off lights and double-checking locks. The alarm was activated and the dogs lay sleeping in Josh and Elizabeth's room. It should be enough, but if not, he'd be here, ready to protect those he loved. And that was exactly what he felt for the three people in this house. Might as well be honest with himself. He'd fallen hard for each of them.

Finally he returned to the guest room and wondered whether he should undress. No. But he could at least take off his boots. He sat on Sebastian's desk chair to pull them off. When he was finished he impulsively leaned over and switched on the antique banker's lamp with the green glass shade. The light cast a soft circle of light over the rumpled daybed.

Good, thought Boone. He and Shelby had spent enough time in darkness. If this could be his only night with Shelby, he wanted to see everything. Most of all he wanted to be able to look into her eyes as he undressed her, to watch those blue eyes sparkle with excitement as he stroked her soft skin, and finally, to see them glow with passion as he pushed slowly, tenderly inside her.

MASON LOWERED his night-vision binoculars. At last his targets were moving toward bedtime. The lights were out in the front of the house, but one had flicked on in a back room. From the pattern of lights he'd figured out where Josh must be sleeping. That light had blinked out an hour ago, sometime around eight.

He could imagine what might be going on in the room with the light. And he figured it would work to his advantage. He hoped the bitch would wear that cowboy out. Heavy-duty sex made a guy sleep like the dead, which was exactly how Mason would like that big lug to sleep tonight. Shelby was doing Mason a favor without even knowing it.

Once the light went out, Mason planned to give them another couple of hours to finish their hanky-panky and fall asleep. Then he'd make his move. First he'd disengage the alarm. As for the dogs, the big cowboy had played into his hands by letting the pooches out right on schedule.

Mason had watched through his binoculars as those dumb canines had wolfed down the hamburger he'd left on the ground where they'd be sure and find it. The tranquilizer buried inside the patties would keep them out of the action until morning.

He could smell success, and damned if it wouldn't be sweeter than going to bed with a willing virgin. The operation seemed almost too easy, but that was because, as usual, people had underestimated Mason Fowler. And by the time they realized their mistake, it would be too late.

BOONE HAD JUST thrown back the covers on the bed when Shelby came into the room. She reappeared so silently that only his sharpened sense of her let him know she was there. He turned to look at her, taking his time, memorizing the way she looked now and imagining how she'd look as he gradually took off her clothes. He didn't plan to rush the process this time.

When he noticed that she'd taken off her shoes and stood there in her socks, he realized why he hadn't heard her come in. So she'd decided to start by taking off her shoes, too, he thought with an inward smile. He loved the idea that she was so eager for him.

But as she stood in the doorway, color tinged her cheeks. For a woman who had acted so boldly not long ago, she seemed hesitant, almost shy.

"Josh had some trouble going back to sleep." She swallowed and made a nervous gesture with her hand. "And I…I checked on Elizabeth, too. She's fine."

"Good. Thank you." He thought of what a wonderful mother Shelby would make. She deserved a baby of her own. He pictured her growing round, her belly becoming almost as big as she was. And he wanted to be the one to plant the seed.

Her cheeks still glowing a rosy pink, she glanced back at the door. "I guess we should close that."

"Yes."

She turned and closed the door with a soft click. Then she faced him again. Like a wild thing struck with curiosity, she slowly ventured farther into the room. He waited, afraid she'd changed her mind and couldn't think how to tell him.

When she hesitated and rested her hand on the desk, his fear grew. "You know, it's easier when you're caught up in the moment," she said, running her finger back and forth along the edge of the desk. Then she cleared her throat. "Now that we've been interrupted, I'm not sure what to do next, Boone."

Pain knifed through him. But if she'd reconsidered, he'd honor that. "You've changed your mind?"

She shook her head. "Oh, no."

Thank God. "Then—"

"My rhythm's messed up, is all. I don't know whether to throw myself into your arms, or do a sexy striptease, or take *your* clothes off, or—"

"Then let me decide," he said with a small smile and a huge feeling of relief. If that was all that was bothering her, he could take care of it. He wanted to take care of it, in fact. He held out his hand.

Holding his gaze, she came toward him and put her hand in his. "I noticed you turned on the light," she said in a breathy voice.

"Yes." His hand dwarfed hers. He brought it to his lips, turned it palm up and placed a kiss there. "You're so small and delicate," he murmured, tracing the shallow creases in her palm. He glanced into her eyes. "Are you afraid? Because I'm so big?"

"No." Her voice had become almost a whisper.

He unfastened the button at her wrist. "You know I'll be careful."

"Yes, I know."

Easing her sleeve back, he slowly kissed his way from the pulse at her wrist to the inside of her elbow. Along the journey he savored the satiny feel of her pale skin and the almost innocent scent of soap and flowers. His angel, who could seem so fragile one minute and so sexually daring the next. She made his head spin.

As he trailed his tongue along the return path to her wrist, she sighed. "That's why I'm not afraid," she murmured. "You are so…" She paused as he relinquished one hand and took the other, unfastening the button there. When he placed his lips against the inside of her other wrist, she sighed again. "So gentle."

He hoped he could live up to that. They were only beginning, and already fine tremors passed relentlessly through him, and beneath his jeans he was hard and hot. Unbuttoning the front of her blouse should have taken only one hand, but desire affected his coordination and he needed two. Gradually the placket gapped open, revealing the lacy cups of her bra. She'd begun breathing faster, and her breasts, cradled in white lace, quivered in response. He licked dry lips.

The light in the barn hadn't been very good. He hadn't been able to see clearly what he'd enjoyed that night, but he would take the time to see now. Pulling the tails of her blouse from the waistband of her jeans, he continued to watch the rapid rise and fall of her breasts as he pushed the blouse off her shoulders. It slid down her arms and whispered to the floor.

His heart hammered in anticipation as he reached

behind her back and unfastened the hooks of her bra. Lifting it by the straps, he pulled it down, and nearly forgot to breathe. He'd remembered the heart-stopping fullness of her breasts and how they'd seemed even fuller contrasted with her small rib cage and narrow waist.

But colors had been muted in the barn. He hadn't seen the delicate tracing of blue veins, or that her nipples were such a tender shade of rose, a shade that deepened as he gazed. The tips grew more erect with each breath she took, and he remembered this was a woman who could climax with only a kiss.

He looked into her eyes and the blue sparkle had turned to intense navy. Cupping a breast in each hand, he shuddered at the delicious weight filling his palms. He had big hands, yet she nearly overflowed his grasp. Just by smoothing his thumbs over her taut nipples, he made her gasp. Instinctively he realized that if he suckled her, even for a moment, she could erupt.

And he didn't want that. Not yet. Instead he leaned down, softly kissed each raspberry tip, and released those heavenly breasts. Her jeans came next, and although he lectured himself to go slow, he took them off much too fast. But he wanted…oh, how he wanted to discover what he'd suspected, that her panties were drenched and fragrant with passion.

With one hand behind her nape, he watched her expression as he spread his hand and placed it firmly against the wet cotton panel between her thighs. A flame leaped in her eyes. He slipped his hand inside her panties and found her slick and hot to the touch.

The fire burned brighter in her eyes, and then she blushed again. Her lashes fluttered down. "You must think I'm…"

"Wonderful?"

"Oversexed."

His hand stilled. The thought had never occurred to him. He'd simply been grateful for her response.

"But I'm not usually so…excitable."

An emotion stronger than gratitude blossomed in him. "You're not?"

She opened her eyes and looked up at him. Then she shook her head.

"Oh, Shelby." Postponing his intimate caress, he cradled her face in both hands and kissed her, putting all that he didn't know how to say into that kiss.

His mouth was tender and reverent against hers. *I love you.* But those were words best not spoken. Not when his future was so uncertain.

Her lips were incredibly sweet. He could be content with this…. But no sooner had the thought come than he knew it was a lie. His fingers were still damp from his intimate caress. As he stroked her cheek, he breathed in the aroma of her passion. The maddeningly erotic scent worked on him until tenderness became urgency and urgency became frenzy. He backed her toward the bed.

If she hadn't matched him in eagerness, he might have regained control, but she fumbled with his shirt buttons and tore at his belt buckle. She had his jeans open before she tumbled backward onto the mattress. Frantic now, he finished the job, nearly groaning in relief as he stepped out of the jeans and briefs and his erection sprang free. By the time he'd grabbed a condom, ripped open the package and rolled it on, she'd torn off her panties and lay waiting for him.

His hungry gaze roamed over the intoxicating sight of her, all flushed and panting and ready. So ready. The bed was short and narrow, but it would have to do. He put a knee between her thighs, his eyes fixed on hers. Despite the forces raging in him, he paused. Now was the time to be careful. Now was the moment they would remember forever, and he wanted it to be right.

"Hurry," she whispered, "I want you so much I feel like I might faint."

"Me, too. But I'm not going to hurry."

"Boone"

"Bend your knees," he murmured.

She drew her knees up.

Bracing a hand on either side of her, he leaned forward and lowered his head to brush her mouth with his. His heart beat like a crazed drummer, yet he had to maintain control. "Don't let me hurt you," he said. "Stop me if I'm hurting you." He slid one hand between her thighs and stroked her damp curls. "Promise me."

"I promise." She gasped as he pressed two fingers deep inside.

"Too much?"

"Not enough," she said, taunting him.

But he knew she was small, knew he would stretch her to her limits. Sitting back on his heels, he cradled a smooth thigh in each hand and guided her knees back and apart. His breath caught. There was the rosy entrance to heaven, glistening and waiting for him.

He leaned forward again, watching her eyes. Always watching her eyes as he slipped his throbbing penis just inside. There. That was the emotion he wanted to see in those blue eyes. He had no right to claim her, but it was all he wanted to do. She was the mate he'd waited a lifetime to find. He trembled as he restrained the overwhelming urge to ram deep.

"Good," she whispered.

Concentrating on the glow in her eyes, he pushed further in. Perfection. His heart ached for what they could have, if only…

A fraction more. He'd had no idea of the ecstasy of being tightly enclosed in her hot sheath. The friction was incredible, and in no time he was balanced on the edge of an orgasm. Or maybe it was more than the friction that had created this powerful need for release. He longed to empty himself in her, in Shelby. To create a child. Dizzy with pleasure, he dared more.

Her eyes widened.

He started to ease back, but she clamped onto his bottom with both hands.

"Keep going," she begged. "Oh, Boone, please keep going."

"Shelby, I'm afraid I'll—" *Lose control. Love you too much to ever let go.*

"Keep going," she begged, her breath coming in quick gasps. "Oh, please."

As he sank further, her body opened to him in a way that he'd never known, hadn't even imagined was possible. She was inviting him into her soul.

Then he felt her first contractions. With a groan of complete surrender he slid deep as they both came wildly undone. He captured her cries against his mouth as they held on tight and rode the whirlwind, locked completely and irretrievably…together.

CHAPTER FIFTEEN

As the waves of Shelby's powerful climax receded, the tears came. She couldn't have held them back if she'd wanted to.

Instantly Boone tensed. "I hurt you."

"No," she choked out, still sobbing. "Just hold me. I need you to hold me."

He cradled her gently, absorbing the torrent without protest or judgment. While he remained solidly within her, as if anchoring her to his strength, she wept in his arms.

She cried for the ugliness she'd endured and she cried for the beauty he'd given her. Months of silent suffering poured out, feelings for which she had no words, sorrows she'd buried deep. He'd uncovered it all.

At last she hiccupped to a stop, exhausted, but feeling a hundred pounds lighter, free of grief she'd bottled up for a long time. Her nose was stuffed up and no doubt her eyes were red.

She gazed up into his beloved face and knew from his tender expression that no apology was necessary. They didn't need to talk it out, or analyze why she'd cried. He knew. She didn't even feel embarrassed about the way she must look, because she knew he didn't care.

Because he loved her. She knew it as surely as she

knew the sun would rise. He didn't need to say it. The truth was in his soft green eyes.

"Lie still," he murmured easing away from her. "I'll get some tissues so you can blow your nose."

She missed him the instant he withdrew and levered his warm body out of the bed. As if he knew that, too, he pulled the comforter over her before he left the room. But a comforter would never substitute for his strong arms. And without him deep inside her, she felt hollow. She wanted him back with her, surrounding her, entering her, being one with her.

No doubt about it, he was immense. She might be a little sore tomorrow, as if that mattered. Given time, her body would adjust to his size. Time—that might be the one thing she would never be given.

He came back into the room—six feet, five inches of the most breathtaking body she'd ever seen. There was much to admire about this man, yet her attention went unerringly to his groin. Even at rest, his male equipment was impressive.

But as he stepped into the light and held out the box of tissues, she noticed the big angry bruise on his shoulder. "You *are* hurt."

He smiled. "Can't feel a thing."

She sat up and the comforter fell away from her breasts. "You should do something for that." She took a tissue and blew her nose. "Ice or something."

"It's probably too late for ice." His gaze lingered on her breasts.

"Then first-aid cream." She noticed the direction of his gaze. She also noticed the twitch of his penis. Her body answered with a quickening of its own, but she was concerned about his shoulder. The bruise was a rainbow of colors. It looked nasty. "There must be something to take the pain away."

"There is." His eyes grew hot as he reached for the comforter.

MUCH LATER, Shelby fell asleep in Boone's arms. The daybed was a tight fit for the two of them, which was exactly how Shelby liked it. Boone seemed quite happy with the arrangement, too, as he turned off the light and wrapped himself protectively around her.

When he cupped her breast and pressed his groin against her bottom, she remembered his embarrassment waking up in the New Mexico motel room in exactly this position. This time, she thought as she drifted to sleep, he wouldn't need to be embarrassed when he woke up with an erection. In fact, she quite looked forward to it.

She awoke to darkness and movement as Boone eased out of bed. Turning over, she saw him pulling on his jeans. She whispered his name.

He leaned down and kissed her. "I heard something. Probably Josh getting up to go potty. I'll go check on him, make sure he didn't pee in the closet. Keep the bed warm."

It probably was Josh, she told herself. Yet something didn't feel right to her. And maybe Josh would need her. As Boone started toward the door, she leaned down and picked up her panties and shirt. She'd slip them on, just in case Boone needed her help with Josh.

Not that Boone needed her help, she thought as she pulled on the underwear and pushed her arms into the shirtsleeves. Josh idolized Boone and would do anything the man asked of him.

Boone stepped into the hallway. "Josh?" he called softly. "What's going on, buddy?"

She had three buttons fastened when she heard Boone fall, hitting the floor in the hallway with enough force to shake the floorboards.

"Boone?" Oh, God, he'd tripped over something. Josh must have left a toy truck in the hall, although she thought they'd picked up everyth—

"Shebby! Shebby, help!"

Her blood ran cold. Something was very wrong. "Josh! I'm coming!"

She barreled into the hall and saw Boone lying motionless, his huge body nearly filling the narrow hall. She fought nausea.

"Shebby! Help me!"

"Shut up, you little monster! I'm your father, and you're coming with me!"

Mason. The blood roared in her ears.

"No! You hurt Boone!" Josh screamed. "You hurt my Boone! Shebby!"

She didn't stop to check on Boone. Mason had Josh. *But why weren't the dogs tearing him apart?* As Elizabeth started wailing, Shelby jumped over Boone and ran into the darkened bedroom.

Inside she faced her worst nightmare. Mason had an arm around Josh's middle while the little boy flailed and kicked at him.

"You hurt Boone!" he screamed. "You hurt my Boone!"

The dogs stood looking from the hysterical baby in the crib to the man and boy struggling next to the bed. They seemed bewildered and sluggish. The facts hit Shelby like bullets. *Mason had found a way to drug the dogs. He'd knocked Boone unconscious or...* No. Her mind couldn't go there.

But for now, she was the only one left to stop him.

A sense of calm resolution came over her. If Mason planned to take that boy out of this house, he would have to kill her first. "Put him down, Mason."

"Not in this lifetime," Mason said with a sneer. "I'm taking him and walking out of this house." He took a step toward her. "Get outta my way, bitch."

As her eyes adjusted to the dim light she could see that he wore camouflage gear and his eyes glittered with an unholy fire. She looked for his weapon and saw some sort of billy club hanging from his belt. No gun. He was probably smart enough to know taking Josh at gunpoint wouldn't look good to the courts. And he was arrogant enough about his physical abilities that he thought he wouldn't need a gun for this job. He probably saw himself as on the kind of mission he imagined when he'd tried so hard to become a SEAL.

She reached behind her for the door handle and flung the door shut. Then she backed against it and turned the lock. "I'm not moving. Put him down."

"You're a joke. I could squash you like a fly."

"Don't hurt my Shebby!" Josh screamed, and he began to cry.

"Shut *up,* I said! Or I'll give you something to cry about!"

Shelby stepped forward, her rage solidifying into cold hate. "You so much as leave a mark on Josh and you'll never get custody, Mason."

He glared at her. "I can sure as hell leave a mark on you. Most judges would understand if I went a little crazy trying to get my precious son back from the crazy woman who snatched him. So stand back and let me pass."

"No." She flexed her knees and tried to remember

what she'd learned in her self-defense course. She seemed pitifully inadequate for the job.

Josh, however, was not. He grabbed Mason's hand and bit him.

Mason yelled in surprise and dropped Josh to the floor. "Son of a bitch!" He drew back his foot as if to kick the little boy.

With a cry of fury Shelby launched herself at him, and to her surprise she knocked him backward onto the bed. The image of his foot drawn back ready to kick Josh brought out primitive instincts she'd never felt before. Lessons in self-defense disappeared in a red haze as she kicked, scratched and clawed. She wanted to kill him.

But she was losing the fight. He grabbed her wrists and shoved her backwards, following her down to the floor with a snarl. Straddling her, he released one of her wrists long enough to backhand her across the face. She saw stars. Then his thumbs closed over her windpipe.

"Stop, stop, stop!" screeched Josh, flailing at Mason.

Shelby caught a glimpse of gold in Josh's hand. He'd picked up his precious stone and was trying to hit his father with it, which might enrage Mason even more. While she struggled to pull Mason's hands away, she tried to tell Josh to stay back, but Mason was choking off her wind.

Josh's aim was bad and his strength puny, but he managed to connect with Mason's ear.

With a yelp of pain, Mason loosened his grip on Shelby's throat, clutched his bleeding ear and twisted toward Josh. "I'll kill you for that, you little runt!"

Desperately Shelby lunged for his face to bring his attention back to her. She succeeded.

"Right after I take care of you, bitch," he said, breathing hard.

"If you kill either of us," she rasped, "you'll never get that money."

"Shut up." He smacked her across the mouth and she tasted blood. "And you're wrong. I have a new plan. I'm gonna burn this place down, all of you in it. So sad. Shouldn't leave live ashes in the fireplace, you know. And guess what? I'm the kid's only surviving parent." His fingers closed around her throat. "Don't worry. I'll get the money. Why do you think I rigged up that little boating *accident?*"

He'd killed her parents and sister. Filled with horror, she fought him as best she could, but her strength was going. The sounds of Josh yelling and Elizabeth crying faded as Mason choked off her air supply. A giant vise seemed to be squeezing her chest. A loud crash sounded somewhere in the distance, but she couldn't make sense of it.

Then came a roar, as if from some enraged beast, and Mason was lifted high in the air. As she struggled to draw breath into her burning lungs she heard furniture splinter. Summoning all her will, she rolled to one side and looked for Josh. She finally saw him. He'd climbed in the crib with Elizabeth and wrapped his arms around her, but she was still crying. Both dogs were cowering under the crib.

Shelby crawled to the crib, put an arm through the slats and wrapped it around Josh. His small body quivered with terror.

"It's okay," she whispered automatically. She didn't know if it was okay or not. The two men fought like animals only a few feet away. She couldn't tell who was winning.

"It's okay," he whispered back, his voice shaking. "Boone gots him."

Sure enough, Boone had the upper hand at last. He held Mason down and his free arm worked like a piston as he pummeled the other man unmercifully.

Shelby remembered how she'd felt when Mason had threatened Josh, and she knew if she didn't do something, Boone wouldn't stop until Mason was dead. She gave Josh a squeeze. "Stay here."

"You, too!"

"No. I have to go. I'll be okay." She crawled closer to the men and tried to make her vocal chords work. *"Boone!"* she cried, but only a squawk came out. She moved even closer, cringing at the crunch of bone against bone as Boone hit Mason again and again.

"Boone!" she squawked again. "Boone, stop! Boone, please stop!"

No response. He seemed oblivious to everything but the task of eliminating Mason Fowler from the face of the earth.

She swallowed and tried again. "If you love me, stop!"

His head came up. His eyes held the wild spark of a predator as he gazed at her, and there was no recognition, as if he couldn't remember who she was. Mason lay unconscious beneath him, his face bloody. But he was still breathing.

"Boone, I love you," she rasped. "Don't kill him. You'll go to jail. We can't be together if you go to jail."

Slowly the killing rage faded from his eyes. He glanced down at Mason.

"He's not going anywhere," Shelby said.

"Josh?" Boone murmured.

"He's okay." She turned toward the crib. "He's taking care of Elizabeth."

Boone looked over at the crib. Then his gaze came back to rest on Shelby's face. He looked disoriented as he reached out a hand and lightly touched her cheek.

Even that gentle touch hurt, but she forced herself not to wince. "I'm fine."

Slowly she stood and held out her hand. "Come on," she said, her voice still hoarse. "Let's get the kids and go call the police."

He put his hand in hers and got to his feet. They walked hand in hand over to the crib. She lifted Elizabeth out and he picked up Josh. But he didn't move. Instead he stood there, as if in shock, while he held tight to Josh and gazed at Shelby and Elizabeth.

Josh looked up into Boone's stricken face and stroked his cheek. "Let's cuddle," he murmured.

With a broken sob Boone reached out and gathered Shelby and Elizabeth into his embrace.

TWO HOURS LATER, the police and the paramedics had come and gone. Fowler was in custody. Boone had given a brief statement telling the officers what he'd heard before he'd broken down the bedroom door. Good thing Fowler had admitted he'd arranged the accident that had killed Shelby's parents, and Boone had regained consciousness in time to hear it. Fowler's chances of getting custody of Josh were finished.

Boone had gathered his charges in the living room by a roaring fire, unable to think of putting Josh or Elizabeth back into the bedroom after what had just happened there. Josh had insisted they all deserved gold stars, so Shelby had dutifully pasted one on each of them. She'd put Elizabeth's on the back of her sleeper so she wouldn't be able to pull it off and eat it.

Josh dozed on the sofa clutching his blankie, and Elizabeth lay asleep in her playpen nearby, her monkey Bruce clutched in one tiny fist. Boone sat on the braided rug with Shelby tucked between his outstretched legs, her back propped against his chest. He knew she wasn't asleep.

Boone supposed the night wasn't really cold enough for a fire, but he was. Every time he thought of Fowler's hands on Shelby's throat he turned to ice inside. He would have killed the bastard if she hadn't stopped him.

As he cradled her in front of the fire he thought of the words she'd used to penetrate his murderous rage. *I love you.*

He'd been thinking about those words ever since the patrol car had pulled away from the house about a half hour ago. They'd run through his head as he and Shelby had hauled Josh and Elizabeth's stuff out to the living room and tucked the kids into bed next to the fire.

Although he and Shelby had talked to Josh and Elizabeth as they'd sung songs and played little games to make things seem okay again, they hadn't talked to each other. After the kids were settled, he'd pulled Shelby down and drawn her up against him. She'd come willingly, but she was very, very quiet.

Boone had to face the fact that everything was changed. So much had happened in only a few hours. First he'd discovered how much he loved Shelby when she'd cried in his arms, and he'd wondered how the hell he'd live without her if Jessica demanded marriage. And then he'd seen Shelby's life nearly snuffed out before his eyes, and he'd realized he couldn't live without her, period.

He had to be with her, see her every morning and sleep next to her every night. His world wouldn't turn unless she was in it. His duty might be to Jessica, and maybe he was supposed to pay for his mistake in getting her pregnant, but he loved Shelby more than duty, and he'd find another way to pay for his mistake.

He took a deep breath and wrapped his arms tighter around Shelby. "Marry me," he said.

She didn't answer for a very long time. Finally she spoke, and she sounded suspiciously close to tears. "Do you mean that?"

"I've never meant anything more in my life."

She scooted around so she could see his face, and sure enough, tears welled in her eyes. Her voice was choked. "I thought you wanted to find out about Jessica, about Elizabeth. I thought everything depended on that."

"It did." He framed her face in his big hands. Every time he looked at the bruise on her cheek and the cut on her lip, his insides twisted. "Until I almost lost you forever. I can't lose you, Shelby." He felt tears burning at the backs of his eyes, too. "I just can't."

She swallowed. "I don't want to lose you, either, Boone."

"I'm no good at fancy speeches." His chest felt tight, full of emotions he didn't know how to explain. "I wish I was. You deserve that. I only know I have to be with you, Shelby. There's no other way."

"I don't need fancy speeches." She reached up and touched his cheek. "Just three little words."

He let out a long, shuddering breath. He knew those words. "I love you." His voice almost broke as he said them. He'd almost lost the chance to tell her.

"Those would be the words." Her eyes glowed as she gazed up at him. "The only ones either of us will ever need." She drew closer, her sweet breath warm on his face. "I love you," she whispered.

The joy that surged through him began to ease the cold chill that had surrounded his heart. He touched her mouth with the tip of his finger. "I want to kiss you, but I don't want to hurt your mouth," he murmured.

"Kiss me," she said, brushing her mouth against his, "and make it better."

He kissed her gently, but she responded with such heat that he nearly forgot to be careful. No telling what might have happened if Josh's childish voice hadn't interrupted them.

"You're *kissing!*" he said.

Boone turned to look at Josh. "Is that okay with you?"

Josh sat up and rubbed at his eyes. "I guess so, but you gots to get married now. Like Travis and Gwen. They kissed in front of all the peoples, and now, bam, they're married."

Boone sighed and glanced at Shelby. "You heard him. I guess we have to."

Her eyes sparkled. "Well, if we have to, we have to."

Boone turned back to Josh. "How would you like that, if Shelby and I got married?"

"Oh, I would," Josh said sleepily, flopping back down.

"Glad to hear it," Boone said with a chuckle.

Josh yawned. "And y'know what?"

"What?"

Josh snuggled into his pillow and closed his eyes. "Bob, he would like it, too."

EPILOGUE

SEVEN ADULTS, a three-year-old boy and a five-month-old baby girl strained the resources of Doc Harrison's waiting room, especially when none of them seemed inclined to stay still. Shelby decided to concentrate on making sure Josh behaved himself.

"Maybe somebody should go outside and wait there until the doc is ready to see us." Sebastian, who was holding baby Elizabeth, glared pointedly at Travis and Boone.

"Not likely." Travis put an arm around Gwen. "We're all in this together, and nobody's going to hear about this paternity test before anybody else."

Josh stopped running his truck over the floor and looked up. "What's a 'ternity test?"

"That's the doctor's test I told you about." Shelby crouched down next to him. "To find out once and for all who's Elizabeth's father."

"My daddy's in jail. He's sick in the head." Josh spoke the fact as if announcing the time of day before going back to his truck race.

Shelby glanced up at Boone. He gazed down at her, offering silent support. They'd decided not to sugarcoat the truth about Mason in some attempt to spare Josh. Fortunately Josh had never formed a real bond with his biological father. Boone was quickly becoming the most important man in his life.

Two weeks had passed since that traumatic night when Mason had broken into the ranch house. Some days Shelby felt impatient that everything hadn't been finalized, but the wedding date was set and the custody hearing scheduled soon afterward. Following that, she and Boone would set the wheels in motion for adoption.

It was just details, paperwork and red tape, she told herself. In all ways that mattered they were already a family. They'd even talked to Sebastian about buying Matty's house and some acreage around it.

Only the question of Elizabeth remained unanswered. With still no word from Jessica, the men had decided to take the step they'd been avoiding and settle the matter medically. The atmosphere in Doc Harrison's waiting room was tense.

"The point I'm trying to make," Sebastian persisted, "is that all these bodies are making it too hot in here for Elizabeth."

"It's how you're holding her," Travis said. "Lizzy prefers a looser grip. And you might try playing peekaboo with her or something. You're such an old sobersides this morning, no wonder she's fussy. Better yet, let me have her."

"No, I'll take her, now." Boone stepped toward Sebastian. "I'm the tallest, so I can hold her up high, where the air's better. And cooler."

Luann Evans edged over toward Sebastian. "Heat rises," she said. "So you'd better give that precious bundle to me. Grandmothers know a few things about tending to a fussy little girl, don't we, sweetheart?"

Sebastian stepped away from the crowd. "She's fine

where she is. Besides, it's my turn. Everybody else has already had her."

"Yeah, but you've had her the longest," Travis grumbled. "Fair is fair, right, Boone?"

Matty rolled her eyes. "I have a watch with a second hand. We could time the baby rotation like a bronc-riding event if it would make you three cowboys happier."

"I'm a cowboy, too!" Josh said happily. "I gots a hat, and I gots boots."

"And they look great," Shelby said.

"Yep. I wanna go ride horsies."

"Sounds good to me, too," Travis said. "I hate this waiting. What's the doc doing in there so long with Nellie, giving her a hip replacement?"

Gwen laid a hand on his arm. "You wouldn't want him to rush his appointment with Nellie."

"Hell if I wouldn't." Travis gave her a rebellious stare. When she frowned at him, he grinned sheepishly. "Just this one time."

"I wouldn't mind if he skipped the bedside manner this morning, myself," Sebastian said. "I mean, I know she's getting up in years, but—"

The examining room door opened and Nellie Coogan shuffled out. She paused to peer through her thick glasses at the crowd in the waiting room.

Shelby stood and walked over to slip her hand inside Boone's. The moment had come. Boone clutched her hand like a lifeline.

"Hey, there, Miz Coogan," Travis said, touching the brim of his hat. "I hope you're in good health on this fine morning."

A chorus of greetings and good wishes followed as everyone else in the room remembered their manners.

"Thank you." Nellie continued to study them with obvious curiosity. Finally she nodded to herself. "I always wondered what they meant by those group health plans. This must be what those folks on the TV are talking about. How smart of you all." Then she shuffled out the door.

Nobody bothered to watch her leave as they turned toward the examining room door where a small, bearded man in a white coat stood quietly.

The silence lengthened.

Finally Sebastian spoke, his voice shaking. "You might as well spit it out, Doc. Which one of us is this baby's father?"

Doc Harrison cleared his throat. "I went over the results several times, because I wanted to make sure. The fact is, gentlemen…"

"Aw, come on, Doc," Travis said. "Don't drag it out."

"Yeah," Boone added. "Just say it. Which one?"

The small doctor adjusted his glasses. "None of you."

* * * * *

LARGER-PRINT BOOKS!

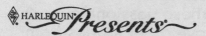

GET 2 FREE LARGER-PRINT NOVELS PLUS 2 FREE GIFTS!

YES! Please send me 2 FREE LARGER-PRINT Harlequin Presents® novels and my 2 FREE gifts (gifts are worth about $10). After receiving them, if I don't wish to receive any more books, I can return the shipping statement marked "cancel". If I don't cancel, I will receive 6 brand-new novels every month and be billed just $4.55 per book in the U.S. or $5.24 per book in Canada. That's a saving of at least 13% off the cover price! It's quite a bargain! Shipping and handling is just 50¢ per book.* I understand that accepting the 2 free books and gifts places me under no obligation to buy anything. I can always return a shipment and cancel at any time. Even if I never buy another book, the two free books and gifts are mine to keep forever.

176/376 HDN E5NG

Name	(PLEASE PRINT)
Address	Apt. #
City	State/Prov.	Zip/Postal Code

Signature (if under 18, a parent or guardian must sign)

Mail to the **Harlequin Reader Service:**
IN U.S.A.: P.O. Box 1867, Buffalo, NY 14240-1867
IN CANADA: P.O. Box 609, Fort Erie, Ontario L2A 5X3

Not valid for current subscribers to Harlequin Presents Larger-Print books.

Are you a subscriber to Harlequin Presents books and want to receive the larger-print edition? Call 1-800-873-8635 today!

* Terms and prices subject to change without notice. Prices do not include applicable taxes. Sales tax applicable in N.Y. Canadian residents will be charged applicable provincial taxes and GST. Offer not valid in Quebec. This offer is limited to one order per household. All orders subject to approval. Credit or debit balances in a customer's account(s) may be offset by any other outstanding balance owed by or to the customer. Please allow 4 to 6 weeks for delivery. Offer available while quantities last.

Your Privacy: Harlequin Books is committed to protecting your privacy. Our Privacy Policy is available online at www.eHarlequin.com or upon request from the Reader Service. From time to time we make our lists of customers available to reputable third parties who may have a product or service of interest to you. If you would prefer we not share your name and address, please check here. ☐

Help us get it right—We strive for accurate, respectful and relevant communications. To clarify or modify your communication preferences, visit us at www.ReaderService.com/consumerchoice.

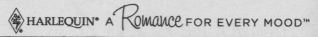

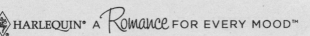

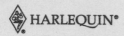 **HARLEQUIN®**

Showcase

On sale May 11, 2010

Reader favorites from the most talented voices in romance

Save $1.00 on the purchase of 1 or more Harlequin® Showcase books.

SAVE $1.00 on the purchase of 1 or more Harlequin® Showcase books.

Coupon expires Oct 31, 2010. Redeemable at participating retail outlets. Limit one coupon per purchase. Valid in the U.S.A. and Canada only.

52609015

5 65373 00076 2   (8100)0 11651

HSCCOUPON-